U0012403

改變人類生活的
創意發明
Eureka!

總編嚴選

お誕生日、おめでとうございます　Tillykke med fodselsdagen

VIESHOW
CINEMAS

8TH nniversary

八年一刻
繼續戀影

2013
09/13-10/13

★ 3C達人禮 09/13~10/13

出示iShow卡消費集點，符合下列參與資格者即有機會抽中指定大獎～

觀賞電影一般版+ 3D版(或4DX版)各乙部	有機會獲得「HTC Butterfly 粉紅限量版」或「iPhone 5」！加購指定套餐還有機會獲得「New HTC One」、「SONY 32型 LED液晶電視」、「半年份免費觀影」、「三個月份免費觀影」！
觀賞IMAX電影	有機會獲得「Samsung Galaxy Note II」或「MacBook Pro 13 吋」！
觀賞GOLD CLASS電影	有機會獲得「Wi-Fi版iPad mini (16GB)」或「力抗錶」！

威秀寶寶家族・EYE ♥ U

09/13~09/26前，強力募集與威秀寶寶家族人偶公開活動合照，參加者除有機會獲得「威秀寶寶家族系列好禮」；票選冠軍還能登上全台威秀影城電漿電視並將「富士 FINEPIX F600EXR 數位相機」帶回家！頭號粉絲缺你不可！

參加者將照片上傳至個人塗鴉牆並設為公開，將姓名、聯絡電話、領獎影城與截圖以facebook訊息發送至威秀影城官方粉絲團www.facebook.com/vieshow即可。

公佈中獎日期：2013/10/04
電漿電視上刊時間：2013/10/04~10/13

普天同慶禮 威秀寶寶生日(09/29)當天

持iShow卡作任何消費集點，符合參與資格者，將有機會獲得「一年份免費觀影」、「半年份免費觀影」或將率性「哈特佛灰狼150機車」騎回家！

點點心意禮 ✚ 09/13-10/13

凡新申辦iShow卡並於活動期間消費滿500元以上，即贈「HAPPY GO卡點數50點」。(不可重覆累計)
注意事項：(1)新申辦iShow卡意指從未申辦過HAPPY GO卡，於威秀影城首次申辦者。 (2)HAPPY GO卡點數統一於11/01入點。

超萌系獻禮 09/13起

iShow點數 88點，免費兌換「DOMI好啾咪造型抱枕」乙個。(兌完為止)

饗餐歡趣禮 09/23起

觀賞任乙部電影加購指定套餐，出示iShow卡消費集點，符合參與資格者即可獲得「這不是電影票N次貼」乙份 (限量珍藏・送完為止)

GOLD CLASS限定 09/27~09/29

凡觀賞GOLD CLASS電影加購指定套餐，出示iShow卡消費集點，符合參與資格者即可獲得「KOSE無限肌緻精潤旅行三件組」乙套 (每日限額・送完為止)

別 放 手

金獎影后 暨 影帝

珊卓布拉克

喬治庫隆尼

鬼才導演 艾方索柯朗 作品

地 心 引 力
GRAVITY

WARNER BROS. PICTURES PRESENTS
AN ESPERANTO FILMOJ/HEYDAY FILMS PRODUCTION AN ALFONSO CUARÓN FILM SANDRA BULLOCK GEORGE CLOONEY "GRAVITY"
MUSIC BY STEVEN PRICE COSTUME DESIGNER JANY TEMIME EDITORS ALFONSO CUARÓN MARK SANGER PRODUCTION DESIGNER ANDY NICHOLSON DIRECTOR OF PHOTOGRAPHY EMMANUEL LUBEZKI, A.S.C., A.M.C.
EXECUTIVE PRODUCERS CHRIS DeFARIA NIKKI PENNY STEPHEN JONES WRITTEN BY ALFONSO CUARÓN & JONÁS CUARÓN PRODUCED BY ALFONSO CUARÓN DAVID HEYMAN DIRECTED BY ALFONSO CUARÓN

www.gravity.com.tw

10/4(五)早場起

3D 太空驚悚鉅作 f 地心引力

國賓巨幕 ATX

DOLBY ATMOS

杜比® 全景聲

10/4 巨幕登場　完美現聲

國賓大戲院
AMBASSADOR THEATRE

目錄 Contents

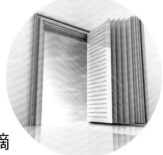

EUREKA! 點子成金

V Vocabulary Bank

1) **intellectual** [ˌɪntəˈlɛktʃuəl] (a.)
知識（分子）的，（需）智力的
Chess is a very intellectual game.
西洋棋是一種非常益智的遊戲。

2) **establish** [ɪˈstæblɪʃ] (v.) 創辦，建立
The university was established in 1926.
這所大學創立於一九二六年。

3) **geometry** [dʒɪˈɑmətri] (n.) 幾何學
Brett failed geometry and had to take it again.
布萊特的幾何學被當掉了，因此他必須重修。

4) **application** [ˌæplɪˈkeʃən] (n.) 應用，運用
Engineering is the application of science to practical problems.
工程學就是科學在實際問題上的應用。

5) **relative** [ˈrɛlətɪv] (n.) 親戚，親屬
How often do you get together with your relatives?
你多久和親戚們聚一次？

6) **ponder** [ˈpɑndɚ] (v.) 思索，仔細考慮，衡量
Do you ever ponder the meaning of life?
你是否曾深思過生命的意義？

7) **displace** [dɪsˈples] (v.) 排（水），（使）移位
(n.) displacement （船）排水量
Floating objects displace an amount of water equal to their weight.
浮在水上的物體所排出的水量就等於它們的重量。

進階字彙

8) **city-state** [ˈsɪtiˌstet] (n.) 城邦
Singapore became a city-state after separating from Malaysia in 1965.
新加坡於一九六五年自馬來西亞獨立，成為一個城邦國家。

9) **goldsmith** [ˈgoldˌsmɪθ] (n.) 金匠
Paula had her wedding ring repaired by a goldsmith.
寶拉把她的婚戒拿給一位金匠修理。

10) **irregular** [ɪˈrɛgjəlɚ] (a.) 不規則的，不平整的，不對稱的
Norway has a long, irregular coastline.
挪威有著長而不平整的海岸線。

11) **submerge** [səbˈmɝdʒ] (a.) 淹沒，把…浸入水中，潛入水中
The small town was submerged by the flood.
這個小鎮被洪水給淹沒了。

Archimedes
and the 阿基米德與第一次的尤里卡時刻
Original Eureka Moment

課文朗讀 MP3 1　　單字朗讀 MP3 2　　英文講解 MP3 3

Archimedes, the famous Greek mathematician, scientist and inventor, was born in 287 B.C. in Syracuse, a Greek [8]**city-state** on the island of Sicily. Although little is known about his early years, Archimedes is said to have pursued his education in Alexandria, Egypt, the [1]**intellectual** capital of the ancient world. After studying mathematics at the school [2]**established** by Euclid, the father of [3]**geometry**, he invented what later became known as Archimedes' screw, a type of water pump that is still in use to this day.

On returning to Sicily, Archimedes devoted his life to mathematics and its [4]application to practical problems. One such problem, given to him by his friend and [5]relative King Hieron of Syracuse, led to the first eureka moment in recorded history. As the story goes, the king provided a bar of pure gold to a [9]goldsmith to make a crown, but later suspected him of replacing some of the gold with silver. Since the crown was the correct weight, and gold is heavier than silver, Archimedes reasoned that the crown would have a larger volume if it was part silver than it would if it was pure gold. But how could he determine the volume of such an [10]irregular shape?

As Archimedes was sitting in the bath one day [6]pondering this problem, he noticed that as he lowered his body, the water in the tub rose. He suddenly realized that he could find the volume of the crown by [11]submerging it in water and measuring the volume of water it [7]displaced. Archimedes was so excited by his discovery that he ran into the street in his birthday suit shouting "Eureka!"—which means "I've found it!" in Ancient Greek.

Mini Quiz 閱讀測驗

■ According to the article, which of the following is NOT true about Archimedes?
(A) He invented a kind of water pump.
(B) He is the father of geometry.
(C) He ran into the street with no clothes on.
(D) He is related to King Hieron.

中 Translation

阿基米德是希臘數學家、科學家及發明家，生於西元前兩百八十七年西西里島的希臘城邦西拉鳩斯。雖然阿基米德的早年事蹟我們知道的並不多，但據傳他在埃及的亞歷山卓受教育，該城是遠古的知識首都。在幾何學之父歐幾里德創辦的學校學習數學後，阿基米德發明了後來被稱為「阿基米德螺泵」的東西，這是一種至今仍為人所用的水泵。

回到西西里島後，阿基米德致力於數學研究並應用在日常問題上。西拉鳩斯的國王海維隆，同時也是其好友與親戚，有天給了阿基米德一道題目，這道題目也帶來了歷史上所記載的第一次「尤里卡時刻」。故事是這樣的，國王請金匠把純金的金條製成皇冠，事後國王懷疑金匠偷摻了一些銀在裡面。然而皇冠重量是正確的，況且金比銀重，阿基米德則推論摻銀的皇冠體積將會大於純金的皇冠，但是他要如何測量不規則狀的皇冠體積呢？

某天當阿基米德一邊泡澡一邊沉思這個問題時，他突然注意到：當他把身體下沉時，浴缸裡的水位就上升了。他頓時悟出皇冠體積的方法，只要將皇冠浸在水裡，測量上升的水即可。阿基米德對於這個發現感到欣喜若狂，裸體衝上大街高喊：「尤里卡！」——在古希臘代表「我發現了」。

答案：閱讀測驗 (B)

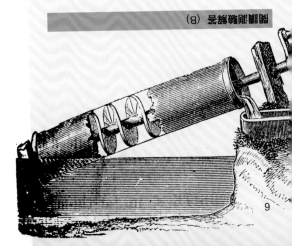

9

古希臘名人堂

希臘文化對歐洲的發展具有深遠的影響。崇尚自由、追求真理、富有創造力 (creativity) 及人文精神 (humanism)，都是該文化的特色。也由於希臘較早發展高等教育，連帶使得當時的文學 (literature)、哲學 (philosophy)、數學獲得高度發展，其中哲學和數學在思維上又有密不可分的關係。

畢達哥拉斯 Pythagoras
（西元前 570 至 495 年）

$a^2 + b^2 = c^2$，相信大家都對這個公式不陌生吧？這個耳熟能詳的「畢氏定理」（Pythagorean theorem，也叫「勾股定理」），其實就是由畢達哥拉斯所發現（雖然相傳古埃及、巴比倫 (Babylon) 和中國很早就知道了）。據說在證明這個定理後，他馬上斬了一百頭牛來慶祝，因此又稱百牛定理。

除了數學外，畢達哥拉斯也是位出色的哲學家，他推崇理性，認為可被理解的東西才是完美的，光靠感知則會有缺陷。這樣的觀念後來被柏拉圖 (Plato) 發揚光大，支配著日後的哲學和神學 (theology) 體系。

泰勒斯 Thales of Miletus
（西元前 624 至 546 年）

是西方史上第一個被記載的數學家和哲學家。曾遊歷埃及鑽研數學，對於天文學 (astronomy) 也有豐富的知識，在當時就知道將一年分為春分、夏至、秋分及冬至。泰勒斯在數學方面的劃時代貢獻就是引入命題證明的思想，他標誌著人們對客觀 (objective) 事物的認識從經驗拓展到理論層面。

歐幾里德 Euclid
（西元前約 325 至 265 年）

Euclid 這個名字在希臘文有「好名聲」(good glory) 的意思。歐幾里德被譽為「幾何學之父」(Father of Geometry) 曾經教導過托勒密一世（Ptolemy I Soter，為埃及托勒密王朝的創建者）幾何學，托勒密一世曾問歐幾里得學習幾何學有沒有捷徑，歐幾里德回答 "There is no royal road to Geometry"（學習幾何沒有帝王之路）。其著作《幾何原本》(Elements) 是數學史上最具影響力的文本之一。歐幾里德留下的生平資料極少，甚至連畫像都是後世藝術家想像而來的。

丟番圖 Diophantus
（約生於西元 200~214 年間，卒於西元 284~298 年間）

原本希臘的數學重心都在幾何，他們認為只有經過幾何論證的命題才可靠，就連代數 (algebra) 也脫離不了幾何，直到丟番圖才將代數獨立出來，擺脫幾何的束縛。他認為代數方法比幾何方法更適合解決問題，解題過程中顯示出的獨創性 (originality)，在希臘數學中獨樹一幟，被後人稱為「代數學之父」，著有《算術》（Arithmetica）一書，專門解代數方程組 (algebraic equation)。同時，他也是第一個承認分數 (fraction) 是屬於數一種的希臘數學家，在數學史上頗具開創性。

希臘詩集上用了個好玩的代學問題來描述丟番圖的一生。若丟番圖一生歲月是 x 年，他有 1/6 的年歲是幼年期，青少年期佔了 1/12，又過了 1/7 才結婚，五年後生了兒子，不過他兒子早他四年過世，壽命只有父親的 1/2。那麼就可以列出以下的公式：

$X/6 + X/12 + X/7 + 5 + X/2 + 4 = X$，計算之後得知 X 等於 84，故得知丟番圖享年八十四歲。

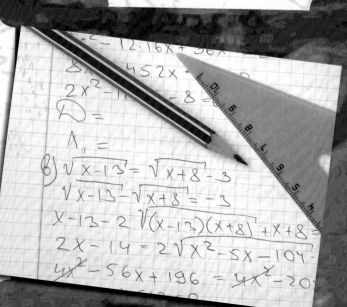

蘇格拉底 Socrates
（西元前 469 至 399 年）

蘇格拉底認為數學可以運用在軍事和哲學上，因為打仗的人必須研究數目的技巧，否則便無法整頓隊伍；而哲學家們想在浩瀚的知識領域中尋出真理，也需要具備良好的算術能力，因而鼓勵城邦中的領袖需學習算術。

身兼哲學家與教育家蘇格拉底，與柏拉圖、亞里斯多德並列「希臘三賢士」，有人甚至還把他比喻為希臘的孔子。他本人並沒有留下任何著作，現在看到的版本都是學生幫他撰寫的。個性鮮明、道德感強烈的他，因「宣揚新的神明，腐化青年人」的罪名被迫服毒自盡。

蘇格拉底作學問最有名的方式就是「辯證法」（dialectic，也叫 Socratic method「蘇格拉底法」），簡單來說就是「打破沙鍋問到底」，藉由不斷地辯論來釐清真相。關於這點有個有趣的小故事，某天他在路上與一位陌生人進行了以下的對話：

蘇格拉底：「大家都覺得誠實無欺的人才算有道德，可是為什麼和敵人作戰時卻要千方百計地欺騙敵人呢？」
路人：「欺騙別人並沒有違背道德，但欺騙自己可就不道德了。」
蘇格拉底：「當我軍被敵軍包圍時，將領欺騙士兵說援軍已經到了，大家奮力突圍出去，結果突圍成功。這種欺騙也不道德嗎？」
路人：「那是因為在戰爭中，迫於無奈才會這樣做，日常生活中這麼做是不道德的。」
蘇格拉底還不死心：「假如你的兒子生病不肯吃藥，你騙他說那不是藥，而是一種可口的食物，這也算不道德嗎？」
路人只好承認：「這種欺騙也是符合道德的。」
蘇格拉底又問：「所以也就是說，道德不能用騙不騙人來證明。那到底要用什麼來說明它呢？可否請你告訴我？」
路人想了想，說：「不知道道德是什麼，就不能變成有道德的人，要知道了道德才能做到道德。」
蘇格拉底開心的說：「您真是個偉大的哲學家，告訴我有關道德的知識，真是太謝謝您了。」

柏拉圖 Plato
（西元前 428 至 348 年）

蘇格拉底的得意門生，在數學方面，特別鍾愛幾何學，他的莊園外還甚至立了「不懂幾何者，不得入內」的牌子。主張宇宙萬物都遵照著數學規律運行，他強調數學應該是觀念上的釐清，而不是只在寫公式或算數字之類的。

柏拉圖同時也是西方第一個高等教育學府——雅典學院 (Academy) 的創辦人，和蘇格拉底、亞里斯多德一同建立起西方的哲學和科學體系。

柏拉圖的知名著作《理想國》(The Republic) 指出，統治者應該具備哲學的思考與力量，否則國將衰退，其中所提出許多具體主張，如共產 (communism)、共妻，雖然看來不可思議，但其深度、廣度，以及分析的謹嚴程度，至今仍無人能出其右。

亞里斯多德 Aristotle
（西元前 384 至 322 年）

是柏拉圖的學生，也曾擔任過亞歷山大大帝 (Alexander the Great) 的老師。在哲學領域的成就不亞於柏拉圖。他在柏拉圖的學校中留了二十年，據說他後來和柏拉圖因想法不合而斷絕關係。他對真理的追尋超越了情理，於是說出了「吾愛吾師，吾尤愛真理」這句名言。

在學術上，最著名的就是對形上學 (metaphysics) 的研究，以及提出「地球是宇宙的中心」和「作用力造成運動速度」等重要的科學見解。他的著作涵括物理 (physics)、形上學、詩集，甚至是動物學 (zoology) 等，首次創造西方哲學完整的系統，包含道德 (ethics)、美學 (aesthetics)、邏輯 (logic)、科學、政治和形上學。

亞里斯多德對學術界的影響甚鉅，一直延伸到整個中世紀，擴及文藝復興時期 (Renaissance)，直到牛頓的物理學說出來後才被取代。他的邏輯理論也整合進十九世紀晚期的模態邏輯 (formal logic) 中，探索那些難以被解讀出來的真相。

V Vocabulary Bank

1) **philosopher** [fəˋlɑsəfə] (n.) 哲學
philosophy 即「哲學」
Aristotle was an ancient Greek philosopher.
亞里斯多德是一位古希臘的哲學家。

2) **inherit** [ɪnˋhɛrɪt] (v.) 遺傳，繼承
Michelle inherited her mother's light blue eyes.
蜜雪兒遺傳了她媽媽的淡藍色眼睛。

3) **classics** [ˋklæsɪks] (n.) 古希臘羅馬文學，古典文學
Teddy Roosevelt studied classics at Harvard.
泰迪羅斯福在哈佛攻讀古希臘羅馬文學。

4) **truce** [trus] (v.) 停戰，休戰
Thousands have died since the truce ended.
數以千計的人在停戰結束後死亡。

5) **spare** [spɛr] (a.) 空閒的，多餘的
We have a spare bed if you want to spend the night.
如果你想在這過夜的話，我們有多一張床。

6) **station** [ˋsteʃən] (v.) 駐紮，部署
My parents met while my dad was stationed in Germany after the war.
我的爸媽是在我爸在戰後駐紮在德國時認識的。

7) **insight** [ˋɪn͵saɪt] (n.) 深入的理解，見解，洞察力
The scholar's work shows great insight.
這位學者的研究展現出許多深入見解。

8) **algebra** [ˋældʒəbrə] (n.) 代數（學）
We learned how to solve equations in algebra class.
我們在代數學的課堂中學習如何解方程式。

9) **coordinate** [koˋɔrdənɪt] (n.) 座標
The police caught the suspect by tracking his cell phone coordinates.
警方靠著追蹤手機座標逮到了那名嫌犯。

10) **invention** [ɪnˋvɛnʃən] (n.) 創造，發明
The kite is a Chinese invention.
風箏是中國的發明。

11) **revolution** [͵rɛvəˋluʃən] (n.) 革命
Millions of people died during the Russian Revolution.
上百萬人在俄國革命期間喪生。

進階字彙

12) **sickly** [ˋsɪklɪ] (a.) 多病的，不健壯的
The girl left school to take care of her sickly mother.
那位女孩為了照顧體弱多病的母親而休學。

13) **mentor** [ˋmɛntə] (n.) 精神導師，良師益友
You should find a mentor to advise you on your career.
你應該找位良師益友來給你一些職涯上的建議。

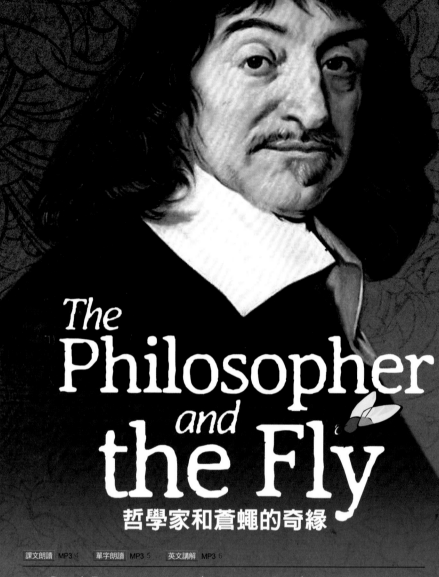

The Philosopher and the Fly
哲學家和蒼蠅的奇緣

課文朗讀 MP3 4　　單字朗讀 MP3 5　　英文講解 MP3 6

René Descartes was born on March 31, 1596 in the French city of La Haye, which was later renamed Descartes in his honor. His mother died when he was just one, and he [2)]**inherited** her poor health. At the age of 11, Descartes entered a Jesuit school in La Flèche, where he studied the [3)]**classics**, and later philosophy and mathematics. Because he was such a [12)]**sickly** child, his teachers let him stay in bed until noon each day, a habit that would stay with him for the rest of his life.

Coming from a family of lawyers, Descartes entered the University of Poitiers in 1615 to study law. Although he received his degree two years later, he had no desire to become a lawyer himself. Instead, he joined the Dutch army, where he worked as a military engineer. Because there was a temporary [4)]**truce** in Holland's war of independence from Spain, Descartes had plenty of [5)]**spare** time to continue his study of philosophy and math.

While ⁶⁾**stationed** in southern Holland, Descartes met Dutch philosopher and scientist Isaac Beeckman, who became his ¹³⁾**mentor**. Impressed by the young man's mathematical ⁷⁾**insights**, Beeckman encouraged him to develop his ideas further. Descartes set his mind to combining geometry and ⁸⁾**algebra** to create a new type of mathematics, but it was his habit of  that led to his eureka moment.

Lying in bed one morning, Descartes noticed a fly crawling on the ceiling. Wondering if it was possible to express the fly's position mathematically, he suddenly realized that all he needed was two numbers: the distance of the fly from the two nearest walls. These numbers, or ⁹⁾**coordinates**, became the basis of analytic geometry, which Descartes developed over the next several years.

Although Descartes is best remembered as a philosopher—his statement, "I think, therefore I am" is the most famous in the history of philosophy—his mathematical ¹⁰⁾**invention** is more significant. Analytic geometry led to the discovery of calculus, which made possible the scientific ¹¹⁾**revolution** that created world we live in today.

Mini Quiz 閱讀測驗

Which of the following is true about Descartes?
(A) He worked as a lawyer after attaining his degree.
(B) He was often ill when he was young.
(C) He developed a habit of staying up late.
(D) He was a mentor to Isaac Beekman.

Translation

勒內笛卡兒在一五九六年三月三十一日生於法國的拉海鎮，後來當地改名為笛卡兒以茲紀念。他的母親在他一歲時就過世了，而他也遺傳到她虛弱的體質。十一歲時，笛卡兒進入拉弗萊契的耶穌會學校就讀，先後修習古典文學、哲學和數學。因為他體弱多病，教師每天都讓他賴床到中午，而這個習慣將跟著他一輩子。

律師家庭出身的笛卡兒在一六一五年進入普瓦捷大學研習法律。雖順利於兩年後拿到學位，他卻一點也不想當律師，反倒加入荷蘭軍隊，擔任軍事工程師。因為當時荷蘭脫離西班牙的獨立戰爭暫時停火，笛卡兒有充分的閒暇時間繼續哲學與數學的研究。

在駐紮荷蘭南部時，笛卡兒結識荷蘭哲學及科學家艾薩克比克曼，他後來成為笛卡兒的精神導師。為這個年輕人對數學的見解深深打動，比克曼鼓勵他進一步發展構想。於是笛卡兒全心投入於結合幾何學與代數學，創造出一種新的數學類別，但促成他靈機一動的，卻是他晚起的習慣。

一天早上，笛卡兒躺在床上，注意到一隻蒼蠅在天花板上爬。他很好奇能否用數學表示蒼蠅的位置，忽然他恍然大悟，他只需要兩個數字：蒼蠅與那兩面最靠近之牆壁的距離。這些數字，即座標，遂成為解析幾何學的基礎，而解析幾何學是笛卡兒接下來幾年所發展出來的。

雖然笛卡兒最為後人記得的是他哲學家的身分──他的「我思，故我在」是哲學史上最著名的一句話，但他在數學上的發明更重要。解析幾何促成微積分的發現，而正是微積分造就科學革命，創造我們今天生活的世界。

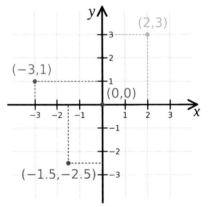

笛卡兒紀念墓碑，位於巴黎的聖日耳曼德佩修道院 (Abbey of Saint-Germain-des-Prés)

我思，故我在

I think, therefore I am

你一定聽過笛卡兒的這句名言，但是你了解這句話表達出什麼樣的思維嗎？這位法國的天才數學家其實讓人印象最深刻的是他在哲學方面的貢獻，就讓我們一同來了解一下這位偉大的哲人吧！

笛卡兒語錄

除了「我思，故我在」，笛卡兒還有說過其他發人深省的名言：

- **The reading of all good books is like a conversation with the finest men of past centuries.**
  所有的好書，讀起來就像與過去許多世紀最傑出的人交談一樣。

- **Each problem that I solved became a rule, which served afterwards to solve other problems.**
  我每解決一個問題，此後都變成解決其他問題的有用準則。

- **It is not enough to have a good mind; the main thing is to use it well.**
  只有良好的心智是不夠的，最主要的是怎麼使用它。

- **If you would be a real seeker after truth, it is necessary that at least once in your life you doubt, as far as possible, all things.**
  如果你是一個追尋真相的人，在你一生中，至少有一次你要盡可能地去懷疑一切。

詭異的三個夢

笛卡兒曾講述了一段富有神秘色彩的經歷。他說他在一六一九年十一月十日的晚上作了三個非常逼真的夢。

第一個夢是夢見自己被一陣強風吹得旋轉起來，隨後被吹到一個陌生的地方。接著他又作了第二夢，在夢中，他聽見了一些爆炸和火花聲，習慣之後，他覺得並不害怕，反倒可以藉由火光看清楚周圍的物體。

作完前兩個夢後，他起床休息了一下，又繼續回去睡，夢見第三個夢。夢裡他在書桌上看到一本詩集，翻開了其中一頁，一看到這句拉丁文—— Quod vitae sectabor iter?（我得遵循什麼樣的生活道路？）他就如醍醐灌頂，得到了啟發，找到了解開自然奧秘的金鑰匙，這把金鑰匙想來指的應該就是「數學」吧！

笛卡兒的哲學思想

笛卡兒被譽為「近代哲學之父」是其來有自的，他的思想支配著十七世紀，所提出的「懷疑論」(skepticism) 是主張運用科學的驗證方法來思考哲學性的問題，強調用理性 (reason) 來檢驗知識與真理。他的整個哲學主張可以大概總結為以下幾點：

● 將事物分成精神 (spiritual) 和物質 (material) 層面去討論，即「二元論」(dualism)。
● 所有看似無懈可擊的知識其實都值得懷疑。
● 將複雜的知識拆解成若干個簡單的部份，把當中模稜兩可、無法確定的知識先排除，然後用最肯定、最不會錯的知識當作基點，逐漸重新建構整個新的知識體系，這樣所構築的知識就會是正確無誤的。
● 我們既然會產生懷疑，表示我們生來是不完美的，但卻可藉由上述的方法獲得完美的觀念。但是不完美的個體，怎麼可能會獲得完美的概念呢？因此我們可以斷定，這些完美的觀念一定來自於他處，來自一個完美的起源，我們姑且將這完美的事物稱之為「神」，所以神是確然存在的。

雖然笛卡兒是個虔誠教徒，堅信上帝的存在，不過他信的是「理性的上帝」，而非一味地崇拜，因此某些觀點還是挑戰到當時的教會，例如他宣稱聖經並非科學知識之源，人類應只接受自己所了解的事物，而且他不認為禱告可以改善人類的生活，一切還是得靠自己創造。因此在他死後，教會將他的書列為禁書，並在一六五〇年巴黎舉辦的喪禮中，禁止他的告別演說。

解碼 r = a(1-sin θ) 中的愛情心臟線

相傳笛卡兒在教導克麗絲蒂娜的期間，兩人之間產生了情愫，譜出一段喧騰一時的師生戀。國王得知後百般阻撓，笛卡兒知道國王會攔截他寫的情書，便將綿綿情話轉為密語，藉此表達他的愛意。國王拿到情書後打開一看，只見裡頭寫著 r = a(1 - sin θ) 這行字，於是找來城裡所有科學家來研究，卻都沒人能解開（因為當時只有他們師生倆會直角座標）。國王實在沒輒，就把信交給克麗絲蒂娜。聰明的克麗絲蒂娜一下就用直角座標系解開了當中的訊息，也就是：

θ = 點和原點 (0,0) 所形成的角度
r = 點到原點的距離
a = 常數
當 θ=0 度時，r=a(1-0)=a，相當於座標上的 (a, 0) 點
當 θ=90 度時，r=a(1-1)=0，相當於座標上的 (0,0) 點
當 θ=180 度時，r=a(1-0)=a，相當於座標上的 (-a, 0) 點
當 θ=270 度時，r=a(1+1)=2a，相當於座標上的 (-2a, 0) 點

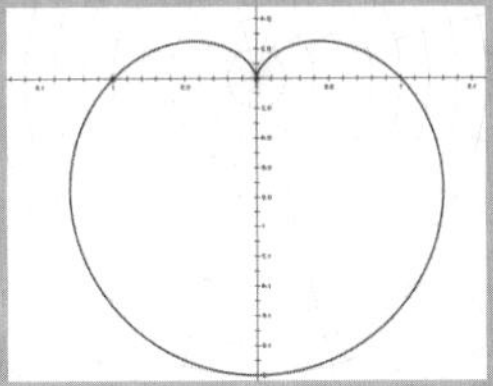

多找幾個點連起來時，就可以在座標圖上得到一個完美的心型圖案。克麗絲蒂娜看到後心花怒放，感動不已，這就是著名的愛情心臟線。

弱不禁風的哲學家

笛卡兒從小就體弱多病，肺部健康狀況尤其差，所以他很怕冷，經常待在火爐旁，而且喜歡賴床，每天都睡到日上三竿。一六四九年，笛卡兒應瑞典克麗絲蒂娜女王 (Queen Christina of Sweden) 的邀約去擔任宮廷教師，這位女王對數學有極高的興趣，常常在一大早天色未明時就把笛卡兒挖起來上數學課。當時十九歲的克麗絲蒂娜身體勇健，能忍受酷寒的天氣，上課時常常堅持要大開窗戶，好讓「可愛的」雪花飄進來。由於瑞典的氣候嚴寒，加上每天得在寒風中早起上課，讓身體孱弱的笛卡兒吃不消，因而染上肺炎，與世長辭。

Ⓥ Vocabulary Bank

1) **empire** [ˋɛmpaɪr] (n.) 帝國
The Roman Empire fell in the 5th century.
羅馬帝國在第五世紀隕落。

2) **take after** [tek ˋæftɚ] (phr.) 像，相似
Which parent do you think you take after?
你覺得你像爸爸還是媽媽？

3) **household** [ˋhaʊs, hold] (a.) 家用的，家庭的
What are your household expenses each
month?
你每個月的家用支出是多少？

4) **appliance** [əˋplaɪəns] (n.) 家電，用具
The store sells kitchen and bathroom
appliances.
這間店販售廚房和衛浴電器。

5) **photographic** [ˌfotəˋgræfɪk] (a.) 攝影的，
照相般的，photographic memory 即為過目不
忘、非常精確的記憶力
The artist painted the scene in almost
photographic detail.
那位藝術家把風景畫得栩栩如生。

6) **accuse** [əˋkjuz] (v.) 指控，控告
Are you accusing me of lying?
你是在指控我說謊嗎？

7) **contract** [kənˋtrækt] (v.) 得（病）
The explorer contracted malaria in the
tropics.
那位探險家在熱帶地區染上了瘧疾。

8) **engineering** [ˌɛndʒəˋnɪrɪŋ] (n.) 工程，工程學
The position requires a degree in electrical
engineering.
這個職位需要具備電機工程學位。

9) **institution** [ˌɪnstɪˋtuʃən] (n.) 機構
This university is the largest educational
institution in the country.
這間大學是國內最大的教育機構。

10) **renowned** [rɪˋnaʊnd] (a.) 有名的
The history textbook was written by a
renowned historian.
這本歷史課本是有名的歷史學家寫的。

11) **demonstrate** [ˋdɛmən, stret] (v./n.) 示範，
說明，展示
The coach demonstrated the correct way to
hold the bat.
教練示範正確的握棒姿勢。

12) **spark** [spɑrk] (n./v.)（冒）火花，（冒）火星
The fire was started by a spark from an
electrical wire.
那起火災的起因是電線走火。

進階字彙

13) **clergy** [ˋklɝgi] (n.)（統稱）神職人員
The couple hopes that their son will enter
the clergy.
這對夫婦希望兒子可以成為神職人員。

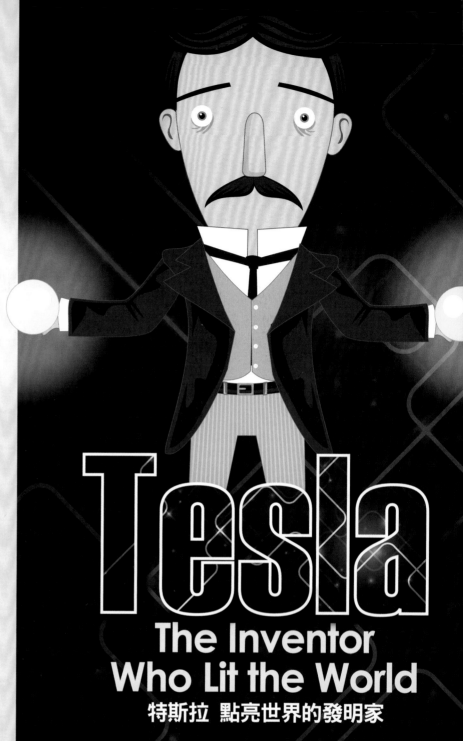

Tesla
The Inventor Who Lit the World
特斯拉 點亮世界的發明家

課文朗讀 MP3　單字朗讀 MP3　英文講解 MP3

Nikola Tesla was born during an electrical storm on July 10, 1856 to Serbian parents in the small village of Smiljan in Croatia, which was then part of the Austrian [1)]**Empire**. His father, an Orthodox Christian priest, hoped that he would join the [13)]**clergy** when he grew up. But the young Nikola [2)]**took after** his mother, a brilliant woman who invented a number of [3)]**household** [4)]**appliances** and memorized long poems. He also showed a talent for inventing as a boy, and his [5)]**photographic** memory enabled him to excel in his studies.

By the time Tesla was in high school, he was solving calculus problems in his head, causing his teachers to [6]**accuse** him of cheating. He **1** had his heart set on becoming an engineer, but his father still wanted him to become a priest. A solution came when Tesla [7]**contracted** cholera at the age of 17. As he lay on his bed near death, his father came in to comfort him. "Perhaps," Tesla said, "I will get well if you let me study [8]**engineering**." "You will go to the best technical [9]**institution** in the world," his father replied.

And so, in 1875, Tesla entered a [10]**renowned** technical college in Graz, Austria to study electrical engineering. In his second year, one of his professors [11]**demonstrated** a newly invented direct current electric motor. When Tesla saw [12]**sparks** flying off the motor, he thought that a better one could be invented using alternating current. While the professor laughed at his idea, Tesla was proved right in the end. But it would be another six years before he had the eureka moment that made his AC motor possible.

Mini Quiz 閱讀測驗

How did Tesla avoid becoming a priest?
(A) By solving calculus problems in his head
(B) By contracting cholera
(C) By attending a technical institution
(D) By making a deal with his father

中 Translation

尼可拉特斯拉在一八五六年七月十日雷電交加的時刻生於當時仍屬奧地利帝國的克羅埃西亞斯米連村，雙親皆為塞爾維亞人。擔任東正教神父的父親希望他長大後從事神職工作。但尼可拉比較像他媽媽：發明多項家用器具、還會背長詩的聰穎女性。他也在小時候就展露了發明的才能，而他過目不忘的記憶力，讓他得以在學校成績亮眼。

進了高中後，特斯拉已能在腦中運算微積分問題，讓老師指他作弊。他一心想當工程師，但父親仍希望他當神父。解決辦法在特斯拉十七歲感染霍亂之際出現。當他臥病在床、瀕臨死亡，他的父親進來安慰他。「說不定，」特斯拉說：「只要你讓我學工程，病就會好起來。」「我會讓你唸世界最好的技術學院，」父親回答。

於是，一八七五年，特斯拉進入奧地利格拉茨知名的技術學院，修習電機工程。大二那年，一名教授示範了新發明的直流電馬達。特斯拉一看到馬達迸射的火花便想，應該可以用交流電發明更好的馬達。教授雖然取笑他的想法，但特斯拉最後證明自己是對的。但要經過六年，讓他靈機一動、催生出交流電馬達的一刻才來臨。

🔑 Tongue-tied No More

1 have one's heart set on sb./sth. 渴望

set 在這裡當形容詞，意思是「下決心的」，因此 have one's heart set on sb./sth. 就用來形容一心想要達成的事情，或是傾心於某物。你也可以說 have one's mind set on sb./sth.，或是把 set 改為動詞用法，說成 set one's mind on sb./sth.。

A: Did you hear? Michael didn't get accepted to Stanford.
你有聽說嗎？麥可沒有被史丹佛錄取。

B: That's too bad. He really had his heart set on going there.
真可惜。他一心一意想上那所學校。

🧭 Language Guide

Orthodox Christian 東正教

與天主教、新教並列為基督教三大宗派，目前東正教信徒多分布於希臘、俄羅斯及東歐。東正教原屬於羅馬天主教會 (Catholic Church)，但在神學議題上與羅馬教庭無法達成共識，屢次爆發衝突。一〇五三年時，當時的君士坦丁堡牧首 (Patriarch of Constantinople) 指責羅馬教宗篡改聖經內容，東正教之後更在一〇五四年正式從天主教（即羅馬公教）分裂出來，並在拜占庭帝國 (Byzantine Empire) 時期達到最高峰。

cholera 霍亂

霍亂源自印度次大陸，後來傳播到歐洲以及世界各地，第一次出現大流行是發生在十九世紀。是一種由霍亂弧菌 (Vibrio cholerae) 引起的急性腸胃炎，常經由水或食物傳染，會有嘔吐 (vomiting)、水性腹瀉 (diarrhea) 及脫水 (dehydration) 的症狀，嚴重甚至造成死亡。

alternating current 交流電

交流電簡稱 AC，電流的方向會來回流動，而出現規律的週期變化，最常見的電流曲線是正弦曲線 (sine wave)，為一般家用插頭配電所使用。直流電（direct current，簡稱 DC）的電流會沿著單一方向流動，只是電壓會隨著距離的增加而減小，不比交流電來得穩定。比交流電來得穩定。

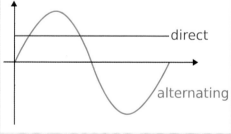

—— direct

—— alternating

© Zureks/Wikipedia

（d）答賴號閱鏖

1) **recite** [rɪˋsaɪt] (v.) 朗誦，背誦，詳述
   We all had to recite a poem in front of the class.
   我們必需在全班面前朗誦一首詩。

2) **diagram** [ˋdaɪəˏɡræm] (n.) 圖解，圖表
   The teacher drew a diagram of the heart on the blackboard.
   老師在黑板上畫了一個心臟解說圖。

3) **companion** [kəmˋpænjən] (n.) 同伴，伴侶
   Dogs and cats make great companions.
   貓和狗是人類最好的伴侶。

4) **continental** [ˏkɑntəˋnɛntəl] (a.) 大陸的，
   （大寫）歐洲大陸的
   There are 48 states in the continental United States.
   美國大陸有四十八州。

5) **invest** [ɪnˋvɛst] (v.) 投資，入股
   (n.) investment [ɪnˋvɛstmənt] 投資（額、標的）
   Now is a good time to invest in the property market.
   現在正是投資股市的好時機。

6) **founder** [ˋfaʊndɚ] (n.) 創立者，創辦人
   Jigoro Kano was the founder of judo.
   嘉納治五郎是柔道的創始人。

7) **happen (to)** [ˋhæpən] (v.) （偶然）發生，碰巧
   I happened to meet an old friend at the post office.
   我在郵局恰巧遇到一位老朋友。

8) **decline** [dɪˋklaɪn] (v./n.) 婉拒，謝絕
   We invited Richard to stay at our house, but he declined.
   我們邀請理查住我們家，但被他婉拒。

9) **generator** [ˋdʒɛnəˏretɚ] (n.) 發電機，產生器
   (n.) generation [ˏdʒɛnəˋreʃən] 產生
   The generator will shut down automatically when power is restored.
   電力恢復後，發電機將自動停止運轉。

10) **bonus** [ˋbonəs] (n.) 獎金，額外津貼
    Did you receive a Christmas bonus this year?
    你今年有拿到年終獎金嗎？

11) **furious** [ˋfjʊrɪəs] (a.) 狂怒的，狂暴的，兇猛的，猛烈的
    My parents were furious when they saw my report card.
    父母看到我的成績單時暴跳如雷。

12) **distribution** [ˏdɪstrəˋbjuʃən] (n.) 分配，配送
    The sale and distribution of cigarettes is heavily restricted.
    香煙的銷售與配銷是被嚴格管制的。

By 1882, Tesla was living in Budapest, Hungary, where he worked as an electrical engineer at the Central Telephone Exchange. One day, while walking in the city park with a friend, [1]**reciting** *Faust*, the answer suddenly came to him. "The idea came like a flash of lightning," said Tesla, "and in an instant the truth was revealed." He then drew a [2]**diagram** of his induction motor in the sand

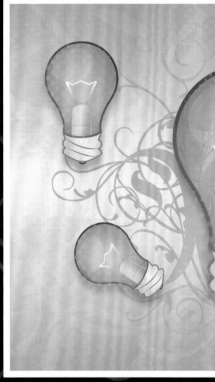

with his walking stick, and it was so clear and complete that his [3]**companion** was able to grasp how it worked.

Tesla soon found a position at [4]**Continental** Edison Company in Paris, but when he couldn't find anyone in Europe to [5]**invest** in his AC motor, he decided to take his idea directly to the company's [6]**founder**, Thomas Edison—who also [7]**happened** to be the world's most successful inventor. When Tesla arrived in New York in June 1885, all he had was four cents and a recommendation letter from Edison's business partner, Charles Batchelor. "I know two great men," the letter read. "One is you and the other is this young man."

Because Edison was already heavily invested in DC power, he [8]**declined** to develop Tesla's AC motor. He did, however, give Tesla a job improving his DC [9]**generators**, promising a $50,000 [10]**bonus** if he succeeded. But when he completed the job, Edison said the bonus was just a joke. Tesla was so

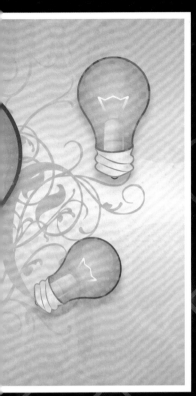

[11]**furious** that he quit and started his own company, where he not only built his AC motor, but also the equipment necessary for the generation and [12]**distribution** of AC power. In 1888, he sold the [13]**patents** for this system to George Westinghouse, which [14]**set off** the War of Currents between Westinghouse and Edison. AC power [15]**eventually** won, and Tesla's power system lights the world to this day.

Mini Quiz 閱讀測驗

■ **Why did Tesla move to America?**
(A) Because he couldn't find work in Europe
(B) Because he wanted to start his own company
(C) Because he couldn't develop his motor in Europe
(D) Because Edison promised to develop his motor

中 Translation

到了一八八二年，特斯拉已住在匈牙利布達佩斯，在中央電信局擔任電力工程師。一天，他和朋友在市立公園散步、吟誦《浮士德》時，答案突然浮現腦海。「那個想法就如靈光一閃，」特斯拉說：「真相立刻水落石出。」他隨即拿手杖在沙地畫下感應馬達圖，清楚、完整到能讓他的同伴理解它如何運作。

特斯拉很快在巴黎大陸愛迪生公司覓得職務，但當他無法在歐洲找到人投資他的交流電馬達時，他決定直接帶著他的構想去找公司創辦人：湯瑪士愛迪生——碰巧也是世界最成功的發明家。當特斯拉於一八八五年六月抵達紐約時，身上只有四分錢，和一封愛迪生事業夥伴查爾斯巴契勒的推薦信。「我認識兩位偉人，」信上寫：「一位是您，另一位就是這個年輕人。」

因為愛迪生已砸下重金投資直流電，他拒絕開發特斯拉的交流電馬達，但他給了特斯拉一份工作改進他的直流電發電機，答應如果成功，就給他五萬美元的獎金。但當特斯拉完成任務，愛迪生卻說獎金只是玩笑。特斯拉憤而離職，自己開公司，不僅打造出他的交流電馬達，也製造了交流電發電和配電所需的設備。一八八八年，他將這個系統的專利賣給喬治威斯汀豪斯，開啟威斯汀豪斯（編註：威斯汀豪斯的公司中文翻譯為「西屋公司」）與愛迪生的「電流戰爭」。最後交流電獲勝，而特斯拉的電力系統，直到今天仍照亮世界。

13) **patent** [ˈpætənt] (n./v.) 專利；申請專利
The patent for this device is owned by Apple.
這項裝置的專利由蘋果公司所有。

14) **set off** [ˈsɛt ˈɔf] (phr.) 引發，導致，引爆
The politician's murder set off violent protests.
這名政治人物的謀殺案引發暴力抗爭。

15) **eventually** [ɪˈvɛntʃuəli] (adv.) 最後，終究
(a.) eventual
Allen and Grace plan to get married and have children eventually.
艾倫和葛麗絲打算最後還是要結婚生子。

Language Guide

Faust 《浮士德》

德國大文豪歌德 (Goethe) 耗盡將近六十年才完成的《浮士德》，這個悲劇作品是根據真實人物浮士德的謠言故事而來。故事大約發生在中世紀，一個完美主義的浮士德博士將自己的靈魂出賣給撒旦，旨在科學與宗教的對立之下，探討著善與惡的主題。故事分為兩部，第一部於一八〇八年出版，第二部則是在一八三一年才完成。相較於第一部，第二部故事更針對現實的社會現象和政治發展。歌德的《浮士德》不僅被認為是德國文學中優秀的作品之一，更被譽為西方文學史上最重要的著作之一，對文學及音樂深具影響力，像是作曲家白遼士 (Berlioz)、詩人拜倫 (Byron) 和作家湯馬斯曼 (Thomas Mann) 等等，都因這部作品得到許多創作靈感。

induction motor 感應馬達

感應馬達的原理若要深入研究其實是很複雜的，因此 EZ TALK 用比較簡單方式來讓大家了解一下。我們都曉得當電流傳送出來會產生磁場，利用同性相斥、異性相吸的原理，因交流電的來回，磁場得以旋轉並驅動馬達。在特斯拉還未發明出交流電的感應馬達時，直流電式的感應馬達，還需將直流電轉換成交流電，過程非常繁複，因此交流電的出現，使得轉換磁場變得容易多了。感應馬達的出現除了造就出許多民生電器的出現，還能應用在工業用的機器上，是近代史上非常重要的發明之一。

瘋狂科學家的經典代表

特斯拉——孤僻的天才科學家，將自己的人生完全奉獻在科學研究上。終身未娶，身邊養了一堆鴿子，討厭人家摸到自己的頭髮，走路的時候還會算自己走了幾步。不僅如此，沒有置產的他，一直住在旅館裡，最後窮困潦倒之時，還是威斯汀豪斯先生幫他支付旅館的費用。個性古怪的他，常被冠上瘋狂科學家的稱號，因此在今日許多電影漫畫中出現的科學家形象，常以他的樣貌為藍圖。

War of Currents
電流之戰──與愛迪生的愛恨情仇

我們都曉得特斯拉曾為愛迪生工作過,在離開愛迪生的公司後,特斯拉並沒有放棄對交流電的研究,甚至自己開了一間公司,開發出一系列交流電的馬達、發電機以及配電設置,最後還與威斯汀豪斯合作,引爆出與愛迪生之間的戰爭。以直流電為至上的愛迪生,非常不屑交流電,為了自己的直流電事業,愛迪生以激烈的手段試圖詆毀交流電的發展。首先,他在大庭廣眾之下用交流電把小句小貓給電死,還想將 Westinghouse 這個字變成「電死(electrocute)小貓小狗」的代名詞。後來還秘密僱用哈洛布萊恩 (Harold P. Brown) 發明電椅,來宣傳交流電比直流電更具危險性,還可致死。一八九○年電椅正式啟用,準備電死威廉凱姆勒 (William Kemmler) 這名囚犯,沒想到卻因為電流不夠,沒有一次將凱姆勒電死,身體著火卻仍有呼吸,受盡折磨,

直到第三次通電才死去。威斯汀豪斯因而譏笑他說,不如直接拿斧頭砍死他還比較快一點。

一八九三年,特斯拉和威斯汀豪斯為芝加哥世界博覽會 (World's Columbian Exhibition) 裝置照明設備,眼紅的愛迪生還不願意將燈泡賣給特斯拉,威斯汀豪斯公司只好連夜趕工,最後在博覽會上將數十個燈泡一次點亮,證明交流電的穩定性及安全性,讓大家更了解交流電。經過電流之戰的激烈競爭,雖然直流電逐漸被交流電取代,愛迪生和威斯汀豪斯兩敗俱傷,兩人的公司都瀕臨倒閉。

至今,交流電已成為你我生活中缺一不可的必需品。雖然電流之戰常被解讀是愛迪生與威斯汀豪斯兩個商人之間的鬥爭,不過其實這背後和美國、歐洲公司投資相互競爭也有很大的關聯。

特斯拉的其他發明

你以為特斯拉只有發明出交流電的感應馬達嗎?其實他發明出來的東西可不是只有這一個,特斯拉一生拿到將近三百個專利,除了感應馬達之外,特斯拉線圈(Tesla coil,一種使用共振原理運作的變壓器)、遙控器、發電機、無線傳訊還有醫療器具 X 光,全都出自他手,說他是天才還真不為過。

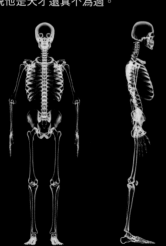

沒有生意頭腦的天才

特斯拉在一九八九年找了當時財力雄厚的銀行家──摩根 (J. P. Morgan),希望他可以投資自己預計在長島建立的沃登克里夫電台 (Wardenclyffe Tower),進行電波傳送資料以及無線傳電的實驗,摩根金援他十五萬美元(超過現在的三百萬美元),但摩根發現特斯拉的理想是想要免費供電給大眾,最後決定撤資,導致整個計劃難產。

21

Newton's Apple 牛頓的蘋果

Vocabulary Bank

1) **influential** [ˌɪnfluˈɛnʃəl] (a.) 有影響力的，有支配力的
The reporter got a job at an influential newspaper.
這位記者在一間有影響力的報社找到工作。

2) **invention** [ɪnˈvɛnʃən] (n.) 發明，創造
The kite is a Chinese invention.
風箏是中國的發明。

3) **component** [kəmˈponənt] (a./n.) 組成的，構成的；構成要素，成分
How can air be separated into its component gases?
要如何把空氣分成它所組成的氣體？

4) **droplet** [ˈdrɑplɪt] (n.) 小滴，微滴
Droplets of dew collected on the tree's leaves.
樹葉結了一滴一滴的露水。

5) **gravity** [ˈɡrævəti] (n.) 重力，引力，地心引力
Rockets must travel at high speeds to escape the Earth's gravity.
火箭必須高速行進來擺脫地球的重力。

6) **come about** [kʌm əˈbaʊt] 發生，產生
How did this problem come about?
這個問題是怎麼發生的？

7) **biography** [baɪˈɑɡrəfi] (n.) 傳記，傳記文學
(n.) biographer 傳記作家
The singer's biography was written by a famous biographer.
這位歌手的傳記由一位知名的傳記作家撰寫。

8) **sideways** [ˈsaɪdˌwez] (adv./a.) （斜）向一邊（的），向旁邊（的）
The car skidded sideways and crashed into a telephone pole.
那輛車朝一邊打滑，撞上電線杆。

9) **assuredly** [əˈʃʊrədli] (adv.) 無疑地，必定，確實
The Labor candidate will assuredly win the election.
這位工黨候選人一定會當選。

10) **orbit** [ˈɔrbɪt] (v./n.) 繞軌道運行；（天體運行）軌道
The Earth orbits the Sun once a year.
地球繞行太陽軌道一年一次。

進階字彙

11) **prism** [ˈprɪzəm] (n.) 棱鏡，棱柱
In science class, we used prisms to learn about light.
我們在理化課時用棱鏡學習光學。

12) **perpendicularly** [ˌpɝpənˈdɪkjələˌli] (adv.) 垂直地，直立地
(a.) perpendicular
Lincoln Street runs perpendicularly to California Street.
林肯街和加州街是垂直的。

課文朗讀 MP3 13　單字朗讀 MP3 14　英文講解 MP3 15

Sir Isaac Newton was born in Lincolnshire, England in 1643. Raised from a young age by his grandmother, he was bright and always at the head of his class. At 19, Newton entered Cambridge University, where he began studying the writings of [1]**influential** thinkers like Galileo and Copernicus. Soon after, he began working on a mathematical theory that led to the [2]**invention** of calculus.

In 1670, Newton switched his attention to optics, or the study of light. He was the first to show how white light can be divided into its [3]**component** colors when shone through a [11]**prism**, and also to explain how a rainbow is caused by sunlight shining through [4]**droplets** of water in the air. However, Newton is best remembered for his *Principia Mathematica*, published in 1687, which includes his three laws of motion and law of universal gravitation.

While it is commonly thought that Newton's idea of [5)]**gravity** [6)]**came about** after he was struck on the head by a falling apple, this isn't entirely true. A 1752 [7)]**biography** reveals that Newton had his Eureka moment while watching an apple fall from a tree in his mother's garden. Why does an apple always fall [12)]**perpendicularly** to the ground instead of going upward or [8)]**sideways**," he asked himself. "[9)]**Assuredly**," he said, "the reason is that the earth draws it."

Building on the idea that gravity causes objects to fall, Newton went on to explain why the planets [10)]**orbit** the Sun and why there are ocean tides. Even today, we owe much of our understanding of physics and the world around us to the great Sir Isaac Newton.

Mini Quiz 閱讀測驗

Which of the following is true about Newton?
A) He was stuck on the head by an apple.
B) He invented the prism.
C) He explained what causes a rainbow.
D) He sat in the front row at school.

中 Translation

艾薩克牛頓爵士在一六四三年生於英國林肯郡。從小由祖母帶大的他天資聰穎，總是班上第一名。十九歲進入劍橋大學就讀後，牛頓開始研究伽利略和哥白尼等重要思想家的作品。不久，他便著手發展一套促成微積分的數學理論。

一六七○年，牛頓將注意力轉向光學，即光的研究。他是證明白光在穿過棱鏡時，會分成組成顏色的第一人，也率先解釋彩虹是如何經由陽光穿透空氣中的水珠而形成。但，牛頓最為後人熟知的是他在一六八七年出版的《數學原理》，書中包含他的三大運動定律與萬有引力定律。

一般認為，牛頓是腦袋被掉落的蘋果砸到後，領悟了重力的概念，但這並非完全正確。一部一七五二年出版的傳記透露，牛頓是在母親的花園裡看到蘋果從樹上掉落時靈機一動。「為什麼蘋果會直直掉到地上，而非向上或往旁邊去呢」他問自己。「一定是地球吸引了它」他說。

以重力會致使物品落下的概念為基礎，牛頓進而解釋行星為什麼會繞著太陽轉，以及為什麼海洋會有潮汐。即便到今天，我們能夠如此了解物理學和我們周遭的世界，泰半要歸功於偉大的艾薩克牛頓爵士。

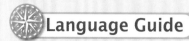

Language Guide

Principia Mathematica
《數學原理》
全書名為拉丁文 *Philosophia Naturalis Principia Mathematica*《自然哲學的數學原理》，意思是 Mathematical Principles of Natural Philosophy，是一套三本書的作品。牛頓在這本書中提出牛頓三大運動定律(three laws of motion)和萬有引力定律(law of universal gravitation)，被認為是科學革命(Scientific Revolution)中最重要的經典著作之一。

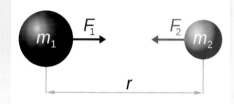

$$F_1 = F_2 = G \frac{m_1 \times m_2}{r^2}$$

牛頓因為一顆蘋果而找出月球繞地球公轉的原因，即「萬有引力定律」，指的是任意兩物體間皆存在著相互吸引的力量，此力量與兩物體的質量(mass)乘積成正比，和距離平方成反比。這個原理更進一步證明出地球上的海洋發生潮汐和太陽與月球間的引力相關。

牛頓發表的三大運動定律被視為經典力學(classical mechanics)的基礎。第一定律為物體的慣性定律，在不受外力的影響之下，物體會保持靜止或是均速的直線運動，也就是靜者恆靜、動者恆動。 例如一顆靜置的球，在未受外力的影響之下，會呈現靜置的狀態；反之，若為滾動狀態，只要未受摩擦的阻力，則會一直滾動下去。第二定律是指物體承受到的力量，與加速度、質量成正比。比如較重的物體從高空落下的速度會比輕物速度還快，力量也更大。第三定律則是作用力與反作用力，也就是施加於物體的力量，同時也會有另一股方向相反但力量相同的作用力產生。就像是當你用手掌拍打桌面的力量，也會有另一股強度相等的力量向手掌返回。

（C）答賴賴賴賴賴

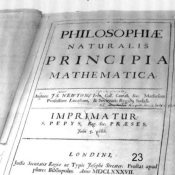

PHILOSOPHIÆ
NATURALIS
PRINCIPIA
MATHEMATICA

Autore *JS. NEWTON*, Trin. Coll. Cantab. Soc. Mathefeos Profeffore Lucafiano, & Societatis Regalis Sodali.

IMPRIMATUR.
S. PEPYS, Reg. Soc. PRÆSES.
Julii 5. 1686.

LONDINI,
Juffu Societatis Regiæ ac Typis Jofephi Streater. Proftat apud plures Bibliopolas. Anno MDCLXXXVII.

©National Portrait Gallery/wikipedia

站在巨人肩膀上的牛頓

謙遜的牛頓說：「如果說我看得比別人遠些，那是因為我站在巨人的肩膀上。」他口中的「巨人」指的就是伽利略、科卜勒、哥白尼等科學巨擘，牛頓的學術研究奠基在這些偉大前人知識體系上。現在就與 EZ TALK 一同躍入牛頓的知識深海中吧！

牛頓的啟蒙者——中世紀四大天文學家

Copernicus 哥白尼 (1473 -1543)

波蘭天文學家 (astronomer)，通曉多國語言，曾任執政官、外交官，同時也是一名經濟學家。他在天文學上最重要的學說則是「日心說」(heliocentric model)，即宇宙的中心為太陽，而不是當時天主教鼓吹的「地心說」(geocentric model)。雖然此一理論日後仍被推翻，不過他卻使得全由宗教主宰的科學觀開始動搖，開啟科學嶄新的一頁。

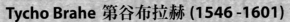

© ArtMechanic/wikipedia

Tycho Brahe 第谷布拉赫 (1546 -1601)

丹麥天文學家，對鍊金術 (alchemy) 和天文學極有興趣，在望遠鏡 (telescope) 尚未發明前就已對天象進行精密的觀測。他學術上的重大成就在於發現了「超新星」(supernova)，以及證實彗星 (comet) 非大氣裡面的現象，而且證明它的軌道在行星之間，粉碎了傳統的觀念。

© ArtMechanic/wikipedia

Galileo 伽利略 (1564 -1642)

義大利物理學家 (physicist) 暨天文學家，被喻為「科學革命的先鋒」。最有名的科學貢獻就是利用光線的折射 (refraction) 原理，用兩片透鏡製造出望遠鏡，並把它用在天文觀測上，開拓人們的天文學視野。而他所作的自由落體實驗也啟發牛頓的三大運動定律。同時，人們也開始跟從他「眼見為憑」的科學精神，成為探索真理的象徵。

© Dmitry Rozhkov/wikipedia

© ArtMechanic

Johannes Kepler 克卜勒 (1571-1630)

德國天文學家，主張地球會不斷移動，且行星的繞行軌道 (orbit) 應為橢圓形 (elliptical) 而非圓形，最著名的成就為「行星運動三大定律」(three laws of planetary motion)，其中第三定律更是牛頓萬有引力定律的基礎，即各行星繞太陽公轉週期的平方和橢圓軌道的半長軸立方成正比。

牛頓的宗教思想

宗教和科學其實有著密不可分的關係，因為宗教對人類來說不僅是心靈支柱，而且也會影響人對於宇宙的生成、發展等觀念。牛頓自小就是虔誠的教徒，不過後人解讀他的手稿後，發現他應該算是異教徒，只不過當時不敢太明目張膽。從他不相信「三位一體」（即聖父、聖靈、聖子皆為神）的教義中可見一斑。

當他越深入研究科學領域，發現無論天文、物理…等法則，都相當精密完美，好似有一隻看不見的手在默默安排，於是他相信，一定有比人類更高等的生命在創造這個世界，於是後來便更醉心宗教，並著有多部宗教作品。而他所主張的宗教思想亦非一般的迷信，而是主張「自然神教」(deism)，認為上帝不過是「有智慧的意志」，祂是世界的造物主，在創世之後就不再干預世界事務，而讓世界按照本身的規律存在與發展，與舊時的「天啟宗教」(revealed religion) 不同。

© Joey Carmichael

牛頓與萊布尼茲的微積分爭議

牛頓和德國的萊布尼茲 (Gottfried Wilhelm Leibniz) 都算是微積分 (calculus) 的始祖，不過由於牛頓曾把微積分運用在物理學上，之後卻看到萊布尼茲竟將他新發現發表於世，因此懷疑他用特殊管道拿到他的資料，指控他抄襲，進而引發學術界爭議，使得英國和德國為了誰先發明微積分而吵得不可開交，使數學界大受打擊。其實並沒有誰抄襲誰的問題，他們兩人只是分別從不同的方向出發（牛頓從微分出發，萊布尼茲從積分出發），兩人不過是殊途同歸罷了。

© www.crystalinks.com

牛頓的小趣事

● 據說有一天牛頓的家鄉出現了一次大風暴，大風把棚欄門吹得碰碰作響，牛頓的母親便叫他趕快去把棚欄的門鎖好。可是過了半個小時仍不見牛頓回來，於是他母親便出去找他。在門口，她看見那扇門已被風吹倒在地上，而她的兒子牛頓卻一下子迎著風往前走，一會兒又逆著風走回來。她覺得很奇怪，便對牛頓大喊：「你怎麼啦？這麼冷還在外面玩！」牛頓聽了母親的話，有點委屈地說：「媽，我不是在玩，我是在計算順風和逆風的速度相差有多大。」由此可知牛頓從小就具備了實事求是的實驗精神。

● 醉心研究的牛頓在實驗室裡工作時，他的家人拿了幾顆雞蛋給他，要他餓了就煮來吃，幾個鐘頭後，家人來收拾餐具，見牛頓還在埋頭做實驗，便輕聲問道：「雞蛋煮熟了嗎？」牛頓頭也不抬地說：「正在煮啊！」家人打開鍋蓋一看，不得了，原來是牛頓誤把他的金錶丟入鍋中煮了。

● 牛頓上小學時，有一次老師在課堂上問學生：「一加一等於多少？」全班同學異口同聲答二，只有牛頓答零。頓時惹來異樣的眼光，老師隔日便找了牛頓的媽媽來，對她說：「您的孩子可能智能有些問題，連最簡單的算術也會錯，請您另請高明，我無法再教導他了」，牛頓便因此慘遭退學。

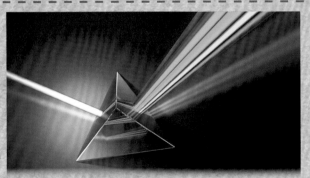

牛頓的光學研究

牛頓從一六六三年起開始對透鏡的結構和性能感興趣，於是開始從事光學 (optics) 研究。在他研究光學大約十年的時間裡，他用稜鏡作實驗，發現陽光是由折射率不同的幾種射線混合而成的，每一種射線都是不能再分解的單純色光。根據這個結論，牛頓又進行了一些實驗，列出了十三條有關光和色的本性的結論。他是第一個科學地解釋了虹的色彩及成因。之後更出版了《光學》(Opticks) 一書來發表他的研究。

V Vocabulary Bank

1) **physician** [fɪˋzɪʃən] (n.)（內科）醫生
You should discuss your sleep problems with your physician.
你應該和你的醫生討論一下你的睡眠問題。

2) **pneumonia** [nʊˋmonjə] (n.) 肺炎
Pneumonia can sometimes be fatal.
肺炎有時會致命。

3) **tuberculosis** [tʊ͵bɜkjəˋlosis] (n.) 結核病
Some types of tuberculosis are resistant to drugs.
某些結核病具有抗藥性。

4) **devote** [dɪˋvot] (v.) 將…奉獻給，致力於
Mother Teresa devoted her life to helping the poor.
德雷莎修女一生致力於幫助窮困的人。

5) **research** [ˋrisɜtʃ / rɪˋsɜtʃ] (n./v.)（學術）研究，調查
(n.) researcher 研究者，調查者
A team of scientists is conducting research on the new virus.
一組科學家正著手對這種新病毒進行研究。

6) **laboratory** [ˋlæbrə͵tɔri] (n.) 實驗室，研究室，亦可寫作 lab
Some people believe that the AIDS virus was created in a laboratory.
有些人相信，愛滋病毒是在實驗室裡製造出來的。

7) **appoint** [əˋpɔɪnt] (a.) 任用，指定
The boy's uncle was appointed his legal guardian after his parents' death.
男孩的雙親死後，他的叔叔被指定擔任他的法定監護人。

8) **professor** [prəˋfɛsə] (n.) 教授
The professor is an expert on Greek history.
這位教授是希臘史的專家。

9) **impulse** [ˋɪmpʌls] (n.)（生理）神經衝動，（電）脈衝
The brain communicates with the body through nerve impulses.
大腦和身體是藉由神經衝動來相互溝通。

10) **transmit** [trænsˋmɪt] (n.) 傳送，播送
The radio set can transmit and receive radio signals.
這台無線電機可以傳送和接收無線電訊號。

11) **messy** [ˋmɛsi] (a.) 凌亂的，邋遢的
Ryan's bedroom is always messy.
萊恩的房間總是很凌亂。

進階字彙

12) **metabolism** [mɛˋtæbə͵lɪzəm] (n.) 新陳代謝
Regular exercise will increase your metabolism.
規律的運動會加速新陳代謝。

13) **hypothesis** [haɪˋpɑθəsɪs] (n.) 假說，假設
The scientist designed an experiment to test his hypothesis.
那位科學家設計了一個實驗來測試他的假設。

14) **scribble** [ˋskrɪbəl] (v.) 潦草地書寫，隨意亂畫
Kelly got in trouble for scribbling in her textbook.
凱莉因為亂畫教科書而惹上麻煩。

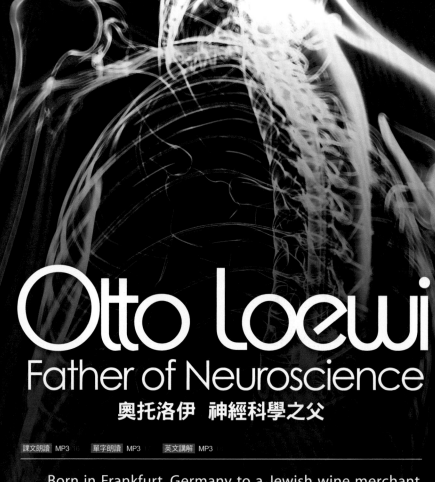

Otto Loewi
Father of Neuroscience
奧托洛伊 神經科學之父

課文朗讀 MP3　單字朗讀 MP3　英文講解 MP3

Born in Frankfurt, Germany to a Jewish wine merchant, Otto Loewi originally planned on becoming a **physician**. After completing medical school at the University of Strasbourg in 1896, he returned to Frankfurt, where he received practical training in internal medicine at the City Hospital. But after watching many **pneumonia** and **tuberculosis** patients die because no treatments were available, he decided he would rather **devote** his career to medical **research**.

Loewi joined the **laboratory** of renowned pharmacologist Hans Horst Meyer in 1898, and spent the next decade studying **metabolism** and the effects of drugs on the internal organs, first at the University of Marburg, and later in Vienna. After Loewi was **appointed professor** of pharmacology at the University of Graz in 1909, the focus of his research turned

to the nervous system. There was a debate at the time about whether nerve **impulses** were **transmitted** electrically or chemically, but nobody had been able to provide proof either way. Loewi suspected that the chemical **hypothesis** was correct, but it wasn't until 1920 that he had his eureka moment.

On the night before Easter Sunday, Loewi dreamed of an experiment that could prove how nerve impulses are transmitted. He woke up in the middle of the night, **scribbled** the experiment down, and went back to sleep. But when he got up the next morning, he found that his notes were too **messy** to read. Luckily, he had the same dream the following night. This time, he rushed to his lab at 3:00 a.m. and performed the experiment while it was still fresh in his mind. For his famous frog heart experiment, which proved that nerve impulses are transmitted chemically, Loewi received the Nobel Prize in 1936.

Mini Quiz 閱讀測驗

■ **Why did Loewi switch careers?**
(A) Because he was unable to complete his medical training
(B) Because he never obtained his medical degree
(C) Because he wanted to work on disease treatments
(D) Because he had no interest in the medical field

中 Translation

生於德國法蘭克福、父為猶太葡萄酒商的奧托洛伊本來打算當醫生。一八九六年,在史特拉斯堡大學唸完醫學院後,他回到法蘭克福,在市立醫院接受內科的實習訓練。但在看到許多肺炎及結核病患因沒有治療方法而病死之後,他決定將生涯投入醫學研究。

洛伊在一八九八年加入知名藥理學家漢斯赫斯特梅爾的研究室,接下來十年都在研究新陳代謝和藥物對內臟的影響,先在馬柏格大學,後赴維也納。一九○九年獲聘為格拉茨大學藥理學教授之後,他的研究重心轉向神經系統。當時,該領域的人士正在辯論神經衝動是由電流還是化學物質傳導,但兩者都沒有人能夠證明。洛伊認為化學派的假設是正確的,但他靈機一動的時刻,直到一九二○年才來臨。

在復活節星期天前夕,洛伊夢到一項能夠證明神經衝動如何傳導的實驗。他在夜半醒來,把實驗草草記錄下來,便回去睡覺。但隔天早上起床時,他發現他的筆記太亂,無法看懂。幸好,隔晚上他又做了同樣的夢。這一次,他在凌晨三點趕往實驗室,趁腦中還有鮮明印象時進行實驗。著名的青蛙心臟實驗證明了神經衝動是由化學物質傳導,也讓洛伊獲得一九三六年的諾貝爾獎。

27

Language Guide

nervous system 神經系統

神經系統是由許許多多的神經細胞(neuron)組成,負責將生物體所受到的刺激(stimulation)傳到大腦或其他部位,進而因應環境做出適當的身體反應。人的神經系統可分為由大腦和脊髓(spinal cord)組成的中樞神經系統(central nervous system),以及周邊神經系統(peripheral nervous system),兩者藉由神經纖維連結,以協調各個組織和器官。

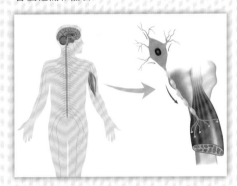

frog heart experiment
青蛙心跳實驗

這是奧托洛伊在一九二○年所做的實驗。將兩隻青蛙的心臟分別置於兩個相通的盒子內,編號一的心臟及其迷走神經(vagus nerve)均浸泡在生理食鹽水(saline solution)中,通電刺激後,使編號一的心跳(heart rate)減緩,再採集一號心臟附近的液體,將其滴到編號二的心臟,進而發現二號心臟的心跳居然也慢了下來,證實二號心臟減緩跳動是因為神經受刺激後釋出的一種化學物質,而非藉由電流來傳導。洛伊將該化學物質命名為 vagusstoff,也就是我們所說的神經傳導物質——乙醯膽鹼(acetylcholine)。

© Nrets/Wikipedia

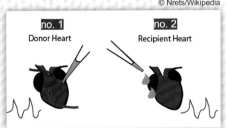

圖說測驗解答:(C)

STARBUCKS
A Company with Soul

星巴克 有靈魂的企業

Vocabulary Bank

1) **fracture** [ˈfræktʃə] (v./n.) 分裂，斷裂
Many families were fractured by the war.
許多家庭都因戰爭而分崩離析。

2) **scholarship** [ˈskɑləˌʃɪp] (n.) 獎學金
Scholarships are available to students with superior grades.
獎學金是提供給那些成績優異的學生。

3) **visa** [ˈvizə] (n.) 簽證
You can't cross the border without a visa.
沒有簽證，你就不能穿越國境。

4) **worship** [ˈwɝʃɪp] (v./n.) 拜神，做禮拜
Which church do you worship at?
你在哪個教堂做禮拜？

5) **convince** [kənˈvɪns] (v.) 說服
The kids convinced their parents to let them have pizza for dinner.
孩子們說服爸媽讓他們吃披薩當晚餐。

6) **exotic** [ɪgˈzɑtɪk] (a.) 異國（風味）的，奇特的
The living room was decorated with exotic furniture.
那間客廳以異國風的傢俱來佈置。

7) **inviting** [ɪnˈvaɪtɪŋ] (a.) 吸引人的，誘人的
The hotel has an inviting swimming pool.
那間飯店有著吸引人的游泳池。

8) **pass away** [pæs əˈwe] (phr.) 過世
Stephen's father passed away last year.
史蒂芬的父親去年過世了。

9) **insurance** [ɪnˈʃʊrəns] (n.) 保險
Do you have fire insurance on your home?
你的房子有保火災險嗎？

10) **afford** [əˈfɔrd] (v.) 負擔得起，買得起
We can't afford to take a vacation this year.
我們今年付不起渡假的費用。

課文朗讀 MP3 19　　單字朗讀 MP3 20　　英文講解 MP3 21

　　Howard Schultz grew up poor in the 1950s in a housing project in Brooklyn. When his father broke his leg at work, he received no benefits, and the family became even poorer. "I saw the 1)**fracturing** of the American dream 11)**firsthand** at the age of seven," recalls Howard. A football 2)**scholarship** served as his exit 3)**visa**, and he became the first college graduate in his family.

　　While working at a 12)**kitchenware** company, Howard became curious about a small coffee bean 13)**retailer** that was ordering large numbers of coffeemakers, so he decided to fly to Seattle and pay it a visit. "I stepped inside and saw what looked like a temple for the 4)**worship** of coffee," he remembers. The store, which was founded in 1971 by three aging 14)**hippies**, was called Starbucks, after the coffee-drinking first mate in *Moby-Dick*. Howard 5)**convinced** the owners to hire him as a manager, and moved his family to Seattle.

On a trip to Italy in 1983, Howard had his first café latte, and his eureka moment: Starbucks needed to expand from selling beans to serving [6]**exotic** coffees in an [7]**inviting** environment. But the owners didn't agree, so he left to open his own café. When Starbucks was **1 put up for sale** in 1987, Howard bought it and combined the two businesses. Another turning point came when his father [8]**passed away**. Not wanting his employees to be treated like his father had been, he began providing full benefits, including health [9]**insurance** for part-time workers. This may be expensive, but Howard can [10]**afford** it—he's now worth over a billion dollars, and Starbucks is the largest coffee chain in the world.

Mini Quiz 閱讀測驗

■ **Which of the following is true about Howard Schultz?**
(A) He is the founder of Starbucks.
(B) He was the first manager of Starbucks.
(C) He is the owner of Starbucks.
(D) He was the one who named Starbucks.

中 Translation

霍華舒茲在一九五〇年代的布魯克林國宅長大。他的父親在工作時摔斷腿，卻沒有得到任何公司福利的補償金，於是一家人變得更窮困。「我七歲時親眼見到美國夢碎，」霍華回憶道。一筆美式足球獎學金讓他得以脫離貧窮，他也成為家裡第一個大學畢業生。

在一家廚具公司工作時，霍華對一家訂購大量咖啡機的小型咖啡豆零售商感到好奇，於是決定飛往西雅圖拜訪。「我踏進去，看到裡面宛如一座膜拜咖啡的廟宇。」他回憶道。那家店是三位年長的嬉皮於一九七一年成立的，店名叫星巴克，出自《白鯨記》中那位愛喝咖啡的大副名字。霍華說服老闆們聘請他擔任經理，並舉家遷至西雅圖。

一九八三年到義大利旅遊時，霍華喝到生平第一杯拿鐵，他靈機一動：星巴克必須拓展生意，從只賣咖啡豆擴展成一個提供異國風味咖啡的誘人環境。但老闆們不同意，所以他離開公司，開了自己的咖啡館。一九八七年星巴克頂讓出售時，霍華把它買下來，將兩家公司合而為一。另一個轉折點在他父親過世時到來。他不希望員工受到父親以往那般的對待，於是開始提供完整的福利，包括為兼職員工提供醫療保險。這或許要花大筆費用，但霍華付得起——他現在身價超過十億美元，星巴克也成了全球規模最大的咖啡連鎖店。

© Postdlf 位於美國華盛頓州西雅圖的星巴克創始店

進階字彙

11) **firsthand** [ˈfɝstˋhænd] (adv./a.) 親自地；第一手的
We heard about the riot firsthand from a witness.
我們從目擊者那裡聽到了第一手有關那場暴動的消息。

12) **kitchenware** [ˈkɪtʃənˌwɛr] (n.) （總稱）廚房用具
This store specializes in European kitchenware.
這間店專門賣歐洲廚具。

13) **retailer** [ˈritelɚ] (n.) 零售商
(n./a./v.) retail [ˈritel] 零售（業）
Retailers are doing better than expected this quarter.
零售業在這一季的表現比預期要來得好。

14) **hippie** [ˈhɪpi] (n.) 嬉皮
Lots of hippies became yuppies in the 1980s.
許多嬉皮在一九八〇年代都成了雅痞。

☞ Tongue-tied No More

1 put (sth.) up for sale 將……拍賣，販售

put up 這個片語因為本身有很多意義，如：「建造，架設」、「提名」，讓人乍看之下不知道究竟是什麼意思。這裡 put up 後方接上了 for sale「出售」，應該就不難猜測 put up 是「提供，拿出」販賣物的意思。這個片語類似的說法還有 put (sth.) up for auction。

A: I heard you guys are moving to Denver soon.
我聽說你們就要搬到丹佛了。

B: Yeah. We've already put our house up for sale.
是啊。我們已經把房子拿出來賣了。

✦ Language Guide

星巴克名稱的由來

星巴克 Starbucks 這個名字，來自於梅爾維爾 (Herman Melville) 的《白鯨記》(Moby-Dick)。《白鯨記》堪稱西洋文學史上最重要的海洋文學之一，基本上已呼應到美國早期咖啡貿易的海運背景。更重要的是，作品中具有理性沈著的正面形象的大副——史塔巴克(Starbuck)，對咖啡情有獨鍾。根據小說情節，每當船靠岸，這位大副就會循著咖啡香味去尋找休憩的地方。星巴克咖啡的創辦人在這位大副名字後方加了 s，為的就是期許所有的員工都能像 史塔巴克一樣，對咖啡和工作充滿熱愛。雖然咖啡在這部作品中並不是主要的意象，但是其背景和人物的連結著實替這個咖啡品牌添加了一道文藝光環。

（C）：答解鹼版關

V Vocabulary Bank

1) **popularity** [ˌpɑpjəˋlærəti] (n.) 普及，流行，廣受歡迎
The popularity of video games continues to grow.
電玩遊戲受歡迎的程度日益成長。

2) **fiction** [ˋfɪkʃən] (n.) 小說，虛構（的事）。
science fiction 意即「科幻小說」
Who is your favorite science fiction author?
你最愛的科幻小說作家是哪一位？

3) **addicted** [əˋdɪktɪd] (a.) 上癮的，入迷的
(n.) addiction [əˋdɪkʃən] 成癮，癮頭
(a.) addictive [əˋdɪktɪv] 會使人成癮的
Samantha is addicted to chocolate.
莎曼莎對巧克力上癮。

4) **inspiration** [ˌɪnspəˋreʃən] (n.) 靈感，啟發
Many poets seek inspiration from the natural world.
許多詩人從大自然界尋求靈感。

5) **ingredient** [ɪnˋgridiənt] (n.)（烹飪）食材
Do you have all the ingredients you need to make the cake?
你有做蛋糕的所有材料嗎？

6) **condition** [kənˋdɪʃən] (n.) 疾病，症狀；（健康）狀況
Michael's father has a heart condition.
麥克的爸爸心臟有問題。

7) **prohibition** [ˌproəˋbɪʃən] (n.) 禁止，禁酒
In many countries, there is increasing debate about drug prohibition.
在很多國家，禁毒的議題越來越引起討論。

8) **formula** [ˋfɔrmjələ] (n.) 配方，公式，方法
The speaker shared his formula for success with the audience.
演講者跟聽眾分享他的成功之道。

進階字彙

9) **carbonated** [ˋkɑrbəˌnetɪd] (a.)（含）二氧化碳的
Most carbonated drinks are high in sugar.
大多數的碳酸飲料含糖量都很高。

10) **morphine** [ˋmɔrfin] (n.) 嗎啡
The patient was given morphine to relieve his pain.
該位病患施打嗎啡，以減輕他的疼痛。

11) **pharmacist** [ˋfɑrmɛsɪst] (n.) 藥劑師
pharmacy [ˋfɑrmɛsi] (n.) 藥房，藥局
There's a new pharmacist working at the pharmacy.
這間藥局新來了一位藥劑師。

12) **cocaine** [koˋken] (n.) 古柯鹼
The drug dealer was caught with a kilo of cocaine in his car.
那名毒販被查獲車上藏有一公斤的古柯鹼。

13) **caffeine** [kɪˋfin] (n.) 咖啡因
Coffee, tea and chocolate all contain caffeine.
咖啡、茶還有巧克力都含有咖啡因。

The Unlikely Origins of Coca-Cola

讓人意想不到的可口可樂由來

課文朗讀 MP3 22　單字朗讀 MP3 23　英文講解 MP3 24

Coca-Cola is recognized as the world's most valuable brand, and is sold in every country around the world except for North Korea and Cuba. Given the great [1]**popularity** of this [9]**carbonated** soft drink, you may be surprised to learn that it started out as a patent medicine in the 19th century. They say that truth is stranger than [2]**fiction**, and in the case of Coke, the truth is strange indeed.

In April 1865, during the final days of the Civil War, a soldier named John Pemberton was injured in battle. He was given [10]**morphine** to ease his pain, and like many wounded soldiers at the time, became [3]**addicted** to the drug. A [11]**pharmacist** by trade, Pemberton began developing patent medicines, likely in an effort to find a cure for his addiction.

After several unsuccessful attempts, Pemberton decided to take [4]**inspiration** from Vin Mariani, one of the world's most successful patent medicines. Made from red wine and coca leaves—the source of [12]**cocaine**—Vin Mariani had many famous fans, including Thomas Edison, Queen Victoria and even the Pope, who awarded it a Vatican Gold Medal. Pemberton created his own coca wine by adding several new [5]**ingredients**, including kola nut, an African fruit that contains more [13]**caffeine** than coffee beans.

Pemberton's French Wine Coca, which he claimed could treat headaches, nervous [6]**conditions** and even drug addiction, was an

instant success when it went on the market in 1885. Considering that the medicine contained three addictive substances, it isn't surprising that customers would keep coming back for more. Unfortunately, Atlanta passed a [7)]**prohibition** law the following year, forcing Pemberton to change his [8)]**formula**.

Mini Quiz 閱讀測驗

Which of the following was NOT an ingredient in French Wine Cola?
(A) Coca leaves
(B) Wine
(C) Cola nut
(D) Coffee beans

中 Translation

可口可樂被公認為全球最具價值的品牌，除了北韓和古巴，世界各國都有販售。基於這種無酒精碳酸飲料大受歡迎的程度，你或許會意外：它最早是十九世紀的一種成藥。人們說：事實比小說更離奇，而以可口可樂這個例子來說，事實確實玄之又玄。

一八六五年四月，正逢南北戰爭的尾聲，一位名叫約翰潘伯頓的士兵在戰場上受了傷。為了緩解痛苦，他被施予嗎啡，就像當時許多受傷士兵一樣，後來他便對那種藥物上癮。可能是為了尋求療方來治療他的藥癮，原本就是藥劑師的潘伯頓開始研發各種成藥。

歷經數度嘗試未果，潘伯頓決定從「馬利安尼酒」這種世上最成功的成藥之一尋找靈感。用紅酒和古柯葉（即古柯鹼的來源）所製成的馬利安尼酒有許多名人粉絲，包括湯瑪士愛迪生、維多利亞女王，甚至還有授予其「梵蒂岡金牌」的教宗。潘伯頓添加數種新原料，製造出他獨創的古柯酒，其中包含有「可樂果」這種咖啡因含量比咖啡豆還高的非洲果實。

潘伯頓聲稱他的「法國古柯酒」能治療頭痛、神經不適，甚至還能對付毒癮，在一八八五年甫一上市即造成轟動。基於這種藥品本身就含有三種會成癮的成分，顧客會不斷回來購買也不足為奇。不幸的是，亞特蘭大於次年通過禁酒令，迫使潘伯頓改變他的配方。

EUREKA! 點子成金

V Vocabulary Bank

1) **syrup** [ˋsɪrəp] (n.) 糖漿
Do you want syrup on your pancakes?
你的鬆餅要淋糖漿嗎？

2) **pronounce** [prəˋnaʊns] (v.) 表示，宣稱，斷言
The doctor pronounced the soldier fit for duty.
醫生表示這位士兵可以執行軍務。

3) **flowing** [ˋfloɪŋ] (a.) 流暢的，流動的
The dancers wore long flowing dresses.
舞者們穿著飄逸的長洋裝。

4) **logo** [ˋlogo] (n.) 商標
The players are all wearing shirts with the sponsor's logo.
這些球員全都穿著上頭有贊助商標誌的球衣。

5) **genius** [ˋdʒinjəs] (n.) 天賦，天才
The artist's genius was only recognized after his death.
這位藝術家的天賦在他過世後才受到肯定。

6) **serving** [ˋsɜvɪŋ] (n.) 一份（食物、飲料）
How many servings does the recipe make?
這個食譜是幾人份的？

進階字彙

7) **contract** [kənˋtrækt] (v.) 得（病）
The explorer contracted malaria in the tropics.
那位探險家在熱帶地區染上了瘧疾。

課文朗讀 MP3 25　　單字朗讀 MP3 26　　英文講解 MP3 27

Back in his home laboratory, Pemberton used suga[r] [1)]**syrup** to replace the sweetness of the wine, and added a number of other secret ingredients to improve the flavor. When he found that the resulting mixture was too sweet, he had his eureka moment. Soda fountains were becoming popular as a result of the prohibition law, so why not mix the syrup with soda water and sell it as a fountain drink instead of a medicine?

In May 1886, Pemberton took a bottle of his new drink down the street for a taste test at Jacob's Pharmacy, where soda fountain customers [2)]**pronounced** it "excellent." But the soft drink still needed a name. A naming contest was held, and Pemberton's business partner Frank Robinson used two of the drink's key ingredients—coca leaves and kola nuts—to come up with the name Coca-Cola. Robinson was also responsible for writing the name in the [3)]**flowing** letters that would become the company [4)]**logo**.

Coca-Cola went on sale at Jacob's Pharmacy for five cents a glass, and was soon being sold at soda fountains around the city. Although Pemberton had finally created a great product, he wouldn't live to see Coke's eventual success. He soon [7)]**contracted** stomach cancer, and passed away two years later. Thanks to the marketing [5)]**genius** of businessman Asa Candler, who bought the rights to Coca-Cola for just $2,300, the drink became a national brand by the end of the century.

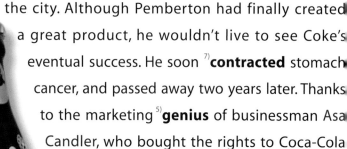

©allieatfood/flickr.com

© harry_nl/flickr.com

Today, 1.8 billion ⁶⁾**servings** of Coke are sold around the world every day!

Mini Quiz 閱讀測驗

Where was Coca-Cola invented?
(A) In a laboratory
(B) At a pharmacy
(C) At Jacob's house
(D) At a soda fountain

中 Translation

回到家中的實驗室後,潘伯頓用糖漿取代葡萄酒的甜味,然後又添加數種秘密原料來增添其風味。當他發現調出來的成品太甜時,他突然靈機一動。在實施禁酒令後,汽水櫃台變得愈來愈受歡迎,所以何不將糖漿和蘇打水混合在一起,然後當成汽水而非藥品來賣?

一八八六年五月,潘伯頓帶了一瓶他的新飲料到同條街上的雅各藥局給人試喝,裡面汽水櫃台的顧客都說誇它「棒得沒話說」。不過這款無酒精飲料還是得取個名字才行。於是潘伯頓便舉辦了一場命名比賽,而他的事業夥伴法蘭克羅賓森就用這款飲料的兩種主成分——古柯葉和可樂果,想出「Coca-Cola」之名。後來成為公司商標的平滑流暢的字樣,也同樣是羅賓森的功勞。

可口可樂以每杯五分錢在雅各藥局販售,並且很快就攻佔了該市各地的汽水櫃台。雖然潘伯頓終於創出了一項成功的商品,卻來不及親眼目睹可樂最後的成功。不久他罹患胃癌,兩年後與世長辭。商人艾薩凱德勒只花兩千三百美元便買斷可口可樂的權利,而拜他的行銷天賦之賜,這款飲料在十九世紀結束時已成為全國品牌。如今,世界各地每天都會賣出十八億份的可口可樂!

✦ Language Guide

soda fountain 汽水櫃台

十九世紀初期的美國,不論大人還是小孩都非常愛喝酒,逐漸地人們開始反省社會嗜酒的風氣,認為應該多喝點健康的飲料,於是汽水櫃台就此誕生。汽水櫃台通常設在藥店內,除了供應碳酸飲料外,有時還會提供冰淇淋等甜點,成了男女老少聚會閒聊的地點,到了一九四〇、五〇年代最為風行。不過後來因為冰淇淋專賣店、瓶裝飲料和快餐店林立,汽水櫃台逐漸式微。而現在較常見的則是自助飲料機 (drink machine),好處是想喝飲料的人可以自己動手,不需有人服務。

Asa Candler 艾薩凱德勒

艾薩凱德勒出生於一八五一年的美國喬治亞州 (Georgia)。他起初經營賣藥和製藥的生意,在一八九二年取得可口可樂的配方和所有權後,開始推出許多促銷活動,附送日曆、時鐘、明信片、剪紙……等贈品,而這些贈品都成了今日可口可樂收藏者的最愛。他曾說過:「要有積極的行銷、獨特的品牌和造型感十足的包裝,才能造就成功的商品。」(Aggressive marketing, unique brands and stylish packaging go a long way.)。因此可口可樂公司邀請印第安那州 (Indiana) 的魯特玻璃公司 (Root Glass Company) 來設計,以《大英百科全書》(Encyclopedia Britannica) 上一幅可可豆莢的圖案發想,創造出全球世人熟知的「可口可樂」曲線瓶。今天可口可樂之所以風靡全球,都要歸功於凱德勒這個具有行銷頭腦的企業家。

© wikipedia

(A) 答網鏈嘅單閱劇[Mini Quiz 答案](A)

33

LEVI'S
FROM Miners TO Movie Stars

走向時尚界的 Levi's 牛仔褲

V Vocabulary Bank

1) **immigrate** [ˈɪməˌgret] (v.) 移民，遷移
   (n./a.) immigrant [ˈɪmɪgrənt] 移民（的）
   Ian's parents immigrated to the U.S. in the 1950s.
   伊恩的父母是在一九五〇年代移民美國的。

2) **tailor** [ˈtelə] (n.) 裁縫師
   I need to take these pants to a tailor to get them taken in.
   我需要把這件褲子拿到裁縫師那裡改小。

3) **miner** [ˈmaɪnə] (n.) 礦工
   Dozens of miners were trapped in the flooded coal mine.
   數十名礦工被困在淹水的煤礦坑裡。

4) **sturdy** [ˈstɝdi] (a.) 堅固的，耐用的
   Be sure to wear sturdy shoes for the hike.
   健行時務必要穿上耐穿的鞋子。

5) **reinforce** [ˌriɪnˈfɔrs] (v.) 加強
   The building was reinforced after the earthquake.
   這棟建築物在地震後被加強。

6) **copper** [ˈkɑpə] (n./a.) 銅
   Copper is often used to make electrical wire.
   銅很常被用來做電線。

7) **harness** [ˈhɑrnəs] (n.) 馬具，挽具
   The horse escaped from its harness and ran away.
   那匹馬掙脫馬具並逃跑了。

8) **fabric** [ˈfæbrɪk] (n.) 布料
   Mom bought some fabric to make a dress.
   媽媽買了一些布料來做洋裝。

9) **partnership** [ˈpɑrtnəˌʃɪp] (n.) 合夥關係，合作
   The two companies formed a partnership to develop the product.
   這兩間公司建立合夥關係來開發產品。

課文朗讀 MP3 28　單字朗讀 MP3 29　英文講解 MP3 30

In the mid-1800s, two European Jews [1]**immigrated** to the United States in search of better lives. Jacob Davis, who was born Jacob Youphes in Latvia, settled in Nevada and opened a [2]**tailor** shop to support his family. Loeb Strauss, who would later be known by his nickname "Levi," left Bavaria for New York to join his two brothers in their [10]**dry goods** business. Sensing opportunity in the California Gold Rush, he moved to San Francisco in 1853 to start his own company, Levi Strauss & Co.

Little did Strauss know, he'd soon be making history with one of his clients—Jacob Davis. One day, a [3]**miner**'s wife came to Davis and asked him to make a [4]**sturdy** pair of pants for her husband, complaining that his pockets frequently tore when he put gold [11]**nuggets** in them. This was his eureka moment—he decided to [5]**reinforce** the pockets and other stress points with the [6]**copper** [12]**rivets** he used to strengthen horse [7]**harnesses**. Davis was soon selling hundreds of pairs, and became alarmed when other tailors began copying his design. Not having enough money to apply for a patent, he wrote to Strauss, who he bought 8)**fabric** from, suggesting that they form a 9)**partnership**.

The two men 13)**took out** the patent together in 1873, and Davis moved to San Francisco to 14)**oversee** production of the new pants. Not long afterward, they switched from white duck cloth to blue denim—blue doesn't show dirt as easily—and the modern blue jean was born. Strauss and Davis, immigrants from humble backgrounds, had created what would later become the most popular type of clothing in the world.

Mini Quiz 閱讀測驗

What was Jacob Davis' original relationship with Loeb Strauss?
(A) He was Strauss' business partner.
(B) He was Strauss' supplier.
(C) He was Strauss' boss.
(D) He was Strauss' customer.

中 Translation

一八〇〇年代中期,兩位歐洲猶太人移民到美國追尋更好的生活。生於拉脫維亞、原名雅各約斐斯的雅各戴維斯落腳於內華達州,開了一家裁縫店來養家活口。洛布史特勞斯——後來別人以其綽號「李維」稱呼他——則離開巴伐利亞赴紐約,加入他兩個哥哥的布匹公司。察覺到加州淘金熱的機會,他於一八五三年遷至舊金山,自己開了李維史特勞斯公司。

史特勞斯不知道的是,他很快就要與他的客戶雅各戴維斯聯手創造歷史。有一天,一位礦工的妻子來找戴維斯,請他幫她的先生製作一件耐穿的長褲,並抱怨他的口袋常因放入金塊而破損。這是戴維斯靈光乍現的一刻——他決定拿他用於加強馬具的銅鉚釘來強化口袋和其他受力集中點。戴維斯很快就賣出好幾百條褲子,也在其他裁縫師開始抄襲他的設計時有所警覺。由於沒有足夠的資金申請專利,他寫信給他的布料供應商史特勞斯,提出合夥的建議。

這兩位男士在一八七三年一起取得專利,戴維斯也搬到舊金山監督新長褲的生產。不久後,他們將白色粗帆布改成藍色丹寧布——藍色比較不容易顯髒——現代藍色牛仔褲於焉誕生。出身卑微的移民史特勞斯和戴維斯,共同創造了後來全球最受歡迎的服飾種類。

© Cullen328 photo by Jim Heaphy (Own work) [CC-BY-SA-3.0]
http://commons.wikimedia.org/wiki/File:Levi_Strauss_sign.
JPG

進階字彙

10) **dry goods** [draɪ gʊdz] (n.) 紡織品,布匹,雜貨
The store sells groceries and dry goods.
這家店販售雜貨和紡織品。

11) **nugget** [ˋnʌgət] (n.) 金屬塊,礦石,塊狀物
The miner went into town to sell his gold nuggets.
那名礦工進城販賣他的金塊。

12) **rivet** [ˋrɪvɪt] (n./v.) 鉚釘;固定,釘牢
The metal frame is held together by rivets.
這個金屬框是用鉚釘固定在一起的。

13) **take out** [tek aʊt] (phr.) 取得(專利、貸款,保單等)
Ron took out a student loan to pay for his tuition.
榮恩申請學生貸款來支付他的學費。

14) **oversee** [͵ovɚˋsi] (v.) 管理,監督
Martha was hired to oversee the sales department.
瑪莎被請來管理業務部。

✧ Language Guide

California Gold Rush 加州淘金熱
加州淘金熱始於西元一八四八年,當時工人在加州沙特磨坊的水車裡發現了金子,消息傳開後,全世界各地民眾紛紛湧入。淘金熱給加州帶來不少影響,舊金山人口從原本的約一千人到一八七〇年成長到十五萬人。人口增加後,加州到東岸間的交通發展加速,新移民帶來了城鎮學校的建設,政治活動開始盛行,與美國其他州關係更密切,促使加州脫離原墨西哥的統治,於一八五〇年九月九號正式成為美國的一州。不過淘金熱也改變了當地原住民的生活環境,造成污染、疾病以及與礦工的對立,逐漸把原住民趕出他們原本居住的地方。

duck cloth 粗帆布
粗帆布一般俗稱 canvas,是一種粗糙的平紋布料,由亞麻或棉製成,有不同的質料和顏色。用於製作衣服、包裝袋、帳篷等物品時,採單紗紡織;用於製造耐壓或耐磨的製品時(好比船用帆布或是覆蓋貨物的帆布)則會用雙經紡織,以加強布料的承受力。

denim 丹寧布
丹寧是一種斜紋厚棉布料,經線為藍色(或其他顏色),緯線為白色,質地堅韌不易破損,最初用於船員、礦工的工作服,現在已成為流行時尚的代表布料。源於法文的「丹寧」原意為 serge de Nîmes(起源自 Nîmes 這個法國城市的布料),在英語中簡化成 denim。「牛仔褲」(jeans)的名稱來源也與法文有關,法文稱呼義大利城市熱那亞 (Genoa) 船員身上的藍褲子為 bleu de Gênes,傳到英文後就寫成發音相似的 jeans。

(D) 答趨鐵鵬讀閱   35

褲中經典 Levi's

首創牛仔褲品牌 Levi's 引領時尚新風潮，最耳熟能詳的便是它的經典褲款 501®。內行人都知道，Levi's 在褲款上不斷推陳出新，從最初的直筒款式演變到後來的喇叭褲，再到現今最夯的合身剪裁，消費者可依自身的體型和個性來搭配不同褲款，將自我風格凸顯到位。現在讓 EZ TALK 帶你一起走向 Levi's 的潮流尖端。

Levi's 以褲子上的布標顏色來區分等級：

紅標：紅底白字，為歷史最悠久的象徵性識別，價格偏高。台灣地區分公司所授權的經銷商皆屬於此。

白標（或稱銀標）：白底黑字，款型較為流行，價格與紅標差不多。

橘標：價位較低，目前多在東南亞地區販售。

501® 經典直筒

絕不退潮的 501® 為 Levi's 首款牛仔褲型號,是最經典的褲款,屬於直筒 (straight leg)、排扣 (button fly) 的設計,由於它經典不敗的地位,因此較有收藏價值。鬆緊度適中,很適合大腿略微肥胖者。除了典型的顏色,現在還推出了粉灰藍、珊瑚紅和卡其色等多種選擇。不過這款褲子洗後會縮百分之七到十,所以要買的話要買比你原先穿的腰圍再多一到三吋左右,褲長也要比一般大三到四吋。店內都會有尺寸表供您參考。

505® 直筒拉鍊款

喜歡 501® 褲款的朋友,一定也會對 505® 愛不釋手,505® 和 501® 款式相近,但和 501® 的排扣設計不同,以便利的拉鍊來取代。該款近年來與多位設計界人士合作,推出變化款,例如與日本設計品牌 Kazuki 的聯名款,在褲子上加入如東方雲紋等圖騰元素,成為潮流人士的最愛。

510® 超緊身 (Skinny Fit)

是所有 Levi's 褲款中褲腿和褲管最窄的款式(褲管大約只有十三點五吋),使用百分之二的人造纖維 (spandex) 來打造纖細質感,褲腿為直筒,而它的類似款 511® 則稍寬一些。

511® 低腰緊身 (Slim Fit)

早期 Levi's 的褲款走的是粗獷寬鬆風,後來因應潮流而出現了比較憋的緊身款式,缺點是較為悶熱不舒服,而這款 511® 的剪裁貼身卻不緊身,錐形褲管配以相應的牛仔褲拉鍊,適合偏瘦的身材。

512® 苗條曲線 (Perfectly Shaping)

此褲款較為高腰的設計可將女生容易突出的小腹包覆起來,達到雕塑的效果。彈性纖維的材質使得褲子更合身,讓妳看起來更纖細、更苗條。此系列還有設計出靴管款和直筒款,是女生打造黃金身型的必備褲款之一。

517® 靴管 (Boot Cut)

之所以稱靴管褲,是因為它的褲管較一般直筒褲寬一些,好容納皮靴 (leather boots) 的厚度,開口的幅度比較小,不像喇叭褲那麼寬,517® 這款靴管褲算是比較不會退流行的安全款,剪裁又頗有修飾效果,適合追求樸素質感的消費者。

528® 雕塑身型 (Curvy Cut)

這款牛仔褲的剪裁可將臀部的完美曲線表現出來,在刷色上也有下功夫,將中間部分刷淡,既顯瘦又有修身效果,深受女性朋友的愛戴。這個型號還出緊身褲型和靴管款式,讓此褲款的愛好者有更多的選擇。

550® 寬鬆牛仔 (Relaxed)

是 Levi's 褲型中剪裁較為寬鬆的一款,適合體格較為壯碩的人穿,簡單的縫線設計,雖然不是典型的靴管褲,造型也不是特別亮眼,但不論是搭配靴子、運動鞋還是平底鞋都有味道,算是百搭款。

立體剪裁 (Engineered Jeans)

這款褲型相當特別,為 Levi's 獨創款式,最大的特色就在於它的車縫技巧。它不採用傳統的剪裁方式,而以 "free to move" 為口號,考慮到人在活動時的舒適度來剪裁,造型也很搶眼,是詢問度相當高的褲款。

公主剪裁 (Lady Style)

為 Levi's 專為亞洲女性所推出的系列,牛仔褲上的每個細節均具巧思,用彈性丹寧布配上合身的側邊剪裁,讓女性的雙腿看起來格外修長,搭配高跟鞋更是如虎添翼。整體走精緻路線,臀部的心型口袋也增添了許多女人味,加上使用銀色的皮牌代替傳統的黃銅色,相當時尚細緻。台灣歌手蔡依琳曾代言此褲款。

Vocabulary Bank

1) **manufacture** [ˏmænjəˋfæktʃə] (v.) 製造
   (n.) manufacturer 製造商
   All of our products are manufactured in China.
   我們的產品皆於中國製造。

2) **hardware** [ˋhɑrdˏwɛr] (n.) 五金器具，金屬器材
   I bought this hammer at the hardware store.
   我這把錘子是在五金行買的。

3) **increasingly** [ɪnˋkrisɪŋli] (adv.) 逐漸地，越來越
   People are increasingly relying on cell phones
   to communicate.
   大家越來越依賴用手機來溝通。

4) **concept** [ˋkɑnsɛpt] (n.) 觀念，概念
   Risk is a difficult concept to understand.
   風險是一種難以瞭解的概念。

5) **go bankrupt** [go ˋbæŋkrʌpt] (phr.) 破產
   (a.) bankrupt 破產的
   Thousands of investors lost money when the
   company went bankrupt.
   數千名投資客都因為那家公司破產而賠錢。

6) **boom** [bum] (n.) 繁榮，景氣好
   The billionaire made his fortune in the real
   estate boom.
   那位億萬富翁因房地產繁榮而致富。

7) **abundance** [əˋbʌndəns] (n.) 豐富，大量
   There was an abundance of food at the
   wedding.
   婚宴上的菜很豐富。

8) **explorer** [ɪkˋsplorə] (n.) 探險家
   (v.) explore [ɪkˋsplor] 探險，探究
   California was first discovered by Spanish
   explorers in the 16th century.
   加州在十六世紀時第一次被西班牙探險家發現。

9) **chemist** [ˋkɛmɪst] (n.) 化學家
   The chemist received an award for his
   contributions to science.
   為了表彰他對科學的貢獻，這位化學家獲贈了某個獎項。

10) **waterproof** [ˋwɔtəˏpruf] (a.) 防水的
    Is this jacket waterproof?
    這件夾克防水嗎？

11) **layer** [ˋleə] (n.) 層
    The wedding cake had four layers.
    那個結婚蛋糕有四疊。

12) **demand** [dɪˋmænd] (n.) 需求，要求
    The demand for organic food is growing rapidly.
    對有機食物的需求正逐漸成長。

進階字彙

13) **sap** [sæp] (n.)（樹等植物的）汁液
    Maple syrup is made from the sap of maple
    trees.
    楓糖是用楓樹的汁液做成的。

Charles Goodyear
Making Rubber Useful

將橡膠發揚光大的
固特異

課文朗讀 MP3 31　　單字朗讀 MP3 32　　英文講解 MP3 33

Charles Goodyear was born in New Haven, Connecticut, on December 29, 1800. His father, Amasa Goodyear, who started his career as a merchant, moved his family to the nearby town of Naugatuck to open a button factory when Charles was seven. Amasa later began [1]**manufacturing** [2]**hardware**, including several farm tools that he invented himself. Growing up in this environment, Charles also developed an interest in manufacturing and invention.

At the age of 17, Charles went to work for a hardware merchant in Philadelphia to learn more about the business. Four years later, he returned to Naugatuck and went into business with his father under the name Amasa Goodyear & Son. The company began producing an [3]**increasingly** wide variety of hardware, and in 1826 Charles returned to Philadelphia and opened the country's first retail hardware store to sell these products. The [4]**concept** was too new to be accepted, however, and the business [5]**went bankrupt** in 1830.

Looking for a new business idea, Charles noted that there was a rubber [6]**boom** going on. Natural rubber was first discovered by Indians in the Amazon region, where rubber trees grow in [7]**abundance**. Cutting into the tree's bark and collecting the white [13]**sap**, the Indians turned it into rubber by smoking it over a fire. While the Indians used rubber mainly to make balls for games, European [8]**explorers** thought it may have more important uses.

Language Guide

Amazon region 亞馬遜流域

位於南美洲(South America)的亞馬遜河(Amazon River)為世上流域最大的河流，面積占了整個南美洲的百分之四十，範圍遍及南美多國，包括祕魯(Peru)、巴西(Brazil)、哥倫比亞(Colombia)、委內瑞拉(Venezuela)、厄瓜多爾(Ecuador)、玻利維亞(Bolivia)等。這條大河所孕育出的亞馬遜熱帶雨林(tropical rainforest)是世界最大的雨林，此處納有數百萬的物種，對地球的生態研究意義不凡。但因人為砍伐，目前超過五分之一的亞馬遜雨林已遭破壞，引起許多環境科學與保育相關的重大議題。

Joseph Priestley 約瑟夫普利斯特里

出生於英國里茲(Leeds)附近的普利斯特里在嚴謹的喀爾文教派(Calvinist)家庭中長大，為了成為牧師而讀書。不知科學為何物的他，在機緣下與美國開國元勛(founding father)兼發明家富蘭克林(Benjamin Franklin)結為好友，開啟了他的科學之路。日後他發現了二氧化碳(carbon dioxide)，並得知把二氧化碳放在水裡會產生特別好喝的氣味，才製造出「汽水」；還從印地安人的口香糖中發現可把鉛筆跡擦掉的「橡皮擦」。但是他沒想到把這兩項發現大量生產販售，竟能在日後創造出極大的商機。

Charles Macintosh 查爾斯麥金托什

蘇格蘭籍的麥金托什從小就對化學有高度的興趣，在化學物工廠工作時也大有成就，找出許多化學物的製作流程，最著名的是融合天然橡膠製成的防水布料，也就是現在的雨衣。而麥金托什最後也成了他所發明的那種橡膠雨衣的代名詞。

In 1770, the substance was named rubber by British [9]chemist Joseph Priestley, who found that it could be used to "rub" pencil marks away. Erasers are called "rubbers" in England to this day. Another British chemist, Charles Macintosh, created a [10]waterproof fabric in 1823 by placing a [11]layer of rubber between two pieces of cloth. Raincoats made from this fabric were soon in great [12]demand in rainy Britain, and a rubber boom was under way.

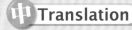

Mini Quiz 閱讀測驗

What is rubber made from?
(A) Erasers
(B) Raincoats
(C) Tree bark
(D) Tree sap

中 Translation

查爾斯固特異於一八○○年十二月二十九日在康乃狄克州紐哈文誕生。他的父親亞馬沙固特異從商起家，在查爾斯七歲時舉家搬到諾加塔克鎮附近，開設鈕扣工廠。亞馬沙後來開始製造五金，包括自己發明的數種農具。在這種環境下長大的查爾斯也培養出製造和發明的興趣。

十七歲時，查爾斯到費城替一名五金商人工作，學習更多做生意的技巧。四年後，他回到諾加塔克，和父親合開亞馬沙固特異父子公司。該公司開始生產種類愈廣的五金，一八二六年，查爾斯回到費城，開了美國第一家零售五金行來銷售那些產品。但這個概念因為太新而未被接受，使得公司在一八三○年走向破產。

在尋找新生意的想法時，查爾斯注意到已經掀起了橡膠熱。天然橡膠最早是由印地安人在橡膠樹大量生長的亞馬遜流域發現。他們先割破樹皮、汲取白色汁液，再用火燻，把汁液變成橡膠。印地安人多半拿橡膠來製作比賽用的球類，歐洲探險家卻認為橡膠或許能有更重要的用途。

一七七○年，英國化學家約瑟夫普利斯特里將此物質取名為「rubber」，因為他發現它可以用來「磨掉（rub）」鉛筆的筆跡。直到今天，橡皮擦在英國仍被稱作「rubber」。另一位英國化學家查爾斯麥金塔則將一層橡膠夾在兩塊布之間，發明了防水布料。用這種布料製成的雨衣很快就在多雨的英國暢銷，橡膠熱就此展開。

Yet, as Charles Goodyear would soon discover, rubber products that worked well in the [9]**temperate** British climate faced greater challenges in America's more extreme weather. In 1834, he bought a rubber [1]**lifesaver** from the Roxbury Rubber Company, and quickly invented an improved [10]**valve** for it. But when Charles presented his design to Roxbury, the manager told him that what really needed improvement was the rubber. The lifesavers were cracking in the winter and melting in the summer, causing many customers to return them.

Although Charles had no scientific background, he spent the next five years experimenting with rubber, adding various chemicals to try and make it more stable. He found that magnesia powder made rubber less sticky, but the boots he made from it melted in the summer heat. Charles next tried dipping rubber in nitric [2]**acid**, and the result was so impressive that the government placed an order for 150 mailbags made from the new rubber. But before the order could be filled, the bags had [11]**disintegrated**, as the acid had only [12]**cured** the surface of the rubber.

Charles' eureka moment finally came in 1839, soon after he'd [3]**purchased** the rights to a process using [4]**sulfur** to treat rubber. This new rubber was an improvement over

V Vocabulary Bank

1) **lifesaver** [ˈlaɪfˌsevɚ] (n.) 救生圈，也叫做 life preserver
The sailor threw the drowning man a lifesaver.
水手丟了一個救生圈給那名遇溺的男子。

2) **acid** [ˈæsɪd] (n.) 〔化〕酸，nitric acid即「硝酸」
Vinegar contains a mild acid.
醋中含有微量的酸。

3) **purchase** [ˈpɚtʃəs] (v./n.) 購買；購買，購買之物
The couple purchased their first home after they got married.
這對夫婦在結婚後買了第一棟房子。

4) **sulfur** [ˈsʌlfɚ] (n.) 硫磺
The sulfur in the hot spring is good for your skin.
溫泉裡的硫磺對你的皮膚有益。

5) **accidentally** [ˌæksəˈdɛntəli] (adv.) 意外地，不小心地
(adj.) accidental [ˌæksəˈdɛntəl] 意外的
Robin accidentally deleted his report and had to rewrite it.
蘿賓不小心將她的報告刪掉，必須重新寫一次。

6) **obtain** [əbˈten] (v.) 取得，獲得
The application form can be obtained online.
那份申請表可以從網路取得。

7) **durable** [ˈdjurəbəl] (a.) 耐用的，耐久的
You should wear durable shoes when you go hiking.
你去健行時應該穿耐走的鞋子。

8) **flexible** [ˈflɛksəbəl] (a.) 有彈性的，柔軟的
Ballet dancers must be very flexible.
芭蕾舞者的柔軟度要非常好。

previous formulas, but it was still too soft and easily affected by temperature. While demonstrating this rubber one day at a store in Woburn, Massachusetts, Charles [5]**accidentally** dropped his sample onto a hot stove. Instead of melting, however, the rubber became firm and smooth like leather.

Although Charles eventually [6]**obtained** a patent for this process—named vulcanization after Vulcan, the Roman god of fire—in 1844, he never made any money from his invention. Large manufacturers stole his formula for [7]**durable**, [8]**flexible** rubber, and he spent all his money trying to protect his patent. When Charles died in 1860, all he left his family was a mountain of debt.

Mini Quiz 閱讀測驗

Why didn't Goodyear make any money from his invention?
(A) Because his rubber was easily affected by temperature
(B) Because he didn't have a patent
(C) Because other companies stole his formula
(D) Because he had to buy the rights to a sulfur treatment process

中 Translation

然而查爾斯固特異很快就發現,這些橡膠製品在氣候溫和的英國擁有良好成效,到了美國卻因天候較為極端而面臨嚴峻的挑戰。一八三四年,他向羅斯貝瑞橡膠公司買了一個橡膠救生圈,很快為它發明改良的氣閥。但當查爾斯把他的設計拿到羅斯貝瑞公司時,經理卻告訴他,真正需要改良的是橡膠。救生圈在冬天會龜裂、在夏天又會融化,很多顧客因此退貨。

即便查爾斯並沒有科學背景,他接下來的五年都拿橡膠來做實驗,加入多種化學物質,試著讓它更穩定。他發現氧化鎂粉可降低橡膠的黏性,但用這種原料製成的靴子卻會受不住夏季的酷熱而融化。查爾斯接著嘗試把橡膠浸在硝酸裡,成果相當不錯,吸引政府訂購一百五十個用這種新橡膠製成的郵袋。但還來不及交貨,郵袋就分解了,因為硝酸只有處理到橡膠表面。

查爾斯靈機一動的時刻於一八三九年終於出現,那時他剛買下用黃硫來處理橡膠這種工序的權利。這種新橡膠的品質優於先前幾種配方,但仍有太軟、易受溫度影響等問題。一天,在麻州伍伯恩一家商店展示這種橡膠時,查爾斯意外讓樣品掉在熱爐上。結果橡膠不但沒有融化,反而變得像皮革一樣堅固、光滑。

雖然查爾斯後來在一八四四年為這種工序取得專利——他以羅馬火神「Vulcan」之名,將工序定名為「vulcanization」(即橡膠硫化)——卻始終沒有靠他的發明賺到錢。大型製造商盜用了他製造耐用、彈性橡膠的配方,而他花光所有積蓄,試圖保護他的專利。查爾斯於一八六〇年過世時,留給家人的只有一屁股債。

Language Guide

magnesia 氧化鎂

一種無臭無味的白色固體,學名為 magnesium oxide,因其有抗酸(antacid)、耐高溫、作用後不會產生二氧化碳的特性,用途相當廣泛。電源導線的絕緣體(insulator)、滅火器(fire extinguisher)內含物、家裡的隔板及天花板、治療胃酸及消化不良(indigestion)的藥物、體操選手止手汗的粉末都可以看見氧化鎂的蹤跡。

vulcanization 橡膠硫化

橡膠和硫化物能透過高壓高溫,將橡膠的分子改造,形成更有彈性且耐磨的硫化膠(vulcanized rubber),一般稱為「交聯作用」(cross-linking),因為首先成為交聯劑的是硫磺,所以也稱作「硫化」。橡膠易受溫度影響的特性源自牠像線一樣的的高分子鏈(polymer chain),硫化則可讓它的線性結構產生交聯,好像線跟線間互相規律地黏在一起般的,變成了網狀結構的分子。結構變成穩定的立體,也就是橡膠不論怎麼被凹曲也會快速恢復原來樣子的最大原因。

Vocabulary Bank

1) **prominent** [ˋprɑmənənt] (a.) 著名的，重要的
The conference was attended by many prominent scholars.
這場會議有許多有名的學者參加。

2) **elite** [ɪˋlit] (a./n.) 菁英的，頂尖的；菁英
Elite troops were sent to rescue the president.
菁英部隊被派去援救總統。

3) **academic** [͵ækəˋdɛmɪk] (a.) 學術的
Shelly has a good academic record.
雪莉的學業成績很優秀。

4) **undergo** [͵ʌndɚˋgo] (v.) 接受（訓練、治療等），經歷
The patient underwent treatment for skin cancer.
那位病患接受了皮膚癌的治療。

5) **rural** [ˋrʊrəl] (a.) 鄉下的，農村的
The typhoon caused heavy flooding in rural areas.
颱風在鄉村地區造成嚴重水災。

6) **software** [ˋsɔft͵wɛr] (n.)（電腦）軟體
What software do you have on your computer?
你的電腦裡有什麼軟體？

7) **occurrence** [əˋkɝəns] (n.) 事情，事件，發生
Traffic accidents are a common occurrence.
交通意外是很常發生的事件。

進階字彙

8) **administration** [əd͵mɪnəˋstreʃən] (n.)（某位總統的）政府、任期
Millions of jobs were created during the Reagan administration.
雷根總統就職期間創造了好幾百萬份工作機會。

9) **Marines** [məˋrinz] (n.)（美國）海軍陸戰隊，全名為 U.S. Marine Corps，Marine 即「海軍陸戰隊員」
The Marines are the smallest of America's armed forces.
美國海軍陸戰隊是美國規模最小的武裝部隊。

10) **cot** [kɑt] (n.) 帆布床，行軍床
The soldiers slept on cots in a large tent.
士兵們睡在大帳篷裡的行軍床上。

11) **thatched** [θætʃt] (a.)（屋頂）茅草蓋的
The farmers live in thatched cottages.
那些農夫住在茅頂屋裡。

12) **start-up** [ˋstɑrt͵ʌp] (n.) 新興企業
Alvin works as an engineer at a tech start-up.
艾文在一間新興的科技公司當工程師。

13) **overdue** [͵ovɚˋdu] (a.) 逾期的，過期的
These library books are overdue.
這些圖書館借來的書都逾期了。

Netflix
觀賞電影的新方法
A New Way to Watch Movies

課文朗讀 MP3 37　　單字朗讀 MP3 38　　英文講解 MP3 39

Wilmot Reed Hastings, Jr. was born in Boston, Massachusetts in 1960. His father, Wilmot Reed Hastings, Sr., was a [1]**prominent** lawyer who served in the Nixon [8]**administration**. After attending [2]**elite** private schools around Boston, the young Reed entered Bowdoin, a small liberal arts college in Maine, where he majored in math. He was a hardworking and talented student, twice receiving math department awards for his [3]**academic** achievements.

Upon graduation, Reed joined the [9]**Marines** and [4]**underwent** officer training. But when he discovered that asking questions wasn't encouraged, he decided that the military life wasn't for him. Reed's desire to serve was still strong, however, so he signed up for the   . From 1983 to 1985, he taught high school math in [5]**rural** Swaziland, where he had no electricity, cooked his meals over a wood fire, and slept on a [10]**cot** in a [11]**thatched** hut.

Back in the U.S., Reed continued his education at Stanford, earning a master's degree in computer science in 1988. It wasn't long before he became one of Silicon Valley's rising tech stars. At the age of 37, he sold his [12]**start-up**, Pure [6]**Software**, for $700 million. As the story goes, Reed was searching for his next big idea when he received a $40 late fee for an [13]**overdue** movie—a cassette of *Apollo 13*. This everyday [7]**occurrence** led to Reed's eureka moment, inspiring the idea that would forever change the way people enjoy watching movies at home.

Mini Quiz 閱讀測驗

 What inspired Reed's eureka moment?
(A) *Apollo 13*
(B) A VHS cassette
(C) A fine
(D) A movie

中 Translation

威摩里德海斯汀二世一九六〇年出生於麻州波士頓。他的父親威摩里德海斯汀一世是任職於尼克森政府的知名律師。念完波士頓附近的菁英私立學校，年輕的里德進入緬因州小規模的鮑登文理學院就讀，主修數學。他是一位既用功又有天分的學生，兩度因學業成績優秀獲頒數學系書卷獎。

里德一畢業後便進入美國海軍陸戰隊服役，接受軍官訓練。然而他卻發現軍方不鼓勵發問，於是他便確定軍事生活不適合他。不過里德為民服務的欲望還是很強烈，因此他報名加入美國和平工作團。從一九八三至一九八五年，他在史瓦濟蘭農村教高中數學，那裡沒有電，只能用木柴生火煮飯，還得睡在茅頂屋的帆布床上。

回到美國後，里德進入史丹佛大學深造，於一九八八年拿到電腦科學碩士學位。不久後，他成為矽谷的科技新星。三十七歲時，他以七億美元轉售他創建的「純粹軟體」公司。後來，里德在尋找下一個不得了的構想時，他因為租電影逾期未歸還（《阿波羅十三》的 VHS 影帶）而被追討四十美元的逾時費。這種稀鬆平常的事讓里德靈機一動，啟發了一個構想，就此改變了人們在家觀賞電影的方式。

EUREKA! 點子成金

V Vocabulary Bank

1) **rental** [`rɛntəl] (n./a.) 租賃（的）
Can you recommend a good car rental company?
你能推薦一家好的租車公司嗎？

2) **work out** [wɔrk aut] (phr.) 健身，鍛鍊身體
Christina works out three times a week.
克莉絲蒂娜每週健身三次。

3) **feasible** [`fizəbl] (a.) 可行的，行得通的
Sending humans to Mars is not feasible at this time.
將人類送上火星一事目前還不可行。

4) **launch** [lɔntʃ] (v./n.) 推出，發行
The designer is launching a new fashion line.
這位設計師將推出新的服裝系列。

5) **title** [`taɪtəl] (n.) 電影、書等作品
Our bookstore has all of the latest titles.
我們這家書店有所有最新的書籍。

6) **go public** [go `pʌblɪk] (phr.)（公司）股票上市
Google went public in August 2004.
谷歌的股票在二○○年的八月上市。

7) **revenue** [`rɛvə͵nu] (n.) 營收，收入
The factory lost revenue during the strike.
這座工廠在罷工期間營收大減。

8) **hit** [hɪt] (a.) 流行的，熱門的
Have you heard Jolin Tsai's latest hit single?
你有聽過蔡依林最新的熱門單曲嗎？

9) **on demand** [ɑn dɪ`mænd] (phr.) 隨選的
The new cable service lets you watch movies and shows on demand.
這項新的第四台服務讓你能夠隨意選看電影和節目。

10) **prime time** [praɪm taɪm] (phr.)（電視、廣播）黃金時段
The interview was broadcast during prime time.
這項新的有線電視方案讓你能夠隨意選看電影和節目。

11) **account for** [ə`kaunt fɔr] (phr.) 佔據
International sales account for nearly half the company's business.
國際銷售幾乎佔了該公司一半的業務。

12) **Internet** [`ɪntə͵nɛt] (n.) 網際網路
You can find all the information you need on the Internet.
你可以在網路上找到所有需要的資訊。

進階字彙

13) **flat** [flæt] (a.)（費用、價格等）均一的，一律的
The bank charges a flat fee of $10 for wire transfers.
銀行的電匯一律收取十元的手續費。

14) **streaming** [strimɪŋ] (n.)（網路）串流，線上即時觀賞、收聽 (v.) stream
My connection is too slow to watch streaming video.
我的連線速度太慢了，無法線上收看影片。

How could the video [1] **rental** store charge a late fee that was three times what the cassette cost in the first place? It just didn't seem fair. Later, on his way to the gym, Reed realized that they had a much better business model. Gym members pay a [13] **flat** fee each month and can [2] **work out** as much—or as little—as they like. So why not apply a similar model to movie rentals? What's more, VHS cassettes were being replaced by DVDs in the late 90s, which would make it [3] **feasible** to mail movies to customers, saving them a trip to the video store. Just like that, the idea for Netflix was born.

With an investment of $2.5 million, Reed and his partners [4] **launched** Netflix in 1998. The idea was simple: members could rent as many DVDs as they wanted for a flat monthly rate, and there were no late fees. At first, Netflix had only 30 employees and 925 [5] **titles** for rent. But the company grew rapidly, [6] **going public** in 2002 and reaching $272 million in [7] **revenues** in 2003. By 2005, Netflix was mailing a million DVDs per day, and in 2007 the company delivered its billionth disc.

Today, Netflix is changing home movie and TV viewing as we know it. With the new Internet video [14] **streaming** service, members can watch [8] **hit** movies and TV shows [9] **on demand**. This service is so popular that during [10] **prime time** hours,

Netflix [11] **accounts for** a third of all North American [12] **Internet** traffic. That's 1 not too shabby for an idea that was inspired by a video rental late fee.

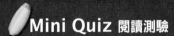

Mini Quiz 閱讀測驗

When can Watch Instantly members view hit movies?
(A) When they are scheduled
(B) Whenever they want
(C) When the DVDs are mailed
(D) Only during prime time

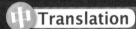

中 Translation

錄影帶店怎麼可以收取影帶原價三倍的逾時費？這一點也不公平。後來，在前往健身房的途中，里德想到他們有更好的經營模式。健身房會員可以每個月付均一費用，然後想健身多少次就去多少次。那麼影片出租為什麼不能用類似的模式呢？此外，至九〇年代晚期，VHS 影帶已逐漸被 DVD 所取代，這讓把影片郵寄給顧客這件事變得可行，顧客可以不必親自到錄影帶店。Netflix 的概念於焉誕生。

里德投資兩百五十萬美金，與合夥人在一九九八年創立 Netflix。概念很簡單：會員只要每月繳定額的費用，想租多少影片就可租多少影片，且不必支付逾時費。當時 Netflix 只有三十名員工和九百二十五部片子。但公司成長迅速，在二〇〇二年公開上市後，二〇〇三年的營收達到兩億七千兩百萬美元。到了二〇〇五年，Netflix 每天要寄送一百萬片 DVD，二〇〇七年，該公司寄出第十億片光碟。

今天，Netflix 仍在改變家家戶戶觀賞電影與電視的習慣。有了最新的網路視訊串流服務，會員可依需求選看熱門電影及電視影集。「立即收視」服務在黃金時段極受歡迎，使 Netflix 占了北美網路總流量的三分之一。就一個由影帶出租逾時費啟發的構想而言，這數字還不賴。

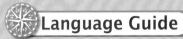

EUREKA! 點子成金

V Vocabulary Bank

1) **wholesale** [ˋhol͵sel] (a./n.) 批發的，成批售出的；批發
   Store owners buy wholesale, so they can earn a decent profit.
   店家購買批發品，因此能賺到相當的利潤。

2) **start over** [stɑrt ˋovɚ] (phr.) 重新開始，展開新的生涯、人生
   I'd like to switch careers, but I'm too old to start over.
   我想轉換跑道，但重展人生對我來說已經太晚了。

3) **agent** [ˋedʒənt] (n.) 經紀人，代理人
   The real estate agent showed us several houses in the area.
   房屋仲介帶我們去看這區的幾間房子。

4) **encounter** [ɪnˋkaʊntɚ] (v./n.) 遇到，遇見
   Laura was surprised when she encountered her ex-boyfriend at the mall.
   蘿菈很驚訝會在購物中心遇見她的前男友。

5) **salesman** [ˋselzmən] (n.)（男）推銷員，業務員，traveling salesman 意即「旅行推銷員」
   You should never trust a used car salesman.
   絕對不能相信二手車推銷員。

6) **acquire** [əˋkwaɪr] (v.) 獲得，得到，購買
   James acquired the property when he father died.
   詹姆斯在父親過逝後拿到了遺產。

7) **cork** [kɔrk] (n.) 軟木塞，軟木
   Bob pulled the cork out of the wine bottle.
   鮑伯將酒瓶的軟木塞拉開。

8) **disposable** [dɪˋspozəbəl] (a.) 用完即丟棄的，拋棄式的
   Disposable diapers are harmful to the environment.
   用過即丟的尿布對環境有害。

9) **consumer** [kənˋsumɚ] (n.) 消費者
   Consumers are spending less during the recession.
   消費者在經濟不景氣時花費較少。

10) **irritated** [ˋɪrə͵tetɪd] (a.) 惱怒的，煩躁的
    The sales clerks were trained how to handle irritated customers.
    店員都被訓練如何應付惱怒的顧客。

11) **sharpen** [ˋʃɑrpən] (n.) 磨銳，鋒利
    These scissors need to be sharpened.
    這把剪刀需要磨利。

12) **visualize** [ˋvɪʒuə͵laɪz] (v.) 想像，假想，設想
    You need to visualize success before you can achieve it.
    你必須要先具體想像成功的樣子才能達成。

13) **clamp** [klæmp] (v./n.) 夾住；夾子
    I want a lamp I can clamp on my desk.
    我想要一個可以夾在書桌上的檯燈。

14) **bear** [bɛr] (v.) 俱有，擁有
    The five dollar bill bears the image of President Lincoln.
    五元硬幣上印有林肯總統的圖像。

GILLETTE
The King of Razors
吉列 王牌刮鬍刀

課文朗讀 MP3 43　　單字朗讀 MP3 44　　英文講解 MP3 45

Born in Fond du Lac, Wisconsin, King Camp Gillette grew up in Chicago, where his father ran a [1)] **wholesale** hardware business. When the business was destroyed in the Great Chicago Fire of 1871, the family moved to New York City to [2)] **start over**. Gillette's father found a job as a patent [3)] **agent**, and often discussed the inventions he [4)] **encountered** in his work at the dinner table. Gillette was inspired to become a successful inventor, but first he had to make a living.

At the age of 17, Gillette left home and became a traveling [5)] **salesman**. It wasn't his dream job, but he had plenty of time on the road to think, and often **1 tried his hand at** improving the products he sold door to door. But the years went by, and although he [6)] **acquired** four patents, none of them brought him success. It wasn't until 1895, at the age of 40, that Gillette had his eureka moment. He was working for Crown **Cork** and Seal Company, whose founder, William Painter, had invented the **crown cap**. Painter gave Gillette just the advice he needed, telling him to invent something similar—a **disposable** product that would keep **consumers** coming back for more.

Gillette went through the alphabet looking for the right product idea, but the answer came to him while he was shaving one morning. **Irritated** that his straight razor was dull and needed to be sent for **sharpening**, he suddenly **visualized** a razor with a small disposable blade **clamped** between two plates. The razor would be much safer than **straight razors**—also known as "cut throat" razors—and the blades could be easily replaced when dull. Was his idea a success? When Gillette died in 1932, the company that **bears** his name had sold over 60 million razors and 4 billion blades!

Mini Quiz 閱讀測驗

What did Gillette invent?
(A) A disposable razor
(B) A razor with a disposable blade
(C) A disposable straight razor
(D) A safer straight razor

中 Translation

出生於威斯康辛州豐迪拉克的金坎普吉列在芝加哥長大，父親在那裡經營五金批發公司。當公司在一八七一年的芝加哥大火付之一炬，全家人遷往紐約重新開始。吉列的父親找到專利代理人的工作，常在晚餐時討論他在工作上碰到的發明。吉列受到啟發，很想成為成功的發明家，但他得先養活自己才行。

十七歲時，吉列離開家中，成為旅行推銷員。這不是他夢想的工作，但他在路上有充分的時間思考，也常著手嘗試改善他挨家挨戶兜售的產品。好幾年過去，雖然他申請到四個專利，但沒有一個帶給他成功，直到一八九五年四十歲時，吉列心靈機一動。當時他正為皇冠瓶塞封口公司工作，公司創辦人威廉潘特正是金屬瓶蓋的發明人。潘特給了吉列所需的建議，要他發明類似的產品──用完即丟、消費者會一再回來買的商品。

吉列依英文字母順序尋找恰當的產品構想，但答案卻是在他一天早上刮鬍子時湧現。摺疊式剃刀的刀片鈍了，必須送去磨利，吉列對此感到煩惱，忽然間，腦海浮現一支刮鬍刀的畫面，有著拋棄式的小刀片鉗在兩片薄板間。這種刮鬍刀比摺疊式剃刀──亦稱「割喉」剃刀──安全多了，刀片鈍了也容易更換。他的構想成功了嗎？當吉列於一九三二年過世時，以其姓氏為名的公司已賣了超過六千萬支刮鬍刀，和四十億支刀片！

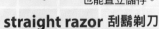
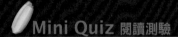

© Kyle May/flickr.com

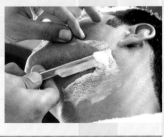
47

EUREKA! 點子成金

V Vocabulary Bank

1) **diner** [ˈdaɪnə] (n.) （餐車式）簡餐店，餐車
The food at that diner is really greasy.
那間簡餐店的菜很油膩。

2) **prosper** [ˈprɑspə] (v.) 繁榮，成功
The company has continued to prosper under the new CEO.
那間公司在新的總裁領導下持續蒸蒸日上。

3) **deli** [ˈdɛli] (n.) 熟食店，小吃店，即 delicatessen的簡稱
That deli makes tasty sandwiches.
那間熟食店有美味的三明治。

4) **dispenser** [dɪˈspɛnsə] (n.) 分配器，自動販賣機
There's a cup dispenser next to the drink machine.
在冷飲機旁邊有紙杯架。

5) **clog** [klɑg] (v.) 堵塞，阻塞的
The bathtub drain is clogged with hair.
浴缸的排水孔被毛髮給堵住了。

6) **packet** [ˈpækɪt] (n.) 小包，小袋
Could I have an extra packet of ketchup?
可不可以再給我一包番茄醬？

7) **substitute** [ˈsʌbstɪˌtut] (n./v.) 替代的人事物；替代
You can use milk as a substitute for cream in the recipe.
這個食譜上，可以用牛奶來代替鮮奶油。

8) **diabetes** [ˌdaɪəˈbitiz] (n.) 糖尿病
There is no cure for diabetes.
沒有能夠根治糖尿病的療法。

9) **chemistry** [ˈkɛmɪstri] (n.) 化學
Brian got a chemistry set for his birthday.
布萊恩生日收到化學實驗組。

10) **lyric** [ˈlɪrɪk] (n.) 歌詞（通常用複數 lyrics）
You can look up the lyrics to the song online.
你可以在網路上找到這首歌的歌詞。

© Roadsidepictures/ flickr.com

Sweet'N Low
Have Your Cake and Eat It Too

纖而樂 代糖
甜食與苗條兼得

課文朗讀 MP3 46　　單字朗讀 MP3 47　　英文講解 MP3 48

Benjamin Eisenstadt was born in New York City in 1906. His father, a Jewish immigrant from Russia, died when Ben was eight, leaving his family deep in debt. As a result, Ben had to **1 fend for himself** growing up. When he was 25, he married Betty Gellman, and the couple had four children together. During World War II, they opened a ¹⁾**diner** next to a navy depot. Business was good and the couple ²⁾**prospered**.

The depot closed after the war, however, and the diner was forced to close. Ben tried his luck packing and selling tea bags, but he couldn't compete with the big producers. One day in 1947, while the couple was having lunch at a local ³⁾**deli**, Betty was served tea in a pink mug. The sugar ⁴⁾**dispenser** was ⁵⁾**clogged**, so Betty started banging it on the table. Just then, Ben had his eureka moment: instead of tea bags, he could package sugar, putting it in convenient disposable ⁶⁾**packets**.

Ben approached Domino Sugar with his idea, but they never **2 got back to** him. Soon enough, though, white packets began appearing on store shelves. Ben had failed to patent his idea, and got nothing. But a few years later, a second opportunity presented itself. A company asked Ben to develop a sugar ⁷⁾**substitute** for people with ⁸⁾**diabetes**. Ben and his son Marvin, who studied chemistry in college, came up with a product based on saccharin, but at that point the company was no longer interested.

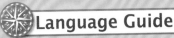
saccharin 糖精

糖精是一種不含卡路里(calorie)的人造甜味劑,甜度為蔗糖(sucrose)的三百倍以上,品嚐過後會有輕微的苦味殘留在舌頭上,一九〇〇年後被廣泛使用於標榜低卡的食品和飲料中,美國農業部(USDA)在一九七二年想要明令禁用卻告失敗,由於實驗發現服下糖精後的老鼠罹癌比例相當高,因此在糖包上加了警告標語。但兩千年時又證實糖精對人體來說並非致癌物,後來便將警告標示拿掉了。

Tongue-tied No More

1 fend for oneself 自力更生,照顧自己

fend 當動詞時指「供給、裝備」,fend for oneself 就是自己能養活自己,能獨立生活。

A: I wish we could go on a trip without the kids.
我希望我們倆可以自己出遊,不帶孩子。

B: We'll have to wait till they're old enough to fend for themselves.
我們必須等到他們長大,能夠照顧好自己才行。

2 get back to sb. 回覆某人

get back to 表示「回覆」的意思,可以是口頭答覆,也能指電話或信件上的回覆。

A: Can I get a discount on that?
能幫我打折嗎?

B: I'll have to check with my boss and get back to you later.
我必須先跟老闆確認,等會兒再回覆你。

And so Ben decided to market the sugar substitute on his own. He called it Sweet'N Low, after the [10]**lyrics** to an old song. Today, the pink packets (inspired by Betty's tea mug) and familiar treble-clef logo are famous the world over and a favorite of dieters and diabetics alike.

Mini Quiz 閱讀測驗

What did Domino Sugar do with Ben's idea for disposable sugar packets?
(A) They copied it.
(B) The paid him for it.
(C) They patented it.
(D) They gave it back.

Translation

班哲明艾森史達特一九〇六年生於紐約市。他的父親是從俄羅斯來的猶太移民,在班八歲時過世,留給家人龐大的債務。因此,班從小就必須自謀生計。班二十五歲時娶了貝蒂蓋爾曼為妻,夫妻倆共生了四個孩子。二次世界大戰期間,他們在海軍補給站旁邊開了一家餐館。生意不錯,夫妻倆過著幸福的日子。

但補給站在大戰之後關閉,餐館也被迫歇業。班嘗試包裝及銷售茶包碰碰運氣,但無法與大廠商競爭。一九四七年的一天,夫妻倆在當地一家熟食店吃午餐,貝蒂點的茶被倒在粉紅色的馬克杯裡送來。砂糖罐堵塞了,貝蒂只好拿來在桌上敲。就在這時,班靈機一動:他不要再包裝茶包了,可以改包裝砂糖,包成便於使用的隨手包。

班找多米諾製糖公司洽談他的構想,但他們始終沒給回音。但不久後,白色的糖包開始出現在商店的架上。班未能為構想申請專利,因此一無所獲。但幾年後,第二個機會出現。一家公司請班研發給糖尿病患使用的代糖。班和在大學主修化學的兒子馬文提出一種以糖精為主原料的產品,但這時那家公司又不感興趣了。

所以班決定自己行銷那一款代糖。他依一首老歌的歌詞,取名為「纖而樂」。今天,粉紅色的糖包(靈感來自貝蒂的馬克杯)和熟悉的高音譜記號商標舉世聞名,是減肥者和糖尿病患的最愛。

treble-clef 高音譜記號

答案解析詳見 (A)

Vocabulary Bank

1) **mechanical** [mə`kænɪkəl] (a.) 機械的
Our flight was delayed due to mechanical problems.
我們的班機因為機械故障而誤點。

2) **construction** [kən`strʌkʃən] (n.) 建設，營造，施工
There was an accident at the construction site.
在工地有一場意外發生。

3) **scooter** [`skutə] (n.)（車輪小的）機車，速克達
Kevin rides his scooter to school every day.
凱文每天都騎機車上學。

4) **communist** [`kɑmjənɪst] (n./a.)（常為大寫）共產黨員，共產主義者；共產黨的 The Chinese Communists came to power in 1949.
中國共產黨在一九四九年取得政權。

5) **extended** [ɪk`stɛndɪd] (a.) 長期的，持久的
I'm planning on taking an extended vacation.
我打算放個長假。

6) **break down** [brek daʊn] (phr.) 故障，停止運轉
My motorcycle broke down just outside of town.
我的摩托車剛騎出城就拋錨了。

7) **plumbing** [`plʌmɪŋ] (n.) 水管（設備），管線，配管系統
We had new plumbing installed in our bathroom.
我們的浴室裝了新的管線。

進階字彙

8) **refinery** [rɪ`faɪnəri] (n.) 提煉廠，煉油廠
The oil refinery was fined for air pollution.
煉油廠因造成空氣污染而遭罰。

9) **pliers** [`plaɪəz] (n.)（用作單數或複數）箝子
Do you have a pair of pliers in your toolbox?
你的工具箱裡有沒有箝子？

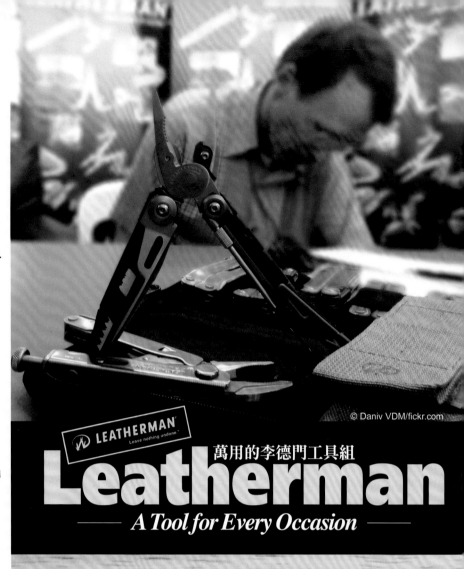

© Daniv VDM/fickr.com

LEATHERMAN Leave nothing undone.

萬用的李德門工具組

Leatherman
— *A Tool for Every Occasion* —

課文朗讀 MP3 49　　單字朗讀 MP3 50　　英文講解 MP3 51

After graduating from Oregon State University in 1970 with a degree in 1)**mechanical** engineering, Tim Leatherman found a job in Los Angeles designing pipe systems for oil 8)**refineries**. But he couldn't stand sitting at a table all day drawing pipes for refineries that he never even saw, so he quit after a year and returned to Oregon. Back in his hometown of Portland, Tim worked in 2)**construction** while he waited for his girlfriend Chau—an exchange student from Vietnam—to finish university.

In 1972, Tim followed Chau to Vietnam, where the couple got married. While working as an English teacher in Saigon, Tim was impressed by how good the locals were at repairing their 3)**scooters**. Regretting his lack of practical engineering knowledge, he began taking small appliances apart to see how they worked. But the Vietnam War brought Tim's life in his wife's country to an early end. As 4)**Communist** forces were approaching Saigon in 1975, Tim and Chau made the decision to return and live in the U.S.

Not yet sure what he wanted to do with the rest of his life, Tim took his wife on an 5)**extended** trip to Europe. The couple didn't have much money, so they bought a $300 car in Amsterdam, and stayed in the cheapest hotels they could find. While traveling 1 **on such a tight budget** was challenging, it also led to Tim's eureka moment. Because the car kept 6)**breaking down** and the hotel 7)**plumbing** often didn't work, he was constantly making small repairs with his pocketknife. But what he really needed was a pair of 9)**pliers**. "Why not combine pliers with a pocketknife?" Tim thought to himself one day.

Mini Quiz 閱讀測驗

Why did Tim Leatherman go to Vietnam?
(A) To work as an English teacher.
(B) To fight in the Vietnam War
(C) To be with his girlfriend
(D) To gain practical engineering knowledge

中 Translation

一九七〇年從奧勒岡州立大學以機械工程學位畢業後,提姆李德門在洛杉磯找到為煉油廠設計輸油管系統的工作。但他無法忍受成天坐在桌前,為他從沒見過的煉油廠畫輸油管,所以幹了一年便離職,回到奧勒岡州。回到波特蘭的家鄉後,提姆在營造業工作,等待他叫「珠」的女友(越南交換學生)念完大學。

一九七二年,提姆跟著珠到越南,兩人在那裡結婚。一邊在西貢擔任英文老師,提姆對當地人善於修理機車之事印象深刻。有感於自己缺乏實務工程知識,他開始拆解小電器,了解它們如何運作。但越戰讓提姆在愛妻國家的生活戛然而止。當越共軍隊於一九七五年迫近西貢,提姆和珠決定返回美國居住。

由於還不確定自己這輩子想做什麼,提姆帶妻子赴歐洲長途旅行。這對夫妻並不富有,所以在阿姆斯特丹買了一部美金三百元的汽車,並盡可能找最便宜的旅館過夜。儘管以如此緊縮的預算旅行非常辛苦,但也為提姆帶來靈機一動的剎那。由於車子一再拋錨,旅館的水管也常不通,他經常拿他的小摺刀做簡單的修理。但他真正需要的是一把鉗子。「為什麼不把鉗子和小摺刀結合起來呢,」提姆一天這麼想。

Vietnam War 越南戰爭

簡稱越戰,為南越(South Vietnam)和北越(North Vietnam)於一九五九到一九七五年發生的內戰,美國當時為了對抗共產主義(Communism)而援助南越,是二戰(WWII)以後美國參戰人數最多、影響最深遠的戰爭。在尼克森總統(Richard Nixon)執政時期,因美國國內反戰聲浪不斷,因此將軍隊慢慢撤出越南。最後,在一九七五年四月三十日的「西貢淪陷」(fall of Saigon)後,由北越贏得這場戰爭,使得越南政權正式轉移。因為越南人認為美軍大肆踐踏他們的家園,干涉別國內政,所以他們稱六〇到七〇年代的越戰為「美戰」(American War)。

pocketknife 小摺刀

大小適合放在口袋中的 pocketknife,最早發現源自於古羅馬時期的西班牙,款式有很多種,有的只有一個刀片,也有集多種刀片於同一刀柄的。有些除了刀片外還附有其他多項工具。用途很多,拆信、切水果或防身等都派得上用場,且大家熟知的瑞士軍用小刀(Swiss army knife)也屬於小摺刀的一種。

Tongue-tied No More

1 on a budget 預算有限

budget 是預算,on a budget 就表示經濟拮据、預算有限。而本文中的 on a tight budget 為加強語氣的說法,tight 一字表「緊縮的」,在此用來形容「預算吃緊」。

A: I want to buy a mountain bike, but I can't really afford it.

我想買一輛登山腳踏車,可是我實在負擔不起。

B: Well, if you're on a budget, you should consider buying a used one.

如果你預算有限,你應該考慮買輛二手車。

閱讀測驗解答 (C)

Vocabulary Bank

1) **estimate** [ˈɛstəmɪt] (n.) 估計（數）
(v.) estimate [ˈɛstəˌmet]
According to government estimates, the economy will grow 2.4% this year.
根據政府的估計，今年的經濟將會成長百分之二點四。

2) **obtain** [əbˈten] (v.) 取得，獲得
The application form can be obtained online.
申請表可以從網路取得。

3) **catalog** [ˈkætəˌlɔg] (n.) 目錄，型錄
Could you send me a copy of your product catalog?
你能寄給我一份你們產品的型錄嗎？

4) **production** [prəˈdʌkʃən] (n.) 生產，產量
World coffee production is down this year.
今年全世界的咖啡總產量減少。

5) **end up** [ɛnd ʌp] (phr.) 結果變成，最後
The restaurant was closed, so we ended up eating at the place next door.
那家餐廳打烊了，所以我們後來跑去隔壁的店吃。

進階字彙

6) **prototype** [ˈprotəˌtaɪp] (n.) 原型
A prototype of the new car was revealed at the auto show.
這款新車的原型車在車展亮相。

7) **gadget** [ˈgædʒɪt] (n.) 小裝置，小玩意兒
That store sells all the latest electronic gadgets.
那家店販售所有最新的 3C 產品。

口語補充

8) **buddy** [ˈbʌdi] (n.) 好友，夥伴
Me and my buddies are going fishing this weekend.
我跟朋友這個週末要去釣魚。

Upon returning to Portland, Tim asked his wife if he could build a 6)**prototype** of his idea. When she asked how long it would take, he told her about a month. So Chau found a job and Tim went to work in their garage. His 1)**estimate**, however, turned out to be a little optimistic—it ᴳtook him three years to create a prototype he was satisfied with! Tim's plan at the time was to patent his invention, sell it to a manufacturer for a million dollars and live happily ever after.

But when Tim 2)**obtained** the patent and took his prototype to a knife company, they said, "It's not a knife, it's a tool." Fine, he thought, I'll show it to tool companies. But the tool companies all said, "This isn't a tool, it's a 7)**gadget**—and gadgets don't sell." Not willing to give up, Tim found a job in sales so he could learn more about business and continued to promote his invention in his spare time. But four years went by, and he still hadn't found a buyer for his patent.

At this point, Steve Berliner, a [8]**buddy** of Tim's from college, told him that if he wanted to bring his product to market, he should start a company and make it himself. So Tim and Steve formed a partnership and began looking for customers. Finally, in 1983, they got their first order for 500 tools from a mail order [3]**catalog**, and went into [4]**production**. They hoped to sell 4,000 of their first model—which they named the Pocket Survival Tool—that year, but [5]**ended up** selling 30,000. Within a decade, the Leatherman Tool Group was making and selling a million multi-tools a year.

Mini Quiz 閱讀測驗

Why did Leatherman start his own company?
(A) Because his prototype was a tool, not a knife
(B) To find a manufacturer for his tool
(C) So he could learn more about business
(D) Because nobody would buy his patent

中 Translation

回到波特蘭後，提姆問妻子他能否為自己的構想打造一個模型。她問要多久時間，他告訴她大概一個月。於是珠去找了工作，提姆則在他們的車庫裡做工。結果，他的預估樂觀了一點——他花了三年時間才做成令他滿意的模型！當時提姆的計畫是為發明申請專利，以百萬美元賣給製造商，從此過著幸福快樂的生活。

但當提姆取得專利，帶著他的模型到一家製刀公司時，他們說：「那不是刀子，而是工具。」好吧，他想，那我就拿去給工具公司看。但所有工具公司都說：「這不是工具，這是小玩意兒——而小玩意兒賣不了錢。」不願就此放棄，提姆找了一份業務工作以便學習更多做生意的知識，並繼續在空閒時間推銷他的發明。但四年過去，他的專利仍然沒賣出去。

就在這時，提姆大學時的死黨史提夫柏林納告訴他，如果他想要讓他的產品上市，就該自己開公司，自己製造。於是提姆和史提夫合夥，開始尋找客戶。終於，一九八三年，他們從郵購目錄公司獲得第一批五百件工具的訂單，並開始生產。他們希望那一年，他們的第一個型號能賣出四千件——他們給它命名為「口袋求生工具」——結果賣了三萬件。不到十年，李德門工具集團每年都要產銷一百萬件多功能工具組了。

Grammer Master

「花多久時間」的寫法

「花…時間」可以用 take 或 spend 這兩個動詞。「某人花了…時間做某事」的句型可以是 "It takes sb. + 一段時間 to + 原型動詞" 或 "Sb. spend + 一段時間 + Ving"。這個用法可千萬不能和花錢的動詞 cost 搞混了。

A: How long did it take you to paint the room?
你花了多久時間粉刷房間？
B: I spent about four hours.
我花了大概四個小時。

Language Guide

Leatherman 工具箱

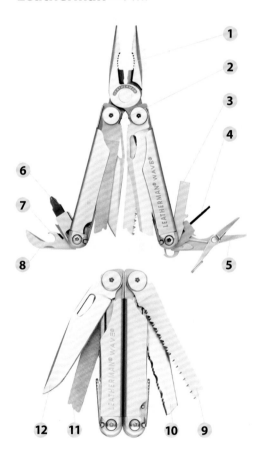

1 **pliers** 箝子
2 **wire cutter** 剪線鉗
3 **large screwdriver** 大螺絲起子
4 **small bit driver** 小鑽頭
5 **scissors** 小剪刀
6 **large bit driver** 大鑽頭
7 **can opener** 開罐器
8 **wire stripper** 剝線鉗
9 **saw** 鋸
10 **serrated knife** 鋸齒刀
11 **wood/metal file** 銼刀
12 **knife** 小刀

（a）答錯驗測讀閱

53

EUREKA! 點子成金

Vocabulary Bank

1) **minister** [ˋmɪnɪstə] (n.) 牧師，神職人員
The minister at our church is retiring next year.
我們教堂的牧師明年要退休了。

2) **rebel** [rɪˋbɛl] (v.) 叛逆，反抗
It's normal for teenagers to rebel against their parents.
青少年反抗父母是很常見的事。

3) **indifferent** [ɪnˋdɪf(ə)rənt] (a.) 平庸的，漠不關心的，狀況差的
Fans were angered by the team's indifferent performance.
球迷因為球隊表現不佳感到氣憤。

4) **transfer** [ˋtrænsfə] (v.) 轉學，調動，調任
Steven is being transferred to the Cleveland branch next month.
史蒂芬下個月會被調到克里夫蘭分公司。

5) **drop out (of)** [drɑp aʊt] (phr.) 輟學
My parents would kill me if I dropped out of school.
如果我輟學的話，我爸媽會宰了我。

6) **publisher** [ˋpʌblɪʃə] (n.) 出版社，發行人
The writer couldn't find a publisher for his novel.
這位作者找不到出版社出版他的小說。

7) **compilation** [ˌkɑmpəˋleʃən] (n.) 叢集，編輯成品
The book is a compilation of the writer's newspaper columns.
這本書集結了那位作家發表在報紙上的專欄。

8) **abandon** [əˋbændən] (v.) 放棄，拋棄
The flood forced thousands to abandon their homes.
水災迫使數千位民眾捨棄他們的家園。

9) **condense** [kənˋdɛns] (v.) 精簡，縮短
Michael condensed his report into a short presentation.
麥可把他的報告濃縮成一個簡短的簡報。

10) **version** [ˋvɝʒən] (n.) 版本
Which version of Windows do you have on your computer?
你電腦用的是哪個版本的微軟視窗軟體？

11) **periodical** [ˌpɪrɪˋɑdɪkəl] (n.) 期刊，雜誌
The library subscribes to hundreds of periodicals.
圖書館訂閱了數百份的期刊。

12) **issue** [ˋɪʃju] (n.) （刊物）期數
Have you seen the latest issue of *Time*?
你看過最新一期的《時代》雜誌了嗎？

圖片提供：
Reader's Digest（East Asia）

Reader's Digest Bringing America to the World 讀者文摘

課文朗讀 MP3 55　　單字朗讀 MP3 56　　英文講解 MP3 57

DeWitt Wallace was born in 1889 to Dr. James Wallace, Presbyterian [1)]**minister** and president of Macalester College in St. Paul, Minnesota. Raised on a diet of endless prayer, DeWitt [2)]**rebelled** by becoming an [3)]**indifferent** student known for [13)]**pranks**. When a cow was discovered in the chapel, all fingers pointed at him. After attending Macalester for two years, he [4)]**transferred** to U.C. Berkeley, where he entered as a freshman. "The freshman year is more fun," he explained.

DeWitt [5)]**dropped out** of college the following year and returned to St. Paul, where he got a job writing for a farming book [6)]**publisher**. Lying in a field one day, he had the idea to create his own book, a [7)]**compilation** of all the free information on farming, so readers could get

[14)]**pertinent** information from a single source. DeWitt quit his job and began selling his books to feed stores, but he barely **1 broke even**, and [8)]**abandoned** the business to serve in World War I. While recovering from an injury in France, he spent his time reading American magazines. He found the articles interesting, but felt that they were too [15)]**lengthy**.

This led to DeWitt's eureka moment—he decided to create a magazine that contained [9)]**condensed** [10)]**versions** of articles from the leading [11)]**periodicals** of the day. He spent the next six months at the library putting together the first [12)]**issue** of *Reader's Digest*, but couldn't find a publisher.

© 達志 / UPI PHOTO

So he decided to publish the magazine himself and sell it by mail order. Although only 5,000 copies of the first issue were printed, *Reader's Digest*, with its Norman Rockwell view of America, soon became one of the most widely read magazines in the world.

Mini Quiz 閱讀測驗

Which of the following is true about DeWitt Wallace?
(A) He lost money in his first business.
(B) He graduated from Macalester College.
(C) He put together the first issue of *Reader's Digest* in France.
(D) He was blamed for putting a cow in a chapel.

中 Translation

德威特華勒斯生於一八八九年，父親詹姆士華勒斯博士是長老教會牧師，也是明尼蘇達聖保羅麥凱勒斯特學院院長。在無窮無盡的禱告生活中長大的德威特，求學時開始叛逆，變成凡事不在乎的學生，還以惡作劇出名。一次，禮拜堂裡出現一頭牛，每個人都認為是他幹的。就讀麥凱勒斯特學院兩年後，他轉學到加州大學柏克萊分校，重當大一新鮮人。「大一的生活比較有趣，」他解釋道。

次年德威特即輟學回到聖保羅，在那裡找到一份工作，替一家農業書籍出版社寫稿。一天，躺在田間時，他突發奇想，打算自己製作一本書，彙整所有免費的農業資訊，讓讀者能夠從單一來源就得到相關資訊。德威特去工作，開始把他的書賣給飼料店，但僅能勉強損益兩平，於是便放棄生意從軍去，參與一次世界大戰。他在法國受了傷，養傷期間都在讀美國雜誌，他發現那些文章很有趣，但覺得太過冗長。

這讓德威特靈機一動——他決定創造一本雜誌，刊登當紅期刊文章的濃縮精華版。接下來六個月，他在圖書館拼湊出《讀者文摘》第一期，但找不到出版商出版，於是他決定自力出版，並透過郵購銷售。雖然第一期只印了五千本，但《讀者文摘》——以諾曼洛克威爾式的美國觀——很快就成為全世界最廣為閱讀的雜誌之一。

進階字彙

13) **prank** [præŋk] (n.) 惡作劇
The witness provided the police with
Billie likes playing pranks on his friends.
比利喜歡捉弄他的朋友。

14) **pertinent** [ˈpɝtɪnənt] (a.) 相關的，切題的
The witness provided the police with pertinent information about the crime.
目擊者提供警方有關該起案件的相關資訊。

15) **lengthy** [ˈlɛŋθi] (a.) 冗長的
The treaty was finally signed after lengthy negotiations.
條約在經過冗長的協商後終於簽定了。

🔑 Tongue-tied No More

① break even 損益平衡

文章中的 break even 不是指打破了什麼東西，而是「不賺不賠」的意思。至於「賺錢」跟「賠錢」則可以用 make a profit 跟 lose money 來表達。

A: How long did it take for your restaurant to break even?
你的餐廳花了多久時間才開始損益兩平？

B: Nearly two years.
將近兩年。

🧭 Language Guide

The Wallace Foundation
華勒斯基金會

華勒斯夫婦一生致力於慈善事業，兩人在一九五一年曾因此登上《時代》雜誌封面。以他們名字建立的基金會贊助了各式藝術、文化及教育的計畫，華勒斯先生身後所留下來的讀者文摘股份，也皆由基金會用於公益用途上。

Norman Rockwell
諾曼洛克威爾

洛克威爾是美國二十世紀重要的插畫家，曾長期為《星期六晚間郵報》繪製封面插圖。他的繪畫內容包含美國各個階級的各式生活及歷史上各類重大事件，忠實記錄下美國的演變。文中便是以這個畫家無所不包的題材跟《讀者文摘》相呼應，因為他畫中溫馨又富有趣味的筆調與《讀者文摘》相同，正是兩者大受歡迎的原因。

閱讀測驗解答：(D)

55

Vocabulary Bank

1) **weary** [ˋwɪrɪ] (a.) 疲倦的，weary of 即「厭煩於」
Voters have grown weary of the government's excuses.
選民對政府的藉口已經感到很厭煩了。

2) **crib** [krɪb] (n.) 嬰兒床
Does your baby sleep in a crib?
你的寶寶是睡在嬰兒床上的嗎？

3) **vacuum** [ˋvækjum] (n.) 真空，真空裝置。
vacuum cleaner 即「吸塵器」。
Nothing can live in the vacuum of space.
沒有生物能在外太空的真空狀態下存活。

4) **application** [ˌæpləˋkeʃən] (n.) 應用，運用
Engineering is the application of science to practical problems.
工程學是解決實際問題的一門應用科學。

5) **venture** [ˋvɛntʃə] (n.) 新創事業，投資事業
There are many joint ventures between American and Chinese companies.
有很多美國企業和中國企業的合資事業。

6) **statistics** [stəˋtɪstɪks] (n.) 統計（數字），統計學
Statistics show that women in the area live longer than men.
統計顯示出該區的女性活得比男性久。

7) **commerce** [ˋkɑmɝs] (n.) 商業，貿易
Gary Locke is currently serving as the U.S. Secretary of Commerce.
駱家輝是現任的美國商務部長。

8) **determine** [dɪˋtɝmɪn] (v.) 判斷，確定，決定
Investigators were unable to determine the victim's time of death.
調查員無法確認受害者死亡的時間。

9) **virtual** [ˋvɝtʃuəl] (a.) 虛擬的
Steve hired a virtual assistant to help him set up his online business.
史帝夫雇了一名虛擬助手來幫他架設線上事業。

10) **operation** [ˌɑpəˋreʃən] (n.) 營運，作業
The senior vice president is in charge of company operations.
這位資深副總負責掌管公司的營運。

11) **implement** [ˋɪmpləˌmɛnt] (v.) 實行，執行
The new tax law will be implemented next year.
新的稅法將會在明年施行。

The Rise of Amazon
亞馬遜網路書店

課文朗讀 MP3 58　單字朗讀 MP3 59　英文講解 MP3 60

　　Born in Albuquerque, New Mexico in 1964, Jeff Bezos showed signs of being a [12] **prodigy** at an early age. At three, [1] **weary** of his sleeping arrangement, he took his [2] **crib** apart with a screwdriver. At age fourteen, he tried to build a hovercraft out of a [3] **vacuum** cleaner. Jeff fell in love with computers in high school, and later graduated from Princeton *summa cum laude* with a degree in computer science and electrical engineering.

　　After graduation, Jeff got a job at D. E. Shaw, a Wall Street [13] **hedge** fund specializing in the [4] **application** of computer science to the stock market. He ❶ **rose** quickly **through the ranks**, and was soon promoted to senior vice president. In 1994, while surfing the Web for new business [5] **ventures** for his company, Jeff discovered that Internet use was growing by 2,300% a year! This [6] **statistic** led to his eureka moment: the real investment was in the Internet itself.

　　The company president didn't agree, so Jeff decided to start his own e-[7] **commerce** venture. But what to sell? He [8] **determined** that the best thing to sell online was books, because he would be able to offer more titles than any traditional bookstore. Jeff next moved to Seattle and set up what he called "the world's largest bookstoreî in his

進階字彙

12) **prodigy** [ˋprɑdədʒɪ] (n.) 神童，奇才
The piano prodigy began playing at the age of three.
那位鋼琴神童三歲就開始彈鋼琴了。

13) **hedge** [hɛdʒ] (n./v.)（兩面下注以）避險，hedge fund 即「避險基金」
The hedge fund requires a minimum investment of a million dollars.
那支避險基金的最低投資額為一百萬元。

14) **fine-tune** [ˋfaɪnˋtun] (v.) 進行微調，使漸趨穩定
The mechanics fine-tuned the racecar's engine before the race.
那些技師在賽車開始前對引擎進行微調。

15) **verification** [ˏvɛrəfɪˋkeʃən] (n.) 確認，認證
Documents must be submitted to the embassy for verification.
文件都必須交到大使館做認證。

garage. In 1995, Amazon.com opened its 9)**virtual** doors, offering a million titles. As sales grew and grew, Jeff kept 14)**fine-tuning** his 10)**operation**, 11)**implementing** novel ideas like one-click shopping and e-mail 15)**verification**. In the process, he became one of the first Internet billionaires.

Mini Quiz 閱讀測驗

According to the article, which of the following is true about Jeff Bezos?
(A) He started Amazon while working at D. E. Shaw.
(B) He grew up in Seattle.
(C) He didn't like sleeping in a crib.
(D) He established Amazon in 1994.

中 Translation

一九六四年出生在新墨西哥州阿布奎基市，傑夫貝佐斯很小就展露神童的跡象。三歲時，由於厭倦他的睡眠環境，他拿螺絲起子拆了他的嬰兒床。十四歲時，他試著把吸塵器打造成一艘氣墊船。傑夫就讀高中時愛上電腦，後來以最優等成績從普林斯頓大學畢業，拿到電腦科學與電機工程雙學位。

畢業後，傑夫在華爾街避險基金公司 D. E. 邵爾任職，這家公司專司將電腦科學應用於股市上。他步步高升，很快便被拔擢到資深副總裁的位子。一九九四年，上網替公司找尋新創事業時，傑夫發現網際網路的使用每年成長百分之兩千三百！這個統計數字讓他靈機一動：真正的投資機會就在網際網路本身。

邵爾公司的總裁不認同，所以傑夫決定成立自己的電子商務公司。但，賣什麼好呢？他判斷，最適合在網路上銷售的東西是書，因為他能比任何傳統書店提供更多書籍。接下來傑夫搬到西雅圖，在他的車庫裡建立他自稱「世界最大的書店」。一九九五年，亞馬遜網路書店正式「開門」營業，提供百萬種圖書。隨著銷售量節節上升，傑夫持續微調營運，實行嶄新的構想，例如「一指訂購」和電子郵件認證。在這段過程中，他成為第一批網路億萬富翁之一。

Language Guide

summa cum laude 以最高榮譽畢業

summa cum laude [ˋsumə kum ˋlaude] 是拉丁文「最優等」的意思，可以當副詞 (graduated summa cum laude)，也能當形容詞 (a summa cum laude graduate)。在美國，高於平均分數的成績分為三個等第：cum laude [kum ˋlaude]（以優等成績畢業）、magna cum laude [ˋmægnə kum ˋlaude]（以優異成績畢業），summa cum laude 則為最高等級。

Tongue-tied No More

1 rise through the ranks 步步高昇

rise 在這裡有「往上爬」的意思，rank 則是「位階、地位」。rise through the ranks 是指「在組織裡的職稱扶搖直上、步步高昇」。你也可以說 move up the ranks 或是 rise up the ranks。

A: Any advice on how to rise through the ranks?
有什麼可以升官的建議？

B: The best way is to bring in more money for the company.
幫公司賺更多錢就是最好的辦法。

Vocabulary Bank

1) **literature** [ˋlɪtərətʃə] (n.) 文學，文學作品
   (a.) literary [ˋlɪtəˏrɛri] 文學的，文藝的
   Donna studied French literature in grad school.
   多娜在研究所攻讀法國文學。

2) **surname** [ˋsɝˏnem] (n.) 姓氏，同 last name 和 family name
   Judging from his surname, I'd guess that he's French.
   從他的姓氏看來，我猜他是法國人

3) **publishing** [ˋpʌblɪʃɪŋ] (n.) 出版（業）
   (v.) publish
   (n.) publication [ˏpʌblɪˋkeʃən] 出版，出版物，刊物
   Karen works as an editor at a publishing company.
   凱倫在一家出版公司當編輯。

4) **content** [ˋkɑntɛnt] (n.) 內容
   The film contains adult content.
   這部電影包含成人內容。

5) **prosecution** [ˏprɑsɪˋkjuʃən] (n.) 起訴，告發
   (v.) prosecute [ˋprɑsɪˏkjut]
   There's been an increase in prosecutions for violent crimes.
   因暴力犯罪而被起訴的案件越來越多。

6) **worthwhile** [ˋwɝθˋwaɪl] (a.) 值得花時間、金錢、精神等的，有價值的
   Did you find the course worthwhile?
   你覺得上這門課值得嗎？

7) **bulky** [ˋbʌlkɪ] (a.) 笨重的，體積大的
   The couch was too bulky to carry up the stairs.
   這個沙發笨重到無法搬上樓。

8) **inheritance** [ɪnˋhɛrɪtəns] (n.) 遺產，繼承物
   The wealthy man left a large inheritance to his children.
   那位富翁留下大筆遺產給他的孩子。

9) **launch** [lɔntʃ] (v./n.) 展開，發起
   The police have launched an investigation into the murder.
   警方已針對該起謀殺案展開調查。

10) **revolution** [ˏrɛvəˋluʃən] (n.) 革命，大變革
    Millions of people died during the Russian Revolution.
    上百萬人在俄國革命期間喪生。

進階字彙

11) **obscene** [əbˋsin] (a.) 淫穢的，猥褻的
    The student was suspended for using obscene language.
    那名學生因言猥褻而被罰暫時停學。

Penguin Books
Literature for the Masses
適合普羅大眾的企鵝讀本

課文朗讀 MP3 61　單字朗讀 MP3 62　英文講解 MP3 63

Growing up in Bristol, England in the early 20th century, Allen Williams was an average student. His uncle, John Lane, had no children of his own and offered to adopt Allen if he agreed to change his [2]**surname** to Lane. Eager to leave Bristol, Allen followed John to London, where he began working at his uncle's [3]**publishing** house, Bodley Head. He rose up the ranks, and upon John's death in 1923, took over the business.

One of Allen Lane's first big moves as managing editor was his decision to publish the Irish novelist James Joyce's *Ulysses*, which had been banned in the U.S. for its [11]**obscene** [4]**content**. Fearing [5]**prosecution**, the Bodley Head board of directors was against the decision. Nevertheless, the publication of *Ulysses* turned out to be a literary and commercial success.

One day in 1934, while returning from a visit to Agatha Christie in Devon, Allen found himself at Exeter Station with nothing [6]**worthwhile** to read. Back then, serious literature was only available in [12]**hardcover** editions, which were [7]**bulky** and expensive. It was right then that Allen had his eureka moment: he could publish inexpensive [13]**paperbacks** that could be easily carried in one's pocket. "A man who may be poor in money," he reasoned, "is not necessarily poor in intellectual qualities."

58

© thepenguinpostcardproject.wordpress.com

Again, the board failed to back him, so Allen gave up his [8]**inheritance** and founded his own publishing house in 1935. The name Penguin was chosen for the bird's "[14]**dignified** but [15]**flippant**" manner. Penguin Books [9]**launched** a paperback [10]**revolution**, and has been bringing quality literature to the masses ever since.

Mini Quiz 閱讀測驗

Why did Allen Lane found Penguin Books?
(A) Because he lost his inheritance
(B) Because penguins are dignified but flippant
(C) Because paperbacks didn't exist at the time
(D) To make literature more easily available

中 Translation

二十世紀初成長於英國布里斯托的艾倫威廉斯是個中等生。他的舅舅約翰蘭恩膝下無子，表示如果艾倫願意改姓蘭恩就收養他。於是亟欲離開布里斯托的艾倫跟著舅舅來到倫敦，開始在約翰的博德利海德出版社工作。他的職位步步高升，而在約翰於一九二三年過世後，艾倫接掌了公司。

艾倫蘭恩接任總編輯後的其中一個大動作就是決定出版愛爾蘭小說家詹姆士喬伊斯的《尤里西斯》，該書因內容淫穢而在美國遭禁。因為害怕遭到起訴，博德利海德的董事會反對這個決定。結果，《尤里西斯》出版後叫好又叫座，既成為文學巨著，也創下銷售佳績。

在一九三四年的一天，赴德文郡拜訪阿嘉莎克莉絲蒂的回程途中，艾倫發現自己在艾克瑟特火車站沒有好書可讀。當時，市面上的嚴肅文學只有精裝本，既笨重又昂貴。就在這時艾倫靈機一動：他可以出版價格便宜、且便於放在口袋攜帶的平裝本。「手頭拮据的人，」他推想：「未必缺乏智識能力。」

這一次，董事會再度不予支持，因此艾倫放棄了遺產，在一九三五年自己成立出版社。「企鵝」一名取自這種鳥類「尊貴但輕率」的舉止。企鵝圖書發動平裝本革命，此後持續為大眾推出優質文學。

12) **hardcover** [ˈhɑrdˌkʌvɚ] (a./n.) 精裝（書）的；精裝書，也可稱作 hardback
Do you have a hardcover copy of this book?
你有這本書的精裝版嗎？

13) **paperback** [ˈpepɚˌbæk] (n./a.) 平裝書；平裝（書）
Holly bought a paperback to read at the beach.
荷莉買了一本平裝書在沙灘上看。

14) **dignified** [ˈdɪgnəˌfaɪd] (a.) 有尊嚴的，莊嚴的，高貴的
Michael looks very dignified in his new suit.
穿上新西裝的麥可看起來相當體面。

15) **flippant** [ˈflɪpənt] (a.) 輕率的，不認真的，無禮的
I don't appreciate your flippant attitude.
我不欣賞你輕挑的態度。

Language Guide

James Joyce 詹姆士喬伊斯

詹姆士喬伊斯為愛爾蘭作家兼詩人，為二十世紀最重要的現代主義(Modernism)作家之一，寫作時常以愛爾蘭當作背景，再融入其他國家的元素，風格相當豐富多元，著名的作品有《一位青年藝術家的畫像》(A Portrait of the Artist as a Young Man)和《芬尼根守靈夜》(Finnegans Wake)。而文中提到的《尤里西斯》(Ulysses)是他在一九五五年出版的長篇小說。該部小說以荷馬史詩《奧得賽》(Odyssey)為寫作藍本，因此書中人物多與《奧得賽》中的角色相互呼應。故事是在描述主人翁 Leopold Bloom 在都柏林（Dublin，即愛爾蘭首都）一天內的各種經歷。這種以時間為主軸，細膩描述角色內心獨白的寫作方式，被喻為意識流(stream of consciousness)小說的代表。不過由於內容被認為過於淫穢敗俗，使得該書在美國遭禁長達十五年之久，直到一九三三年才解禁。

Agatha Christie 阿嘉莎克莉絲蒂

阿嘉莎克莉絲蒂是英國知名偵探小說(detective novel)的作家，全名為 Dame Agatha Mary Clarissa Christie，她另一個專門用來寫愛情小說的筆名是 Lady Mallowan（馬洛溫爵夫人）。根據金氏世界紀錄統計，其作品銷售量僅次於聖經(Bible)及莎士比亞(Shakespeare)，為史上最暢銷的作家。「密室殺人法」(locked room mystery)是她小說中常見的犯案手法，也就是乍看之下，凶手或兇器就像蒸發一樣，完全沒有留下任何殺人證據，直到最後一刻才真相大白，這種故事走向常被日後的其他偵探小說家仿效。代表作品有《東方快車謀殺案》(Murder on the Orient Express)、《尼羅河謀殺案》(Death on the Nile)、《一個都不留》(And Then There Were None)等。

閱讀測驗解答：(D)

Vocabulary Bank

1) **round** [raʊnd] (n.) （常為複數）巡視，巡迴
   Doctors at the hospital make their rounds twice a day.
   醫院裡的醫生一天要巡視病人兩次。

2) **sketch** [skɛtʃ] (n./v.) 素描；畫素描，寫生
   The artist drew a quick sketch of the vase.
   那位藝術家快速畫了一張花瓶的素描。

3) **illustration** [ˌɪləˈstreʃən] (n.) 插畫，圖解
   The encyclopedia has thousands of color illustrations.
   百科全書裡有成千張彩色圖解。

4) **editor in chief** [ˈɛdɪtə ɪn tʃif] (n.) 總編，
   亦作 editor-in-chief
   The newspaper's senior editor was promoted to editor in chief.
   報社的資深編輯被升為總編。

5) **reign** [ren] (n./v.) 在位，統治，當道
   The king's reign lasted for 30 years.
   這個國王在位長達三十年。

6) **dorm** [dɔrm] (n.) 宿舍，即dormitory的簡稱
   Would you rather live in the dorms or rent an apartment?
   你寧願住宿舍還是在外面租房子？

7) **era** [ˈɛrə] (n.) 時代，年代，紀元
   The president has promised a new era of peace.
   這位總統允諾會帶來和平的新時代。

8) **extracurricular** [ˌɛkstrəkəˈrɪkjələ] (a.)
   課外的，課餘的
   I don't have time for extracurricular activities this semester.
   這學期我沒有多餘的時間參加課外活動。

9) **maiden** [ˈmedən] (a.) 未婚的，maiden name
   即「娘家姓」
   Anne decided to keep her maiden name when she got married.
   安結婚時決定保留她娘家的姓氏。

10) **drop out (of)** [drɑp aʊt] (phr.) 輟學
    My parents would kill me if I dropped out of school.
    如果我輟學，我爸媽會殺了我。

進階字彙

11) **superintendent** [ˌsupərɪnˈtɛndənt] (n.) 管理
    員，負責人
    All budget decisions are made by the organization's superintendent.
    所有經費的決定都是由這個組織的負責人做的。

12) **doodle** [ˈdudəl] (v.) （無聊、心不在焉地）亂
    畫，亂塗
    I just doodled in my notebook during the lecture.
    我上課時都在筆記本裡面塗鴉。

How Theodor Geisel Became Dr. Seuss

看希歐多蓋索如何化身為蘇斯博士

課文朗讀 MP3 64　單字朗讀 MP3 65　英文講解 MP3 66

Theodor Geisel was born in Springfield, Massachusetts to Theodor Robert and Henrietta Geisel, both children of German immigrants. Theodor's father worked as a [11)]**superintendent** at Forest Park, and as a boy he often went with his father when he made his [1)]**rounds**. His favorite part of the park was the zoo, where he loved to make [2)]**sketches** of all the animals. If Geisel's father helped inspire his interest in drawing, his mother—who read him stories in both English and German—gave him a love of language.

In 1921, Geisel entered Dartmouth University, where he majored in English. He also drew cartoons and [3)]**illustrations** for the campus humor magazine, *Jack-O-Lantern*, and was elected [4)]**editor in chief** in his junior year. But his [5)]**reign** at the magazine ended when he was caught throwing a drinking party in his [6)]**dorm** room. Because this was the Prohibition [7]**era**, Geisel was forced to give up all [8]**extracurricular** activities. But he continued contributing to *Jack-O-Lantern* in secret under the pen name "Seuss," which was his mother's [9]**maiden** name.

After graduating from Dartmouth, Geisel traveled to England to study at Oxford, intending to earn a Ph.D. in English literature and become a professor. But he was often bored in class, and spent his time [12]**doodling** instead of taking notes. When fellow American student Helen Palmer

© Greg Williams/ Wikipedia

saw his drawings, she told him he should be an artist rather than a professor. He took her advice and, soon after, her hand in marriage. Geisel [10]**dropped out** of Oxford, and in 1927 the couple got married and moved to New York.

Mini Quiz 閱讀測驗

Where did Theodor Geisel's pen name come from?
(A) It was a nickname his mother gave him.
(B) It was the name of a maiden his mother knew.
(C) It was his mother's first name.
(D) It was his mother's original last name.

中 Translation

希歐多蓋索出生於麻州春田市，父親希歐多羅伯特和母親韓莉塔蓋索都是德國移民的子女。希歐多的父親是森林公園的管理員，從小他就常和父親一起巡邏。他最喜歡公園裡的動物園，喜歡在那裡畫所有動物的素描。若說蓋索的父親有助於啟發他對繪畫的興趣，那麼他的母親──會用英語和德語唸故事給他聽──就賦予他對語言的熱愛。

一九二一年，蓋索進入達特茅斯大學就讀，主修英文。他也為校園的幽默雜誌《傑克南瓜燈》畫漫畫和插圖，並在大三那年被選為主編。但當他被抓到在宿舍房間開飲酒派對，他在雜誌的領導職務便告終止。因為當時是禁酒時期，蓋索被迫放棄所有課外活動。但他繼續以母親的娘家姓「蘇斯」為筆名，秘密供稿給《傑克南瓜燈》。

從達特茅斯畢業後，蓋索前往英國進牛津大學就讀，打算攻讀英國文學博士並當教授。但他常在課堂上覺得無聊，老是亂塗亂畫而不做筆記。同樣來自美國的同學海倫帕瑪看到他的畫，直說他該當畫家而不是教授。他接受了她的建議，不久，也牽起她的手步入婚姻。蓋索從牛津退學，一九二七年，兩人結為連理，搬到紐約。

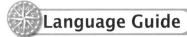

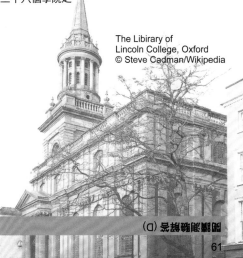
61

EUREKA! 點子成金

V Vocabulary Bank

1) **submit** [səb`mɪt] (v.) 呈送，提交，投稿
   All applications must be submitted by September 30.
   申請書必須在九月三十號前呈交。

2) **executive** [ɪg`zɛkjətɪv] (n.) 高階主管，高級官員
   Many company executives received large bonuses this year.
   公司很多高階主管今年都領了高額獎金。

3) **salary** [`sæləri] (n.) 薪資
   It's hard to support a family on such a low salary.
   這麼低的薪水很難維持家計。

4) **cruise** [kruz] (n.) 巡航，搭船旅行
   Let's go for a cruise in the Caribbean.
   我們去搭船遊加勒比海吧。

5) **fascinate** [`fæsə,net] (v.) 著迷，使神魂顛倒
   Let's go for a cruise in the Caribbean.
   羅貝塔一直對亞洲文化深深著迷。

6) **rhythm** [`rɪðəm] (n.) 節奏，韻律
   You need a good sense of rhythm to dance well.
   需要有很好的節奏感才能把舞跳得好。

7) **fantastic** [fæn`tæstɪk] (a.) 奇異的，古怪的
   The wind and sea have worn the rock into fantastic shapes.
   風和海水把石頭磨成奇怪的形狀。

8) **publisher** [`pʌblɪʃə] (n.) 出版社，發行人
   The writer couldn't find a publisher for his novel.
   猜猜我在郵局遇到誰？

9) **run into** [`rʌn `ɪntu] (phr.) 巧遇
   Guess who I ran into at the post office?
   這位記者在一間有影響力的報社找到工作。

進階字彙

10) **insecticide** [ɪn`sɛktə,saɪd] (n.) 殺蟲劑，農藥
    The farmer sprayed insecticide on his crops.
    這位農夫在作物上噴農藥。

© catwalker/Shutterstock.com

課文朗讀 MP3 67　單字朗讀 MP3 68　英文講解 MP3 69

Geisel began [1]**submitting** his cartoons to magazines, and after having one published by the *Saturday Evening Post*, he was offered a job at *Judge* magazine. At Judge, he began signing his cartoons "Dr. Seuss" to ❶**make fun of** himself for not completing his Ph.D. One of the cartoons he drew there—showing a knight using Flit bug spray to get rid of dragons—led to another career change. [2]**Executives** at Standard Oil, which made the [10]**insecticide**, were so impressed that they offered him a job in their advertising department, where he worked for the next decade.

Working in advertising gave Geisel a high [3]**salary** and plenty of time to travel, and it was on a [4]**cruise** to Europe in 1936 that he had his eureka moment. On the return trip, stormy weather kept passengers off the deck, and Geisel passed the time in the ship's bar. While drinking vodka on the rocks, he became [5]**fascinated** by the sound of the engines, and began reciting silly verses to the [6]**rhythm**. One verse, "And that is a story that no one can beat, and to think that I saw it on Mulberry Street," kept repeating in his head after the trip. So he kept adding more verses—along with illustrations—until he had a story about a parade of [7]**fantastic** creatures that a boy imagines while walking home.

And to Think That I Saw It on Mulberry Street was rejected by 27 [8]**publishers** before Geisel's luck changed. He was just about to give up when he [9]**ran** into an old Dartmouth

© catwalker/Shutterstock.com

classmate on the street. His classmate had just been made editor at Vanguard Press, and agreed to publish his book **2on the spot.** Geisel went on to write dozens of children's classics during his long career, and some, including *The Cat in the Hat* and *How the Grinch Stole Christmas!*, have even been made into Hollywood movies.

Mini Quiz 閱讀測驗

What was Geisel doing when he had his eureka moment?
A) Going to Europe
B) Writing silly verses
C) Drinking alcohol
D) Singing at a bar

中 Translation

蓋索開始向各家雜誌投遞他的漫畫，在一篇獲得《週六晚郵報》刊登後，《審判》雜誌給了他一個職務。在《審判》雜誌，他開始為他的漫畫署名「蘇斯博士」，嘲弄自己沒有完成博士學業。他在那裡畫的一篇漫畫──一名騎士拿「飛利脫」殺蟲劑對付惡龍──促成他再次轉換跑道。飛利脫製造商標準石油公司的高階主管對那篇漫畫印象深刻，於是聘請他進該公司廣告部門任職，接下來十年，他都在那裡工作。

從事廣告工作給了蓋索相當高的待遇和許多時間旅遊，而正是一九三六年航往歐洲之旅，讓他靈機一動。回程，狂風暴雨讓乘客上不了甲板，蓋索只好在郵輪的酒吧消磨時間，在飲用加冰伏特加時，他聽引擎的聲音聽得入迷，開始配合韻律吟誦愚蠢的韻文。其中一句：「而那故事無人敵得過，想起我在桑樹街上見過」，在旅行結束後仍縈繞在他腦海。所以他增添了更多韻文──以及插畫──最後完成一篇敘述一個男孩在走路回家途中，想像出一系列荒誕怪物的故事。

《想起我在桑樹街上見過》接連被二十七家出版社拒絕，蓋索的運氣才好轉。就在他準備放棄之際，他在街上遇到一個達特茅斯的老同學。這位同學才剛接任先鋒出版社的編輯，當場一口答應幫他出書。在他長久的生涯，蓋索繼續寫了數十部童書經典，其中《魔法靈貓》和《鬼靈精》等作品，更被拍成好萊塢電影。

✂ Tongue-tied No More

1 make fun of 嘲笑，戲弄

fun 意思是「娛樂、開心」，make fun of 就是說「取笑或戲弄別人當做娛樂」。

A: This boy in my class keeps making fun of me.
我們班有個男生總是喜歡取笑我。

B: He probably likes you.
他大概喜歡你。

2 on the spot 當場，當下

慣用語 on the spot 有 immediately「立刻，馬上」的意味。spot 有「地點、位子」的意思，因此 on the spot 是一種強調語氣的用法，描述當你還沒離開這個位子之前就發生了這件事情，也就是某件事「馬上發生，發生就在當下」。

A: So did you ask Karen out yesterday?
你昨天有約凱倫出去嗎？

B: Yeah. She turned me down on the spot.
有啊。她當場拒絕我了。

✦ Language Guide

And to Think That I Saw It on Mulberry Street《桑樹街漫遊記》

於一九三七年出版的《桑樹街漫遊記》，為蘇斯博士的第一本童書。距離蘇斯博士同年家鄉不到一公里的桑樹街，成為他故事筆下的場景，故事裡的小男孩馬可（Marco，這個名字正是從他編輯的兒子而來的），放學回家途中在桑樹街上的所見所聞，幻化成自己想像的情景。一輛普通的馬車在馬可的眼中變成大象載著一大群樂隊，還有許多動物都加入了這像極嘉年華會的遊行活動，這麼盛大的隊伍，還得麻煩警察先生來幫忙開路！這麼精彩的情結，馬可卻只以一輛普通的馬車簡單帶過，並未告訴父親任何想像故事。馬可甚至還成為蘇斯博士另一本童書──《麥艾林格特的泳池》(McEilligot's Pool)裡的主角。

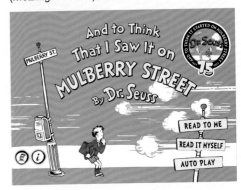

© xJason.Rogersx/flickr.com

© joesuspense/flickr.com

© joesuspense/flickr

美國兒童界的莎士比亞

你可能不知道蘇斯博士是誰，但對美國人來說，他可是位想像力豐富的創作大師，沒有一個人沒讀過他寫的童話故事，這些故事可說是陪伴他們一起長大的重要玩伴。總共寫出了四十四本童書的蘇斯博士，曾在一九八四年得到普利茲文學獎 (Pulitzer Prize)，這些經典故事不僅被拍成卡通，甚至成為好萊塢優質的動畫電影。雖然蘇斯博士已在一九九一年辭世，但他留下的作品始終是全球最暢銷的童書。現在讓 EZ TALK 帶大家一起進入蘇斯博士的童話想像世界吧！

 荷頓大象故事系列

© ladybugbkt/flickr.com

Horton Hears a Who!《荷頓奇遇記》

本書為蘇斯博士於一九五四年再次以大象荷頓為主角所寫出的故事，並在二〇〇八年被拍成動畫電影。故事中，荷頓聽見一顆塵埃微弱到幾乎快聽不見的求救聲，原來塵埃上有個稱作「Who-Ville」的小鎮，他們的鎮長希望荷頓可以幫他們找到一個安身立命的地方，於是荷頓便將這顆小塵埃放在苜蓿花上，打算帶他們到叢林中的一座山頭上安頓下來。然而，聽不見塵埃聲響的其他森林動物，不相信荷頓說的話，以為荷頓患了幻想症，千方百計想從他身邊把花搶走，甚至還將荷頓關進籠子裡。此時，塵埃上的居民也努力發出聲響，想讓塵埃以外的動物們聽見，只是似乎沒有什麼效果。JoJo 是鎮上唯一一個沒有發出噪音的人，最後他也加入發出聲響，使得大家發出的聲音大到可以讓森林動物都聽見，大家這才相信，原來塵埃上真的住了一群人。故事寓意旨在地球其實也只是宇宙中的一顆小塵埃，就如同這顆在地球上的小塵埃一般。

兩千年時，這兩個以荷頓為要角的故事作成了音樂劇——Seussical，搬上了百老匯 (Broadway) 的大舞台，並在美國及英國巡迴演出，深受學校和當地劇院的喜愛。

Horton Hatches the Egg 《荷頓孵蛋》

《荷頓孵蛋》以一隻名叫荷頓的大象為故事中心，為蘇斯博士於一九四〇年所出版的童書。懶惰的小鳥梅茲 (Mayzie)，覺得孵蛋是件無趣又空虛的事，因此她拜託荷頓，希望荷頓可以代替她孵蛋，讓她好好度假、放鬆一下。沒想到荷頓居然答應了，一隻大象在樹上孵鳥蛋的景象惹來大家一陣恥笑，但荷頓始終堅守自己的承諾，繼續做他答應梅茲的事情。荷頓受盡苦難，跟著巡迴馬戲團來到了棕櫚灘 (Palm Beach) 附近的城鎮，在那裡遇見了梅茲。梅茲想和荷頓要回快孵出的鳥蛋。但當蛋終於孵出來時，結果卻是荷頓和梅茲的綜合體——一隻大象鳥。最後，梅茲什麼東西都沒有得到，而那隻大象鳥則和荷頓回到森林快樂地生活。

識字系列

Green Eggs and Ham《綠蛋和火腿》

你喜歡綠色蔬菜嗎？如果你不喜歡，那麼我猜綠色的蛋和火腿應該也無法讓你下嚥！故事中的 Sam-I-Am 先生追著不吃綠蛋和火腿的故事敘述者，逼問他願不願意在各種地方，如屋裡、樹上還是火車上，或是配合其他動物吃下綠蛋和火腿。

童書《綠蛋和火腿》於一九六〇年出版，為 Beginner Books 系列中的一本，這個書系是蘇斯博士因應出版社的要求，以初學識字該學的兩百五十個重要字彙編寫而成，裡頭出現的單字都相當簡單。而這本書裡總共只出現五十個英文單字，像是 box、and、car、do 或是 boat 等等。這個書系中除了《綠蛋和火腿》，用兩百三十六個字完成的《魔法靈貓》(The Cat in the Hat) 也深受家長和老師的喜愛，並在二〇〇三年被拍成動畫電影。

蘇斯博士生涯中最後著作

Oh, the Places You'll Go!
《喔，你要去的地方！》

以開放式結局 (open ending) 做結尾的《喔，你要去的地方！》是蘇斯博士離開人世前所寫的最後一本書，出版於一九九〇年，主要是針對人生旅途上的冒險和挑戰。寫作風格與《綠蛋和火腿》、

《魔法靈貓》相似，但增添了更多不同的角色身份。故事從旁白開始，不具名的主角離開城鎮踏上旅程，旅行在各種幾何圖形造型的地方，最後意外去到一個時間完全不會流逝的地方——The Waiting Place，但主角後來選擇離開那裡，繼續他的探險之旅。這本書常被送給即將畢業的學生當作禮物，希望可以幫助他們在人生即將展開的下一步做準備。

發人深省的故事

The Butter Battle Book
《奶油之戰》

《奶油之戰》是蘇斯博士有感於冷戰 (Cold War) 時期，美國和蘇聯以核武 (nuclear weapons) 相互威脅所寫出反戰 (anti-war) 意識的諷刺故事，於一九八四年出版。故事是這樣的：身穿藍衣的 Yooks 和身穿黃衣 Zooks 是兩個文化對立的族群，以一道高牆為界分開居住（此高牆暗喻柏林圍牆），生活習慣相反的他們，連奶油裏麵包的方式都不同，Yooks 喜歡吃奶油面朝上的麵包，Zooks 則是喜歡朝下的，於是紛爭就這樣發生了，他們開始以武力相互攻擊，衝突日趨緊張，後來高牆因為一枚炸彈引爆而倒下，但蘇斯博士並沒有把故事的最後交代清楚，而是讓讀者自己去深思、探討。

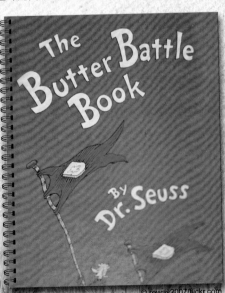

The Lorax《羅雷司》

電影《羅雷司》是環球電影 (Universal Pictures) 根據蘇斯博士在一九七一年出版的同名童話所改編，除了這部電影，《羅雷司》在一九七二年也曾被翻拍成為電視卡通。故事發生在所有物品全為人造的高科技城市中，一位名叫泰德 (Ted) 的小男孩想為了奧黛莉 (Audrey) 找出一顆真正的樹，找上了當年為追求利益而將樹木全砍掉，使森林守護者羅雷司消聲匿跡的萬事樂 (Once-ler)。良心發現的萬事樂想藉由泰德使森林復甦，不過另一個唯利是圖的商人歐洋氣 (O'Hare) 會讓他們稱心如意嗎？

情節和綠化、環保議題緊緊相扣，無疑是現代社會的寫照，大自然的存續與科技發展，兩者間該如何取得平衡，蘇斯博士很早就想藉由《羅雷司》來引發大家省思。特別的是，蘇斯博士的原著是以萬事樂為說故事的人，而且在書裡及卡通中都看不到萬事樂的樣子，最多只有出現手臂而已，而他完整的樣貌則在電影中首次被描繪出來。

The Tao of Pooh 小熊維尼之道

© 達志 / UPI PHOTO

Vocabulary Bank

1) **run** [rʌn] (v.) 經營，管理
The company is run by the founder's son.
這家公司是由創辦者的兒子所經營的。

2) **entertain** [ˌɛntɚˋten] (v.) 娛樂，招待
A magician was hired to entertain the children.
一位魔術師被請來逗孩子們開心。

3) **make up** [mek ʌp] (phr.) 編造，捏造
Is that story true, or did you just make it up?
那故事是真的，還是你編出來的？

4) **stuffed** [stʌft] (a.) 填充的
I bought my girlfriend a stuffed panda for her birthday.
我買了一隻填充貓熊玩偶送我女友當生日禮物。

5) **setting** [ˋsɛtɪŋ] (n.) （文學、戲劇、電影等作品的）時空背景、場景
The setting of the movie is Chicago in the 1920s.
這部電影的背景設在一九二〇年代的芝加哥。

6) **illustrator** [ˋɪləˌstretɚ] (n.) 插畫家
Jimmy dreams of becoming a comic book illustrator.
吉米夢想成為一位漫畫插畫家。

7) **translate** [ˋtrænslet] (v.) 翻譯
Can you translate this document into English for me?
你可以幫我把這份文件翻成英文嗎？

課文朗讀 MP3 70　單字朗讀 MP3 71　英文講解 MP3 72

As a child, Alan Alexander Milne, creator of Winnie the Pooh, attended a small London school [1]**run** by his father. One of his teachers there, H.G. Wells, would become the father of science fiction. Although Milne later attended Cambridge on a mathematics scholarship, he returned to London after graduation to pursue a literary career.

Milne began writing articles for humor magazine *Punch*, and was hired as an assistant editor in 1906. He fell in love with the editor's goddaughter, Dorothy, and the couple soon married and had a son, who they named Christopher Robin. For his first birthday, his parents gave him a teddy bear called Edward. Inspired by Winnipeg, a Canadian black bear at the London Zoo, Christopher later changed his name to Winnie. The bear was followed by a pig named Piglet, a tiger named Tigger, a donkey named Eeyore, a kangaroo named Kanga, and her son Roo.

When Christopher was six, his father bought a country home south of London. The whole family stayed there on

66

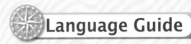

weekends and holidays, spending long hours exploring nearby Ashdown Forest. To keep his son [2]**entertained**, Milne would [3]**make up** stories about Winnie and the other [4]**stuffed** animals. The hero of the stories, of course, was Christopher, and the [5]**setting** was the Hundred Acre Wood, which was based on Ashdown Forest. This led to Milne's eureka moment: the tales he told his son could be the basis for a children's book.

Partnering with *Punch* [6]**illustrator** E.H. Shepard, A.A. Milne published *Winnie-the-Pooh* in 1926 and *The House at Pooh Corner* in 1928. The books quickly became classics of children's literature, and have since been [7]**translated** into over 40 languages.

Mini Quiz 閱讀測驗

What was Christopher Robin's toy Winnie named after?
(A) A stuffed animal
(B) A black bear
(C) A Canadian city
(D) A story character

Translation

創造小熊維尼的亞倫亞力山德米恩，小時候在父親經營的一所倫敦小型學校就讀，他的一位老師，名叫做威爾斯，之後成為科幻小說之父。雖然米恩後來拿數學獎學金進入劍橋大學求學，但畢業後他回到倫敦從事文學工作。

米恩開始為趣味雜誌《珠璣》撰寫文章，並且在一九〇六年的時候獲聘為助理編輯。他和總編輯的乾女兒桃樂絲相戀，這對情侶很快就結婚並生了一個兒子，取名為克里斯多夫羅賓。克里斯多夫一歲生日時，他爸媽送他一隻名為愛德華的泰迪熊。從倫敦動物園一隻加拿大黑熊的名字溫尼伯得到靈感，克里斯多夫後來把泰迪熊改名為維尼。隨著維尼熊之後而來的，還有小豬皮傑、跳跳虎、驢子依唷、袋鼠媽媽和她兒子小荳。

克里斯多夫六歲時，他爸爸買了一幢在倫敦南部的鄉間別墅。一家人在那兒度週末和度假，花很多時光探索附近的艾許當森林。為了逗兒子開心，米恩編了維尼熊和其他填充動物玩偶的故事。故事主角當然是克里斯多夫，而故事場景「百畝林」是以艾許當森林為藍本。這觸發米恩靈機一動：他講給兒子聽的這些故事可以做為一本童書的依據！

米恩和《珠璣》雜誌的插畫家謝培德聯手合作，分別在一九二六年和一九二八年出版了《小熊維尼》和《小熊維尼和老灰驢的家》（編註：老灰驢就是驢子依唷）。這兩本書很快就成為兒童文學的經典，至今已有四十多國語言的翻譯版本。

閱讀測驗解答：(B)

原始的維尼角色玩偶，
現在被收藏於紐約市立圖書館

© Kirill Levin / flickr.com

Pooh & His Pals
維尼和牠的夥伴們

有誰不認識維尼啊？牠那呆呆傻傻、成天老想著吃蜂蜜的可愛模樣，真的讓人很難不喜歡牠耶。看完前面的文章，相信大家都對這個角色的背景更加瞭解，不過別忘了，除了維尼以外，他在百畝林那群可愛的朋友也是很受歡迎的！

© http://wondersofdisney.disneyfansites.com/

Winnie the Pooh 小熊維尼

We'll be friends until forever, just you wait and see.
我們將會是永遠的朋友，你等著瞧吧！

故事的主角，一隻黃色的泰迪熊 (Teddy bear)，那件紅色小 T 恤還有圓滾滾的肚子就是牠的正字標記。維尼的腦子呆呆笨笨的，反應也很慢，不過心地卻很善良，每當朋友有難，牠總是義不容辭地伸出援手。同時，牠也自有一套樂觀豁達的生活哲學，常邊走邊隨性地哼著自己亂編的旋律。幸福、快樂與友誼就是牠一生最重視的事。維尼最愛吃的食物是蜂蜜（不過牠每次都把 honey 拼成 hunny），牠總是滿足的舔著手上的蜂蜜，直到一滴不剩為止。

維尼還發明了一個好玩的遊戲，叫做 Poohsticks，玩法非常簡單，就是大家一起從橋上各自丟下一根樹枝，然後趕快跑到橋的另一頭，比賽看看誰丟的樹枝先漂過來。百畝林的動物們都很愛玩這個遊戲，連牠的主人克里斯多夫羅賓也不例外。

Christopher Robin 克里斯多夫羅賓

Promise me, you'll always remember: You're braver than you believe, and stronger than you seem, and smarter than you think.
答應我，你會永遠記住：你比你所認為的還要勇敢，比你看到的還要堅強，也比你所想的還要聰明。

以作者兒子為藍本所創造出來的角色，是當中唯一真正存在的人物。克里斯多夫羅賓是個貼心懂事的小男孩，也是大家的好朋友，不過百畝林中跟他最親近的動物是維尼。熱心助人的他會幫維尼取得蜂蜜、營救被困在樹上的跳跳虎和小袋鼠、拯救遇溺的小豬等，總之遇到問題找他準沒錯。他經常把手放在維尼的肩膀上，叫牠一聲 silly old bear（小笨熊），然後輕柔地對牠說話。克里斯多夫最愛吃蛋糕，最喜歡做的事就是辦派對，不過嚴格說來，他最擅長的應該是發呆才對。

Piglet 皮傑

皮傑這隻粉紅色小豬應該算是維尼最好的動物朋友吧！牠的特徵就是總是穿著橫條紋上衣，體型相當嬌小，整個百畝林裡大概只有袋鼠小荳跟牠的體型差不多，所以每當牠鑽進去袋鼠媽媽的袋 (pouch) 中時，袋鼠媽媽根本搞不清楚袋中的是自己的寶寶還是牠。也因為牠比較小隻，所以性格特別膽小 (timid)，還帶點神經質。不過，雖然牠看來怯懦，其實內心相當堅強，因為牠堅信友情會帶給牠力量。牠的興趣就是和維尼結伴去探險，牠自己最喜歡做的事則是玩氣球，還有把蒲公英 (dandelion) 給吹散，同時，牠最愛的食物是橡實（acorns，在書中常拼寫成 haycorns）。還有，牠的口頭禪就是 "Oh, dear! Oh, dear, oh, dearie, dearie, dear!"（喔，天啊！喔，天啊，喔，天啊天啊天啊！）

Weeds are flowers, too, once you get to know them.
一但你有機會認識它們，你會發現雜草也可以是花朵。

Tigger 跳跳虎

就如牠的名字一般，跳跳虎總是蹦蹦跳跳的，一刻也靜不下來。牠對自己身上美麗的斑紋引以為傲，也很喜歡交朋友，同時牠還有一項專長，那就是牠從來不會迷路，每次都可以沿著腳印找到回家的路。跳跳虎覺得蹦蹦跳跳是很棒的一件事，因為牠可以用這種方式來散播歡樂，逗朋友開心，不過這樣的性格也常替牠帶來麻煩，而且牠有時會誇大事實 (exaggerate)，有點臭屁。牠最好的朋友是袋鼠小豆，最愛的食物是麥精 (malt extract)。

> I wouldn't trade it for anything. Never, no, never. Your friendship is the best present ever.
> 我絕不會拿它跟任何事物交換。絕不，對，絕不。你的友情就是我收過最棒的禮物。

Eeyore 依唷

> A little consideration, a little thought for others, makes all the difference.
> 只要多一點點體諒，稍微考慮到別人，就能讓一切截然不同。

一隻帶有憂鬱氣息的驢子，經常愁眉苦臉、垂頭喪氣的，不管什麼事情總是先做最壞的打算，多虧有了維尼這群關心牠的好友給牠溫暖，為牠的生活帶來一絲歡笑，因此牠總是會默默的守護在朋友身邊。依唷雖然話不多，不過卻相當有智慧 (wisdom)，很常到把頭垂向一邊沈思。悲觀的牠認為所有事情都處處和牠作對，不但牠的房子常常倒塌，尾巴也常掉下來（此時好心的克里斯多夫就會用圖釘幫牠固定）。牠最開心的事情就是有人記得牠的生日，而牠最喜愛的食物是薊花（thistle，也就是蘇格蘭的國花）。

Rabbit 瑞比

瑞比是隻勤勞的兔子，總是汲汲營營，努力打理牠的紅蘿蔔園，急性子的牠總忍不住把每件事安排好，也很喜歡指揮和鞭策別人，是團體中的領導者。牠和貓頭鷹算是森林裡最聰明的兩隻動物（牠自己也很愛強調這一點），鬼點子很多。瑞比對園藝很有興趣，牠最愛的食物是蔬菜。

> Owl, you and I have brains. The others have fluff. If there is any thinking to be done in this forest—and when I say thinking I mean thinking—you and I must do it.
> 貓頭鷹，只有你和我有腦袋。其他人都不切實際。如果這座森林裡有需要思考的事物——我是說真正的思考，那勢必得由我們去做了。

Owl 貓頭鷹

> My spelling is wobbly. It's good spelling but it wobbles, and the letters get in the wrong places.
> 我的拼字零零落落的。拼字很好，只是有點不穩，而且字母會跑錯地方了。

一隻十分多話的貓頭鷹，常滔滔不絕地說個沒完，被認為是森林中最聰明的動物，不過常常因看錯字而惹出麻煩，牠囉唆的性格常讓森林裡其他動物吃不消，而且牠所講的內容大部份別人都聽不太懂。總之牠的興趣就是到處跟人說故事，向別人分析事情的運作方式，儼然一副學者的模樣。

Kanga & Roo 袋鼠媽媽與小荳

> Do be careful, dear.
> 要小心喔，寶貝。

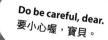

> I like the bouncy old tiger best!
> 我最喜歡跳跳虎了！

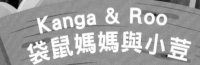

小荳是一隻調皮的小袋鼠，性格活潑開朗，喜歡和大伙一起玩拋樹枝大賽，覺得自己很能幹，最好的朋友就是跳跳虎。牠對跳跳虎說過：「我們是最好的跳躍選手！」而 Kanga 是牠的媽媽，就像跟全天下的媽媽一樣，牠的生活重心都在照顧小荳，催小荳洗澡、吃飯一類的事情。

EUREKA! 點子成金

V Vocabulary Bank

1) **route** [raʊt/rut] (n.) 路徑，路線，paper route 即「送報生的工作」
Which route do you usually take to work?
你上班通常都走哪一條路？

2) **institute** [ˋɪnstɪˌtut] (n.) 學院，機構
Bradley works as a researcher at a scientific institute.
布萊德利在科學機構當研究員。

3) **underage** [ˌʌndəˋedʒ] (a.) 未成年的
The bar was fined for serving alcohol to underage drinkers.
這間酒吧因為賣酒給未成年的顧客而遭罰。

4) **ambulance** [ˋæmbjələns] (n.) 救護車
When you hear an ambulance coming, you should pull over and let it pass.
當聽到有救護車要來，你應該要停在路邊並讓它過。

5) **field** [fild] (n.) 領域，專業
The scientist made important contributions to his field.
這位科學家在他的專業領域做出重要貢獻。

6) **animation** [ˌænəˋmeʃən] (n.) 動畫
(a.) animated [ˋænəˌmetɪd] 動畫（片）的
Japanese animation is becoming increasingly popular in the U.S.
日本動畫在美國越來越受歡迎。

7) **lifelong** [ˋlaɪfˌlɔŋ] (a.) 一生的
The designer had a lifelong love of fashion.
該位設計師一生熱愛時尚。

8) **creation** [krɪˋeʃən] (n.) 創作（品），產物
The artist's latest creations are on display at the gallery.
這位藝術家的最新創作在畫廊裡展示。

9) **distribute** [dɪˋstrɪbjut] (v.) 發行，經銷
The company markets and distributes its products to retail stores.
那間公司的產品都配銷到零售店裡。

10) **premiere** [prɪˋmɪr] (n./v.) 首映會；初次上演
Did you watch the season premiere of *Gossip Girl*?
妳有看這一季《花邊教主》的首播嗎？

進階字彙

11) **collaborator** [kəˋlæbəˌretə] (n.) 合作者，共同研究者
The scientist thanked all his collaborators when he received the award.
那位科學家得獎時感謝了所有和他一起參與研究的人員。

12) **talkie** [ˋtɔki] (n.) 有聲電影（此為早期的稱呼，也稱為 sound film）
Silent films were replaced by talkies in the 1930s.
默劇在一九三〇年代被有聲電影取代。

13) **rodent** [ˋrodənt] (n.) 齧齒類動物
Did you know that squirrels are rodents?
你知道松鼠是齧齒類動物嗎？

WALT DISNEY
華 特 迪 士 尼
米老鼠的創作者
A Mouse Is Born

©akva / Shutterstock.com

© Debby Wong / Shutterstock

課文朗讀 MP3 73　　單字朗讀 MP3 74　　英文講解 MP3 75

　　Born in Chicago on December 5, 1901, Walter Elias Disney spent his childhood on a farm in Missouri. Inspired by the animals around him, the young Walt began to draw at an early age, selling sketches to his neighbors when he was just seven. The Disneys next lived in Kansas City, where his father ran a paper [1)]**route**, returning to Chicago in 1917 when his father invested in a jelly factory there. During high school, Walt took night classes at the Chicago Art [2)]**Institute** and drew cartoons for the school paper.

　　At the age of 16, Walt dropped out of school to serve in World War I. Rejected by the Army because he was [3)]**underage**, he joined the Red Cross and drove an [4)]**ambulance** in France. After the war, Walt returned to Kansas City to pursue a career as a cartoonist. He soon became interested in the new [5)]**field** of [6)]**animation**, and founded

Laugh-O-Gram Studio to create animated cartoons. Unfortunately, the studio soon went bankrupt, and Walt decided to **1 try his luck** in Hollywood. With $250 in capital, he and his brother Roy started Disney Brothers Cartoon Studio in 1923. His first employees included Ub Iwerks, who became Walt's [7)]**lifelong** [11)]**collaborator**, and Lillian Bounds, who became his wife.

When Walt and Ub's first [8)]**creation**, Oswald the Lucky Rabbit, was stolen by the studio that [9)]**distributed** it, they decided to create their own character. Walt came up with a cheerful mouse named Mortimer, but Lillian thought Mickey sounded better. The [10)]**premiere** of *The Jazz Singer*—the world's first "[12)]**talkie**"—provided him with his eureka moment. Walt decided to give Mickey Mouse a voice, and the famous [13)]**rodent** has been talking ever since.

Mini Quiz 閱讀測驗

Which of the following is true about Mickey Mouse?
(A) He appeared in the first talkie.
(B) He was invented by Walt's wife Lillian.
(C) He was originally named Mortimer.
(D) He was originally a rabbit.

中 Translation

一九〇一年十二月五日，華特伊利亞斯迪士尼出生於芝加哥，童年都在密蘇里州的農場上度過。受到生活周遭動物的啟發，華特在很小的時候便開始畫圖，年僅七歲就把他的素描畫賣給鄰居。迪士尼一家　人之後搬到堪薩斯市，華特的父親在那以送報維生。一九一七年搬回芝加哥，因為當時華特的父親在那投資一間果醬工廠。高中時期，華特在芝加哥藝術學院就讀夜間部，同時間幫校刊畫漫畫。

十六歲那年，華特輟學，準備要從軍投入一次大戰。陸軍以不足齡為由拒絕他之後，他加入紅十字會，到法國駕駛救護車。戰爭結束後，華特回到堪薩斯市想以漫畫家為業。不久後，他對動畫這個新領域產生興趣，於是成立 Laugh-O-Gram 工作室從事卡通影片的創作。不幸地，這工作室沒多久後即宣告破產，於是華特決定到好萊塢碰碰運氣。帶著兩百五十元資金，華特和他的哥哥洛伊於一九二三年創立迪士尼兄弟卡通工作室。他最初的雇員中，有後來成為他終身工作夥伴的厄伯艾沃克，以及成為他妻子的莉蓮邦茲。

當華特和厄伯的第一個創作——奧斯華幸運兔——被負責發行的片廠搶走後，他們決定自行創作卡通人物。華特想出一隻開心的老鼠，取名為莫迪默，不過莉蓮認為米奇比較好聽。世界首部有聲電影《爵士歌手》的首映會讓華特靈機一動，他決定賦予米老鼠一個聲音，從此這隻知名的齧齒動物的話從此沒停過。

🎙 Tongue-tied No More

☐ try one's luck 碰碰運氣

這個片語用來表達做了某件事情，希望得到成功的結果。

A: I haven't met anybody on that dating site.
我在那個交友網站上沒遇到任何對象。
B: Maybe you should try your luck on another site.
也許你該到另一個網站碰碰運氣。

🧭 Language Guide

Oswald the Lucky Rabbit
奧斯華幸運兔

華特和厄伯在一九二七年至二八年製作了二十六部奧斯華幸運兔的黑白無聲短片。奧斯華幸運兔是第一個用於商品開發的迪士尼角色，商品包括糖果棒、圖騰及別針。這個角色的構想來自於迪士尼影片發行人查理斯梅茲，因為當時環球電影公司正在尋找一部以兔子為主角的卡通系列。迪士尼工作　室追求高品質的同時，製作卡通奧斯華幸運兔的成本隨之提高。一九二八年二月，華特到紐約跟梅茲談增加酬勞，卻反因超支預算被扣下百分之二十的酬勞，甚至喪失奧斯華幸運兔的所有權。華特在這次的損失中吸取教訓，從此以後非常重視人物及影片的版權。在離開紐約返回家中的路上，他創作了至今仍風靡全球的卡通人物米老鼠。

The Jazz Singer 《爵士歌手》

《爵士歌手》這部一九二七年上映的美國歌舞片，是世界上第一部有聲電影。故事敘述主角傑克對於家族信仰和繼承傳統不感興趣，他熱中的是爵士樂和拉格泰姆 (ragtime) 音樂，這一點讓在猶太教堂擔任司會 (cantor) 的父親極度不滿。某天，傑克和父親激烈爭執，迫使他離家出走。經過幾年拮据的生活後，他得到著名舞台劇演員瑪莉的協助，並且與她陷入熱戀。這時候傑克卻體會到，在事業、感情和家庭上，他必須做出痛苦的抉擇。

（C）案答驗測讀閱

© Iknowthegoods

Laugh-o-Gram Studio

EUREKA! 點子成金

Barbie 好一個芭比娃娃 What a Doll!

©達志/ UPI PHOTO

V Vocabulary Bank

1) **flee** [fli] (v.) 逃跑，逃脫
   The robber fled from the scene of the crime.
   那名搶匪逃離了犯罪現場。

2) **frame** [frem] (n.) 架構，骨架，結構，picture frame 意即「相框」
   The bicycle has an aluminum frame.
   這台腳踏車有鋁製車架。

3) **profitable** [ˈprɑfɪtəbəl] (a.) 有利可圖的，賺錢的
   (n.) profit 利潤，盈利
   Investing in real estate can be quite profitable.
   投資房地產可能會賺大錢。

進階字彙

4) **persecution** [ˌpɜsɪˈkjuʃən] (n.) 迫害
   (v.) persecute
   The Nazi persecution of the Jews began in 1933.
   納粹對猶太人的迫害始於一九三三年。

5) **interest** [ˈɪntrəst] (n.) 股份
   The president owns the largest interest in the firm.
   總裁擁有這間公司最大的股份。

6) **leftover** [ˈlɛftˌovə] (a./n.) 殘餘的；殘餘物。leftovers 即「剩菜」
   We had leftover meatloaf for dinner last night.
   我們昨晚吃剩下的烤肉餅當晚餐。

7) **curvy** [ˈkɜvi] (a.) 凹凸有致的，有曲線的
   Jake likes girls with curvy figures.
   傑克喜歡身材凹凸有致的女孩。

課文朗讀 MP3 76　單字朗讀 MP3 77　英文講解 MP3 78

Ruth Moskowicz was born in Denver, Colorado on November 4, 1916 to Jacob and Ida, Jewish immigrants who had [1)]**fled** to the U.S. from Poland to escape [4)]**persecution**. She met Elliot Handler at a B'nai B'rith dance when she was sixteen, and the couple later got married and moved to Los Angeles.

In L.A., Elliot went into business with Harold "Matt" Matson, starting a company called Mattel (a combination of their names) to manufacture picture [2)]**frames**. When Matson sold his [5)]**interest** in the company thee following year, Ruth took over his position. They began to use [6)]**leftover** wood to make doll furniture, and when it proved more [3)]**profitable** than the frames, they turned Mattel into a toy company.

The Handlers had two children, daughter Barbara and son Kenneth. One day, Ruth observed her daughter playing with paper dolls, which she gave adult roles. This led to her eureka moment: the market was ready for a grown-up doll with a grown-up figure. Elliot didn't think an adult doll would sell, but Ruth found a Bild Lilli—a 7)**curvy** German doll—at a shop on a trip to Switzerland and brought it home with her. Using Lilli as a model, she designed a grown-up doll for American girls, which she named Barbie after her daughter.

Launched at a New York toy fair in 1959, Barbie was an instant 8)**hit**, selling over 350,000 the first year. And since popular girls always have boyfriends, the Handlers introduced Ken, named after their son, in 1961. To date, over a billion Barbies have been sold, making the doll a true American 9)**icon**.

Mini Quiz 閱讀測驗

What made Barbie different from the American dolls that came before her?
(A) She was designed for grown-ups.
(B) She had an adult body.
(C) She had her own furniture.
(D) She was designed by adults.

Translation

露絲莫斯柯維奇於一九一六年十一月四日出生在科羅拉多州丹佛市,雙親雅各及艾達都是為逃離迫害而從波蘭逃至美國的猶太移民。她十六歲時在一場「聖約之子」舞會上邂逅艾略特韓德勒,兩人後來結為連理,並遷居洛杉磯。

在洛杉磯,艾略特和哈羅德「麥特」馬特森一起創業,合開一家名為「美泰兒」(結合兩人之名)的公司(編註:Matt+Elliot),製造相框。次年,馬特森賣掉他的股份,露絲便接替他的位置。他們開始運用剩餘木材製造洋娃娃的家具,結果這項業務的獲利高於相框,於是他們便將美泰兒轉型為玩具公司。

韓德勒夫婦育有一女一子,分別名為芭芭拉和肯尼斯。一天,露絲看到她的女兒在玩紙娃娃,並賦予它成人的角色。這使她靈機一動:市場已經可以接受成人身形的成人娃娃。艾略特不認為成人娃娃會暢銷,但露絲赴瑞士旅行途中在一家商店發現凹凸有致的德國玩偶「莉莉」,把它買回家。她以莉莉當範本,為美國女孩設計了一款成人娃娃,並以女兒之名命名為芭比。

芭比娃娃在一九五九年紐約一場玩具展正式推出,立刻造成轟動,第一年就賣了三十五萬個以上。而且因為受歡迎的女孩一定有男友,於是韓德勒夫婦在一九六一年推出肯尼,以他們兒子之名來命名。到今天,芭比娃娃已售出超過十億個,成為名副其實的美國偶像。

8) **hit** [hɪt] (n.) 成功、受歡迎的事物
The clown was a big hit at Timmy's birthday party.
那個小丑在堤米的慶生會上大受歡迎。

9) **icon** [ˈaɪkɑn] (n.) 偶像,代表性的人事物
Clint Eastwood is a Hollywood icon.
克林伊威斯特是一位好萊塢偶像。

Language Guide

B'nai B'rith 聖約之子會

B'nai B'rith [bəˈne brɪθ] 為歷史最悠久的猶太人服務組織,一八三四年成立於紐約,致力於各種社會服務及福利活動,遍布全球各國有上百個分支,以促進當地猶太人福利為宗旨,性質類似台灣人在海外的台灣同鄉會。

Bild Lilli

Bild Lilli 原是德國連環漫畫裡的卡通人物,漫畫家委託玩具公司將 Lilli 製成人偶販售,一炮而紅。Bild Lilli 擁有三項全新的人偶製作專利:頭部可自由轉動、髮絲以隱藏螺絲緊緊鎖住頭皮、兩腿不會因坐姿而分開。Bild Lilli 一開始是在酒吧和菸草店當作廉價禮物販售,主要對象為成人,但最後卻非常受兒童歡迎,而有越來越多玩具商因為製作 Bild Lilli 娃娃屋、屋內擺飾、家具等專屬配件而大發利市。Bild Lilli 販售期間始於一九五五年,而後被芭比的製作公司 Mattel 買下,並停止生產。對某些收藏家來說,Bild Lilli 現在是價值上千歐元的珍品。

© Science Museum / Science & Society Picture Library

(B) 景趣鏈動關閱

你所不知道的 Barbie

大家都知道,如今芭比娃娃已不僅是小女孩愛不釋手的玩具,更是時尚潮流的指標、收藏家的最愛。除此之外,這一路走來還有許多你不知道的事情喔,就讓 EZ TALK 帶你看看和芭比有關的小事蹟吧!

- 芭比原本眼睛是看向一邊的,直到一九七一年才改成向前望。

- 芭比是最先用電視宣傳的玩具,售於一百五十個國家以上,據說當時每秒鐘就可以賣出三個芭比娃娃。

- 一九七四年,紐約時代廣場(Times Square)的一部份被名命為「芭比大道」(Barbie Boulevard)一星期,以歡慶芭比的十六歲生日。

- 一九八五年,後現代藝術家安迪沃荷(Andy Warhol)製作了芭比的圖象。

- 芭比曾出現在一系列的卡通中,並於一九九九年的動畫電影《玩具總動員 2》(Toy Story 2)中客串。

Designer Barbies 設計師系列

Ralph Lauren 芭比

年份:1996

美式休閒品牌首席設計師 Ralph Lauren 替這款芭比打造了優雅的美式風格,完全展現出當代經典的衣著態度。穿著雙排釦(double-breasted)的海軍藍混羊毛(wool-blend)外套,上頭有著 RL 品牌標誌,裡面穿的則是高領(turtleneck)緊身衣;下半身穿羊毛格子褲,繫上一條黑色皮帶,另外還搭上一件駝色(camel)大衣,無論質感或造型都極具水準。

Calvin Klein 芭比

年份:1996

從頭到腳穿的全都是 Calvin Klein 設計的衣服,非常時髦。全套的丹寧(denim)外套和裙子,就連裡面的灰色棉 T-shirt 也相當經典,仔細看,就連底褲的褲頭上都看得到 CK 的標誌喔!

Vera Wang 芭比

年份:2008

講到婚紗,Vera Wang 絕對是每個女孩夢寐以求的品牌。芭比身上這套平口無肩帶(strapless)的婚紗,腰身剪裁極為合身,薄紗(tulle)澎澎裙並非傳統的純白,而是淡淡的粉膚色,上頭還有一些花朵圖案,華麗但不俗氣,質感一流。

Christian Dior 芭比

年份:1997

這款芭比如實重現了一九四七年 Dior 的經典潮流造型。窄肩上衣和膨膨長裙的搭配,再加上巴黎風編織帽(straw hat)、珍珠項鍊(pearl necklace),以及內搭網襪及吊襪帶(garter),保守中不失性感,優雅的氣質完全展現,整個就是 Dior 的經典 look。

蝙蝠俠 (Batman) 肯尼

年份：2013
蝙蝠俠這個角色最早發跡於漫畫，後來改編成電視劇，爾後又拍一系列賣座電影。為了保衛高譚市 (Gotham City)，這位俗稱斗篷鬥士 (Caped Crusader)的面具英雄總在危急之際挺身而出，成功解救高譚市的市民。如今肯尼(Ken)穿上了早期電視劇中的蝙蝠俠裝，看起來是否既帥氣又帶點懷舊感呢？

Hollywood Barbies 好萊塢系列

瑪麗蓮夢露 (Marilyn Monroe) 芭比

年份：1997
看看這身造型，白色三角背心 (halter)洋裝、飄逸的裙襬和金色捲髮，再擺上電影《七年之癢》(The Seven Year Itch)中的經典姿勢，不用說也知道這是瑪麗蓮夢露芭比吧

《暮光之城：破曉》 (The Twilight Saga: Breaking Dawn) 角色芭比

年份：2001
紅透半邊天的《暮光之城》也推出了系列芭比！貝拉(Bella)在第二集中的吸血鬼(vampire)造型令人印象深刻，她身穿黑色皮衣(leather jacket)與內搭褲(leggings)，而迷人的艾德華(Edward)則穿著長袖襯衫與牛仔褲，兩人看起來極為登對，相信暮光迷們一定愛不釋手，很想買來收藏吧！

World Culture 世界文化系列

自由女神 (Statue of Liberty) 芭比

年份：2010
為慶祝世界芭比系列三十週年所推出的款式，將自由女神的圖像穿上身，裙襬的細節和頭上的皇冠畫龍點睛，完全可以感受到紐約這座城市的活力。

雪梨歌劇院 (Sydney Opera House) 芭比

年份：2011
服裝靈感來自於澳洲雪梨歌劇院的建築外觀，上衣代表帆型的屋頂，而圍繞歌劇院的下方水域則用水藍色雪紡紗(chiffon)展現。這款芭比證明了建築的美學概念使用在服飾上仍舊不失其美，令人驚艷。

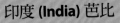

印度 (India) 芭比

年份：2012
「哈囉，歡迎來到印度！」看看芭比穿的服飾，是不是常在寶萊塢(Bollywood)的電影看到呀？黃色的莎麗服(Sari)配上傳統印度婦女會戴的頭巾(headscarf)，烏溜溜的黑髮和較深的膚色，東方世界的芭比也是很美麗的！

部落 (Tribal) 芭比

芭比全身上下穿得繁複華麗，上身是羽毛露腰裝(midriff)和金色匈甲(breastplate)，誇張的耳環和手鐲，手上拿著斑馬權杖(scepter)，全身散發出非洲公主的貴族氣息。

芭比還有這麼多系列…

Couture Collection　高級時裝系列
Barbie Fashion Model Collection　超級名模系列
Classique Collection　經典收藏系列
Diva Collection　女伶典藏系列
FAO Exclusives　FAO 玩具獨賣系列
Fashion Savvy　新潮時尚系列
Flowers in Fashion Collection　花語系列
Grand Entrance Series　晚宴禮服系列
Great Fashions of the 20th Century　二十世紀系列
Model of the Moment Collection　當紅名模系列
Portrait Collection Series　名畫典藏系列
Royal Jewel Collection　皇家寶石系列
Service Merchandise Exclusives　獨家商品系列
Society Hound Collection　芭比與愛犬系列
Style Set Collection　風格集合系列
Ballroom Beauties　舞姿儷影系列
Barbie Loves Pop Culture　芭比流行文化系列
Barbie Loves Sports　芭比運動系列
Pin-Up Girls Collection　海報女郎系列
COCA-COLA Barbie Series　可口可樂芭比系列
Grand Ole Opry Series　華麗鄉村歌手系列
Harley-Davidson Barbie Dolls　哈雷機車系列

Ⓥ Vocabulary Bank

1) **assign** [ə`saɪn] (v.) 分配，分派
The soldier was assigned to guard duty.
這名士兵被分配至衛兵哨。

2) **naval** [`nevəl] (a.) 海軍的，軍艦的，船的
The naval battle was won by the Russians.
俄國人贏得了這場海上戰爭。

3) **delicate** [`dɛlɪkət] (a.) 精密的，精細的
The delicate equipment must be stored in a cool, dry place.
這些精密儀器需保存在乾冷處。

4) **tumble** [`tʌmbəl] (v.) 打滾，跌倒，翻跟斗
The man slipped and tumbled down the hill.
這名男子滑倒然後滾下山坡。

5) **tension** (n.) [`tɛnʃən] 張力，緊張
You tune a guitar by adjusting the tension of the strings.
吉他是藉由調整弦的鬆緊來調音的。

6) **browse** [brauz] (v.) 翻閱，瀏覽
Susan browsed through a magazine while waiting for her dentist appointment.
蘇珊翻雜誌來打發等待牙醫的時間。

7) **convince** [kən`vɪns] (v.) 說服，使人信服
The kids convinced their parents to let them have pizza for dinner.
孩子們說服父母讓他們晚餐吃披薩。

8) **enthusiasm** [ɪn`θuzɪ͵æzəm] (n.) 熱忱，熱衷的事物
Eric always faces challenges with energy and enthusiasm.
艾瑞克總是用活力漢熱忱來面對挑戰。

9) **counter** [`kauntɚ] (n.) 櫃台，吧台，流理台
Please come to the counter when your name is called.
叫到名字請到櫃台報到。

進階字彙

10) **prototype** [`protə͵taɪp] (n.) 原型
A prototype of the new car was revealed at the auto show.
這款新車的原型車在車展亮相。

口語補充

11) **break** [brek] (n.) 大好機會，幸運的轉折
The band is still waiting for its big break.
這個樂團還在等待成名的機會。

The Slinky 讓彈簧活起來
Bringing a Spring to Life

© RHiNO NEAL/f

課文朗讀 MP3 79　單字朗讀 MP3 80　英文講解 MP3 81

Having graduated from Penn State with a degree in mechanical engineering, Richard James was [1)]**assigned** to work at a Philadelphia [2)]**naval** yard during WWII. In 1943, the young engineer was given the task of developing springs to keep [3)]**delicate** instruments steady in high seas. One day, a spring suddenly fell off his desk and went bouncing and [4)]**tumbling** across the floor. That was Richard's eureka moment. "Why not turn the spring into a toy?" he thought.

Richard took the spring home that evening and gave it to his two-year-old son Tommy to play with. To everyone's surprise, when his son pushed the spring off the top of the stairs, it "walked" and over all the way to the bottom. Soon, every kid in the neighborhood was coming to their house to play with the "walking spring."

Over the next two years, Richard made springs out of many different kinds of wire. "Our house was a mess while I experimented," he admitted. Eventually, he found that flat wire with no [5)]**tension** worked best. By the summer of 1945, the [10)]**prototype** was ready: a two-and-a-half inch spring wound from 80 feet of Swedish steel wire. Now all the toy needed was a name. [6)]**Browsing** through the dictionary, his wife Betty found a word that best described the way the spring moved: "slinky."

After Richard [7)]**convinced** an auto parts manufacturer to produce 400 Slinkies—all he could afford—he took them to toy stores all over Philadelphia. Toy buyers, however, didn't share his [8)]**enthusiasm**. His [11)]**break** came when Gimbel's Department Store gave him [9)]**counter** space to demonstrate his product during the 1945 Christmas season.

 Mini Quiz 閱讀測驗

Where did Richard James have his eureka moment?
(A) At his office
(B) At home
(C) On a ship
(D) At a naval yard

中 Translation

從賓州州立大學拿到機械工程學位畢業後，理查詹姆士在二次世界大戰期間被派往費城的海軍造船廠工作。一九四三年，這位年輕的工程師被賦予一項任務：發展出能夠讓精密儀器在大海上保持穩定的彈簧。一天，一個彈簧突然從他桌上掉落，在地板上彈了又彈、滾了又滾。理查就在這時靈機一動。「為什麼不把彈簧變成玩具呢？」他想。

當晚理查便把彈簧帶回家，拿給他兩歲的兒子湯米玩。出乎大家意料的是，當他兒子把彈簧從樓梯上端推下去時，它竟一路頭尾交替地「走」下樓梯。沒多久，附近每一個孩子都到他家玩「會走路的彈簧」了。

接下來兩年，理查用各種不同的鐵絲做彈簧。「我做實驗的時候，家裡可說亂七八糟，」他坦承。最後，他發現沒有張力的扁鐵絲最適合。一九四五年夏天，原型製作完畢：用八十呎瑞典鋼絲製成的兩吋半彈簧。現在，這種玩具就差沒有名字。妻子貝蒂翻遍字典，找到一個字最為貼切地描述這種彈簧的運動方式：「slinky」。

在理查說服一家汽車零件製造商生產四百個 Slinky 後（他只負擔得起這麼多），他把它們帶去費城各地的玩具店。但玩具採購人員沒給他熱情的響應。一九四五年耶誕季節，金貝爾百貨給他櫃台空間展示產品，他的機會才來了。

 Language Guide

end over end 翻滾
end 在這裡有「頂端」的意思，over 則是「越過」，因此 end over end 就是用來形容從此端翻越至彼端，重複翻轉的狀態。比如體操選手 (gymnast) 在進行翻滾 (tumble) 動作時，是從人體的頭頂端翻轉到下肢的末端，不斷重複而形成的翻滾動作。

Slinky 彈簧玩具
最早期的 Slinky 玩具是以瑞典的鋼鐵製成，之後才改用美國鋼，後來 Slinky 也跳脫金屬來料，開始出現塑膠材質。塑膠的 Slinky 彈簧圈數沒有金屬材質來得多，變形能力也沒有金屬材質來的好，但這樣的特質反而讓塑膠的 Slinky 更好翻滾且不易打結，通常會以七彩的塑膠組合而成。之後還發展出更多樣式的 Slinky 玩具，如眼鏡裝著以 Slinky 彈簧連結眼球的 Crazy Eyes 還有因《玩具總動員》(Toy Story Series) 系列電影又掀起一波風潮的 Slinky Dog 等等。

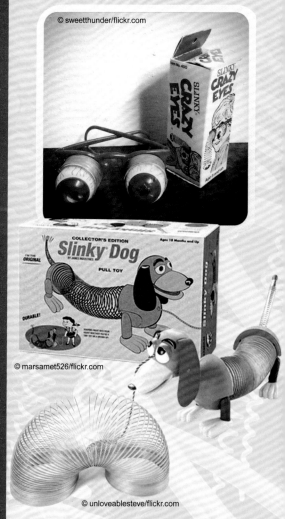

© sweetthunder/flickr.com

© marsamet526/flickr.com

© unloveablesteve/flickr.com

（C）：案答驗測讀閱

EUREKA! 點子成金

V Vocabulary Bank

1) **stock** (n.) [stɑk] 存貨，庫存
Our entire stock is half off this week.
我們所有的存貨在這星期半價。

2) **sell out** [sɛl aʊt] (phr.) 銷售一空，賣光
You should hurry up and buy tickets before they sell out.
你應該要在票賣完前趕快買票。

3) **mass-produce** [ˈmæsprəˈdus] (v.) 大量生產
The toys the company sells are mass-produced in China.
那間公司賣的玩具在中國大量生產。

4) **exposure** [ɪkˈspoʒɚ] (n.) 曝光，暴露
The two candidates are competing for media exposure.
兩位候選人都在搶媒體曝光。

5) **soar** [sor] (v.) 高漲，暴漲
The divorce rate in Japan is soaring.
日本的離婚率正在飆高。

6) **estate** [ɪˈstet] (n.) 地產，莊園
The estate includes a big house, a tennis court and a swimming pool.
這個莊園包含了一間大房子、網球場和游泳池。

7) **material** [məˈtɪrɪəl] (a.) 物質的，實質性的
The poor villagers have few material comforts.
這些貧窮的村民物質匱乏。

8) **financial** [faɪˈnænʃəl] (a.) 金融的，財務的
There's a rumor that the company is having financial difficulties.
謠傳這家公司正面臨財務困難。

9) **contribution** [ˌkɑntrəˈbjuʃən] 捐獻（的錢、物品），貢獻
The millionaire made a large contribution to the charity.
那位百萬富翁捐了一大筆錢給慈善機構。

10) **bankrupt** [ˈbæŋkrʌpt] (a.) 破產的
Thousands of investors lost money when the company went bankrupt.
那家公司破產時，數千名投資客賠了錢。

11) **boost** [bust] (v.) 加強，提升
The tax cut is supposed to boost the economy.
減稅方案旨在提振經濟成長。

進階字彙

12) **gesture** [ˈdʒɛstʃɚ] (n.) 表示心意的行為、舉止
Offering to let us stay at your house was a nice gesture.
你讓我們借住你家真是太好心了。

13) **cult** [kʌlt] (n.) 邪教，（洗腦信徒的）教派
The couple tried to rescue their daughter from the cult.
那對夫婦極力想救出他們被邪教吸收的女兒。

As Richard nervously set up his display on the rainy evening of November 27, his wife went to get coffee. Worried that her husband wouldn't make any sales, Betty gave a stranger a dollar to buy a Slinky from him. When she returned, she realized that her [12)]**gesture** was unnecessary. The counter was crowded with customers, money in hand. Within 90 minutes, their entire [1)]**stock** of Slinkies had [2)]**sold out**.

Knowing they had a hit on their hands, the couple borrowed $500 and started a company to [3)]**mass-produce** the toy. Richard designed a machine that could produce a Slinky every 10 seconds, and applied for a patent to protect his invention. The Slinky gained national [4)]**exposure** at the 1946 American Toy Fair, and sales began to [5)]**soar**.

By the late 1950s, Richard and Betty were living with their six children on a 12-acre [6)]**estate** in the wealthy suburb of Bryn Mawr. But Richard didn't seem satisfied by his [7)]**material** success. He cheated on his wife, and then joined a Bolivian religious [13)]**cult** and began making large [8)]**financial** [9)]**contributions**. By the time Richard left Betty and his children and moved to Bolivia in 1960, the company was nearly [10)]**bankrupt**.

© Lucho Molina/flickr.com

© Hosam AL-Hwid/flickr.com

Luckily, Betty had a good head for business. As the new CEO, she cut costs by switching to cheaper American steel and used TV commercials to [11]**boost** sales. Within no time, the company was back on its feet. When Betty finally retired and sold the business in 1998, nearly a quarter of a billion Slinkies had been sold.

 Mini Quiz 閱讀測驗

Why did Richard and Betty's business nearly go bankrupt?
(A) Because they didn't spend enough on advertising
(B) Because Richard cheated on his wife
(C) Because Richard gave large amounts of money to a cult
(D) Because Richard left Betty and moved to Bolivia

中 Translation

十一月二十七日,下雨的夜晚,當理查焦急地擺出他的陳列品時,他的妻子出去買咖啡。擔心她的先生連一個也賣不出去,貝蒂給了一個陌生人一美元,請他跟理查買Slinky。當她回來時,她發現她完全沒有必要那麼做。櫃台已擠滿顧客,手拿著錢。不到九十分鐘,他們的 Slinky 存貨便銷售一空。

知道自己的產品紅了,這對夫妻借了五百美元,開了一家公司大量生產這個玩具。理查設計出一種機器,每十秒就能製造一個 Slinky,並申請專利來保護他的發明。Slinky 在一九四六年美國玩具展呈現在全國眼前,銷售開始一飛沖天。

到一九五○年代後期,理查和貝蒂已跟他們的六個孩子住在富裕的布林莫爾郊區廣達十二英畝的莊園。但理查似乎不以他的物質成就為滿足。他搞婚外情,然後加入一個玻利維亞的異教派,開始做大筆捐獻。在理查一九六○年離開妻小、搬到玻利維亞時,公司幾近破產。

所幸,貝蒂很有生意頭腦。接任新執行長,她改用較便宜的美國鋼來降低成本,並利用電視廣告來提振銷售。一轉眼,公司已東山再起。在一九九八年,貝蒂終於退休、轉售公司之際,Slinky 已賣了將近兩億五千萬個。

 Language Guide

American Toy Fair 美國玩具博覽會
通常被稱為紐約玩具展 (New York Toy Fair) 的美國玩具博覽會,是由紐約市的玩具工業協會 (TIA) 所主辦,每年二月在曼哈頓 (Manhattan) 的賈維茨會展中心 (Jacob K. Javits Convention Center) 舉行,堪稱是西半球最大的國際玩具展。主要是給來自世界各地的玩具製造商 (toy manufacturer) 和遊戲發行商 (game publisher) 參加,因此不開放給一般民眾。

© insidethemagic/flickr.com

Bryn Mawr 布林莫爾
布林莫爾是賓州 (Philadelphia) 近郊著名的高級社區之一,位在「費城黃金通道」(Main Line) 的中央,風景優美,Bryn Mawr 這個名字來自威爾斯語 (Welsh),原意為「大山丘」。一六八六年時,在北威爾斯多爾蓋萊 (Dolgellau) 附近的某個莊園主人為逃離宗教迫害,從多爾蓋萊移居賓州,才將此名傳入。很多人可能不知道布林莫爾原來也是座城鎮,因為坐落於此的布林莫爾學院 (Bryn Mawr College) 名氣大過這個地方。布林莫爾學院是間女校,課程設備都在水準之上,堪稱是全美數一數二的文理學院。

閱讀測驗解答:(D)

© smallbones/wikipedia

Mount Rushmore
A Eureka Moment Carved in Stone
拉什莫爾
總統雕像山

Vocabulary Bank

1) **sculpt** [skʌlpt] (v.) 雕刻，造型
   (n.) sculptor 雕刻家
   The statue was sculpted from marble.
   這座雕像是用大理石雕刻而成的。

2) **expand** [ɪkˋspænd] (v.) 擴大，擴展
   The company has plans to expand into Asia.
   這公司有擴展至亞洲的計畫。

3) **carving** [ˋkɑrvɪŋ] (n.) 雕刻品，雕刻物
   The tribe is famous for its beautiful wood carvings.
   這個部落以美麗的木雕聞名。

4) **monument** [ˋmɑnjəmənt] (n.) 紀念碑、塔、館
   A monument was built in honor of those who died in the war.
   紀念碑是為了表彰在戰時捐軀的人而建造的。

5) **cliff** [klɪf] (n.) 懸崖，峭壁
   The man committed suicide by jumping off a cliff.
   那名男子跳崖自殺。

6) **opposition** [ˌɑpəˋzɪʃən] (n.) 反對，對抗
   The proposed law faces strong opposition.
   該項法案面臨到強烈的反對聲浪。

7) **environmentalist** [ɪnˌvaɪərnˋmɛntəlɪst] (n.) 環保人士
   (a.) environmental 自然環境的
   A group of environmentalists protested in front of the factory.
   一群環保人士在工廠前抗議。

8) **dynamite** [ˋdaɪnəˌmaɪt] (n.) 炸藥
   The soldiers used dynamite to blow up the bridge.
   士兵們用炸藥來炸毀橋墩。

9) **notably** [ˋnotəblɪ] (adv.) 值得一提，特別，尤其
   There have been many layoffs, most notably in the manufacturing sector.
   近來很多人被裁員，尤其都是在製造業。

課文朗讀 MP3 85　　單字朗讀 MP3 86　　英文講解 MP3 87

In 1909, a leader of the Daughters of the Confederacy named Helen Plane gazed at Stone Mountain in Georgia and had a eureka moment: the mountain would be the perfect place to ¹⁾**sculpt** her hero, Confederate General Robert E. Lee. When famous Danish-American sculptor Gutzon Borglum was hired for the project, he convinced the Daughters to ²⁾**expand** the ³⁾**carving** into a scene of General Lee, Jefferson Davis and Thomas "Stonewall" Jackson riding across the mountain on horseback. Due to various delays, work on the ⁴⁾**monument**—which was funded by the Ku Klux Klan—didn't begin until 1923, and Borglum left the project before completion because of creative differences.

But thanks to another eureka moment, Borglum wasn't out of work for long. Inspired by an article about Stone Mountain, South Dakota state historian Doane Robinson decided that carving ¹⁰⁾**likenesses** of Western heroes in the Black Hills would be a great way to promote tourism. When he invited Borglum to South Dakota, however, the sculptor had different ideas. Insisting on figures of national importance, Borglum chose George Washington, Thomas

Jefferson, Abraham Lincoln and Theodore Roosevelt—four presidents who he felt represented the country's birth, growth and ideals. He also picked the site for the monument: Mount Rushmore, a tall granite ⁵⁾**cliff** with southeastern ¹¹⁾**exposure**.

After overcoming ⁶⁾**opposition** from ⁷⁾**environmentalists** and Native Americans, Borglum obtained funding with the help of no other than President Calvin Coolidge, who ¹²⁾**dedicated** the site while summering in the Black Hills in August 1927. With a staff of 400 workers using drills, chisels and ⁸⁾**dynamite**, the Mount Rushmore National Memorial was completed in 1941 at a cost of $989,922. ⁹⁾**Notably** for such a large project, there were few injuries and no deaths.

Mini Quiz 閱讀測驗

According to the passage, which of the following statement is false?
(A) Due to various delays, the work on the monument didn't begin until 1923.
(B) Doane Robinson invited Borglum to South Dakota to carve President Calvin Coolidge.
(C) George Washington, Thomas Jefferson, Abraham Lincoln and Theodore Roosevelt represent the country's growth and ideals.
(D) The Mount Rushmore National Memorial was completed in 1941 at a cost of $989,922.

Translation

一九〇九年，邦聯之女聯合會一位名叫海倫普藍的領導人注視著喬治亞州的石頭山，突然靈機一動：這座山是雕刻她心目中的英雄，同盟軍將軍羅伯特李，的絕佳地點。當知名的丹麥裔美籍雕刻家古茲儂波格隆獲聘進行這項計畫時，他說服聯合會擴增雕刻的人物和範圍：讓李將軍、傑佛遜戴維斯和湯瑪士「石牆」傑克遜騎馬超過險峭山脊。由於數度延誤，興建紀念雕像的工程——由三K黨資助——到一九二三年才開始，而由於創作理念上的差異，波格隆在完工前便離開計畫。

但多虧另一次靈機一動，波格隆並未失業太久。受到一篇有關石頭山的文章啟發，南達科他州政府的歷史學家多安羅賓遜認為，在黑山雕刻西部英雄的雕像是推廣觀光的絕佳方式。但當他邀請波格隆到南達科他州時，這位雕刻家卻有不同的想法。波格隆堅持要刻國家最重要的人物，於是選擇了喬治華盛頓、湯瑪士傑佛遜、亞伯拉罕林肯和西奧多羅斯福——四位他認為能代表美國誕生、成長和理想的總統。他也選定紀念園區的位置：拉什莫爾山，一座面朝東南、高峻的花崗岩峭壁。

在克服環保人士與美洲原住民的反對後，波格隆透過卡文柯立芝總統本人的協助取得資金，柯立芝也趁一九二七年八月於黑山避暑時為該地舉行動工典禮。在四百名工人用鑽頭、鑿子和炸藥的努力之下，羅斯摩爾山國家紀念公園於一九四一年完工，造價九十八萬九千九百二十二美元。儘管工程如此浩大，卻幾乎沒有人受傷，無人喪命。

進階字彙
10) **likeness** [ˈlaɪknɪs] (n.) 肖像，畫像，雕像
A likeness of his grandfather hung above the fireplace.
他祖父的畫像掛在壁爐上方。

11) **exposure** [ɪkˈspoʒɚ] (n.)（山、住家等的）朝向，方位
The room is sunny because of its southern exposure.
這間房採光很好，因為它面向南方。

12) **dedicate** [ˈdɛdɪˌket] (v.) 為（建築物等）舉行落成典禮
The Empire State Building was dedicated on May 1st, 1931.
帝國大廈於一九三一年五月一號落成。

Language Guide

美國人最景仰的總統
總統山上的雕像由左至右分別是：
· George Washington 喬治華盛頓（1732~1799）
· Thomas Jefferson 湯瑪士傑佛遜（1743~1826）
· Theodore Roosevelt 西奧多羅斯（1858~1919）
· Abraham Lincoln 亞伯拉罕林肯（1809~1865）

Ku Klux Klan 三K黨
三K黨（Ku Klux Klan，縮寫為KKK）是一個主張白人至上的美國民間團體，為美國種族主義的代表性組織。初期是由南北戰爭中戰敗的老兵組成，以反對改善黑人待遇的政策為宗旨，經常透過暴力來達成目的。這個組織於一八七一年遭到掃蕩之後，於一九一五年另起爐灶，鼓吹白種新教徒具有比黑人、天主教徒、猶太人、亞裔及其他移民更優越的地位，依然以各種暴力方式運作，但經歷兩次世界大戰及經濟大蕭條之後，勢力大為減弱。六〇年代開始，有數個以三K黨為名號的團體均以暴力手段打擊民權運動，激起極大的輿論反感，反而促進了一九六四年民權法案的通過。案的通過。

（B）答解錄測讀閱

美國總統介紹

湯瑪斯傑佛遜 ▼
Thomas Jefferson

美國第三任總統
任期：1801~1809
重大事蹟：起草《獨立宣言》、
　　　　　路易西安納購地案

湯瑪斯傑佛遜最為眾人所知的身分即為美國《獨立宣言》起草人，他先後擔任了美國第一任國務卿、第二任副總統與第三任總統。傑佛遜創立並領導民主共和黨，成為今日民主黨前身。他在任期間不僅減少了國債，並通過路易西安納購地案，使美國國土面積擴大近一倍。

亞伯拉罕林肯 ▲
Abraham Lincoln

美國第十六任總統
任期：1861~1865
事蹟：起草《解放黑人奴隸宣言》、簽署
　　　《宅地法》
格言：人生最美好的東西，就是他同別人
　　　的友誼。

亞伯拉罕林肯任內，美國爆發了南北戰爭。林肯帶領美國度過艱困的內戰時期，擊敗了南方勢力，透過頒布《解放奴隸宣言》使四百萬奴隸獲得自由，並簽署《宅地法》使百姓皆能獲得土地，加速美國西部開發。在他遇刺後，美國正式廢除奴隸制度。

喬治華盛頓 ▲
George Washington

美國第一任總統
任期：1789~1797
事蹟：宣布美國獨立

美國首任總統喬治華盛頓，在美國獨立戰爭時率領大陸軍擊敗英殖民軍，贏得美國獨立。他於一七八七年主持了制憲會議並組織聯邦政府，被尊稱為美國國父。一七八九年，他當選美國首任總統，於一七九三年連任，在兩屆任期結束後便自願放棄續任，也建立了美國總統不超過兩任的傳統，影響了世上許多民主國家的元首選舉制度。

西奧多羅斯福Theodore Roosevelt ▼

美國第二十六任總統
任期：1901~1909
事蹟：開鑿巴拿馬運河、推行公平交易
綽號：Teddy T.R.

西奧多羅斯福，人稱老羅斯福，美國軍事家及政治家，一九〇一年威廉麥金萊總統遇刺後，羅斯福繼任，年僅四十二歲，成為美國歷史上最年輕的總統。

羅斯福開鑿了巴拿馬運河，將紐約與舊金山之間的水路航程大幅縮短。他也致力於生態環境保護，他所設立的國家公園和自然保護區面積比歷任總統都來得多。他因調停解決日俄戰爭而獲頒諾貝爾和平獎。

伍得羅威爾遜Woodrow Wilson ▲

美國第二十八任總統
任期：1913~1921
事蹟：降低關稅、反壟斷法、通過聯邦儲備法案

伍得羅威爾遜於一九一三年勝出後，第二任期即面臨第一次世界大戰，儘管他在競選時打出遠離戰爭的口號，但美國中立政策仍未持久。一戰最後階段，威爾遜主導了對德交涉並協定停火。他於一九一九年赴巴黎籌建國際聯盟，之後被授予諾貝爾和平獎。威爾遜所秉持的理想國際主義，也被後人稱為「威爾遜主義」，主張美國登上世界舞台，來為民主戰鬥。

富蘭克林羅斯福 ▼
Franklin D. Roosevelt

美國第三十二任總統

任期：1933~1945

事蹟：領美走出經濟大蕭條、
　　　結束美國孤立主義

綽號：FDR、小羅斯福

富蘭克林羅斯福的遠房堂兄為美國第二十六任總統——西奧多羅斯福，人常稱富蘭克林羅斯福為小羅斯福。羅斯福為美國歷任總統中任期最長的總統。分別於一九三三年、一九三七年與一九四一年連任成功，是美國唯一單聯四屆（第四屆未任滿）的總統。羅斯福在二十世紀的經濟大蕭條與第二次世界大戰中扮演了舉足輕重的角色。

哈瑞杜魯門 ▲
Harry S. Truman

美國第三十三任總統

任期：1945~1953

事蹟：結束二次大戰

格言：If you can't stand the heat,
　　　get out of the kitchen.
　　　「怕熱就別進廚房」

哈瑞杜魯門總統任內發生了許多重大事件，先是盟軍戰勝德國、盟軍在廣島及長崎投下原子彈、日本投降、二次大戰正式結束。緊接著冷戰開始及韓戰爆發，韓戰使美國付出了沉痛的代價，直接影響杜魯門的連任計畫。儘管各界對於杜魯門總統的評價不一，但面臨險峻的國際情勢，他仍以果斷的性格克服許多挑戰。

杜懷特艾森豪 ▼
Dwight D. Eisenhower

美國第三十四任總統

任期：1953~1961

事蹟：二次大戰盟軍最高指揮官、
　　　冷戰期間使用圍堵政策

杜懷特艾森豪於一九五二年競選總統成功，並連任兩屆。他所面對的是剛自韓戰抽身的美國政府，為了儘速結束韓戰，他也曾表示不惜動用核武。在艾森豪任內先後簽訂了《朝鮮停戰協定》及《美韓共同防禦條約》。此外，自一九四五年至一九九〇年，以美國為首的北大西洋公約組織，與蘇聯為首的華沙公約組織，形成長達四十五年的冷戰，艾森豪可謂此局勢的關鍵人物。艾森豪支持所以反蘇聯政權為唯一於任期內訪問中華民國的總統。

約翰甘迺迪John F. Kennedy ▼

美國第三十五任總統

任期：1961~1963

事蹟：古巴飛彈危機、封鎖古巴

約翰甘迺迪是歷任總統中唯一獲得普立茲獎的總統。在他任內發生的重大事件包含：豬灣入侵事件、古巴飛彈危機、建立柏林圍牆及越戰活動。其中，甘迺迪對於古巴飛彈危機的妥善處理贏得許多讚譽，美蘇領袖相互妥協，避免了一場核戰爆發，成為危機處理的最佳典範。甘迺迪於一九六三年十一月二十二日在德克薩斯州達拉斯市遇刺身亡。

羅納德雷根Ronald Reagan ▲

美國第四十任總統

任期：1981~1989

事蹟：推行經濟政策，使經濟大幅茁壯

羅納德雷根為美國歷任總統中唯一一位演員出身的總統。他在任內成功推行了許多經濟政策，人稱雷根經濟學；他降低所得稅、減少通貨膨脹、排除稅賦漏洞等，在美國歷經經濟衰退，一九八二年後經濟漸有起色。雷根總統的任期影響了美國一九八〇年代，也因此常將此年代稱為「雷根時代」。

EUREKA! 點子成金

Madame Tussaud
A [1] Legend in Wax
杜莎夫人與永垂不朽的蠟像

© anka@happyhangaround、Klaith Zhang / flickr.com © Gertjan R.、Rudolph.A.furtado、Mvkulkarni23 / commons.wikimedia.org

V Vocabulary Bank

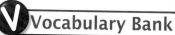

1) **legend** [ˋlɛdʒənd] (n.) 傳奇，傳說
The Loch Ness Monster is just a legend.
尼斯湖水怪只是個傳說。

2) **exhibit** [ɪgˋzɪbɪt] (v./n.) 展示，展覽
The museum will exhibit the artist's paintings next month.
博物館將會在下個月展出該位畫家的畫作。

3) **apprentice** [əˋprɛntɪs] (n.) 學徒
Gary found a job as a plumber's apprentice.
蓋瑞找到了水管工的學徒工作。

4) **craft** [ˋkræft] (v.) 精巧地製作
The furniture is crafted from fine oak.
這個家具是用最好的橡木精製而成的。

5) **victim** [ˋvɪktɪm] (n.) 受害者，遇難者
Bombing victims were treated at a local hospital.
爆炸事件受害者在當地醫院接受治療。

6) **attraction** [əˋtrækʃən] (n.) 景點，具吸引力的特色
The National Palace Museum and Taipei 101 are two major tourist attractions in Taiwan.
故宮博物院和台北一○一是台灣著名的兩個觀光景點。

7) **idol** [ˋaɪdəl] (n.) 偶像
Korean idols are popular all over Asia.
韓國偶像風靡了全亞洲。

進階字彙

8) **anatomy** [əˋnætəmi] (n.) 解剖結構，解剖學
The professor teaches a course in plant anatomy.
那位教授教的是植物解剖學。

課文朗讀 MP3 88　單字朗讀 MP3 89　英文講解 MP3 90

Two months before Marie Grosholtz was born in Strasbourg, France on December 1, 1761, her father was killed in battle. To **1 make ends meet**, her mother Anne moved to Bern, Switzerland, where she worked as a housekeeper for Dr. Philippe Curtius, a physician who was skilled at making wax models of human [8] **anatomy**.

Dr. Curtius later gave up his medical [9] **practice** and moved to Paris, where he made his living creating and [2] **exhibiting** wax figures of famous people. He took the young Marie as his [3] **apprentice**, and before long she was [4] **crafting** figures of Rousseau, Voltaire and Benjamin Franklin. She showed such great talent that Louis XVI hired her as a tutor for his sister, moving her to the royal palace at Versailles. The good times ended, however, with the arrival of the French Revolution in 1789. Luckily, Marie's wax modeling skills saved her from the [10] **guillotine**—the revolutionaries employed her to create death masks of famous [5] **victims** like her former boss Louis, Marie Antoinette and Robespierre.

When the Reign of Terror ended, Marie married François Tussaud, becoming Madame Tussaud. In 1802, she was invited to display her wax figures at the Lyceum Theatre in London. The Napoleonic Wars prevented her from returning to France, and she spent the next several decades touring the U.K. with her collection. Finally, in 1835, Marie had her eureka moment: too old and tired to continue her traveling show, she decided to open a wax museum on Baker Street in London.

Madam Tussauds was a huge success from the start, and is still one of London's top tourist ⁶⁾**attractions**, ¹¹⁾**drawing** 2.8 million visitors a year. The museum now has branches all over the world, and displays figures of Hollywood stars, pop singers and sports ⁷⁾**idols**.

Mini Quiz 閱讀測驗

Which of the following is NOT true about Madame Tussaud?
(A) She lived in the U.K. for many years.
(B) She learned wax modeling from a doctor.
(C) Her father died before she was born.
(D) She tutored Louis XVI.

中 Translation

瑪麗格勞舒茲於一七六一年十二月一日出生於法國的斯特拉斯堡，出生前兩個月父親就死於戰場，為了餬口，她的母親安搬到瑞士的伯恩，替擅長製作人體結構蠟像的菲利浦柯提斯醫生擔任管家。

柯提斯醫生後來放棄行醫，搬到巴黎，以創作、展示名人的蠟像維生。他收年輕的瑪麗為徒，沒多久，瑪麗就能打造出盧梭、伏爾泰和富蘭克林的人像。她展現出過人的天分，路易十六甚至聘請她當他妹妹的家教，並讓她搬進凡爾賽皇宮。然而，好日子卻隨著一七八九年法國大革命的到來而終止。幸好，瑪麗製作蠟像的技能救了她，使她免於登上斷頭台—革命份子要她製作知名罹難者面具，像是她的前老闆國王路易、皇后瑪麗安托瓦內特、羅伯斯比爾（法國大革命首腦之一）。

當恐怖統治結束之後，瑪麗嫁給了法蘭柯斯杜莎，成為杜莎夫人。在一八〇二年，她受邀到倫敦的蘭心劇院展出她的蠟像作品，但拿破崙戰爭卻讓她無法回法國，於是她接下來數十年都帶著作品英國巡迴展出。最後在一八三五年，瑪麗靈機一動：她老了也累了，無法再繼續巡迴展覽，所以她決定在倫敦貝克街開設一個蠟像博物館。

杜莎夫人蠟像館從一開幕就很成功，現在仍是倫敦數一數二觀光景點，每年吸引兩千八百萬名觀光客。如今蠟像博物館在世界各地都設有分館，展示好萊塢巨星、流行歌星和運動偶像的蠟像。

9) **practice** [ˋpræktɪs] (n.)（醫生、律師等專業人士的）執業，事業
Dean joined his father's legal practice after graduating from law school.
尼恩在法律學院畢業後加入了他爸的法律事務所。

10) **guillotine** [ˋgiəˏtin/ˋgɪləˏtin] (n.) 斷頭臺
The guillotine was used in France until 1981.
到一九八一年，法國都還在用斷頭台執行死刑。

11) **draw** [drɔ] (v.) 吸引，招徠
The royal wedding drew huge crowds to the streets of London.
那場皇室婚禮吸引眾多人潮聚集在倫敦的街道上。

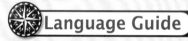

Tongue-tied No More

❶ make ends meet 維持生計

此片語照字面上解釋是「使兩端相接」，大家可以想成記帳時「收入」與「支出」兩欄的數字至少要「入能敷出」，才不會還沒月底就月光光、心慌慌，所以 make ends meet 可解釋為「收支平衡、勉強餬口」等。

A: How's the pay at your company?
你在這間公司的薪資待遇如何？
B: Pretty bad. I'm barely making enough to make ends meet.
很差。我賺的錢少到幾乎無法維持生計。

Language Guide

Lyceum Theatre 蘭心劇院

蘭心劇院建於一七六五年，起初有過一些音樂表演、馬戲團演出及杜莎夫人蠟像展，同時也是莫札特的歌劇《女人皆如此》的倫敦首演場地。劇院歷經數次改建後，現為倫敦西區 (West End) 的著名劇院之一，可容納兩千名觀眾。音樂劇《獅子王》為蘭心劇院的常態劇作，從一九九九年開始至二〇〇九年已吸引超過八百萬名觀眾前來觀賞。

Napoleonic Wars 拿破崙戰爭

拿破崙戰爭是歐洲各國和拿破崙政府所爆發多次戰役的統稱，時間約為一八〇一年到一八一五年，始於法國大革命後拿破崙取得政權，終於滑鐵盧戰役。從奧國加入英、俄等國，共同阻成第三次反法同盟開始，拿破崙政府前後曾與西班牙、普魯士、匈牙利等國為敵。戰爭後歐洲各國版圖重整，為日後的民族國家奠下基礎，也使封建體制遭到破壞，進而加速資本主義的發展。

© Annek_B / flickr.com

Vocabulary Bank

1) **convert** [kən`vɜt] (v.) 改變形態、用途
The sofa can convert into a bed.
這座沙發可以變成一張床。

2) **manual** [`mænjuəl] (a.) 用手操作的，手動的，手的
Being a dentist requires a high level of manual skill.
當牙醫需要很高超的手技。

3) **device** [dɪ`vaɪs] (n.) 裝置，設備
Our store sells all the latest wireless devices.
我們店有賣所有最新的無線裝置。

4) **plow** [plau] (v./n.) 耕；犁
The farmer used an ox to plow the field.
農夫用牛來耕田。

5) **scan** [skæn] (v./n.) 掃描
You should scan your computer for viruses regularly.
你應該定期為你的電腦掃毒。

6) **investor** [ɪn`vɛstə] (n.) 投資者，出資者
Investors lost billions of dollars in the market crash.
股市崩盤時，投資者損失了好幾十億。

7) **unknown** [ʌn`non] (a./n.) 沒沒無聞的（人），未知的（事物）
The director chose an unknown actor to play the leading role.
導演選了一位沒沒無聞的演員飾演主角。

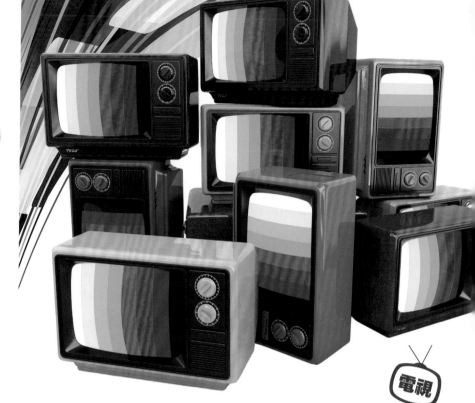

THE TELEVISION
From Potato Field to Couch Potato
電視
從馬鈴薯田到沙發馬鈴薯

課文朗讀 MP3 91　單字朗讀 MP3 92　英文講解 MP3 93

Like Abraham Lincoln, Philo Farnsworth was born in a log cabin. Although he was the son of humble Mormon farmers, he showed a strong [8)]**affinity** for technology as a child. When his family moved from Beaver, Utah to a farm near Rigby, Idaho in 1918, the young Philo was excited to find that their new home was wired for electricity, which was rare in rural America at that time. He quickly learned how to repair the family's generator, and when he found an old electric motor, he used it to [1)]**convert** his mother's washing machine from [2)]**manual** to electric.

At the age of 14, Philo read a magazine article about scientists who were developing mechanical [3)]**devices** to send images through the air, just like radios send sound. ⒼReasoning that machines wouldn't be able to move fast enough to transmit pictures accurately, he concluded that such a device should be electronic, not mechanical. A few days later, Philo had his eureka moment while ⁴⁾**plowing** the family's potato field. Looking at the neat lines made by the plow, he suddenly realized that a picture could be sent in the same way— ⁵⁾**scanned** line by line, sent through the ⁹⁾**airwaves**, and then put back together by a receiving device on the other end.

But theory and practice are two different things, and years passed before Philo was able to find ⁶⁾**investors** and turn his concept into reality. On September 27, 1927, in his small lab above a garage in San Francisco, he successfully transmitted an image of a simple line from a video camera tube to a small screen in the next room. "We've done it," he cried. "There you have electronic television!" Unfortunately, Philo spent the next decade in a patent war with RCA, which stole many of his ideas. Although RCA was eventually required to pay ¹⁰⁾**royalties** to Philo, he died poor and ⁷⁾**unknown** in 1971.

Mini Quiz 閱讀測驗

Which of the following did Philo Farnsworth invent?
(A) The electronic scanner
(B) The electric washing machine
(C) The mechanical television
(D) The electronic television

Translation

菲洛范斯沃斯跟林肯總統一樣在小木屋出生。雖然雙親是中下階層的摩門教農人，他從小就展現對技術的強烈喜好。一九一八年，他們全家從猶他州畢佛搬到愛達荷州利格比附近的農場，年輕的菲洛興奮地發現他們的新家有裝電線，這在美國當時的鄉村地區相當罕見。他很快就學會如何修理家裡的發電機，而在他發現一顆舊電動馬達之後，他便利用它將母親的洗衣機從手動改為電動。

十四歲時，菲洛讀到一篇雜誌文章提到科學家正在研發經由空氣傳送影像的機械裝置，就像無線電傳送聲音一樣。推想機器轉動速度不夠快速，無法精確傳送影像，他斷定這樣的裝置必須是電子裝置，而非機械。幾天後，菲洛在犁家中馬鈴薯田的時候靈機一動。看著犁頭劃出整齊的線，他突然領會，影像也可以透過同樣方式傳送——一排一排掃描、透過電波傳送，然後在另一端利用接收裝置重新組合。

不過，理論和實際情況是兩碼子事，菲洛花了多年的時間才找到投資人實現他的概念。一九二七年九月二十七日，他在舊金山車庫樓上的小實驗室成功將一條簡單線段的影像，從攝像管傳輸到隔壁房間的小螢幕。「我們辦到了，」他大叫。「電視大功告成了！」不幸的是，接下來十年，菲洛都在與竊用他許多構想的 RCA 公司打專利戰。儘管最後 RCA 被要求付給菲洛權利金，但菲洛在一九七一年過世時仍舊一文不名、沒沒無聞。

進階字彙

8) **affinity** [əˋfɪnətɪ] (n.)（自然的）喜好，傾向
Ducks have an affinity for water.
鴨子們都喜歡水。

9) **airwaves** [ˋɛr͵wevz] (n.)（電台或電視）廣播
During the election, the airwaves were filled with political ads.
選舉期間的廣播都充斥著政治廣告。

10) **royalty** [ˋrɔɪəltɪ] (n.) 權力金，版稅
Songwriters receive royalties each time one of their tunes is played on the radio.
每次只要電台播放作曲者的歌曲，他們就可拿到版稅。

Language Guide

couch potato 沙發馬鈴薯

這個詞是用來形容整天窩在沙發上看電視吃東西、不愛活動的懶人。這個說法並沒有確切的出處與來由，不過大部份的人都很喜歡一邊看電視一邊吃薯片(potato chips)，而且吃多了又會發福，身材就像馬鈴薯一樣圓滾滾的，所以應該不難和這個詞聯想在一起吧！如今，有很多人整天都黏在電腦前，因此也出現了 mouse potato（滑鼠馬鈴薯）這個詞彙，和 couch potato 有異曲同工之妙。

Grammar Master

用分詞句構來簡化句子

本文中 "Reasoning that..., he concluded that..." 這句其實可以拆成兩句：

1. He reasoned that machines wouldn't be able to move fast enough to transmit pictures accurately.

2. He concluded that such a device should be electronic, not mechanical.

這兩句都是同一個主詞(He)，不管是用連接詞合併或是分成兩句都太冗長了，所以就用分詞句構來簡化。

步驟1：省略第一句的主詞

~~He~~ reasoned that machines wouldn't be able to move fast enough to transmit pictures accurately.

步驟2：判斷主詞後的動詞是「主動」還是「被動」

主動→動詞改為「現在分詞」(Ving)
被動→動詞改為「過去分詞」(p.p.)

Reasoning that machines wouldn't be able to move fast enough to transmit pictures accurately.

簡化結果

Reasoning that machines wouldn't be able to move fast enough to transmit pictures accurately, he concluded that such a device should be electronic, not mechanical.

閱讀測驗解答：(D)

87

The Microwave Oven
A Hot Invention
微波爐 火熱的發明

Born in 1894 in the small town of Howland, Maine, Percy Spencer was [1]**orphaned** at an early age. After his father died and his mother abandoned him, Spencer was raised by a poor aunt and uncle. Unable to complete [2]**elementary** school, he joined a mill as an apprentice at the age of 12, and later became a [3]**self-taught** [4]**electrician**. In 1912, Spencer joined the U.S. Navy, where he was trained as a radio operator. To [5]**make up for** his lack of education, he read math and science textbooks while standing [6]**watch**.

In the late 1920s, Spencer joined the growing Raytheon company in Massachusetts, where he soon became an expert on vacuum tubes, a key component of early radios. During WWII, the company's focus switched to another kind of radio radar. Raytheon won a government contract to produce magnetrons—high-powered vacuum tubes that [7]**generate** microwaves for radar, and Spencer increased production from 17 a day to over 2,600 by the end of the war. But it was after the war that he had his eureka moment. One day while standing next to a magnetron, Spencer had a strange feeling and noticed that the candy bar in his pocket was melting. He quickly sent for a bag of popcorn, which began popping away when placed in front of the magnetron. The microwave oven was born.

The first commercial model—the Radar Range—was the size of a refrigerator and cost $5,000. No wonder it was used mostly in restaurants. When smaller, cheaper home

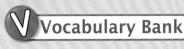

Vocabulary Bank

1) **orphan** [ˋɔrfən] (v./n.) 使成為孤兒；孤兒
Many children were orphaned during the war.
很多小孩在戰爭時期成為孤兒。

2) **elementary** [ˏɛləˋmɛnt(ə)ri] (a.) 基本的，初級的，基礎的。elementary school 即「小學」
Free elementary education is a basic right.
免費的小學教育是基本的權利。

3) **self-taught** [ˋsɛlfˋtɔt] (a.) 自學的
The members of the band are all self-taught musicians.
這個樂團的成員都是自學的樂手。

4) **electrician** [ɪlɛkˋtrɪʃən] (n.) 電工
Andrew called an electrician to fix her fuse box.
安德魯打電話請一位電工來修他的電箱。

5) **make up for** [mek ʌp fɔr] (phr.) 彌補，補償
Nothing can make up for the death of a child.
沒有任何東西可以彌補一個孩子的死。

6) **watch** [wɑtʃ] (n./v.) 守衛，看守。stand watch 即「站崗」
Two guards stood watch at the embassy gates.
有兩名警衛守在大使館的門口。

7) **generate** [ˋdʒɛnəˏret] (v.) 產生（光、熱、電能等）
Waves can generate electronic power.
海浪可用來發電。

進階字彙

8) **take off** [tek ɔf] (phr.) 起飛，蔚為風潮，大受歡迎
The star's career took off when she was nominated for an Oscar.
那位明星在獲奧斯卡提名後星路大開。

88

models were introduced in the 1960s, the market for these fast cooking ovens 8)**took off**. Today, microwave ovens can be found in over 90% of American homes.

Mini Quiz 閱讀測驗

What is a magnetron?
(A) A kind of microwave
(B) A form of radar
(C) A type of vacuum tube
(D) A kind of radio

中 Translation

一八九四在緬因州豪蘭鎮出生的波西史班瑟，從小是個孤兒。在父親去世，母親拋棄他以後，他由貧窮的嬸嬸及叔叔撫養。史班瑟沒辦法讀完小學，於是在十二歲時進入一家磨坊當學徒，後來成為一位自學的電工。一九一二年，史班瑟加入美國海軍，在此被訓練為無線電操作員。為了彌補所受教育的不足，他在站崗時念數學和自然教科書。

在一九二○年代晚期，史班瑟加入了位於麻波州正在擴張的瑞錫恩公司，在此他很快就成為真空管專家，也就是早期無線電的一種重要組件。二次大戰期間，該公司的重心轉移到另一種無線電：雷達。瑞錫恩公司拿下政府的合約來製造磁控管——一種為雷達微波的高能量真空管，而且到戰爭結束時，史班瑟已將產量由一天十七個提高到二千六百個。不過，他靈光乍現的時刻是在戰後。有一天他站在磁控管旁邊，察覺有一絲異樣，發現口袋裡的巧克力棒融化了。他馬上要來一袋爆米花，爆米花放在磁控管前就劈哩啪啦爆開來。微波爐就此誕生。

第一部量產的微波爐——「雷達爐」，尺寸有冰箱那麼大，而且要價五千美元，難怪當時大多使用於餐館。等到尺寸較小、較便宜的家用微波爐在一九六○年代問世後，這種快速烹調爐在市場上大受歡迎。如今，美國有超過九成的家庭都有微波爐。

EUREKA! 點子成金

V Vocabulary Bank

1) **photography** [fə`tɑɡrəfi] (n.) 攝影，照相
National Geographic is famous for its photography.
《國家地理》雜誌以攝影著稱。

2) **pioneer** [ˌpaɪə`nɪr] (n.) 先驅，倡導者
The scientist was a pioneer in his field.
這位科學家是他這個領域的先鋒。

3) **excel** [ɪk`sɛl] (v.) 擅長於，表現優異
Lisa excels in math and science.
麗莎在數學和理化表現優異。

4) **freshman** [`frɛʃmən] (a./n.) （高中、大學）一年級生（的）
I can't believe you failed freshman English.
我不敢相信你大一的英文被當掉。

5) **vibrate** [`vaɪbret] (v./n.) 震動，（手機）震動模式
The whole house vibrates whenever a train passes by.
每次火車經過的時候整棟房子都在震動。

6) **sneak** [snik] (v.) 偷偷地走，溜
Carrie snuck out of the house to meet her boyfriend.
凱莉為了跟男友見面而偷溜出家裡。

7) **breakthrough** [`brek͵θru] (n.) 突破性進展
Police are still waiting for a breakthrough in the investigation.
警察仍等待調查有所突破。

8) **crystal** [`krɪstəl] (n.) 晶體，水晶
Some clouds are made of tiny ice crystals.
有些雲是由細小的冰晶體組成的。

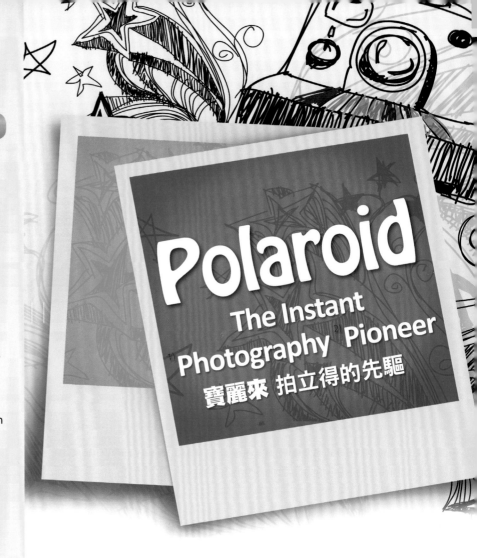

Polaroid
The Instant Photography Pioneer
寶麗來 拍立得的先驅

課文朗讀 MP3 97　單字朗讀 MP3 98　英文講解 MP3 99

Edward Herbert Land was born in Bridgeport, Connecticut in 1909. After graduating from high school, where he 3)**excelled** at science, Land entered Harvard University to study chemistry. In his 4)**freshman** year, he became so interested in polarized light—light whose waves all 5)**vibrate** in a single plane—that he left to pursue full-time research on polarizing materials.

Land moved to New York, where he read scientific works at the public library by day and 6)**snuck** into a lab at Columbia University to do experiments by night. His 7)**breakthrough** came when he realized that instead of using large 8)**crystals**—which were expensive and hard to come by—to polarize light, he could achieve the same effect with lots of tiny crystals 11)**embedded** in a sheet of clear plastic. Land then returned to

Harvard to perfect his new polarizing material, and in 1932 founded Land-Wheelwright Laboratories with one of his [9]**physics** teachers. By 1937, the company—renamed the Polaroid Corporation—was producing polarizers for a variety of uses, including sunglasses and camera lens [10]**filters**.

But land's real eureka moment came during a vacation to Santa Fe in 1943. After taking a family photo, his three-year-old daughter asked why she couldn't see it right away. On a walk that afternoon, he **1 came up with** a solution—why not combine the film and chemicals used to develop it? So Land designed special sheets of film with [12]**pouches** of chemicals on one side that would be spread across the negative by [13]**rollers** after the picture was taken. The first Polaroid camera, introduced in 1948, could produce a black-and-white print in 60 seconds. The color Polaroid cameras of the '60s and '70s sold so well that Land was a billionaire when he retired in 1982.

Mini Quiz 閱讀測驗

What inspired Edward Land to invent the Polaroid camera?
(A) His research on polarizing materials
(B) A vacation to Santa Fe in 1943
(C) Working with one of his physics teachers
(D) A question asked by his daughter

Translation

愛德華賀伯蘭德一九〇九年生於康乃迪克州布里吉波。高中科學成績十分優異的蘭德，畢業後進入哈佛大學研讀化學。大一那年，他開始對偏振光——在同一平面振動的光——深感興趣，於是離開學校，全力投入偏光材料的研究。

蘭德搬到紐約，白天在公立圖書館閱讀科學著作，晚上則偷偷溜進哥倫比亞大學的實驗室做實驗。當他發現要使光發生偏振不必使用大塊晶體——那又貴又難取得，改用嵌入許多小晶體的透明塑膠片就能達到同樣效果，他的研究有了突破性的發展。接著蘭德回到哈佛大學精進他新的偏光材料，並於一九三二年和他的一位物理學老師創立蘭德惠萊特實驗室。一九三七年，這間公司——易名為寶麗來公司——開始為多種用途製造偏光鏡，包括太陽眼鏡和照相機的濾鏡。

但蘭德真正靈機一動的時刻是他一九四三年到聖塔菲度假期間。拍了一張全家福合照之後，他三歲大的女兒問，為什麼不能馬上看到照片。當天下午散步時，他想到一個辦法——為什麼不把底片和沖洗底片的化學藥劑結合起來呢？於是，蘭德設計了一款特別的底片，一側附上裝有化學藥劑的囊袋，照片一拍攝，滾軸便會將化學藥劑塗滿底片上。第一部拍立得相機在一九四八年問世，可於六十秒內產生一張黑白照片。六〇及七〇年代的彩色拍立得相機非常暢銷，使蘭德在一九八二年退休時已是億萬富翁。

9) **physics** [ˋfɪzɪks] (n.) 物理學
Einstein made many important discoveries in physics.
愛因斯坦在物理學上有很多重大發現。

10) **filter** [ˋfɪltɚ] (n.) 過濾裝置，濾網，濾心
Coffee filters are on sale at the supermarket.
超市正在促銷咖啡濾紙。

進階字彙

11) **embed** [ɪmˋbɛd] (v.) 嵌入，埋入
There were many fossils embedded in the rock layer.
有許多化石被埋在岩石層。

12) **pouch** [pautʃ] (n.) 小袋，囊
I gave my dad a tobacco pouch for his birthday.
我送一個菸草袋給我爸當生日禮物。

13) **roller** [ˋrolɚ] (n.) 滾軸，滾筒
We used paint rollers to paint the room.
我們用滾輪刷來粉刷這間房間。

Tongue-tied No More

1 come up with（針對問題）想出、提出

片語 come up with 解釋為「提出、想出（主意、解決辦法、計畫等）」，所以在句子中 with 後面通常會接 idea、solution、plan 等字。另外，come up with 也可以表示「提供別人想要的東西」。例如 "We'll be in big trouble if we don't come up with six grand by three p.m."（要是沒在下午三點前弄到六千美元，我們就麻煩大了）。

A: I have no idea what to give Dad for his birthday.
我真不知道要買給爸爸什麼樣的生日禮物。
B: Don't worry. I'm sure you'll come up with something.
別擔心，我相信你會想出來的。

Language Guide

polarized light 偏振光

因為光線的前進並不會有任何特定的方向，朝四面八方前進，因此經過折射或反射後，能使不同方向的光線限定在同一個平面，這就被稱作為偏振光。換句話說，光的偏振性是指行進中的光具有規律的方向。攝影時常用的偏光鏡，全名是偏振光濾色鏡 (polarizing filter)，過濾出某些反光或散射光，消除後可增強色彩的飽和度，使得照片的景深更有層次感。

polarize 當動詞時，有極化的意思還有使光偏振的意思；polarizer 則是當名詞使用，是偏光鏡的意思。

EUREKA! 點子成金

Post-it Notes
便利貼 黏東西的最佳幫手
Making the Best of a Sticky Situation

Vocabulary Bank

1) **definitely** [ˋdɛfənɪtlɪ] (adv.) 一定地，絕對地
I'm definitely going to the concert.
我一定會去那場演唱會。

2) **undergraduate** [ˌʌndəˋgrædʒuɪt] (n./a.)
大學生（的），graduate 即「研究生」
All undergraduates are required to take at least one science course.
所有的大學生都至少要修一堂理工課程。

3) **researcher** [rɪˋsɜtʃə] (n.) 研究員，調查者
(n./v.) research 研究，調查
The researchers published their results in a scientific journal.
研究人員在科學期刊上發表他們的研究結果。

4) **mining** [ˋmaɪnɪŋ] (n.) 採礦，礦業
Copper mining is Chile's largest industry.
開採銅礦是智利最大的產業。

5) **organic** [ɔrˋgænɪk] (a.) 有機的
Where can I buy organic produce around here?
這附近哪裡可以買到有機蔬果？

6) **seminar** [ˋsɛməˌnɑr] (n.) 研討會，專題討論會
All employees are required to attend the training seminar.
所有員工都必須參加訓練研討會。

7) **hymn** [hɪm] (n.) 聖歌，讚美詩
Do you sing hymns at your church?
你會在你去的教堂唱聖歌嗎？

8) **sermon** [ˋsɜmən] (n.) 佈道，說教
The priest gave a sermon on the importance of kindness.
牧師佈道談論仁慈的重要性。

9) **pass out** [pæs aut] (phr.) 分發，派送
The teacher asked Billy to pass out the test sheets.
老師要比利幫忙發考卷。

進階字彙

10) **adhesive** [ədˋhisɪv] (n./a.) 黏著劑；黏著的
Bill used a strong adhesive to fix the chair.
比爾用強烈黏著劑來修復那張椅子。

課文朗讀 MP3 100　單字朗讀 MP3 101　英文講解 MP3 102

You've probably never heard of Art Fry or Spencer Silver. But you've [1)]**definitely** heard of, and used, their famous invention. What is it? Possibly the most important office supply product since the paperclip!

Art Fry loved to build things as a child, so it was natural that he study engineering in college. In 1953, while still an [2)]**undergraduate** in Chemical Engineering at the University of Minnesota, he found a job as a new product development [3)]**researcher** at 3M—then known as Minnesota [4)]**Mining** & Manufacturing.

Spencer Silver followed a similar path, joining 3M's Central Research Labs as a chemist in 1966 after studying [5)]**organic** chemistry at the University of Colorado. In 1968, while trying to invent a better [10)]**adhesive** for tape, Silver came up with something truly revolutionary—a reusable adhesive that was sticky enough to hold sheets of paper together, but not sticky enough to make them tear when you pulled them apart. The only thing was, he'd invented a solution without a problem.

Until, that is, Art Fry learned about Silver's new adhesive at a company [6]**seminar** five years later. Fry enjoyed singing at church, but he had a problem—the pieces of paper he used to mark his place often fell out when he opened his [7]**hymn** book. One day, while sitting through a boring [8]**sermon**, he had his eureka moment: he could use Silver's adhesive to make a bookmark that would stay in place without damaging the pages.

When Fry [9]**passed out** these bookmarks to his co-workers, they began using them to write notes on, and the Post-it was born. Introduced in the U.S. in 1980, and Canada and Europe a year later, Post-its can now be found stuck to computers, desks and doors in offices and homes all over the world.

Mini Quiz 閱讀測驗

■ **Where did Art Fry have his eureka moment?**
(A) At a seminar
(B) At a church
(C) At a research lab
(D) At work

中 Translation

你可能從來沒聽過亞瑟傅萊或史賓瑟席佛，可是你一定聽過、也用過他們著名的發明。是什麼呢？那可能是繼迴紋針之後最重要的辦公用品喔！

亞瑟傅萊從小就喜歡做東西，所以上大學很自然就念工程系。一九五三年，當他還是明尼蘇達大學化工系的學生時，他就在 3M 找到了新產品研發人員的工作，當時那家公司不叫 3M，而是明尼蘇達礦業與製造公司。

史賓瑟席佛從業的過程也類似，他從科羅拉多大學有機化學系畢業後，於一九六六年加入 3M 中央研究實驗室擔任化學研究員。一九六八年，席佛正試著發明一種較好的膠帶黏膠，他想出了非常革命性的發明──可重複使用、讓紙張黏在一起，但撕下來卻不會把紙撕破的黏膠。只是，他發明了解決方法，但卻沒有問題好對付。

一直到五年後，亞瑟傅萊在一場公司的研討會得知席佛的新黏膠。傅萊喜歡在教會唱詩歌，可是他有個困擾－每次打開詩歌集，他用來標示位置的紙片就會掉下來。有一天，聽著無聊的佈道時，他突然靈光一現：他可以用席佛的黏膠來做一種可以固定位置、卻不會弄傷書頁的書籤。

當傅萊將這種書籤發給同事時，他們開始在上頭寫筆記，於是便利貼就誕生了。便利貼一九八〇年在美國上市，隔年引進加拿大和歐洲，現在世界各地公司和住家的電腦、書桌和門上都可見到它的蹤跡。

Language Guide

paperclip 的發明人

便條紙尚未問世之前，要固定零散的紙片和便條，總少不了各種大大小小的夾子和釘子。迴紋針一度被認為由挪威人約翰瓦萊 (Johan Vaaler) 所發明，事實是瓦萊在一八九九年開發出第一支三角形迴紋針，並於德國取得專利權（當時挪威沒有專利法），但早在一八六七年美國的山謬費 (Samuel B. Fay) 就已經申請過類似的專利。現在常見的雙橢圓形迴紋針，是由英國寶石公司 (Gem Manufacturing Company) 在一八九〇年所生產，設計人為美國的威廉米德爾布魯克 (William Middlebrook)，米德爾布魯克並於一八九九年申請製作迴紋針機器的專利。

辦公室文具

paperclip 雖名為「迴紋針」，但 clip 卻是「夾子」的意思。你是否曉得其他固定用的夾子、圖釘等文具的說法呢？

● **binder clip** 長尾夾

● **spring clip / bulldog clip** 彈簧夾

● **thumbtack** 扁式圖釘

● **pushpin** 大頭圖釘

● **straight pin** 大頭針

● **safety pin** 安全別針

EUREKA! 點子成金

V Vocabulary Bank

1) **promise** [ˈprɑmɪs] (n.) 前途，指望
The young athlete shows great promise.
那位年輕的運動員很有前途。

2) **divorce** [dɪˈvors] (v./n.) 離婚
Mark's wife refuses to divorce him.
馬克的太太拒絕與他離婚。

3) **spare** [spɛr] (a.) 空閒的，多餘的
We have a spare bed if you want to spend the night.
如果你要留下來過夜的話，我們有多一張床。

4) **executive** [ɪgˈzɛkjətɪv] (a.) 執行的，主管級的
Roberta works as an executive secretary.
羅貝塔擔任執行秘書的工作。

5) **chairman** [ˈtʃɛrmən] (n.) 主席，主任，董事長，chairman of the board 亦即「董事長」
The chairman called a meeting of the committee.
那位主席召開了委員會議。

6) **exception** [ɪkˈsɛpʃən] (n.) 例外
Every rule has an exception.
每個規則都有例外。

7) **batch** [bætʃ] (n.) 一批生產出來的量
How many batches of brownies did you make?
你烤了幾盤布朗尼？

8) **blender** [ˈblɛndə] (n.) 果汁機
You need a blender to make smoothies.
做冰沙要有果汁機才行。

進階字彙

9) **keystroke** [ˈkiˌstrok] (n.)（一次）敲擊鍵盤
You can add the date to your document with a single keystroke.
你只要按一次鍵就可以在文件中加入日期。

Bette McMurray
© aquirkyblog.com

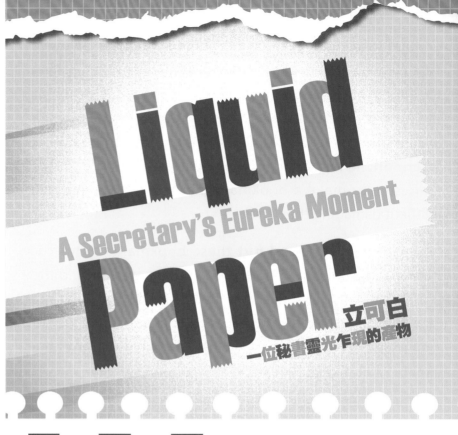

Liquid Paper 立可白
A Secretary's Eureka Moment
一位秘書靈光乍現的產物

課文朗讀 MP3 103　單字朗讀 MP3 104　英文講解 MP3 105

Growing up in San Antonio, Texas, Bette McMurray didn't show any particular [1]**promise**. She dropped out of school at the age of 17, and married her high school sweetheart, Warren Nesmith, two years later. Her husband left to fight in WWII soon afterward, and Bette gave birth to their son Michael while he was away. After Warren returned from the war, however, the couple [2]**divorced**, and she was left to raise Michael on her own.

When Bette's father passed away and left her property in Dallas, she decided to move there with her son and make a fresh start. To make ends meet, she found a position as a secretary at the Texas Bank & Trust. She also developed an interest in art, and enjoyed painting and drawing in her [3]**spare** time. Bette was a hard worker, and by 1951 she was working as [4]**executive** secretary to the [5]**chairman** of the board.

In the early 1950s, many companies began switching to electric typewriters, and Bette's office was no [6]**exception**. These new typewriters were faster and easier to use, but they also brought a new challenge. While mistakes made on a manual typewriter could be removed with an eraser, the more powerful [9]**keystrokes** of electric models made this difficult. Basically, the only choices were to **1** **x** the error **out** or type the whole page over.

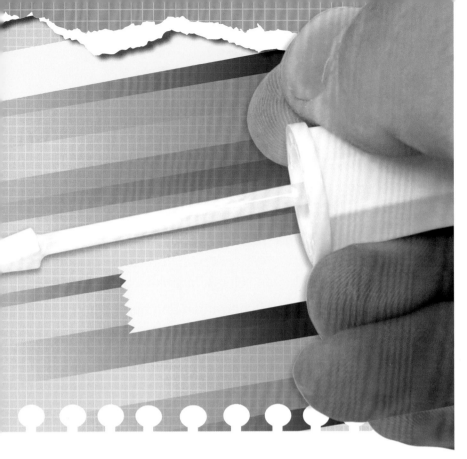

Bette thought that there must be a better way to correct mistakes, and it was her artistic hobby that provided her eureka moment. When she made a mistake while painting, she didn't start over again—she just painted over it. So why not use the same method when she was typing? That evening, she mixed up a [7]**batch** of white tempera paint in her [8]**blender**, then put it in a bottle and took it with her to work the next day.

 **Mini Quiz** 閱讀測驗

Which of the following is NOT true about Bette?
(A) She was a single mother.
(B) She liked to paint and draw in her free time.
(C) She graduated from high school.
(D) She inherited property from her father.

Translation

在德州聖安東尼奧長大的貝蒂麥克莫瑞,看不出會有什麼璀璨的前途。她十七歲時便輟學,並在兩年後嫁給她高中的青梅竹馬華倫奈史密斯。不久後,她的丈夫便離家參與二次世界大戰,而貝蒂則在他離家這段期間生下他們的兒子麥可。然而,這對夫妻在華倫自戰場返家後便離婚了,剩下她獨自一人撫養麥可。

貝蒂的夫親去世後留給她位於達拉斯的房產,於是她決定帶兒子搬去那裡重新開始。為維持生活開銷,她在德州信託銀行找了秘書的職務。她也開始對藝術燃起興趣,喜歡在閒暇之餘畫畫。貝蒂是位勤勞的員工,到了一九五一年時已升為董事長執行秘書。

一九五〇年代初期,許多公司開始改用電動打字機,貝蒂的辦公室也不例外。新款打字機速度較快、較易於使用,但也帶來新的挑戰。手動打字機的錯字可用橡皮擦去除,而電動打字機鍵敲得較重,打錯字就很難擦掉了。基本上,出錯只有兩種選擇:劃掉或整頁重打。

貝蒂認為一定有更好的方法修正錯誤,而她的藝術愛好讓她靈機一動。每當她畫畫出錯時,她不會重頭來過,只會覆蓋上去。那麼,何不在打字時運用同樣的方法呢?那天晚上,她用果汁機調製了白色的蛋彩顏料,然後裝進瓶子,隔天再帶去上班。

閱讀測驗解答:(C)

95

課文朗讀 MP3 106　單字朗讀 MP3 107　英文講解 MP3 108

Whenever Bette made a [5]**typo**, she just painted over it with a small brush and retyped the word. To her surprise, her solution worked so well that her boss never even noticed. Soon, other secretaries at the office began asking her for bottles of her [1]**correction** [2]**fluid**, and she knew she had a good business idea.

In 1956, Bette began selling "Mistake Out" in her free time, mixing the liquid in her kitchen and hiring her son and his friends to bottle it and make deliveries. When Bette was fired from her job—she accidentally typed her company's name instead of the bank's on a letter—she was able to devote her full efforts to her new venture. She improved the formula, changed the name to Liquid Paper, and was soon selling 500 bottles a month.

Bette married Robert Graham in 1967, and the two ran the growing company as a team. By 1975, the year of her second divorce, the Liquid Paper factory was [6]**churning** out 500 bottles a minute! Bette sold her company to Gillette in 1979 for nearly 50 million dollars, but was unable to enjoy her fortune—she died

Vocabulary Bank

1) **correction** [kə`rɛkʃən] (n.) 修改，校正
There are several errors in the report that need correction.
這份報告有好幾處錯誤需要修正。

2) **fluid** [`fluɪd] (n.) 流體，液體
The doctor removed the fluid from the patient's lungs.
醫生把病人肺部的積水給抽出來。

3) **live on** [lɪv ɑn] (phr.) 活下去，繼續存在
The memory of Michael Jackson lives on in the hearts of his fans.
對麥可傑克森的記憶永存在他粉絲心中。

4) **credit (with)** [`krɛdɪt] (v.) 把…歸功於
Thomas Edison is often credited with inventing the light bulb.
湯瑪士愛迪生常被譽為發明燈泡的大功臣。

進階字彙

5) **typo** [`taɪpo] (n.) 打字錯誤（全稱為 typographical error）
The menu at the restaurant was full of typos.
那間餐廳的菜單上打錯了一堆字。

6) **churn out** [tʃɜn aʊt] (phr.) 大量、快速地生產
The author churns out a new novel almost every year.
這位作家幾乎每年都出新書。

just six months later. At least her creative spirit [3)] **lived on** in her son. Michael Nesmith, who became famous in the 1960s as a member of the Monkees, is [4)] **credited** with inventing the music video.

Mini Quiz 閱讀測驗

What was Liquid Paper originally called?
(A) tempera paint
(B) Mistake Out
(C) typo
(D) correction fluid

Translation

每當貝蒂打錯字，她只要用小筆塗掉，再重打那個字就好。令她意外的是，她的解決方法非常有效，老闆始終沒有發現。沒過多久，辦公室其他秘書開始向她要修正液來用，於是她知道自己有了一個不錯的生意點子。

一九五六年，貝蒂開始在閒暇時賣「除錯」產品，在自家廚房調製液體，並雇用兒子和他的朋友裝瓶和運貨。後來貝蒂被公司炒魷魚——她本來要在一封信上打上銀行名稱，卻不小心打成自己公司的名字——因此她反而能全心全意投入她的新事業了。她改進配方，更名為「立可白」，沒多久，一個月內就可以賣到五百瓶了。

貝蒂在一九六七年嫁給羅伯特葛拉罕，兩人合力經營這間持續成長的公司。一九七五年，也就是她第二次離婚的那年，立可白工廠每分鐘就可製造五百瓶！貝蒂在一九七九年以將近五千萬美元的價格把公司賣給吉列集團，但卻無福享用這筆財富——她在六個月後就過世了。不過至少她將她的創意精神傳給了她的兒子。身為頑童合唱團的一員、於一九六○年代聲名大噪的麥可奈史密斯，被公認為音樂錄影帶的發明者。

Language Guide

頑童合唱團與麥克奈斯密

頑童合唱團 (The Monkees) 為一九七○年代紅極一時的男孩團體，走的是英式搖滾風，電視製作人找了四名歌手來演唱流行歌曲及演出電視劇，包括美籍歌手米奇杜列茲 (Micky Dolenz)、彼得托克 (Peter Tork) 和麥可奈斯密 (Michael Nesmith)，以及英國的德維瓊斯 (Davy Jones)。The Monkees 原先只是電視節目中的虛擬樂團，他們飾演一群企圖打敗披頭四 (The Beatles) 卻從未成功的樂團。（beetle 為英文「甲蟲」之意，而 The Monkees 便模仿他們，取用英文的「猴子」monkey 來命名）。該樂團隨後便正式成立為一個實質的團體，由麥可奈斯密擔綱大部分作曲和編曲的工作，並且在一九六七年達到事業巔峰，擊敗披頭四和滾石合唱團 (The Rolling Stones) 等搖滾樂團。他們留下了不少膾炙人口的經典好歌，例如 "Last Train to Clarksville"、後來成為電影《史瑞克》(Shrek) 主題曲的 "I'm a believer"，以及出現在香港電影《歲月神偷》(Echoes of the Rainbow) 中的 "I wanna be free"。雖然該團在成立短短五年後便宣告解散，但直到二○一二年都還有舉辦巡迴演唱會。

其中，麥可奈斯密正是本文介紹立可白發明人的兒子，相較於他的母親，奈斯密反而還比較出名，他在單飛後仍持續從事音樂創作，並且於一九七七年製作出他首支音樂錄影帶 "Rio"，成了 MTV 的創始人。他把母親發明立可白的獲益拿來投資電視節目 Elephant Parts，於一九八一年拿下葛萊美年度錄影帶獎。之後又於一九八七年幫麥可傑克森的單曲 "The Way You Make Me Feel" 製作音樂錄影帶，無論在音樂或電視節目方面都有相當亮眼的成績。

Vocabulary Bank

1) **spectacle** [ˋspɛktəkəl] (n.) 壯觀的場面，奇觀
The New Year's fireworks were quite a spectacle.
那場新年煙火果真壯觀。

2) **competitor** [kəmˋpɛtɪtə] (n.) 參賽者，競爭對手
Over 3,000 competitors participated in the race.
這項競賽有超過三千位參賽者參加。

3) **strive** [straɪv] (v.) 努力，奮鬥
My parents taught me to strive for success.
我的父母教導我要為了成功而奮鬥。

4) **accomplishment** [əˋkɑmplɪʃmənt] (n.) 成就，成績
The discovery of DNA was a major scientific accomplishment.
DNA 的發現是一項重大的科學成就。

5) **wrestling** [ˋrɛslɪŋ] (n.) 摔角運動
(v.) wrestle [ˋrɛsəl] 摔角，角力
Jake was on the wrestling team in high school.
傑克高中時參加學校的摔角隊。

6) **boxing** [ˋbɑksɪŋ] (n.) 拳擊運動
(n.) boxer 拳擊手
Boxing is a dangerous sport.
拳擊是一項危險的運動。

7) **die out** [daɪ aʊt] (phr.) 逐漸消失，絕跡，滅絕
The tribe's traditional culture is dying out.
這個部落的傳統文化正逐漸消失。

8) **ban** [bæn] (v./n.) 禁止，取締
The city is considering banning smoking in restaurants.
該市正考慮禁止在餐廳吸菸。

9) **confidence** [ˋkɑnfɪdəns] (n.) 自信，信心
Consumer confidence is starting to rise.
消費者信心開始上升。

10) **defeat** [dɪˋfit] (n./v.) 擊敗，戰敗
The party suffered a major defeat in the election.
該政黨在這場選舉中大敗。

11) **physical** [ˋfɪzɪkəl] (a.) 身體的，肉體的
Stress can affect your physical and mental health.
壓力會影響你的身心健康。

12) **witness** [ˋwɪtnəs] (v.) 目擊，見證
Dozens of people witnessed the accident.
有幾十個人目睹了那場意外。

13) **revival** [rɪˋvaɪvəl] (n.) 復興，復甦
The city is showing signs of economic revival.
這座城市顯示出經濟復甦的跡象。

14) **resistance** [rɪˋzɪstəns] (n.) 反對，阻力，反抗
The president's proposal ran into resistance in Congress.
總統的提案在國會中面臨到反對聲浪。

15) **persist** [pəˋsɪst] (v.) 堅持，執意
The reporter persisted in questioning the politician.
記者堅持對那名政治人物提出質疑。

Pierre de Coubertin

皮耶古柏坦　現代奧運的推手

Bringing the Olympics into the Modern Age

課文朗讀 MP3 109　單字朗讀 MP3 110　英文講解 MP3 111

Every four years, the world's greatest athletes gather for a two-week-long ¹⁾**spectacle** of sports. Many of them have trained their whole lives just to participate. ᴳWith the world watching, the ²⁾**competitors** ³⁾**strive** to jump higher, run faster, and be stronger than the rest. Simply participating is an ⁴⁾**accomplishment** in itself, but the athletes who succeed will be forever remembered as Olympic champions.

The first Olympic Games were held in ancient Greece almost 3,000 years ago. Held in honor of the Greek god Zeus, they included ⁵⁾**wrestling**, ⁶⁾**boxing** and running events. The tradition ⁷⁾**died out**, however, after Theodosius I ⁸⁾**banned** them in 394 AD as part of his efforts to promote Christianity throughout the Roman Empire.

Fast forward to the late 19th century, when a French noble named Pierre de Coubertin was searching for ways to rebuild his country's strength and ⁹⁾**confidence** following its ¹⁰⁾**defeat** in the Franco-Prussian War. An admirer of the British, he traveled to England in 1890 to observe how they taught ¹¹⁾**physical** education. While visiting the town of Much Wenlock in Shropshire, de Coubertin ¹²⁾**witnessed** a ¹³⁾**revival** of the Olympic Games started by Dr. William Penny Brookes. This led to de Coubertin's eureka moment: he could use the Olympics not only to strengthen French schools but also bring the world together through sports.

At first, his idea was met with [14]**resistance** back in France. But de Coubertin [15]**persisted**, and in 1894 the International Olympic Committee (IOC) was formed. The first modern Olympics were held in Athens two years later, and the sporting tradition has continued ever since.

Mini Quiz 閱讀測驗

When did the Olympic Games begin?
(A) Once every four years
(B) Nearly 3,000 years ago
(C) In 1896
(D) In the late 19th century

中 Translation

每隔四年,世界最頂尖的運動員都會齊聚一堂,進行為期兩週的運動盛會。其中許多選手訓練一輩子就只為了參加奧運。在全世界關注下,選手們無不努力比別人跳得更高、跑得更快、擁有更強壯的體魄。光是參加奧運本身就是莫大的成就,而獲勝的運動員更將以「奧運金牌得主」的身分,永遠被世人記得。

史上第一次奧林匹克運動會大約在三千年前的古希臘舉行。這項為榮耀希臘神明宙斯而辦的盛會包含摔角、拳擊和賽跑等項目。然而,在西元三九四年羅馬皇帝狄奧多西一世為了於帝國全境推廣基督教而停辦奧運之後,這項傳統戛然而止。

時間快轉到十九世紀末,法國一個名叫皮耶古柏坦的貴族,正在想辦法重建國家於普法戰爭失利後的國力與信心。向來崇拜英國人的他,於一八九〇年來到英國觀察當地人怎麼教體育。在造訪施洛普郡的文洛克鎮時,古柏坦目睹威廉潘尼布魯克斯醫師發起的奧運復興運動。這讓古柏坦靈機一動:他不僅能利用奧運讓法國學生身強體壯,還能透過運動將世界團結在一起。

一開始,他的想法在法國遭遇抵制,但古柏坦非常堅持,於是一八九四年,國際奧林匹克委員會(國際奧會)正式成立。兩年後,第一屆現代奧運會於雅典舉行,自那時起,這項運動傳統便一直延續至今。

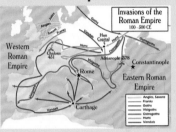
閱讀測驗解答:(B)

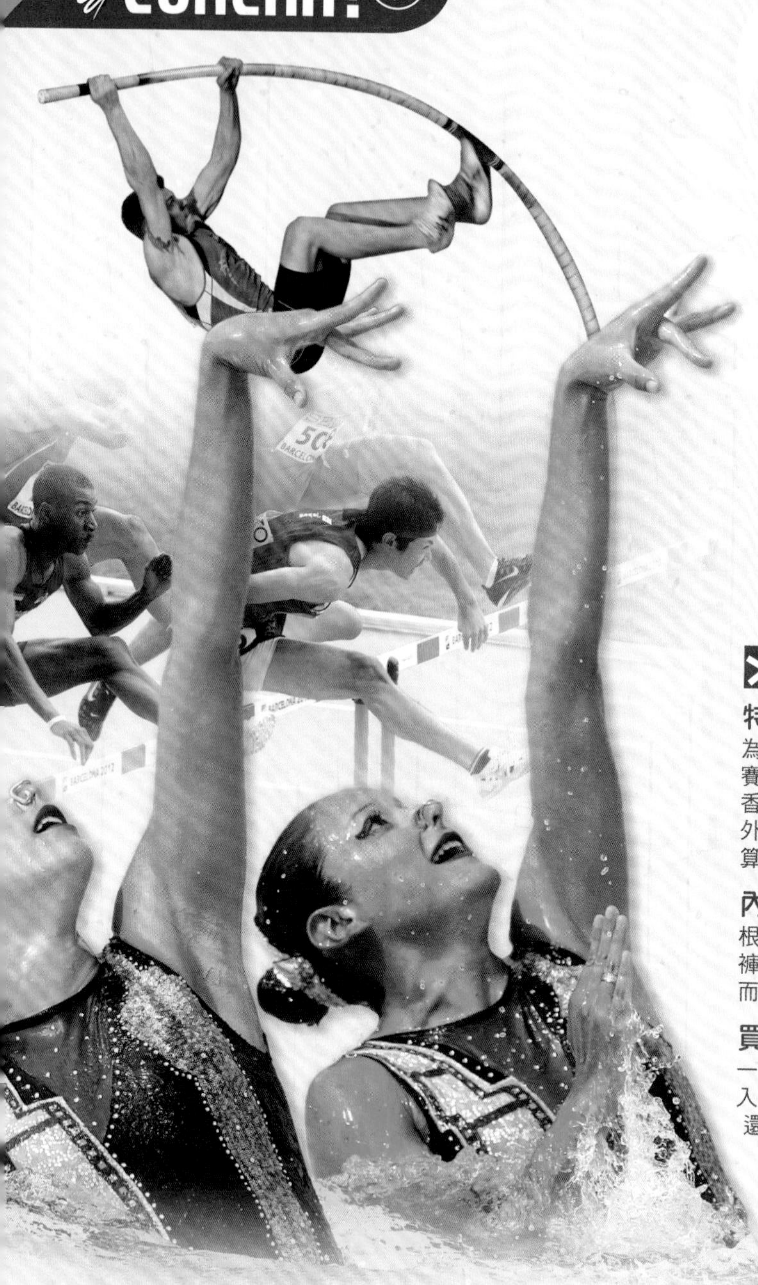

運動界的盛會 奧林匹克運動會

無論你是不是運動狂熱者，相信都曾感受過全民瘋奧運的熱鬧氛圍，四年一度的奧運不但能夠凝聚國人的向心力，同時也是各國展現和平友愛的好時機，更別提它帶來的龐大商機了。除了運動員在場上展現出的力與美，其文化意涵以及賽程中的小插曲也成為大家津津樂道的話題。

好玩的插曲

特殊的獎勵

為了獎勵自己國家的運動員，白俄羅斯 (Belarus) 一家肉品公司提供給參賽的奧運選手，無論他們有沒有獲得獎牌，都可以終身免費享用該公司的香腸。蒙古奧運柔道 (judo) 選手布辛巴亞爾除了獲得蒙古政府的高額獎金外，另外當地的電信公司還另外提供 9999-9999 這串電話號碼，這在當地算是相當吉祥的數字。

內褲顏色不對也要罰？

根據奧運草地曲棍球 (field hockey) 比賽規定，球員上場時所穿的運動短褲和內褲的顏色必須一致。而某次，有三名紐西蘭選手因不符合這項規定而受罰，而他們的球隊教練也只能在看台上觀看與德國隊的晉級關鍵賽。

買票入場

一九五六年洛杉磯的奧運會初賽中，美國跳高選手因為通行證不見而無法入場，只好自己買了一張門票進場，最後不但順利打進奧運，奪得冠軍，還打破了世界紀錄。

尷尬的一刻

一九七六年蒙特婁奧運中，當美國摔角選手在量體重時，指示燈因為他的體重超標而亮起，他趕快脫去背心、扔掉太陽鏡…直到吐掉了嘴裏的口香糖後，體重計上的指示燈才熄滅。

發燒吉祥物

造型有趣的吉祥物 (mascot) 在奧運中扮演相當重要的角色，提升整個奧運熱潮，周邊商品更是帶來龐大的商機，營造良好的活動氣氛。這些吉祥物通常是當地特有、具有文化代表性的動物，快來看看曾經出現過哪些吉祥物吧！

1

第一個正式的吉祥物出現在一九七二年慕尼黑 (Munich) 的夏季奧運，一隻名為 Waldi 的臘腸狗 (dachshund)，牠身上的顏色就是當時慕尼黑奧運的主色，傳達出運動員不可或缺的幾個要素：耐力 (endurance)、堅忍 (tenacity) 和靈活 (agility)，造型相當可愛。

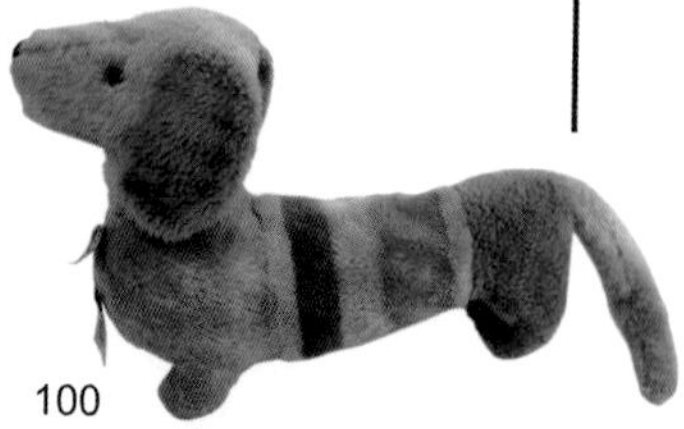

2

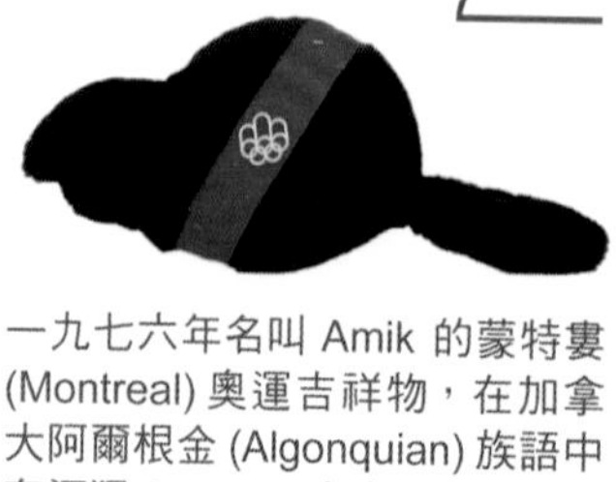

一九七六年名叫 Amik 的蒙特婁 (Montreal) 奧運吉祥物，在加拿大阿爾根金 (Algonquian) 族語中有河狸 (beaver) 之意。勤奮努力是這種動物的特性，身上的紅色腰帶則代表獎牌上的緞帶，同時也象徵參賽國的友好情誼。

3

一九八八的首爾 (Seoul) 奧運選用頗具東方色彩的老虎作為吉祥物，取名為 Hodori，牠頭上戴著韓國傳統農民的帽子，帽子上纏繞成 S 形的彩帶即為 Seoul（首爾）的字首。

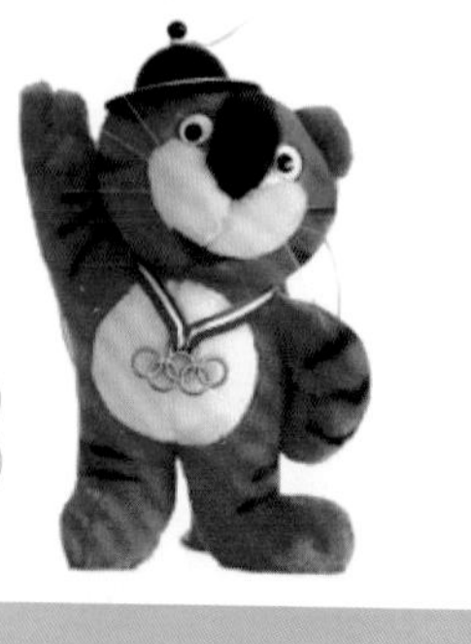

4

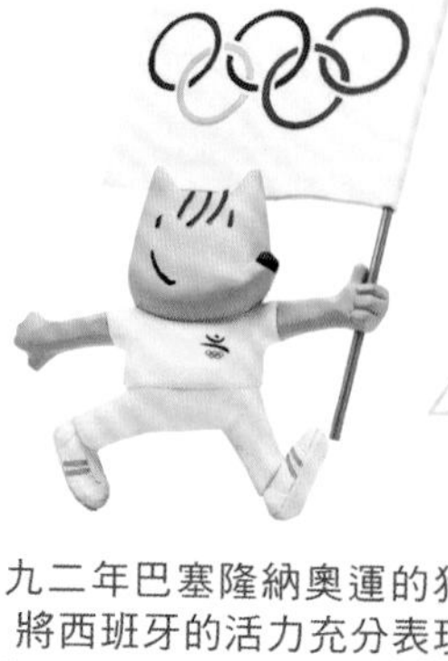

一九九二年巴塞隆納奧運的狗狗 Cobi 將西班牙的活力充分表現出來，為了炒熱氣氛和製造話題，甚至還有電視台以牠為主角製作連續劇呢！

☒ 搞怪的奧運比賽項目

奧運雖是正式比賽，但也出現過許多令人匪夷所思的比賽項目，這些比賽現在都已停辦，不過回憶起來還是相當有趣。

熱氣球比賽 (hot air ballooning)

出現於一九〇〇年的巴黎奧運，比的是看誰的熱氣球飛最遠、在空中停留最久，且能在指定的地點著陸。

爬繩比賽 (rope climbing)

舉辦於一八九六到一九三二年間，為夏季奧運會體操項目的子項目之一，評判的標準包括姿勢、速度以及選手是否能夠爬到繩索的頂端（高度約十三米）。

鴿子射擊比賽 (live pigeon shooting)

這項比賽同樣也出現在一九〇〇年的巴黎奧運上。比賽規則非常直接，就是放出一大堆鴿子，在規定時間內射殺最多鴿子的人即為贏家，射擊失誤達兩次者即被淘汰。

單人花式游泳 (solo synchronized swimming)

這項比賽出現於一九八四到一九九二年間，有別於其他水上項目，單人花式游泳並不強調快速和敏捷，而是著重在節奏感上，也就是與音樂的協調一致性。

☒ 奧運的亮點——聖火 (Olympic Flame)

在古希臘神話中，火是神聖不可侵犯的，因此古奧運的點火儀式其實是為了紀念宙斯而舉辦，宗教意味濃厚，且火炬在比賽過程中也必須保持不滅。一九二八年現代奧運便重現這段神話，同時也象徵著奧運比賽的精髓——光明、團結和勇敢。

聖火傳遞 (torch relay) 的儀式最早則出現在一九三六年起的柏林 (Berlin) 奧運會，爾後每屆奧運的主辦國無不極力在點燃方式和傳遞路線上煞費苦心，例如一九九二年巴賽隆納 (Barcelona) 的射箭點火、兩千年雪梨 (Sydney) 奧運的水池點火以及二〇〇八年北京 (Beijing) 的飛人點火等，都是點火儀式創意的展現。

在開幕典禮數月前，奧運聖火會先從希臘奧運發源地奧林匹亞 (Olympia) 利用凹面鏡 (parabolic mirror) 匯集陽光而取得，接下來便透過接力 (relay) 的方式傳到下一屆奧運主辦城市。

聖火傳遞者 (torchbearer) 來自不同領域，可能是運動員或名人，傳遞的動作在奧運開幕式 (opening ceremony) 舉行時劃下句點，由最後一位傳遞者點燃聖火，一直到奧運比賽結束的那天才熄滅。

☒ 奧運主辦國是怎麼選出來的？

奧運主辦國 (host country) 通常會在該屆奧運舉辦的前七年就選出，想要主辦的國家可自行向國際奧委會 (IOC) 提出申請，申辦的整個過程大約要兩年。國際奧委會會針對住宿 (accommodations)、環境、場地等方面進行審查，初步評估通過的城市為申請城市 (applicant city)，之後過關的就正式成為候選城市 (candidate city)，最後一關則是國際奧委會的委員以不記名投票 (secret ballot) 方式進行多輪投票，得票超過半數以上的即為主辦城市。根據統計，目前主辦奧運次數最多的城市，前三名依序為倫敦、雅典 (Athens) 和洛杉磯。

兩千年雪梨奧運的吉祥物是以澳洲特有的三種動物做代表，分別是鴨嘴獸 (duck-billed platypus)、笑翠鳥 (kookaburra)，以及頻臨絕種的針鼴 (spiny anteater)，分別取名為 Syd、Olly 和 Millie，為「雪梨」、「奧林匹克」及「千禧年 (millennium)」的字首來作為吉祥物的名字。

5

6

二〇〇八年北京奧運的吉祥物福娃 (Fuwa)，融入了魚、熊貓、藏羚羊 (Tibetan antelope)、燕子以及奧林匹克聖火的元素來造型，名字分別是貝貝、晶晶、歡歡、迎迎、妮妮，合起來就是「北京歡迎你」的諧音。

二〇一二年倫敦奧運及殘障奧運 (Paralympics) 的 Wenlock 和 Mandeville，前者得名於奧運靈感發源地 Much Wenlock，後者則得名於殘障奧運的促成者 Stock Mandeville，運用的元素是鋼筋和攝影機。

7

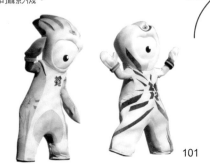

The Birth of Basketball
籃球的誕生

V Vocabulary Bank

1) **chore** [tʃor] (n.) 家事，例行工作
My parents give me an allowance if I do all my chores.
如果我做好所有分內的家事，我爸媽就會給我零用錢。

2) **involve** [ɪn`vɑlv] (v.) 需要，包含
Does the job involve a lot of overtime?
這份工作需要常加班嗎？

3) **combine** [kəm`baɪn] (v.) 結合，聯合
Many factors combined to cause the economic recession.
經濟蕭條是許多因素共同造成的。

4) **position** [pə`zɪʃən] (n.) 職位，工作
Denise applied for a position at the bank.
丹妮絲應徵那間銀行的職位。

5) **minimize** [`mɪnə,maɪz] (v.) 減至最小
Wearing a seat belt minimizes the risk of injury.
繫安全帶能將受傷的風險降至最低。

6) **out of reach** [aut əv ritʃ] (phr.) 拿不到，無法取得
If you don't put the cookies out of reach, the kids will eat them all.
如果你不把餅乾放在拿不到的地方，孩子們會把它們全都吃了。

進階字彙

7) **typhoid** [`taɪfɔɪd] (n.) 傷寒，亦作 typhoid fever
Bill caught typhoid after eating at a night market.
比爾在夜市吃東西後染上了風寒。

課文朗讀 MP3 112　單字朗讀 MP3 113　英文講解 MP3 114

　　Born in a small town in Ontario, Canada in 1861, James A. Naismith lost his parents to [7]**typhoid** when he was nine years old. He went to live on an uncle's farm, where he helped with [1]**chores** and spent his free time playing with a group of local boys. They enjoyed all kinds of sports, but their favorite game was "duck on the rock," which [2]**involved** trying to knock a stone off of a tall rock by throwing smaller stones up at it.

　　Naismith's interest in sports continued during his studies at McGill University, where he played on the football, rugby and soccer teams and earned a B.A. in physical education. After next earning a master's in religion at Presbyterian College, he [3]**combined** his two areas of study by accepting a [4]**position** as a P.E. teacher at the YMCA Training School in Massachusetts. In 1891, the department head asked Naismith to come up with a safe indoor game to keep students busy during the cold winter months between football and baseball seasons.

　　Thinking about popular games like football, soccer and baseball, Naismith decided to make his new game safe by using a soft soccer ball and requiring players to pass it instead of running with it to [5)]**minimize** physical contact. While considering how to reduce contact around the goal, he suddenly remembered the "duck on the rock" game he'd played as a child. This was his eureka moment: why not place the goals [6)]**out of reach** above the players' heads? And so Naismith hung a peach basket at both ends of the gym and invited his students to play his new game, which he called "basket ball." Later shortened to one word, basketball is now one of the most popular sports in the world.

Mini Quiz 閱讀測驗

Why did Naismith decide to place the goals above the players' heads?
(A) So they could play "duck on the rock"
(B) To reduce physical contact
(C) To make scoring more difficult
(D) Because players couldn't run with the ball

中 Translation

一八六一年生於加拿大安大略省一個小鎮的詹姆斯奈史密斯，九歲時父母因傷寒過世。他前往一個叔叔的農場居住，協助料理雜務，閒暇時則和當地一群男孩嬉戲。他們喜歡各式各樣的運動，但他們最喜歡的遊戲是「擊落石頭」。玩法是以岩石高處上的一塊石頭為目標，試著投擲較小的石頭將之擊落。

就讀麥克基爾大學期間，奈史密斯仍維持著對運動的興趣，他在學校踢美式足球、橄欖球和足球校隊，並獲得體育學學士。接下來，在長老會學院拿到宗教學碩士之後，他結合了他的兩個研究領域，接受麻薩諸塞州基督教青年會提供的體育老師教職。一八九一年，部門主管請奈史密斯設計一種安全的室內遊戲，讓學生在美式足球季及棒球季之間數個寒冬月份有事可忙。

思考了美式足球、足球和棒球等受歡迎的運動，奈史密斯決定讓他的新遊戲安全無虞：採用質地軟的足球，並要求選手傳球、不可帶球跑，以將肢體接觸減到最少。在思考如何減少球門附近的肢體接觸時，他忽然想起小時候玩過的「擊落石頭」遊戲，這就是他靈機一動的時刻：何不把球門設在選手構不著的頭上呢？於是奈史密斯在體育館兩端掛上裝桃子的籃子，然後邀請學生玩他取名為「籃球」(basket ball)的新遊戲。後來縮短為一個字之後，籃球現在是世界最受歡迎的運動之一。

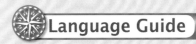
美國第一大籃球賽事：NBA 美國職籃

NBA 的全文是 National Basketball Association（國家籃球協會），一般翻譯直接稱NBA、美國職籃或 NBA 籃球聯賽。協會一共擁有三十支球隊，分屬東區聯盟 (Eastern Conference) 和西區聯盟 (Western Conference)，而每個聯盟各由三個分區 (division) 組成，每個分區有五支球隊。三十支球隊當中有一支來自加拿大，其餘都位於美國本土。

NBA 正式賽季於每年十一月開打，分為 regular season（常規賽）和 playoffs（季後賽）。包括各分區冠軍在內，每個聯盟的前八名，即可進入季後賽。季後賽採用七戰四勝制，共分四輪；季後賽的最後一輪也稱為 NBA Finals「總決賽」，由兩個聯盟冠軍爭奪 NBA 總冠軍。

籃球場位置

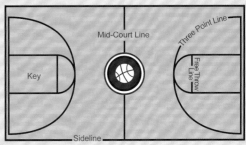

- Mid-Court Line 中線
- Sideline 邊線
- Three Point Line 三分線
- Free Throw Line 罰球線
- Key 禁區

籃球員位置

- Center (C) 中鋒
- Point Guard (PG) 控球後衛
- Power Forward (PF) 大前鋒
- Shooting Guard (SG) 得分後衛
- Small Forward (SF) 小前鋒

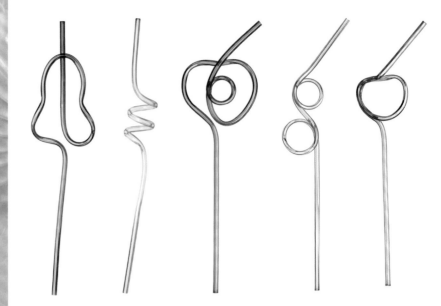

Vocabulary Bank

1) **attach** [ə`tætʃ] (v.) 裝上，貼上
Remember to attach a photo to your application.
記得在你的申請表附上照片。

2) **real estate** [`riəl ɪ`stet] (n.) 房地產，不動產
The real estate agent showed us several properties.
房屋仲介帶我們看了幾間房子。

3) **parlor** [`pɑrlə] (n.)（用來構成複合詞）店、館
Our family runs a funeral parlor.
我們家是經營葬儀社的。

4) **amusement** [ə`mjuzmənt] (n.) 娛樂（活動），遊樂，趣味
We took the kids to the amusement park last weekend.
我們上星期帶孩子去遊樂園玩。

5) **insert** [ɪn`sɜt] (v.) 插入，投入
Please insert the correct change into the slot.
請將正確的幣值投入投幣孔中。

6) **dental floss** [`dɛntəl flɔs] (n.) 牙線
You should use dental floss at least once a day.
你每天至少該用一次牙線。

7) **cut off** [kʌt ɔf] (phr.) 切斷，中斷
The phone company cut off my phone service because I didn't pay the bill.
電信公司把我的電話停話，因為我沒繳帳單。

8) **establish** [ɪ`stæblɪʃ] (v.) 創辦，建立
The university was established in 1926.
這所大學於一九二六年創立。

9) **corporation** [.kɔrpə`reʃən] (n.) 股份（有限）公司，企業
Karen plans to work for a large corporation after she graduates.
凱倫打算在畢業後到大企業上班。

進階字彙

10) **knack** [næk] (n.) 本領；訣竅
Daniel has a knack for finding simple solutions to complicated problems.
丹尼爾有本事可以找出複雜問題的簡單解決方法。

11) **gauge** [gedʒ] (n.) 測量儀器，錶，計
I bought a bicycle pump with a pressure gauge.
我買了一個附有氣壓計的腳踏車打氣筒。

12) **broker** [`brokə] (n.) 經紀人，中間人
My broker said I should buy Apple stock.
我的股票經紀人說我應該買蘋果公司的股票。

13) **groove** [gruv] (n.) 溝，槽，紋道
The window slides along a groove in the frame.
那扇窗可沿著溝槽來開關。

Joseph Friedman
An Inventor with a Flexible Mind
約瑟夫弗里曼 頭腦會「轉彎」的發明家

課文朗讀 MP3 115　單字朗讀 MP3 116　英文講解 MP3 117

Born in Cleveland, Ohio in 1900, Joseph Friedman showed an early 10)**knack** for inventing. At the age of 14, Friedman invented the "pencilite"—a pencil with a light 1)**attached** for writing in the dark. Although he didn't have the money to apply for a patent at the time, he did receive a patent for an ink 11)**gauge** for fountain pens in 1922, which he later sold to the Sheaffer Pen Company in the 1930s.

By this time, Friedman had moved to California and started a family. He found a job as a 2)**real estate** 12)**broker** to support his wife and children, but continued his inventing career on the side. One day, Friedman was sitting at an ice cream 3)**parlor** in San Francisco watching his young daughter Judith trying to drink a milkshake with a straw. Too short to reach the top of the straw, she bent it down to reach her mouth. But this caused the straw to fold in half, blocking the flow of milkshake.

While this scene would have been a source of 4)**amusement** for most people, for Friedman it was a eureka moment. Pondering the problem of how to make a straw bend without folding, he quickly came up with a solution. Friedman [5]**inserted** a screw into a paper straw and then wound [6]**dental floss** around the screw's threads, creating [13]**grooves** in the paper. After removing the screw, he found that the grooves had formed a flexible "elbow" that could be bent without [7]**cutting off** the flow of liquid.

Friedman [8]**established** the Flexible Straw Company in 1939, but wasn't able to start production until after WWII. First sold to hospitals—where they allowed patients to drink lying down—his flexible straws became increasingly popular in the 1950s. Maryland Cup [9]**Corporation**, which bought the rights to the straws, now sells 500 million a year!

Mini Quiz 閱讀測驗

Which of the following is true about Joseph Friedman?
(A) He invented a pen that can write in the dark.
(B) He had his eureka moment while drinking a milkshake.
(C) He showed a talent for inventing as a child.
(D) He started the Flexible Straw Company after WWII.

中 Translation

一九〇〇年出生在俄亥俄州克里夫蘭市的約瑟夫弗里德曼，很早就展現發明的本領。十四歲時，弗里曼就發明了「亮鉛筆」——附了燈、可以在黑暗中書寫的鉛筆。雖然當時他沒有錢申請專利，但一九二二年，他就獲得一項鋼筆墨水刻度計的專利，後於一九三〇年代賣給西華鋼筆公司。

在這個時候，弗里曼已遷居加州，並建立家庭。他找了房屋仲介的工作扶養妻小，一邊繼續發明的志業。一天，弗里曼坐在舊金山一家冰淇淋店看著小女兒茱蒂絲試著用吸管喝奶昔。她因為個子太矮，碰不到吸管的頂端，只好把吸管彎下來放進嘴巴。但此舉造成吸管折成兩截，阻礙了奶昔的流動。

雖然這個畫面可能會讓多數人莞爾一笑，對弗里曼來說，它卻是靈機一動的片刻。他思考著如何讓吸管彎曲又不會折到的問題，結果很快就想出了辦法。弗里曼把一根螺絲釘塞進紙吸管，然後用牙線纏繞螺紋，在紙上壓出溝槽。移除螺絲釘後，他發現溝槽已經形成可彎曲的「手肘」，彎曲後不會阻礙液體流動。

弗里曼在一九三九年創辦彎吸管公司，但直到二次世界大戰結束才開始生產。先賣到醫院，讓病患得以躺著喝東西——他的產品在一九五〇年代愈來愈受歡迎。買斷彎吸管權利的馬里蘭杯子公司，現在每年會賣出五億支！

鋼筆為什麼稱作 fountain pen?

鋼筆最初是以沾墨的方式書寫，只是這樣容易漏墨且弄髒文件，因此後來便發展出蓄墨鋼筆。蓄墨鋼筆是運用毛細管作用(capillary action)的原理，讓筆桿裡的儲墨裝置可吸滿墨水，再利用重力(gravity)將裡頭的墨水送出，由於墨水就像是水流的源頭一般，不斷流入筆頭，因而被稱作 fountain pen。填充墨水的方式有很多種，例如用滴管補充的滴墨式或是直接更換墨水匣等，都很常見。如今，鋼筆甚至成為身分的象徵，有些品質優良的鋼筆，價格可不太平易近人呢！

吸管成長史

吸管的英文 straw 也有「稻草」的意思，可想而知，一開始的吸管其實用稻草做的，只是稻草製的吸管禁不起液體長時間停留，常變得軟爛(soggy)且容易積垢，之後便開始用其他材料來製作，像是玻璃或紙張等。現今的吸管則大多為塑膠製，由於近來環保意識高漲，這些用過即丟的拋棄式(disposable)塑膠吸管，被認為不適當，因此掀起了一股使用玻璃吸管的復古風潮。

說到吸管，你就一定要知道 crazy straw，不過什麼是 crazy straw 呢？讓 EZ TALK 來為你解答。crazy straw 得名於吸管品牌名稱——Krazy Straw，起初 crazy straw 是以透明塑膠做成，在吸管的嘴頭上會有好幾個彎，飲料會依照吸管的形狀流過，讓喝飲料的過程中多了許多的樂趣。如今，市面上還出現了各式各樣的造型吸管，如眼鏡造型的瘋狂吸管等。

© steakpinball/flickr.com

閱讀測驗解答：(C)

V Vocabulary Bank

1) **currency** [ˋkɝənsi] (n.) 貨幣，錢
What currency should I take with me on my trip?
我去旅行應該帶什麼錢比較好？

2) **senior** [ˋsinjɚ] (a.) 資深的，地位較高的
Robert was recently promoted to senior vice president.
羅伯特最近被晉升為資深副總裁。

3) **drop by** [drɑp baɪ] (phr.) 順道去拜訪
Feel free to drop by any time for a cup of coffee.
沒事儘管來找我喝杯咖啡。

4) **cash** [kæʃ] (v.) 把（支票、匯票等）兌現
Where can I get this check cashed?
哪裡可以辦理支票兌現？

5) **annoy** [əˋnɔɪ] (n.) 惹惱，令人討厭
Rude behavior really annoys me.
失禮的行為真的很令我討厭。

6) **inconvenience** [͵ɪnkənˋvinjəns] (n.) 不便，麻煩
The security checks at the airport are a real inconvenience.
機場的安檢真的很麻煩。

7) **withdraw** [wɪðˋdrɔ] (v.) 提取，提領
(n.) withdrawal [wɪðˋdrɔəl]
How much money did you withdraw from your account?
你從戶頭領了多少錢？

8) **ponder** [ˋpɑndɚ] (v.) 思索，仔細考慮，衡量
Do you ever ponder the meaning of life?
你有仔細思索過人生的意義嗎？

9) **vending machine** [vɛndɪŋ məˋʃin] (phr.) 自動販賣機
I think the vending machine is out of order.
這台自動販賣機好像故障了。

10) **around the clock** [əˋraʊnd ðə klɑk] (phr.) 一天二十四小時，日以繼夜
That convenience store is open around the clock.
那間便利商店二十四小時不打烊。

進階字彙

11) **airborne** [ˋɛr͵born] (a.) （軍方）空降的，空運的
The soldier was injured during an airborne training exercise.
這位士兵在進行空降訓練時受傷了。

12) **trainee** [treˋni] (n.) 受訓者，練習生
Our company hires several sales trainees each year.
我們公司每年都會招募幾個業務實習生進來。

The ATM
Making
Cash
Convenient

提款機
讓領錢更方便

課文朗讀 MP3 118　單字朗讀 MP3 119　英文講解 MP3 120

John Shepherd-Barron was born in India on June 23, 1925 to Scottish parents. His father Wilfred was an engineer, and his mother Dorothy was an Olympic tennis player and Wimbledon champion. After completing his education at Edinburgh University and Cambridge, John served as an [11]**airborne** officer in the Second World War.

In 1950, John joined De La Rue, a company that prints and provides paper for many of the world's [1]**currencies**. Starting out as a management [12]**trainee**, he moved quickly up the ranks. John established the company's North American operations in the late 1950s, and then returned to England to take up a [2]**senior** management position.

John had the habit of [3]**dropping by** the bank each Saturday to [4]**cash** checks. But one day he was **1 running late**, and arrived at the bank one minute after closing time. He realized that he would be without cash for the weekend, and was [5]**annoyed** at the [6]**inconvenience**. "It's my money," he thought to himself. "Why can't I [7]**withdraw** it whenever I want?"

Like Archimedes before him, John has his eureka moment while taking a bath. Sitting in the tub that evening, he continued to [8]**ponder** the problem. He thought of the chocolate [9]**vending** machines that were common on the platforms at British train stations, and that's when the answer came to him. If there were machines that provided chocolate bars [10]**around** the clock, why couldn't someone invent a similar machine to provide money?

Mini Quiz 閱讀測驗

Why did John go to the bank each Saturday?
(A) To deposit cash
(B) To get money
(C) To pick up checks
(D) To write checks

中 Translation

約翰薛佛巴倫在一九二五年六月二十三日誕生於印度，雙親都是蘇格蘭人。父親威弗烈是工程師，母親桃樂西是奧運網球選手，還拿過溫布頓冠軍。在愛丁堡大學和劍橋完成學業後，約翰便入伍服役，擔任第二次世界大戰的空降官。

一九五〇年，約翰加入替許多國家印刷貨幣及提供用紙的德拉魯公司。他一開始只是儲備幹部，後來便扶搖直上。約翰在一九五〇年代晚期為公司設立北美分公司，然後回到英國擔任高級主管。

約翰有每星期六到銀行兌現支票的習慣。不過，有一天他來不及了，人到銀行時已經過了打烊時間一分鐘。他知道自己那個周末將沒有現金可用，這種不便讓他又氣又惱。「那是我的錢，」他心想。「我為什麼不能隨心所欲的想領就領？」

一如古代的阿基米德，約翰也在洗澡時靈機一動。那一晚，他坐在浴缸裡，繼續思忖這個問題。他想到英國火車站月台上常見的巧克力自動販賣機，於是解答就此誕生。如果有機器夜以繼日的供應巧克力，為什麼沒有人能發明類似的機器讓人領錢呢？

107

EUREKA! 點子成金

V Vocabulary Bank

1) **slot** [slɑt] (n.)（投幣、投信等）狹長口
Which slot is for local mail?
本地郵件要投哪一個孔？

2) **on hand** [ɑn hænd] (phr.) 出席的，在場的，在手邊的
The director will be on hand to answer questions after the film.
導演會在電影結束後現場回答問題。

3) **maximum** [ˋmæksəməm] (a./n) 最大的，對多的；最大量、數等
The maximum sentence for murder is life in prison.
殺人罪的最重刑責是無期徒刑。

4) **code** [kod] (v./n.) 編碼；代號，代碼，密碼
Each product is coded before leaving the factory.
每項產品在送離工廠前都會被編碼。

5) **mildly** [ˋmaɪldli] (adv.) 略微地，適度地
(a.) mild 輕微的，溫和的
I was mildly surprised that our team lost the game.
我們球隊輸掉這場比賽讓我有點意外。

6) **identification** [aɪˏdɛntəfəˋkeʃən] (n.)
身分證明
To open an account, two forms of identification are required.
開戶需準備兩份身份證明。

7) **globe** [glob] (n.) 地球，地球儀，球體
Who was the first pilot to circle the globe?
誰是第一位環繞地球的飛行員？

進階字彙

8) **pitch** [pɪtʃ] (v.) 口頭推銷（生意點子）
The director pitched his movie idea to the producer.
導演向製片推銷拍攝電影的新點子。

9) **sitcom** [ˋsɪtˏkɑm] (n.)（電視）情境喜劇，為 situation comedy 的簡稱
Friends is my favorite sitcom.
《六人行》是我最喜歡的情境喜劇。

10) **radioactive** [ˏredioˋæktɪv] (a.) 放射性的
Nuclear waste remains radioactive for thousands of years.
核廢料在數千年後還是具有放射性。

課文朗讀 MP3 121　單字朗讀 MP3 122　英文講解 MP3 123

When John met a Barclays Bank executive at a party later that year, he asked for 90 seconds to [8)]**pitch** his cash machine idea. He described how a customer would be able to put a Barclays check in a [1)]**slot** on the side of the bank at any time of the day or night, and then receive cash in return. "If you can build a machine like that," said the impressed executive, "I'll buy it."

Barclays ordered six of John's cash machines, which he called ATMs, or automated teller machines. The first ATM was installed at a Barclays branch in the north London suburb of Enfield on June 27, 1967. To promote the event, actor Reg Varney, the star of a popular British [9)]**sitcom**, was [2)]**on hand** to make the first cash withdrawal.

Using John's machine, bank customers were able to withdraw a [3)]**maximum** of 10 pounds, an amount he considered "quite enough for a wild weekend." After placing a special check [4)]**coded** with [5)]**mildly** [10)]**radioactive** carbon 14 in one drawer and entering a four-digit PIN, or personal [6)]**identification** number, the customers received cash from another drawer. When asked about health concerns, John stated that you would have to eat 136,000 such checks for it to have any negative effect on you.

Barclays Bank
© Kake Pugh/flickr.com

John's ATM was an immediate success, and before long competitors in England and other countries were producing similar machines. Today, there are nearly two million ATMs—which now use plastic cards instead of radioactive checks—around the [7]**globe**. In 2005, John was awarded the Order of the British Empire for his services to the banking industry.

Mini Quiz 閱讀測驗

How did customers prove their identity when using John's ATM?
(A) With a PIN
(B) With a check
(C) With a radioactive code
(D) With a fingerprint

中 Translation

同年稍晚，當約翰在一場晚宴上遇到巴克萊銀行的高級主管，他爭取到九十秒鐘來竭力推銷他的提款機概念。他形容客戶如何可以不分晝夜、在任何時間把巴克萊的支票塞進銀行旁邊的狹縫，然後立刻拿到現金。「如果你能造出這樣的機器，」心動的主管說：「我就跟你買。」

巴克萊跟約翰訂了六部領鈔機。約翰稱它作 ATM，即「自動櫃員機」。第一部 ATM 於一九六七年六月二十七日安裝在倫敦北部郊區恩菲德的巴克萊分行。為了替這個創舉打廣告，他們邀請備受歡迎的英國情境喜劇明星雷格法尼到場，成為第一個用 ATM 領取現金的人。

使用約翰的機器，銀行客戶最多可以提領十鎊，他認為這金額「足以度個瘋狂的週末。」客戶只要將附有輕微放射線碳十四的特製支票置入抽屜，輸入四位數 PIN，即「個人身份識別碼」，就能從另一個抽屜拿到現金。被問及健康顧慮時，約翰指出，你要吃下十三萬六千張這樣的支票，才會對你產生負面影響。

約翰的 ATM 立刻大獲成功，不久，英國和其他國家的競爭對手紛紛製造類似的機器。如今全球將有近兩百萬部 ATM ——現在是用塑膠卡片取代具有放射性的支票。二〇〇五年，約翰因為他對銀行業的貢獻而獲頒大英帝國勳章。

Language Guide

ATM 提款機

提款機的出現使得銀行邁向另一個新時代，就算銀行沒有營業、沒有任何行員(bank teller)可以協助辦理，只要找到提款機，許多問題都能迎刃而解。提款機會藉由卡片上的磁條(magnetic strip)或晶片(IC chip)辨認身分，輸入正確的密碼(PIN)後，就能使用領錢(withdraw)、存款(deposit)、轉帳(transfer)及確認帳戶餘額(balance inquiry)等基本功能。而且現在銀行的網絡系統非常發達，就算提款機的所屬銀行和你的存款銀行不同，也不會影響你使用基本的功能，只要負擔一些手續費(fee)即可，辦理成功之後，還能將明細(receipt)列印出來，非常方便。

carbon 14 碳十四

碳十四是碳元素具放射性的同位素(isotope)，由加州大學柏克萊分校放射性實驗室(UC Berkeley Radiation Laboratory)的馬丁卡門(Martin Kamen)和薩姆魯本(Sam Ruben)發現，也可稱作 radiocarbon。其實所有的有機物(organic matter)皆含有碳十四，而它在有機材料中的濃度衰退時間長達五千七百三十年之久，因此只要研究出歷史古蹟、生物化石(fossil)或地質樣本的碳十四，就可以確認其大致的年代，稱為「放射性碳定年法」(radiocarbon dating)，對於考古學(archeology)的發展有極大的助益。

Vocabulary Bank

1) **economics** [ˌɛkəˈnɑmɪks] (n.) 經濟學
William wants to pursue a major in economics.
威廉想要主修經濟學。

2) **team up** [tim ʌp] (phr.) 與…合作，組成團隊
The two companies teamed up to develop a new video game.
這兩家公司合作開發一款新的電玩遊戲。

3) **sole** [sol] (a.) 唯一的，專屬的
The sole survivor of the accident was taken to the hospital.
這起意外唯一的生還者被送往醫院。

4) **staple** [ˈstepəl] (n.) 主食，必需品
Rice is a staple in many Asian countries.
米飯是許多亞洲國家的主食。

5) **bulk** [bʌlk] (n./a.) 未分裝、秤重的（商品），大量（的）
Do you sell almonds in bulk?
你們這裡有賣未分裝的杏仁果嗎？

6) **container** [kənˈtenə] (n.) 容器
You can put your lunch in this container.
你可以把你的午餐放進這個容器裡。

7) **fragile** [ˈfrædʒəl] (a.) 脆弱的，虛弱的
Be careful with that glass bowl—it's very fragile.
小心這個玻璃碗，它很容易破。

8) **carton** [ˈkɑrtən] (n.) 紙盒，紙箱
How much does a carton of eggs cost?
一盒雞蛋要多少錢？

9) **rectangular** [rɛkˈtæŋjələ] (a.) 長方形的，矩形的
The watch has a rectangular face.
那隻錶的表面是長方形的。

進階字彙

10) **perishable** [ˈpɛrɪʃəbəl] (a.) 易腐爛的，易腐敗的
Perishable food should be stored in a refrigerator.
易腐敗的食物應該放冰箱。

11) **refrigeration** [rɪˌfrɪdʒəˈreʃən] (n.) 冷藏（技術）
(v.) refrigerate
How did people keep food cold before refrigeration was invented?
在發明冷藏技術以前食物是怎麼保冷的？

Tetra 利樂包
Leader of the Pack
包裝的領導者

課文朗讀 MP3 124　　單字朗讀 MP3 125　　英文講解 MP3 126

While studying [1]**economics** at Colombia University in the early 1920s, a young Swede named Ruben Rausing was impressed by America's self-service grocery stores, and especially the individual packages that food was sold in. Guessing that there would soon be a demand for convenient packaged food in Europe, on returning to Sweden he [2]**teamed up** with businessman Erik Åkerlund to found Åkerlund & Rausing, the first packaging company in Scandinavia. The company failed to break even in its first few years, however, and in 1933 Åkerlund sold his interest to Rausing, who became the [3]**sole** owner.

At first, Åkerlund & Rausing produced packaging for dry [4]**staples** like flour and sugar, which were originally sold in [5]**bulk** at that time. Then, in the late '30s, Rausing began thinking about a more challenging problem: how to create better [6]**containers** for [10]**perishable** liquids like milk, which usually came in heavy, [7]**fragile** glass bottles. Over the next several years, the company began developing light, durable paper [8]**cartons** that were easy to transport, but Rausing's eureka moment didn't come until 1943.

Rausing was sitting in the kitchen watching his wife stuff sausages one day, and he thought, "Why not package milk in a similar manner?" By filling a paper tube with milk and then dividing it into cartons, the milk could be kept

©Tetra Pak/flickr.com

from coming into contact with air or germs, allowing it to be stored without [11]**refrigeration**. After nearly a decade of R&D, Rausing started a new company, Tetra Pak—named after the tetrahedron shape of his cartons. These cartons were first used to package cream from a local dairy in 1952. The Tetra Brik—a [9]**rectangular** carton more convenient for storing and shipping—was introduced in 1963. Today, 85 billion Tetra Pak cartons are produced each year.

Mini Quiz 閱讀測驗

Which of the following is true about Descartes?
(A) He worked as a lawyer after attaining his degree.
(B) He was often ill when he was young.
(C) He developed a habit of staying up late.
(D) He was a mentor to Isaac Beekman.

中 Translation

年輕的瑞典人魯本勞辛在一九二〇年代出於哥倫比亞大學攻讀經濟學時,對美國的自助式超市印象深刻,尤其是賣食物的獨立包裝。心想歐洲很快也會有便利包裝食品的需求,他回到瑞典後便與商人艾瑞克艾克倫合資成立北歐第一家包裝公司:艾克倫勞辛。該公司前面幾年無法收支平衡,於是一九三三年艾克倫將股份賣給勞辛,勞辛遂成為唯一的所有人。

起初,艾克倫勞辛公司生產麵粉和糖等乾貨的包裝,當時這類食品都是秤重販售。然後,三〇年代晚期,勞辛開始思考一個更具挑戰性的問題:如何製造更好的容器來裝牛乳等容易變質、通常裝在又重又脆弱的玻璃瓶裡銷售的飲品。接下來幾年,該公司開始研發輕巧、耐用且易於運輸的紙盒,但勞辛靈機一動的一刻,到一九四三年才來臨。

一天,勞辛坐在廚房裡看著妻子灌香腸,他想:「為什麼不能以類似的方式包裝牛乳?」先在紙管裡注滿牛乳,再分成一個一個的紙盒,就能避免牛乳接觸到空氣或病菌,不必冷藏也能保存。歷經近十年的研發,勞辛成立了新的利樂包公司──以紙盒的四面體形狀為名。利樂磚──更方便存放及運送的長方盒──則在一九六三年推出。今天,每年生產的利樂包多達八百五十億個。

(B) 答解題測讀閱

Vocabulary Bank

1) **agricultural** [ˌæɡrɪˋkʌltʃərəl] (a.) 農業的，農學的，農用的
The farmers turned the desert into agricultural land.
農人把這片沙漠變成了農地。

2) **federal** [ˋfɛdərəl] (a.) 聯邦政府的
Employees have to pay both federal and state taxes.
員工必須納稅給聯邦政府和州政府。

3) **microscope** [ˋmaɪkrəˌskop] (n.) 顯微鏡
In biology class, we looked at cells through a microscope.
上生物課時，我們透過顯微鏡來觀察細胞。

4) **hook** [hʊk] (v./n.) （用鉤）鉤住；鉤子，釣魚鉤
Jack hooked the umbrella over his arm and went outside.
傑克把雨傘鉤在手臂上然後出門去了。

5) **catch (on)** [kætʃ] (v.) 鉤住，卡住，夾住
My sleeve caught on a nail and tore.
我的袖子鉤到釘子鉤破了。

6) **textile** [ˋtɛkstaɪl] (n.) 紡織品
The textile factory exports most of its products.
這間紡織廠大部份的產品都外銷。

7) **nylon** [ˋnaɪlɑn] (n.) 尼龍
Most stockings are made of nylon.
大部份的絲襪都是尼龍製的。

8) **combination** [ˌkɑmbəˋneʃən] (n.) 結合，組合
Purple is a combination of red and blue.
紫色是紅色加藍色調配而成。

Velcro

The Invention that Hooked the World
魔鬼氈　鉤住世界的發明

課文朗讀 MP3 127　單字朗讀 MP3 128　英文講解 MP3 129

George de Mestral was born in a small village near Lausanne, Switzerland in June 1907. The son of an [1]**agricultural** engineer, he showed an interest in inventing at an early age. In fact, he received his first patent—for a model airplane—when he was just 12. After later graduating from the [2]**Federal** Institute of Technology in Lausanne, de Mestral found a job working in a machine shop at an engineering firm.

On a summer day in 1941, de Mestral returned from a hike in the woods to find that his clothes, and his dog's fur, were covered with thistle burrs. Curious about how the burrs could attach so easily—and also be removed and reattached—he took a burr and examined it under a [3]**microscope**. To his surprise, he discovered that it had hundreds of tiny ⁴⁾**hooks** on its surface, allowing it to ⁵⁾**catch** on ¹¹⁾**loops** of fabric or fur. This was de Mestral's eureka moment: by designing a similar "hook and loop" system, he could create a clothing fastener that was easier to use than buttons, and wouldn't jam like a zipper.

When de Mestral first took his idea to Lyon, France's main ⁶⁾**textile** center, most people laughed at him. But with the help of a local weaver, he eventually succeeding in creating two strips of ⁷⁾**nylon** fabric—one with hooks and the other with loops—that could be stuck together and pulled apart. After receiving a patent in 1955, de Mestral started a company to manufacture his new product, which he called Velcro—a ⁸⁾**combination** of two French words, velours ⁹⁾(**velvet**) and crochet (hook). Today, Velcro can be found on everything from clothes and shoes to wallets and even ¹⁰⁾**spacecraft**!

Mini Quiz 閱讀測驗

According to the article, what is "crochet"?
(A) Another name for Velcro
(B) A type of nylon fabric
(C) A French word for "hook"
(D) An English term for "hook"

中 Translation

喬治迪梅斯楚於一九〇七年六月出生在瑞士洛桑附近一個小村落。身為農業工程師之子，他很小就展現出發明的興趣。事實上，他年僅十二歲便取得他的第一項專利——一架模型飛機。後來自洛桑的聯邦技術學院畢業後，迪梅斯楚於一家工程公司找到任職機械工廠的工作。

一九四一年一個夏日，迪梅斯楚從森林健行回來，發現他的衣服和狗的毛上都黏滿了薊草的刺果。他很好奇那些刺果是如何這麼容易就附著上去——去除之後還可重新附著——他便拿了一顆刺果，在顯微鏡下檢視。他驚訝地發現刺果表面有數百個微小的鉤子，使之得以鉤住布料或毛髮上的環。這時迪梅斯楚靈機一動：如果設計出類似的「鉤環」系統，他便能製造出比鈕扣容易使用，也不會像拉鍊一樣卡住的衣物扣件。

梅斯楚剛將構想帶到法國紡織重鎮里昂時，大多數人都嘲笑他。但在當地一位織布工的幫助下，他終於成功製作出兩條尼龍布——一條有鉤，一條有環——可以黏在一起再拉開。一九五五年取得專利後，迪梅斯楚開了一家公司製造他的新產品，他稱之為「魔鬼氈」（Velcro）——結合了「velour」（絲絨）和「crochet」（鉤子）兩個法文字。如今，從衣服、鞋子到皮夾甚至太空船，到處都見得到魔鬼氈的蹤影！

Language Guide

burr 刺果

burr 為植物的刺果，亦作 bur。刺果是具有鉤狀組織特性的種子，在很多類型的植物裡都可以看見，像是薊花或是牛蒡類植物等等。易於鉤住皮毛的特性，刺果能輕易地附著在動物及人類身上，藉由動物及人類帶動傳播，幫助刺果類植物開枝散葉。針刺狀的外表更能保護它們，驅趕食草性動物，提高存活的機率。

Velcro S.A. 魔鬼氈公司

一九五五年得到 Velcro 專利後，迪梅斯楚便在瑞士成立魔鬼氈公司——Velcro S.A.。迪梅斯楚開始將魔鬼氈向外發展，拓展海外，不僅在英國和美國都有分公司，加拿大分公司甚至開始將魔鬼氈銷售至亞洲地區。魔鬼氈的普及，Velcro 與 hook and loop fastener 被大眾劃上等號。Velcro 開始一系列的廣告，喊出 "the first, the best" 的口號，告訴所有消費者，Velcro 才是擁有專利的開發者，品質一定是最好的。

閱讀測驗解答：(C)

EUREKA! 點子成金

V Vocabulary Bank

1) **first aid** [fɜst ed] (phr.) 急救（護理）
We always take a first aid kit when we go camping.
我們去露營時總是會帶上急救箱。

2) **assign** [əˋsaɪn] (v.) 指定，分派
The teacher didn't assign any homework today.
老師今天沒有出任何功課。

3) **atomic** [əˋtɑmɪk] (a.) 原子的，原子能的
Japan relies heavily on atomic energy.
日本非常依賴原子能。

4) **track** [træk] (n.)（專輯）歌曲
What's your favorite track on the album?
你最喜歡這張專輯裡的哪一首歌？

5) **forbid** [fɚˋbɪd] (v.) 禁止，不許
Sam's parents forbid him to play video games.
山姆的父母不准他玩電玩遊戲。

6) **instructor** [ɪnˋstrʌktɚ] (n.) 教員，指導者，教練
My golf instructor has really helped me improve my game.
我的高爾夫球教練大大地幫我增進球技。

7) **convinced** [kənˋvɪnsd] (a.) 堅信的
Mary was convinced that what she saw was a ghost, not a shadow!
瑪莉堅信自己看到的是鬼而不是黑影。

進階字彙

8) **Mafia** [ˋmɑfɪə] (n.)（大寫）黑手黨，黑道
Some people believe President Kennedy was killed by the Mafia.
有些人相信甘迺迪總統是被黑手黨殺死的。

9) **dean** [din] (n.)（大學）學院院長，教務長
The dean of the law school is retiring next year.
法學院的院長明年即將退休。

10) **checkout** [ˋtʃɛk͵aʊt] (n.) 結帳（櫃台）
The checkout lines are really long on weekends.
在週末時，結帳都要大排長龍。

From Lines in the Sand to the Bar Code 條碼沙紋帶來的靈感

課文朗讀 MP3 130　單字朗讀 MP3 131　英文講解 MP3 132

Norman Joseph Woodland was born in Atlantic City on Sept. 6, 1921, the older of two boys. As a child, he joined the Boy Scouts, where he learned [1] **first aid**, Morse code and other survival skills. After graduating from Atlantic City High School in 1939, Woodland entered the Drexel Institute of Technology, now Drexel University, to study mechanical engineering. His education was interrupted by the Second World War, when he was [2] **assigned** to work on the Manhattan Project, which developed the first [3] **atomic** bomb.

While still an undergraduate, Woodland invented a new system for delivering elevator music using [4] **tracks** recorded on 35mm film, which was much more effective than systems that used records or tape. He planned on starting a company to manufacture and sell this technology, but his father, who believed that elevator music was controlled by the [8] **Mafia**,

[5)]**forbid** him to pursue the idea any further. So Woodland gave up this project and returned to Drexel as a graduate student and [6)]**instructor.**

One day in 1948, a local supermarket executive visited the campus to talk to the [9)]**dean** of engineering about the possibility of developing product codes that could be read automatically to make sorting and [10)]**checkout** more efficient. While the dean showed no interest in the idea, Woodland's classmate Bernard Silver overheard the conversation, and the two grad students began looking for solutions. Although their first few efforts were unsuccessful, Woodward was so [7)]**convinced** the problem could be solved that he quit grad school and went to stay at his grandparents' house in Miami Beach.

Mini Quiz 閱讀測驗

Which of the following is true about Norman Woodland?
(A) He invented elevator music.
(B) He had a younger brother.
(C) He started a company while in college.
(D) He was a professor at Drexel.

中 Translation

諾曼約瑟夫伍德蘭一九二一年九月六日出生於大西洋城,下面有個弟弟。小時候他參加過童軍團,在那裡學會急救、摩斯電碼和其他生存技能。一九三九年自大西洋城高中畢業後,伍德蘭進入卓克索理工學院,即現在的卓克索大學修習機械工程。他的學業因二次世界大戰中斷,當時,他被分派參與曼哈頓計畫,也就是研發第一枚原子彈的計畫。

還在唸大學時,伍德蘭發明了播放氛圍音樂的新系統:利用錄製於三十五釐米底片的音軌,這比使用唱片或錄音帶的系統有效率多。他打算開一家公司來製造及銷售這種技術,但他的父親相信氛圍音樂控制在黑手黨手中,因此不准他進一步推展這個構想。所以伍德蘭放棄了這個計畫,回卓克索唸研究所並擔任講師。

一九四八年的一天,當地的超市高階主管拜訪校園和工學院院長討論研究產品條碼的可能性,有了能自動判讀的條碼,便能提升產品分類和結帳的效率。院長對此構想不感興趣,但伍德蘭的同學伯納希佛偶然聽到他們的對話,於是這兩位研究生開始想辦法。雖然最初幾次努力並未成功,伍德蘭卻堅信問題一定能解決,於是離開研究所,前往祖父母位於邁阿密海灘的房子居住。

Language Guide

Morse Code 摩斯電碼

為美國人摩斯(Samuel Morse)於一八三六年發明的編碼方式,運用長、短不同的訊號(signal)來組成字母、數字或符號,藉以互相溝通。長訊號的符碼用「線」(dash)表示,短訊號則為「點」(dot)。後來則常用於戰爭、災難等時機。據說當年鐵達尼號郵輪(Titanic)首航遇險時,就是使用摩斯電碼發出標準求救信號SOS(‧‧‧－－－‧‧‧),成為世上第一艘發出 SOS 電碼的船隻。

Manhattan Project 曼哈頓計劃

曼哈頓計畫是美國總統羅斯福(Roosevelt)在一九四二年到四六年間,為二戰原子彈和英國、加拿大聯合的研發計畫。這項計畫始因於美國捲入二戰時,納粹德國已開始發展核武計畫來運用在戰爭之中。所以一些美國科學家提出,要搶先於納粹德國之前研發出原子彈。最後研發成功,並在廣島(Hiroshima)和長崎(Nagasaki)兩地投下原子彈而結束戰爭。

elevator music 氛圍音樂

常會在賣場(shopping mall)、商店或百貨公司聽見這樣的音樂,通常旋律輕柔、反覆播放,僅用樂器演奏卻沒有歌詞,目的在於堆砌氣氛,讓人感覺輕鬆,進而刺激消費或生產量。這種音樂又稱為 Muzak,因為第一個發展並提供此類音樂的公司就叫作 Muzak。

During the winter of 1949-49, Woodland spent his days sitting in a chair on the beach [8]**brainstorming**. To represent information [1]**visually**, he would need a simple code, and the only one he knew was the one he'd learned as a Boy Scout. He began thinking about the dots and dashes of Morse code, and that's when his eureka moment struck. "I [2]**poked** my four fingers into the sand and for whatever reason—I didn't know—I pulled my hand toward me and drew four lines," Woodland said in a later interview. "[9]**Golly**! Now I have four lines, and they could be wide lines and narrow lines instead of dots and dashes."

Norman Joseph Woodland)

Woodland then took a further step and turned his lines into a [3]**series** of circles, like the rings on a target, with information contained in the width of the rings. He filed a patent application for his code in 1949, and joined IBM in 1951, hoping the company would develop his idea. But the equipment required to scan products was too large and expensive for use at supermarket checkouts, so Woodland eventually sold his patent to Philco, which [4]**in turn** sold it to RCA.

By the early 1970s, new [5]**laser** scanning technology was beginning to make Woodland's invention more

V Vocabulary Bank

1) **visually** [ˋvɪʒʊəlɪ] (adv.) 視覺上，視力上
(a.) visual
The critic called *Life of Pi* a visually exciting movie.
影評把《少年Pi的奇幻漂流》稱為一部視覺效果令人驚艷的電影。

2) **poke** [pok] (v.) 戳
My dad poked me in the ribs when I fell asleep in church.
我在教堂睡著時，我爸戳了戳我的腰際。

3) **series** [ˋsɪrɪz] (n.) 系列，連續
J.K. Rowling is the creator of the Harry Potter series.
J.K. 羅琳創造出哈利波特系列小說。

4) **in turn** [ɪn tɝn] (phr.) 既而，因而
Smoking makes your mouth dry, which in turn causes bad breath.
抽菸會讓你口乾，進而導致口臭。

5) **laser** [ˋlezɚ] (n.) 雷射
I'm thinking of buying a laser printer.
我在考慮要買一台雷射印表機。

6) **demonstration** [ˌdɛmənˋstreʃən] (n.) 證明，示範
The trial results are a demonstration that the drug is safe.
試驗結果證明這種藥物是安全的。

7) **expire** [ɪkˋspaɪr] (v.) 到期，滿期
When does your passport expire?
你的護照什麼時候到期？

進階字彙

8) **brainstorm** [ˋbrenˌstɔrm] (v.) 腦力激盪，集思廣益
Let's brainstorm and see if we can find a creative solution.
我們來集思廣益一下，看能不能找到一個創新的解決辦法。

口語補充

9) **golly** [ˋgɑlɪ] (int.) 天啊（God的婉轉表示法）
Golly, what a long day!
天啊，好漫長的一天！

feasible. IBM executives saw a successful [6)]**demonstration** of RCA's product code at an industry meeting, and since the patent had [7)]**expired** by then, they put Woodland to work developing a better version. Woodland's new code, which used bars instead of rings—making it easier to print and read—was selected as the industry standard in 1973. Today, bar codes can be found on everything from grocery products and books to luggage and hospital patients, and are scanned over 5 billion times every day!

Mini Quiz 閱讀測驗

■ Why wasn't Woodland's idea developed in the 1950s?
(A) Because nobody was interested in the patent
(B) Because scanning technology wasn't advanced enough
(C) Because Philco and RCA refused to develop it
(D) Because there was no need for product codes

中 Translation

一九四八到四九年的冬天，伍德蘭成天都坐在海灘的椅子上腦力激盪。要將資訊以視覺的方式呈現，他需要簡單的代碼，而他唯一知道的就是他當童軍時學到的那種。他開始思考摩斯電碼中的點和橫線，然後，靈光乍現的時刻來了。「我把四隻手指插進沙子裡，而不知怎麼地——我不知道為什麼——我把手向身體拉回來，畫出四條線，」伍德蘭後來接受訪問時表示：「天啊！現在我有四條線，而且它們可以是寬窄不一的線，不必是點和橫線。」

接著伍德蘭更進一步，將他的線轉變成一連串的圓圈，就像標靶上的圓環，而資訊就包含在圓環的寬度中。他在一九四九年為他的代碼申請專利，後於一九五一年加入 IBM 公司，希望該公司能發展他的構想。但掃描產品所需的設備太過龐大且昂貴，無法在超市結帳櫃台使用，所以伍德蘭最後把專利賣給飛歌公司，後來飛歌又轉賣給 RCA。

一九七○年代初期，新的雷射掃描技術開始讓伍德蘭的發明更加可行。IBM 高階主管在一場產業會議上見到 RCA 產品碼的成功示範，由於當時專利已經過期，他們便請伍德蘭研發更好的版本。伍德蘭以長條取代圓環的新代碼更易於印刷及讀取，在一九七三年被選為產業標準。如今，從超市商品、書籍到行李和醫院的病患身上，所有的物品都看得到條碼的蹤跡，每天被掃描超過五十億次！

Language Guide

一維條碼與二維條碼

bar 這個英文字為「條」的意思，所以 bar code 中文才會叫做「條碼」。條碼在日常生活中的應用相當普遍，可以記錄許多資訊，不過如今已步入資訊爆炸的年代，若想容納更多資訊，條碼勢必得越拉越長，於是便發明了第二代條碼技術，也就是二維條碼(2D Barcode，2D 表 two dimensional)，這種編碼方式可以連結到文字、聲音和圖形等資料，容量也較大，為黑白交錯的矩陣式（matrix）或條狀圖形。目前最常見的就是日本發明的 QR code（QR 表 quick response），只要下載掃描器，就可從中讀取網站、影音等資訊，相當方便。

答：閱讀測驗解答 (B)

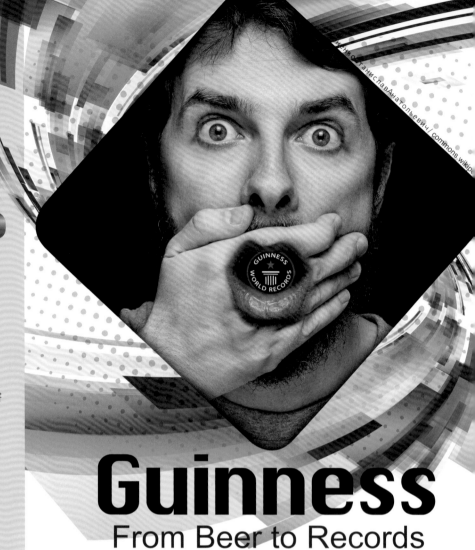

Vocabulary Bank

1) **extensive** [ɪk`stɛnsɪv] (a.) 廣泛的，廣大的
The professor has extensive knowledge of Greek history.
這位教授對希臘歷史有相當廣泛的了解。

2) **consult** [kən`sʌlt] (v.) 查閱
We consulted the train schedule to see when our train was arriving.
我們查閱了火車時刻表來看看我們的火車何時會抵達。

3) **encyclopedia** [ɪn͵saɪklə`pidɪə] (n.) 百科全書
The encyclopedia has an excellent article on the Industrial Revolution.
這部百科全書中有一篇關於工業革命的文章寫得很棒。

4) **definitive** [dɪ`fɪnɪtɪv] (a.) 決定性的，最可靠的，最完整的
The court lacks definitive proof of the suspect's guilt.
法庭缺少了該名嫌疑人犯罪的鐵證。

5) **reference** [`rɛf(ə)rəns] (n.) 參考（資料、書籍等）
Dictionaries can be found in the reference section of the library.
字典都放在圖書館的參考資料區。

6) **brew** [bru] (v.) 釀酒，泡茶，煮咖啡
(n.) brewery [`bruəri] 啤酒廠
Would you like me to brew some coffee?
你要我幫你煮杯咖啡嗎？

7) **agency** [`edʒənsi] (n.) 代理商
Which travel agency did you book your tour with?
你的旅遊行程是跟哪一家旅行社訂的？

8) **compile** [kəm`paɪl] (v.) 彙整，編輯
Steven is busy compiling information for his presentation.
史蒂分正忙著匯整他簡報要用的資料。

Guinness
From Beer to Records
金氏世界紀錄

課文朗讀 MP3 136　　單字朗讀 MP3 137　　英文講解 MP3 138

While out hunting on the coast of Ireland in 1951, Sir Hugh Beaver, managing director of Guinness Brewery, got in a debate about which game bird was the fastest in Europe. Sir Hugh claimed that it was the plover (probably because he couldn't hit one), but his friends insisted it was the grouse. That evening, he searched for the answer in his host's [1]**extensive** library, but came up empty-handed.

Back in England, Sir Hugh [2]**consulted** all the [3]**encyclopedias** he could find, but still had no luck. This led to his eureka moment: there should be a [4]**definitive** [5]**reference** book to settle the similar debates that must be going on in pubs all over Britain and Ireland. In addition, it would be a great marketing tool—drinkers who could say "I told you so!" would be more likely to drink beer [6]**brewed** by the publishers of the book that proved them right.

Next, Sir Hugh found the perfect partners, Norris and Ross McWhirter, twins with photographic memories who ran an [7]**agency** supplying sports [9]**trivia** to British newspapers. The twins went to work [8]**compiling** the world's largest, smallest, fastest and tallest, completing the first edition of the *Guinness Book of Records* in just 16 weeks. The [10]**almanac** rolled off the presses in August 1955, and was at the top of the British bestseller list by Christmas.

The Guinness Book of Records was launched in the U.S. the following year, selling 70,000 copies. Because of the book's growing success, the publishers decided to [11]**put out** a new edition each year. Now known as *Guinness World Records*, the almanac is available in 26 languages in 100 countries around the world.

Mini Quiz 閱讀測驗

According to the article, which of the following is true?
(A) The first edition of the Guinness Book of Records was available in 26 languages.
(B) The Guinness Book of Records became a bestseller in August 1955.
(C) The plover flies faster than the grouse.
(D) The first edition of the Guinness Book of Records took 4 months to complete.

中 Translation

一九五一年，健力士酒廠的總經理休比佛爵士在愛爾蘭海岸打獵時，與友人爭論歐洲哪一種打獵時常見的鳥類飛得最快。休爵士堅稱是千鳥（大概是他沒打中過），但友人堅持是松雞。那天晚上，他在東道主藏書豐富的圖書室裡查詢解答，可是卻徒勞無功。

回到英格蘭，休爵士翻遍所有他找得到的百科全書，仍毫無所獲，這導致他靈機一動：應該要有一本最可靠的參考書來解決這些想必在全英國和愛爾蘭酒吧會不斷上演的類似爭論。此外，這也會是一個很棒的行銷工具：能夠說出「我就跟你說嘛！」這句話的酒客，會更願意喝這本證明他們無誤的書籍出版商所釀造的酒。

接著，休爵士找到一對絕佳夥伴，諾里斯和羅斯麥克沃特，這對學生兄弟有過目不忘的能力，經營一間專為英國報社提供運動冷知識的代理商。於是，這對雙胞胎著手編寫世界上的最大、最小、最快、最高記錄，僅花十六週就完成《金氏世界紀錄大全》第一版。一九五五年八月，這本年鑑發行，在耶誕節之前就登上全英國最暢銷排行榜首。

隔年，這本《金氏世界紀錄大全》在美國發行，賣出七萬本。因為銷售成長的關係，出版商決定每年推出新版。現今，這部書改名為《金氏世界紀錄》，有二十六種語言的版本，遍布全球一百個國家。

✳ Language Guide

Guinness Brewery 健力士啤酒公司

為一七五九年在愛爾蘭都柏林(Dublin, Ireland)成立的一家釀酒廠，創始人為 Arthur Guinness，該酒廠專門釀造一種烈性黑啤酒(stout)，名為健力士啤酒(Guinness draught)。健力士酒廠到一八三八年時已成為愛爾蘭最大的釀酒廠，到了一九一四年更居於全球之冠，佔地六十四英畝。雖然現已不是規模最大的啤酒廠，但其出產的黑啤酒仍熱銷全球。

© littleny / Shutterstock.com

© littleny / Shutterstock.com

閱讀測驗解答：(D)

我們現在所說的金氏世界紀錄，其實是一本名為《金氏世界紀錄大全》(Guinness World Records) 的書，裡頭記載著各種千奇百怪的世界紀錄，像是指甲最長的人、最高的瀑布、最大尾的蛇以及三分鐘內用鼻子吹出最多顆氣球的紀錄⋯等等，任何你想得到或想不到的世界之最全都在這裡。《金氏世界紀錄大全》每年都會更新版本，不用怕資訊落伍，跟不上時代。現在讓 EZ TALK 帶大家來瞧瞧一些有趣的世界紀錄吧。

台北 101 曾得過金氏世界紀錄，你知道嗎？

原來台北 101 不只是高度 (altitude) 驚人，連電梯也要最神速。它所裝置的是日本東芝 (Toshiba) 的電梯系統，從一樓到八十九樓（約三百八十二公尺）只需四十秒，相當於時速六十點六公里，榮登金氏世界紀錄排行中最快的電梯。不只如此，電梯的空氣節壓系統，還能讓人擺脫高空氣壓對人體所產生的不舒適感，如耳鳴 (tinnitus) 等症狀。

Guinness
World Records
———— 令人驚豔的世界之最 ————

© EtherH/flickr.com

男女誰長舌？

一位名叫香奈兒泰波 (Chanel Tapper) 的美國加州女孩於二〇一〇年榮登世界上舌頭最長的女人，她的舌頭有九點七五公分長，為一般人的兩倍，媲美世上最大的蟑螂，也與 iPhone 機身等長，寬度大約與手掌同寬，體積相當於四分之一磅重的漢堡肉片。這項紀錄已正式列入《二〇一二年版金氏世界紀錄》。不過現今的紀錄保持人仍為男性，他是英國人史蒂芬泰勒 (Stephen Taylor)，擁有九點八公分長的舌頭。

女人的夢想就是細腰大胸部？

哪個女生不希望自己身材好？好身材指的不外乎就是小蠻腰和豐腴的胸部，不過你知道全世界最細的腰居然只有十五吋嗎？美國一位名叫凱西榮格 (Cathie Jung) 的女人，穿上馬甲 (corset) 的腰圍居然只有十五吋，就算將馬甲脫掉，二十一吋的腰圍也只是別人的三分之二。凱西對於英國維多利亞女王 (Queen Victoria) 時期的束腰服飾非常熱愛，為了擁有性感的細腰，她從四十五歲時開始全天穿著馬甲，只為將腰圍減下。另一個締造女人奇蹟的是安妮霍金斯特拿 (Annie Hawkins-Turner)，大家對於她的另一個名字諾瑪史蒂茲 (Norma Stitz) 或許比較熟悉。沒錯，她就是世界上胸圍最大的女人，有一百〇九公分、ZZZ 罩杯，光是胸部就有將近一百一十二磅（相當於五十公斤），雖然常使她腰酸背痛，但她從未有縮胸的念頭。

到底是狗高還是馬大？

出遠門怕沒人幫狗狗換水喝嗎？密西根州 (Michigan) 的多爾萊格 (Doorlag) 一家人完全不需要擔心這個問題。他們飼養的大丹狗 (Great Dane) 宙斯 (Zeus)，和一般狗狗不一樣，可以自己到廚房流理台開水龍頭來喝水。宙斯三歲時，從肩膀到腳就有四十四吋，將近一百一十二公分，遠看就像是隻馬。宙斯成為金氏世界紀錄中全世界最高的狗，以僅僅的一吋勝過此項紀錄的保持者——大喬治 (Giant George)。有趣的是，在密蘇里州 (Missouri) 有一隻名叫坦芭莉娜 (Thumbelina) 的馬，Thumbelina 是安徒生 (Hans Christian Andersen) 童話中拇指姑娘的名字，既然名字都叫作拇指姑娘了，我們可以猜想，她的個頭應該不大。坦芭莉娜是全世界最小的馬，只有四十四點五公分高。

© Philkon Phil Konstantin/Wikipedia

刺青達人看這邊

湯姆萊波德 (Tom Leppard) 是世界上刺青最多的男子，身上有百分之九十九點二都刺上滿滿的豹紋，不僅將自己的姓氏從 Woodbridge 改為 Leppard，甚至把牙齒磨成像動物的尖牙 (fang)，遠看就像是一隻豹，常被稱作 Leopard Man（leopard 意思為「豹」）。曾經為軍人的湯姆，非常嚮往野外生活，二十年前決定搬離他所厭惡的喧囂城市，居住在蘇格蘭的斯凱島 (Isle of Skye) 上，因此也常稱呼他為 Leopard Man of Skye。二〇〇六年時，湯姆的紀錄被全身將近百分之百都是刺青的洛基戴蒙里奇 (Lucky Diamond Rich) 打破。

EUREKA! 點子成金

V Vocabulary Bank

1) **fluent** [ˋfluənt] (a.) （語言）流利的
It takes years to become fluent in a foreign language.
外語要流利得花上好幾年的時間。

2) **explosive** [ɪkˋsplosɪv] (n./a.) 爆裂物；爆炸的
(n.) explosion [ɪkˋsploʃən]
The terrorist was caught with explosives in his underwear.
那名恐怖份子被查獲內褲中藏有爆裂物。

3) **stroke** [strok] (n.) 中風
The old man suffered a stroke and was unable to speak.
那位老先生因中風而失去說話能力。

4) **motivate** [ˋmotɪ͵vet] (v.) 激勵，激發
Bonuses are a good way to motivate employees.
發獎金是激勵員工的好方法。

5) **revolutionize** [͵rɛvəˋluʃə͵naɪz] (v.) 徹底變革
Cell phones have revolutionized the way people communicate.
手機徹底革新了人們通訊的方式。

6) **dedication** [͵dɛdɪˋkeʃən] (n.) 投入，專注
Thanks to your dedication, we were able to finish the project on time.
多虧你的投入，我們才能準時完成這項專案。

7) **arm** [ɑrm] (n.) （常用複數）武器，槍砲
The Soviet Union lost the arms race with the United States.
蘇聯在軍備競賽中輸給了美國。

8) **expose (to)** [ɪkˋspoz] (v.) 使接觸到，使暴露於
The goal of the program is to expose students to art.
這個課程的目的是讓學生接觸藝術。

9) **criticism** [ˋkrɪtə͵sɪzəm] (n.) 批評，評論，挑剔
Some people just can't take criticism.
有些人就是無法接受批評。

10) **draft** [dræft] (v.) 起草，草擬
The senator stayed up all night drafting the bill.
這位參議員熬夜草擬法案。

11) **promotion** [prəˋmoʃən] (n.) 促進，發揚，提倡
The organization's main goal is the promotion of free trade.
該組織的主要目標在於提倡自由貿易。

Alfred Nobel's [12)] Legacy 諾貝爾獎

課文朗讀 MP3 139　單字朗讀 MP3 140　英文講解 MP3 141

Born in Stockholm, Sweden in 1833, Alfred Nobel moved with his family to St. Petersburg, Russia at the age of nine. His father Immanuel, an engineer and inventor, became wealthy manufacturing mines for the Russian Navy during the Crimean War. Educated by private tutors, Alfred studied chemistry and physics, and became [1)] **fluent** in five languages.

After the war, Alfred returned to Stockholm with his father and younger brother Emil to start a business developing and manufacturing [2)]**explosives**. The Nobels began experimenting with a [13)]**volatile** substance called nitroglycerine—so volatile, in fact, that Emil was killed in an explosion soon afterward. The business was forced to move outside city limits, and Immanuel had a [3)]**stroke**, leaving Alfred in charge. [4)]**Motivated** by Emil's death, he devoted all his efforts to making nitroglycerine safer to handle. After adding a number of different substances, Alfred finally found one that worked: kieselguhr, a fine sand consisting mostly of silica. The resulting explosive, which he named "dynamite" after the Greek word for power, [5)]**revolutionized** the mining and construction industrdeies.

And yet Alfred's true eureka moment was still to come. As he entered middle age, dynamite and other inventions had made Alfred one of the richest men in the world. But his tireless [6)]**dedication** to his career had left him in poor health, and the use of his inventions in the [7)]**arms** industry had [8)]**exposed** him to severe [9)]**criticism**. Worried about his legacy, Alfred [10)]**drafted** a will in which he left most of

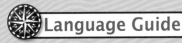

© Euclid vanderKroew / flikr

his wealth to establishing annual prizes for outstanding achievements in physics, chemistry, medicine, literature and the [11)]**promotion** of peace. Since the Nobel Prizes were established in 1901—six years after Alfred's death—they have become the most[14)] **prestigious** awards in the world.

Mini Quiz 閱讀測驗

Which of the following is true about dynamite?
(A) It consists mostly of silica.
(B) It is a Greek word.
(C) It contains the explosive kieselguhr.
(D) It contains nitroglycerine.

中 Translation

阿弗雷德諾貝爾一八三三年生於瑞典斯德哥爾摩，九歲時隨家人搬到俄羅斯的聖彼得堡。他的父親殷曼紐是個工程師暨發明家，在克里米亞戰爭期間替俄羅斯海軍製造地雷而致富。在私人家教指導下，阿弗雷德研習化學和物理，並能流利地說五種語言。

戰後，阿弗雷德和父親及弟弟艾米爾回到斯德哥爾摩，開了一家研發及製造爆裂物的公司。諾貝爾一家開始拿一種名為硝化甘油的爆炸性物質來做實驗——其爆炸性之強烈，事實上，艾米爾因此於不久後死於一場爆炸。公司被迫遷至城市範圍外，且殷曼紐中風，於是由阿弗雷德掌管公司。深受艾米爾之死所刺激，阿弗雷德投注一切心力，設法提升使用硝化甘油的安全性。在添加各種不同物質後，阿弗雷德終於發現一種物質有效：矽藻土，主要由二氧化矽構成的細砂。結果製成的爆裂物——他命名為「dynamite」（即炸藥），取自希臘文的「力量」一字——為礦業及營建業開啟劃時代的革命。

但阿弗雷德真正「靈機一動」的時刻還沒到。在他步入中年後，炸藥和其他發明已使阿弗雷德成為世界首富之一，但他對事業孜孜不倦的投入，卻讓他的身體每下愈況，而且他的發明為軍火業使用，也使他遭受嚴厲的批判。很擔心自己能遺留什麼給後世，阿弗雷德擬了一份遺囑，將大半財富用於設置一年一度的獎金，表揚物理學、化學、醫學、文學與促進和平的傑出成就。諾貝爾獎於一九〇一年設立以來——阿弗雷德逝世六年後——至今已成為全世界最具聲望的獎項。

Language Guide

Crimean War 克里米亞戰爭

克里米亞戰爭是十九世紀歐洲爆發的一場戰爭，為俄羅斯帝國對抗奧斯曼帝國、法蘭西帝國、薩丁尼雅王國和不列顛帝國。其中最重要的戰役發生於克里米亞半島，因而得名。這場戰爭真正的原因是，俄羅斯想趁著奧斯曼帝國內部逐漸瓦解之便，擴大在歐洲的勢力，而英國和法國不希望自己利益受損。

這也是世界史上第一次現代化戰爭，從軍事和政治上改變了歐洲列強之間的地位和關係。在克里米亞戰爭中，現代的爆炸性炮彈第一次被使用，電報(telegraph)首次被使用，火車也首次用來運送補給和增援。

用來製造炸彈的化學物質

• nitroglycerine 硝化甘油

nitroglycerine [ˋnaɪtrəˋglɪsərɪn]是一種爆炸力極強的炸藥。由化學家索布雷洛（Ascanio Sobrero）發明。常有人誤解「硝化甘油」是瑞典化學家阿爾弗雷德諾貝爾發明的，事實上諾貝爾只是當時最大的硝化甘油製造商。

• kieselguh 矽藻土

kieselguhr [ˋkizəl.gur] 是一種淡黃色或淺灰色的生物化學沉積岩；由矽藻的細胞壁沉積而成。是硝化甘油炸藥中硝化甘油的吸附物、殺蟲物質等等。也可當作絕緣物質。

• silica 二氧化矽

silica [ˋsɪlɪkə]（化學式：SiO_2）是一種酸性氧化物，具有硬度大、耐高溫、耐震、電絕緣的性能。空氣中若存有一定濃度的二氧化矽粉粒，會經人類呼吸進入肺部，引發呼吸器官相關疾病，例如塵肺症。

（D）答稱線順題閱 Mini Quiz

© Jonathanriley/wikipedia

諾貝爾究竟有多少個獎項？

根據瑞典化學家阿弗雷德諾貝爾的遺囑，希望表彰對社會做出卓越貢獻及傑出研究的人士，而成立了諾貝爾獎。頒獎典禮自一九〇一年開始，每年於諾貝爾逝世紀念日舉行。一九六九時，瑞典國家銀行為紀念創立三百週年，增設了「紀念阿弗雷諾貝爾瑞典銀行經濟學獎」，一般通稱為諾貝爾經濟學獎，但因為諾貝爾的遺囑中並未提及此為獎勵領域，因此很多人都認為它並不屬於諾貝爾獎。原始遺囑中，諾貝爾將獎項分為以下五個領域：

1 諾貝爾物理學獎

表彰在物理學領域有最重要發現或發明的人。

© cstmweb/flickr

2 諾貝爾化學獎

頒發給在化學方面有最重要發現或新進展的人。

© cstmweb/flickr

3 諾貝爾生理學或醫學獎

表揚在生理學或醫學方面有重大發現的人。

© trindade.joao/flickr

4 諾貝爾文學獎

文學獎一直是備受考驗的獎項，為什麼這麼說呢？在諾貝爾的遺囑當中，文學獎是要頒發給在文學方面創作表現出理想主義且寫出優秀作品的人。但是這樣的標準非常主觀，因此文學獎的得主及作品一直備受爭議。

© cstmweb/flickr

5 諾貝爾和平獎

和平獎是諾貝爾獎中最受矚目的獎項，甚至連頒獎儀式所舉行的地點都與其他四個獎項不同。除了和平獎是在挪威奧斯陸舉行之外，其他獎項都在瑞典斯德哥爾摩頒發。和平獎是為表揚那些屏除武力手段，為國與國之間的友好做出貢獻的人。這個獎項最特別的是，除了諾貝爾委員會主席進行頒獎之外，挪威國王會前往參與典禮，表示對諾貝爾和平獎的重視。

© Chris campbell/flickr

諾貝爾獎特別報導：

什麼？！原來這部電視劇連諾貝爾獎都讚賞

© CarlVanVechten/wikipedia

相信大家一定都聽過《京華煙雲》這部電視劇，此劇改編自林語堂以英語創作的歷史小說 Moment in Peking（譯作《京華煙雲》）。大家可能不知道此電視劇的原著小說曾榮獲諾貝爾文學獎的提名。

這部小說的創作動機源自於《紅樓夢》，當時林語堂原想將《紅樓夢》譯作英文介紹給西方讀者，但《紅樓夢》時代太過遙遠，作者便以此本小說結構撰寫了《京華煙雲》。小說的背景設定在一九〇〇年至一九三八年的中國，一個紛擾戰亂不斷的年代——當時中國正歷經八國聯軍、辛亥革命以及北洋政府軍閥當政。除了滿清朝廷的內憂外患之外，書中也記載了民族主義及共產主義的崛起，以及抗日戰爭發端之時動盪不安的局面，完整勾勒出清末民初近三十多年的中國輪廓。

《京華煙雲》一九三九年底在美國出版，短短半年即行銷五萬多冊，美國《時代雜誌》當時也對其推崇備至，表示此小說極有可能成為描繪中國社會近代史的經典作品。

與和平獎有緣的總統可不只歐巴馬

我們都曉得,美國總統歐巴馬因主張從阿富汗和伊拉克撤軍,獲頒二○○九年諾貝爾和平獎。事實上,台灣也有位總統曾和諾貝爾和平獎擦身而過。他就是台灣首位公民直選總統——李登輝。人民可直選總統是台灣民主改革趨近完整的大指標,也是華人社會民主的表率;由於李登輝在其任內積極修法,促進並落實台灣全面民主化,被美國《時代雜誌》讚譽為「民主先生」。根據當時新聞報導,李登輝在當選第一任民選總統(一九九六年)年底曾獲諾貝爾和平獎提名的殊榮,但一九九七年和平獎最後由美國反地雷人士及其組織得獎。

和平獎的遺珠之憾

美國民權運動領袖馬丁路德金恩 (Martin Luther King) 採用非暴力手法,積極推動美國民權進步,發表最鼓舞美國人民的一場演講——我有一個夢 (I Have a Dream),並迫使美國國會宣佈種族隔離和歧視政策為非法政策,金恩博士也因而獲得一九六四年貝爾和平獎。

公認,同樣以非暴力方式帶領國家走向民主,印度國父甘地,卻是諾貝爾和平獎的遺珠。莫罕達斯甘地 (Mohandas Gandhi),是印度獨立運動的創使人,被尊稱「聖雄甘地」(Mahatma Gandhi)。他終其一生,致力為印度帶來改變。他呼籲印度同胞不論遭遇到任何處境也要以和平、非暴力方式抗爭,並以「不合作主義」帶領國家邁向獨立,脫離英國的殖民統治。甘地的哲學與政治信念是在南非遭受種族歧視時開始成形,而這樣的哲學思想影響了全世界的民族主義者和爭取和平變革的國際運動,也激勵了其他殖民地人民為獨立抗爭的決心,並鼓舞了其他的民主運動人士。甘地於一九四八年初遭到暗殺,諾貝爾基金會的網站暗示原本屬意得獎人是他,但諾貝爾獎原則上僅能授予在世者,故當年的諾貝爾和平獎並未頒發給甘地。

愛因斯坦得諾貝爾獎不是因為相對論?

現代物理學之父艾伯特愛因斯坦 (Albert Einstein) 並不是以他最著名的相對論獲獎,而是以光電效應定律榮獲一九二一年諾貝爾物理學獎。原因是相對論深深撼動了當時居於主導地位的經典物理學說,在物理學界和哲學界掀起軒然大波,招來眾人非議;縱然有許多科學家認為相對論對科學有極大貢獻,但保守的諾貝爾委員會仍對於頒獎給愛因斯坦猶豫不決。不過,迫於擁護愛因斯坦的科學家日趨增多,委員會最後決定繞過相對論這個爭議性太多的障礙,直接以光電效應定律的貢獻將物理學獎授予愛因斯坦。

諾貝爾獎的第一位女得主

瑪麗斯克羅德沃斯卡居禮 (Marie Sklodowska-Curie),通常稱為瑪麗居禮,是放射性現象的研究先驅,不僅為諾貝爾獎的第一位女得主,也是二次獲頒諾貝爾獎的第一人。

她和丈夫皮耶居禮 (Pierre Curie) 經常一起進行放射性物質的研究,不斷提煉瀝青鈾礦石中的放射成份。居里夫婦與亨利貝克勒於一九○三年因發現釙 (Po) 和鐳 (Ra) 這兩種新的放射性元素,共同獲得諾貝爾物理學獎的肯定。因被質疑鐳並非一種純元素,而是化合物,瑪麗居里鍥而不捨積極研究放射化學,最後終於純化出鐳元素而再次獲得諾貝爾化學獎。出乎意外的是,居禮夫人獲得諾貝爾獎之後,並沒有為提煉純淨鐳的方法申請專利,反而將其公布於世,大大推動了放射化學的發展及研究。

EUREKA! 點子成金

V Vocabulary Bank

1) **autobiography** [ˌɔtəbaɪˈɑɡrəfɪ] (n.) 自傳
Have you read Benjamin Franklin's autobiography?
你讀過富蘭克林的自傳嗎？

2) **positive** [ˈpɑzətɪv] (a.) 確定的，確信的
Are you positive you saw my boyfriend with another girl?
你確定你有看到我男友和其他女生在一起嗎？

3) **enroll** [ɪnˈrol] (v.) （註冊）入學
How many students are enrolled at the college?
那所大學有多少學生註冊入學？

4) **tuition** [tuˈɪʃən] (n.) 學費
Students held a protest against the tuition increase.
學生們發動了一場抗議學費調漲的示威活動。

5) **in common (with)** [ɪn ˈkɑmən] (phr.)
（與…）共通的
Rita and I have nothing in common.
芮塔與我毫無共通點。

6) **bond** [bɑnd] (n.) （人之間的）關係，聯繫
The bond between mother and child is very strong.
媽媽和孩子間的連結是非常強烈的。

7) **pocket money** [ˈpɑkɪt ˈmʌnɪ] (n.) 零用錢
Kevin got a part-time job after school to earn pocket money.
凱文放學去打工賺取零用錢。

8) **turning point** [ˈtɜnɪŋ pɔɪnt] (n.) 轉捩點
Getting his first novel published marked a turning point in the author's life.
那位作家的人生轉捩點就在他第一本小說順利出版時。

9) **run into** [rʌn ˈɪntu] (phr.) 巧遇
Guess who I ran into at the post office?
猜猜我在郵局碰到誰？

10) **acquaintance** [əˈkwentəns] (n.)
相識人，舊識
George is a business acquaintance of mine.
喬治是我一位生意上的舊識。

11) **due** [du] (a.) 到期的，預期的。due date 即「預產期」、「到期日」，「期限」等
When is the phone bill due?
你的電話費什麼時候到期？

12) **humiliated** [hjuˈmɪlɪˌetɪd] (v.) （感到）丟臉、羞辱的
I've never felt so humiliated in my whole life!
我一生從沒感到如此丟臉過！

體重管理小尖兵
Weight Watchers

課文朗讀 MP3 142　　單字朗讀 MP3 143　　英文講解 MP3 144

Born in Brooklyn, New York, Jean Slutsky struggled with her weight from an early age. "I don't really remember," she recalls in her [1]**autobiography**, "but I'm [2]**positive** that whenever I cried, my mother gave me something to eat." Jean dreamed of becoming a teacher, but her father died shortly after she [3]**enrolled** in college in 1942. Unable to afford the [4]**tuition**, she was forced to drop out and find full-time work to help support her family.

In 1947, at the age of 24, Jean married Marty Nidetch, a man from her neighborhood who had something [5]**in common** with her. "I was fat and he was fat," says Jean. "It was our common [6]**bond**." The young couple moved to Queens, where Marty worked as a bus driver. Jean became a housewife, had two kids, and sold eggs door to door whenever she needed [7]**pocket money**. She kept gaining weight over the years, and by 1961 she weighed 214 pounds.

Jean's [8]**turning point** came when she [9]**ran into** an [10]**acquaintance** at the supermarket one day. "You look great, Jean," the woman said. "When is your [11]**due** date?" She was so [12]**humiliated** that she visited the New York Department of Health Obesity Clinic the same day. Jean was placed on a

strict diet with lots of fish, fruit and vegetables, and was able to lose 20 pounds in 10 weeks. But then she began cheating, sneaking Mallomars that she hid in a laundry basket late at night. Doubting that the skinny woman who ran the clinic would understand her weakness for cookies, Jean invited six overweight friends to her apartment to discuss her problem.

Mini Quiz 閱讀測驗

What finally motivated Jean to lose weight?
(A) She was worried about her health.
(B) She was embarrassed about her appearance.
(C) Her doctor said it would improve her health.
(D) An acquaintance told her she was too fat.

中 Translation

在紐約布魯克林區出生的珍史拉斯基從年幼時就有體重問題。「我不太記得了，」她在自傳中回憶：「但我確定，小時候只要我一哭，媽媽就會拿東西給我吃。」珍夢想成為一名老師，但在一九四七年時，她的父親在她進入大學就讀不久後便過世了。由於無法負擔學費，她不得不輟學，找份全職的工作來幫忙養家。

一九四七年，二十四歲的珍嫁給了和她同社區的馬提尼德契，一個跟她擁有某項共通點的男人。「我很胖，他也很胖，」珍說。「那是我們的共同聯繫。」這對年輕夫婦搬到皇后區，馬提在那裡擔任公車司機。珍成了家庭主婦，生了兩個孩子，並在需要零用錢時挨家挨戶賣雞蛋。這些年她的體重持續增加，到了一九六一年已高達二百一十四磅。

珍的轉捩點就是某天她在超市遇見熟人的時候。「妳看起來氣色很好，」那個女人說：「預產期什麼時候？」她深深引以為恥，於是當天便去了紐約衛生局的肥胖診所。珍於是開始進行嚴格的飲食控制，只吃大量的魚肉和蔬果，十個星期後減了二十磅。不過隨後她便開始作弊，在半夜偷吃藏在洗衣籃裡的棉花餅。珍很懷疑開那間診所的窈窕女士會諒解她無法抗拒餅乾這件事，因此她便邀請六個體重過重的朋友到家裡討論她遭遇的問題。

Mallomars 棉花餅

這種棉花餅是外裹黑巧克力、內餡由棉花軟糖(marshmallow)及全麥餅乾(graham cracker)組成的高熱量甜點。最早是由納貝斯克公司（Nabisco，由 National Biscuit Company 縮寫而來）於一九一三年開始製造，有鑑於巧克力容易在高溫下融化，棉花餅一開始只有在十月至隔年的四月間才有供應，嗜吃甜食者知道夏天買不著，就會在冬、春兩季屯貨，現今的棉花餅全年供貨無虞，百分之七十在紐約售出。

© ohdearbarb/flickr.com

© SimonP/Wikipedia

New York's Five Boroughs 紐約五個行政區

borough 一字指的是「自治行政區」，而紐約的五個行政區包含曼哈頓區(Manhattan)、布魯克林區(Brooklyn)、皇后區(Queens)、布朗克斯區(The Bronx)、和史坦頓島(Staten Island)。每一個行政區所擁有的行政權與「州」(state)之下的「郡」(county)相同。不過紐約市的管理是由紐約市長執行，立法單位則是紐約市議會所負責，除了曼哈頓區以外，其他區皆各有一位「行政區長」(borough president)作代表。

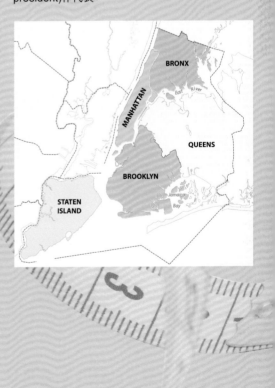

閱讀測驗解答：(B)

EUREKA! 點子成金

V Vocabulary Bank

1) **mutual** [ˈmjutʃuəl] (a.) 互相的，共同的
Our relationship is based on mutual trust.
我們的關係建立在互信的基礎上。

2) **stick to** [stɪk tu] (phr.) 堅持，持續，信守
If you stick to your studies, your grades are sure to improve.
如果你持續用功下去，你的成績一定會進步。

3) **shed** [ʃɛd] (v.) 甩掉（肥肉），（動物）掉毛，（植物）掉（葉）
Karen wants to shed a few pounds before swimsuit season.
凱倫想要在泳裝季節來臨前甩掉幾磅肥肉。

4) **talk into** [tɔlk ɪntu] (phr.) 說服，用言語打動
My roommate talked me into going skydiving with him.
我的室友說服我和他一起去玩跳傘。

5) **astonished** [əˈstɑnɪʃt] (a.) 驚訝的，吃驚的
We were astonished by the size of the Grand Canyon.
我們都對大峽谷的壯闊規模感到驚訝無比。

6) **show up** [ʃo ʌp] (phr.) 出席，出現
We waited for Gail for an hour, but she never showed up.
我們等了蓋兒一個小時，但她沒有出現。

7) **lecturer** [ˈlɛktʃərə] (n.) 講師
Donna is being promoted from lecturer to assistant professor.
唐娜從講師升到了助理教授。

8) **sympathize** [ˈsɪmpəˌθaɪz] (v.) 同情，體諒
I really sympathize with the victims of the terrorist attack.
我實在很同情那些遭受恐怖攻擊的受害者。

9) **take public** [tek ˈpʌblɪk] (phr.) 讓（公司）股票上市
The two founders took Google public in 2004.
谷歌的兩位創辦者在二○○四年讓公司股票上市。

進階字彙

10) **obsession** [əbˈsɛʃən] (n.) 著迷，縈繞於心的慾望
Tim teased his sister about her Hello Kitty obsession.
提姆嘲笑他妹妹對凱蒂貓的癡迷。

11) **franchise** [ˈfræntʃaɪz] (n.) 經銷權，加盟（店）
My parents own a fast food franchise.
我爸媽擁有一間加盟速食店。

課文朗讀 MP3 145　單字朗讀 MP3 146　英文講解 MP3 147

Jean's friends not only gave her encouragement, but also shared their own food [10]**obsessions**. This was her eureka moment: she realized that this kind of [1]**mutual** support was just what overweight people needed to help them [2]**stick to** their diets. Jean and her friends began meeting once a week, and within two months 40 women were squeezing into her tiny living room. Everyone was losing weight, and by October 1962, Jean had [3]**shed** 70 pounds, reaching her target weight of 142 pounds.

Because of her space problems, Jean began driving her Studebaker to other dieters' homes as well. One of these homes belonged to Albert Lippert, a Long Island businessman who lost 40 pounds under her guidance. Convinced that Jean's diet program would make a great business, Albert [4)]**talked** her **into** forming a partnership with him. In May 1963, Weight Watchers opened its first office over a movie theater in Queens. Jean set up 50 chairs in the meeting room, and was [5)]**astonished** when 400 people [6)]**showed up** for the first class.

As their membership kept growing, Albert suggested they start selling Weight Watchers [11)]**franchises**. Jean agreed, but with one condition—all classes must be taught by [7)]**lecturers** who had been through the program themselves and could [8)]**sympathize** with clients. When Jean and Albert [9)]**took** their company **public** in 1968, it had grown to 81 franchises in the U.S. and 10 overseas. Weight Watchers was sold to the H. J. Heinz Company in 1978 for $71.2 million, and is now the largest weight-loss organization in the world, with over a million members attending 40,000 weekly meetings in 30 countries.

Mini Quiz 閱讀測驗

Who teaches Weight Watchers classes?
(A) College lecturers
(B) Sympathetic clients
(C) Former members
(D) Franchise owners

Translation

珍的朋友不僅給予她鼓勵,還和她分享自己最無法抗拒的食物。這時,珍靈機一動:她明白像這種相互支持正是體重過重者所需的,這能幫助他們堅持自己的飲食計畫。珍和她的朋友開始每星期聚會一次,不到兩個月,共有四十位女性擠進她狹小的客廳。每個人的體重都持續下降,到了一九六二年十月,珍已經甩掉七十磅,減到目標體重一百四十二磅。

由於家裡空間不夠,珍也開始開她的斯圖貝克車到其他節食者家中。其中一個就是長島商人亞伯特利波特的家,他也在珍的引導下減了四十磅。亞伯特堅信珍的減重計畫一定能大發利市,於是便說服珍與他合夥。一九六三年五月,「慧優體」在皇后區一間電影院樓上成立第一間辦公室。珍在會議室擺了五十張桌子,之後還驚訝地發現,居然第一堂課就湧進了四百人。

隨著會員人數不斷增加,亞伯特建議開始賣慧優體的加盟權。珍答應了,不過條件是每堂課的講師都必須經歷過他們的減肥計畫,這樣才能對客戶感同身受。當珍與亞伯特在一九六八年讓公司上市時,在美國已有八十一家加盟店,而在海外也有十家。一九七八年慧優體以七千一百二十萬美元轉售給亨氏公司,現在已是全球最大的減重組織,遍及三十個國家,有超過百萬名會員,每週有四萬場聚會。

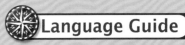
Studebaker 斯圖貝克
為德國移民後代的斯圖貝克兄弟,其實早在一八五二年就在印第安那州(Indiana)製造馬車,一八六八年才成立斯圖貝克兄弟製造公司(Studebaker Bros. Manufacturing Company)。一九○四年的時候加入製造汽車的行列,雖然以高品質著稱,但規模不大的斯圖貝克汽車公司最終不敵美國汽車業三巨頭(Big Three)——福特(Ford)、通用(General Motors)、和克萊斯勒(Chrysler),在強大的競爭之下,最後在一九六七年結束營業。

Long Island 長島
長島是位於北美洲大西洋岸(Atlantic Ocean)的島嶼,屬美國紐約州,也是美國人口最密集的地區之一。長島西部是紐約市五行政區中的布魯克林區(Brooklyn)和皇后區(Queens),其東則有紐約州的納蘇郡(Nassau County)和蘇福克郡(Suffolk County)。一般說來,長島指的是後者兩個郡。長島不僅長且大,東西向長達一百九十公里,南北則有三十七公里之遙。十九世紀時,許多富裕的企業家在長島北岸(North Shore)建立莊園,雖然當時建造的莊園不一定還存在,但這個地區仍是現今的奢華地區。另外,值得一提的是,又名黃金海岸(Gold Coast)的長島北岸,其實就是前一陣子改編自費茲傑羅(F. Scott Fitzgerald)同名小說《大亨小傳》(The Great Gatsby)的故事場景。

State of New York

New York

Long Island

H. J. Heinz Companyr 亨氏公司
亨氏公司於一八六九年成立,以創辦人 Henry J. Heinz 命名,以市占超過百分之五十的番茄醬打響名號,是美國位於賓州(Pennsylvania)的食品加工商,他們生產上千種的食品、行銷逾兩百個國家,在二○一三年以超過兩百三十億美元的市值賣給巴菲特(Warren Buffet)的保險及投資集團——波克夏哈海瑟威公司(Berkshire Hathaway)和 3G 資本公司(3G Capital)。

減肥之路不孤單，
讓盟友們助你一臂之力！

試想一下，當你正在苦哈哈的節食減肥，周遭的人卻都在大吃大喝，你能把持得住嗎？**Weight Watchers** 的成員不僅互相打氣，更在網路上交換自己與肥胖戰鬥的心得和方法，分享減重方面的知識，讓肥胖者充滿信心，不再孤軍奮戰。快來看看減肥盟友們分享了哪些有用的減肥資訊吧！

減肥大哉問，考考你的減肥觀念正不正確

1. 火龍果 (dragon fruit) 和酪梨 (avocado)，哪個熱量比較低？

 VS.

2. 澱粉 (starch) 是肥胖元兇，減肥時最好不要吃主食？

3. 啤酒和紅酒都是酒類，哪個熱量高？

 VS.

4. 為了快速瘦身，餐餐吃得越少越好？

5. 剛運動完千萬不能吃東西，否則就前功盡棄了？

*解答請見右頁下方

BMI 與 體脂肪率

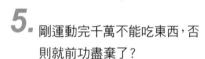

BMI (body mass index) 即「身體質量指數」，因為體重會隨身高而增加，兩者間呈現一個關係常數，故常用來測量人是否過胖，公式為：體重（公斤）÷ 身高（公尺）的平方。

正常範圍應落在 18 到 24 間。不過近年研究顯示，BMI 落在正常範圍，並不能完全代表罹患慢性疾病的機率低或不肥胖；相同的，若大於 24 也不能表示就是過重。「隱形肥胖」帶來的危險才是大家要注意的問題，而最能反應隱形肥胖的就是「體脂肪率」，通常女性體脂率為 20 到 27 間，男性則落在 15 到 20 間為標準。

├「智慧型」減肥法┤

現在什麼都科技化，減肥當然也不例外，使用智慧型手機的人可以下載這些好用的 app 來督促自己，幫助提升減肥效率。

FatSecret 卡路里計算器

可計算每天所攝取食物和運動消耗的熱量，讓您養成良好的生活習慣，對於卡路里斤斤計較的人一定要下載這個計算器！

3D YOGA

不只要瘦，更要打造勻稱曲線。這款 app 特別針對想雕塑身材的人所設計。使用者可以參考軟體中的 3D 示範動畫，學習正確的瑜珈姿勢，該款 app 有中文教學說明，在練習的同時還能播放幫助你放鬆的音樂。

喝水寶

多喝水有助新陳代謝 (metabolism)，對減重有相當助益。這款 app 可幫我們記錄自己的飲水習慣，只需輸入自己現在的體重，它就會幫我們確定體內每天所需的攝水量。當我們喝完一杯水，只需要在上面記錄，軟體就會自動提醒我們下次該喝水的時間，非常適合常忙到連喝水都會忘記的人。

Fitness Pro 健身專家

主要概念就是將所有健身知識濃縮在一個 app 裡，裡面有超過四百五十種運動及體操，同時還可以記錄使用者每日的運動情形，包括慢跑 (jogging) 的路程或重量訓練 (weight training) 的強度，想靠運動減肥的人，它是不可或缺的好幫手。

├ 簡易居家塑身運動 ┤

老是找藉口，說自己沒時間出門運動的人，以下這幾個簡單的動作在家就可以做了，每天一回家就躺在沙發上看電視的你，還不趕快動起來！

chair dips
用椅子訓練上臂三頭肌

lunges
弓箭步

jumping jacks
開合跳

push-ups
扶地挺身

squats
蹲踞

plank
撐舉

├ 解答 ┤

1. 火龍果

你以為不管吃什麼水果都不會變胖嗎？錯！有些糖類指數 (glycemic index，簡寫為 GI) 很高的水果，吃多了也是會發福的。糖類指數就是食物糖分被人體吸收的速度，越容易吸收的 GI 值越高，也越容易發胖，像香蕉、木瓜、酪梨這類水果的 GI 值都不低，減肥者可要多多注意。

2. 減肥期間還是要吃澱粉！

澱粉是提供腦部運作的重要原料，不吃澱粉會讓人精神不濟，長期下來會出現頭暈、想睡覺、精神不集中或是脾氣暴躁等問題，更重要的是，米飯、麵包等穀類含有豐富的維生素 B 群，是身體代謝重要的物質。當我們運動時需要靠澱粉（醣類）來幫助脂肪燃燒，缺乏會使基礎代謝 (basic metabolism) 下降，埋下復胖的因子。

3. 紅酒

大家都知道啤酒的熱量很高，但其實酒類的熱量多寡跟酒精含量成正比，紅酒的酒精含量比啤酒高，當然熱量也較高囉！

4. 減肥不是份量越少就越好

正常來說，一般成年女性一天所需的熱量約為一千五百卡左右（隨年紀和身體狀況而略有不同），男性則為兩千五百卡左右，因此只要攝取量在合理的範圍內即可，吃太少的話反而會降低新陳代謝，日後復胖會更嚴重。

5. 剛運動完還是可以吃東西

這是很多減肥者都有的迷思。運動會消耗體能，運動完身體非常需要補充能量，這時你如果進食，身體會感到滿足，但是並不會囤積；但如果你不吃，身體已經很累了，你還不給它能量，就會把身體推入一種「飢餓模式」，這個模式一旦啟動，你反而更容易囤積脂肪！

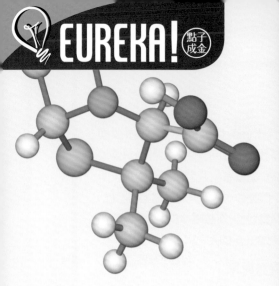

Penicillin
Mold as Medicine
盤尼西林 藥用的黴菌

課文朗讀 MP3 148　單字朗讀 MP3 149　英文講解 MP3 150

Vocabulary Bank

1) **mold** [mold] (n.) 霉，黴菌
There was mold on the bread, so I threw it away.
麵包發霉了，所以我把它丟了。

2) **infection** [ɪnˋfɛkʃən] (n.) 傳染，感染
(v.) infect
The doctor prescribed antibiotics for my throat infection.
醫生開了抗生素來治我的喉嚨感染。

3) **patch** [pætʃ] (n.) 一片，一塊
Watch out for that patch of ice on the road.
小心路上結冰的那塊。

進階字彙

4) **antiseptic** [ˌæntəˋsɛptɪk] (n./a.) 抗菌劑；
抗菌的
The doctor cleaned the wound with an antiseptic.
醫生用抗菌劑清洗傷口。

5) **antibacterial** [ˌæntibækˋtɪriəl] (a.) 抗細菌的
Can you recommend a good antibacterial soap?
你可以推薦好用的抗菌肥皂嗎？

6) **agent** [ˋedʒənt] (n.) （化）劑，作用物
Chemical agents are used to treat cancer.
化學藥劑被用於治療癌症。

7) **enzyme** [ˋɛnzaɪm] (n.) 酵素
Yogurt contains enzymes that aid digestion.
優格含有可幫助消化的酵素。

8) **saliva** [səˋlaɪvə] (n.) 唾液，口水
The doctor took a saliva sample from the patient.
醫生取出病人的唾液檢體。

9) **antibiotic** [ˌæntɪbaɪˋɑtɪk] (n.) 抗生素
Gary is taking antibiotics for his throat infection.
蓋瑞為他的喉嚨發炎服用抗生素。

Alexander Fleming was born in 1881 on a farm in southwestern Scotland. The seventh of eight children, he spent a happy childhood exploring the countryside with his brothers. Fleming was a bright student, and after attending Kilmarnock Academy on a scholarship, he moved to London to live with his older brother Tom, who worked there as a doctor.

In London, Fleming studied at the Royal Polytechnic and then found a job as a shipping clerk. He found the work boring, though, so when he received an inheritance from an uncle, he decided to **1 follow in his brother Tom's footsteps**. Fleming was accepted to St. Mary's Hospital Medical School, where he graduated with honors and became a researcher and lecturer.

When WWI broke out, Fleming joined the Royal Army Medical Corps and served at a field hospital in France. In treating wounded soldiers, he found that **antiseptics** were useless in treating deep wounds, and sometimes even made **infections** worse. This experience inspired Fleming to devote his research to finding a safer **antibacterial agent** after the war.

Fleming's hard work led to the discovery of lysozyme, an antibacterial **enzyme** found in tears and **saliva**—but his most important discovery happened by accident. Returning to his lab from vacation in September 1928, he noticed a **patch** of mold on a Petri dish he was using to grow bacteria. What's more, there was a circle around the mold that was free of bacteria. That was Fleming's eureka moment—he realized that something in the mold was killing the bacteria.

But it wasn't until 1940 that the first [9]**antibiotic**—which Fleming named penicillin after the penicillium mold it came from—was produced in large enough quantities to use as medicine. Since then, this "miracle drug" has saved over 200 million lives!

Mini Quiz 閱讀測驗

What did Fleming decide to do when he received an inheritance?
(A) Study medicine
(B) Become a researcher
(C) Work at a hospital
(D) Serve in WWI

中 Translation

亞歷山大弗萊明於一八八一年出生在蘇格蘭西南部的農場。八名孩子中排行第七的他，和他的手足度過了探索鄉野的快樂童年。弗萊明是位聰穎的學生，受領基馬諾克學院的獎學金後，他就搬去倫敦和在當地行醫的哥哥湯姆同住。

到了倫敦，弗萊明於英國皇家理工學院就讀，接著他找到一份運務員的工作。對這個工作感到無聊，所以當他從叔叔那邊繼承到一筆遺產後，就決定跟隨哥哥湯姆的腳步。於是，弗萊明就得到聖瑪莉醫學院的入學許可，也在那兒光榮畢業成為一名研究員兼講師。

一次大戰爆發時，弗萊明加入了英國皇家陸軍軍醫團，到法國一間野戰醫院服務。為受傷士兵做治療時，他發現抗菌劑對治療深部傷口無效，有時甚至會讓感染情況更加嚴重。這樣的經歷激發了弗萊明在戰後將他的研究致力於找尋一種更安全的抗病菌藥劑。

弗萊明的辛勤研究讓他發現了溶菌酶，一種存在於人的淚水和唾液中的抗菌酵素。不過，他最重要的發現竟是在一次意外中得到的。一九二八年九月，剛放完假返回實驗室時，他注意到用來培養細菌的培養皿上長了一小塊黴菌。而且，有一圈繞著這塊黴菌的地方是沒長細菌的。這就是弗萊明靈光乍現的時刻——因為他明白黴菌中有著某種殺死細菌的東西。

不過直到一九四〇年，第一種抗生素——弗萊明以其來源的青黴菌命名為盤尼西林——才得以大量生產、當藥物使用。至今，這種「奇蹟藥」已救過兩億以上的人命。

Tongue-tied No More

❶ follow in sb's footsteps

footstep 顧名思義即為「腳步，步伐」，而 follow in sb's footsteps 就是追隨某人的腳步、步上某人的後塵。

A: You're going to art school? I thought your dad wanted you to study law.
你要去讀美術？我記得你老爸要你去念法律。

B: Yeah, but I don't want to follow in his footsteps.
是沒錯，但我不想要跟他走一樣的路。

Language Guide

弗萊明的大發現

lyso 是從 lyse 這個動詞發展而來的，有讓細胞溶解的意思；再加上酵素 (enzyme) 組合而成 lysozyme，溶解、破壞細胞的酵素。是 1928 年弗萊明無意間發現一種存在在唾液、眼淚或是蛋白中，可以破壞細菌細胞壁的溶解酵素，這項原理幫助他發明盤尼西林 (penicillin)。盤尼西林從青黴菌 (penicillium) 製作而來，能夠抑制細菌的滋生，產生殺菌作用的一種抗生素。

Petri dish 培養皿

由德國細菌學家 Julius Richard Petri 發明設計，便以他命名為 Petri dish（又稱 Petri plate）。是平面圓盤狀的底部加上蓋子的器皿，在實驗室中常用來培養細菌，通常是用玻璃或透明塑膠材質製作而成。

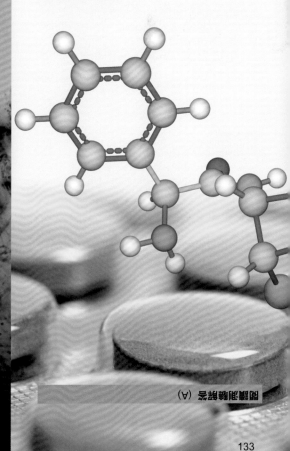

〈A〉答賴競賺：答賴mini

EUREKA! 點子成金

V Vocabulary Bank

1) **invisible** [ɪn`vɪzəbəl] (a.) 肉眼看不見的，無形的
Viruses are invisible to the naked eye.
病毒是肉眼看不見的。

2) **electronics** [ɪlɛk`trɑnɪks] (n.) 電子科技，電子學，電器用品
The tech firm is hiring electronics engineers.
那家科技公司正在招募電子工程師。

3) **surgeon** [`sɜdʒən] (n.) 外科醫生
The operation was performed by an experienced surgeon.
這個手術由經驗豐富的外科醫生操刀。

4) **chamber** [`tʃembɚ] (n.) 室，房間（尤指寢室）
The human heart consists of four chambers.
人類的心臟由四個心房組成。

5) **external** [ɪk`stɜnəl] (a.) 外部的，外面的
The external walls of the house are painted yellow.
這房子的外牆被漆成黃色。

6) **device** [dɪ`vaɪs] (n.) 設備，裝置
Our store sells all the latest wireless devices.
我們店裡銷售各式最新型的無線裝置。

7) **circuit** [`sɜkɪt] (n.) 電路，回路
The circuit board in the camera had to be replaced.
相機的電路板必須更換。

8) **pulse** [pʌls] (n.) 脈衝，脈衝波，脈搏
Strong pulses of energy are released during solar storms.
太陽風暴期間會釋放出強烈的能量脈衝。

9) **accidental** [ˌæksə`dɛntəl] (a.) 偶然的，意外的
The building was destroyed by an accidental fire.
這棟建築被一場意外的大火燒毀了。

進階字彙

10) **implant** [ɪm`plænt] (v.) 植入
(a.) implantable [ɪm`plætəbəl]
The hearing aid was implanted in the patient's ear.
這位病人植入助聽器在耳朵裡。

The Pacemaker
Sometimes Accidents Can Save Lives
心律調節器 有時意外反能救命

課文朗讀 151 單字朗讀 152 英文講解 MP3 153

Born on September 6, 1919 in Buffalo New York, Wilson Greatbatch was fascinated by radios as a child. Wondering how [1]**invisible** waves could carry voice through the air, he studied radio [2]**electronics** on his own and built a short wave radio receiver in his early teens. Greatbatch later joined the Navy, serving as a radio operator in WWII.

After the war, Greatbatch studied electrical engineering at Cornell on the G.I. Bill. While working at a campus animal behavior lab, two visiting [3]**surgeons** told him about a condition called heart block, in which electrical signals from the heart's upper [4]**chambers** fail to reach the lower chambers, leading to an irregular heartbeat that can cause fainting and even death.

At the time, the only way to treat heart block was with a TV-sized [5]**external** pacemaker that delivered painful electric shocks strong enough to burn the skin.

While the young engineer was convinced that he could design a better pacemaker, his eureka moment came completely by accident. In 1956, Greatbatch—now an assistant professor at the University of Buffalo—was working on a [6]**device** to record heart sounds for a nearby medical research institute. But when he installed the wrong resistor in the [7]**circuit** he was building, he found that it produced a steady electrical [8]**pulse** every second—just like a heartbeat!

Realizing that his circuit could be used to create a pacemaker small enough to [10]**implant** in patients, Greatbatch quit his job and spent the next two years in his workshop perfecting his invention. His implantable pacemaker was introduced in 1961, and an improved version—with a lithium battery that extended its life from two years to 10—in 1970. Since then, Greatbatch's [9]**accidental** invention has saved millions of lives worldwide.

Mini Quiz 閱讀測驗

Which of the following did Greatbatch invent?
(A) A shortwave radio receiver
(B) The lithium battery
(C) The external pacemaker
(D) The implantable pacemaker

中 Translation

一九一九年九月六日出生於紐約水牛城的威爾森葛瑞巴契從小就對無線電深深著迷。他很好奇看不見的電波是如何能透過空氣傳送聲音,於是自己研習無線電電子學,十多歲便打造出一部無線電短波接收器。後來葛瑞巴契入海軍服役,並於二次世界大戰期間擔任無線電士。

戰後,葛瑞巴契依據美國軍人權利法,到康乃爾大學修習電子工程。在大學裡的動物行為實驗室工作時,兩名客座外科醫師告訴他一種名為「心臟傳導阻滯」的病症,在這種情況下,心房的電子信號將無法送抵心室,導致心律不整進而可能造成昏厥甚至死亡。當時,治療心臟傳導阻滯的唯一方法是用電視大小的外部心律調整器提供會引發疼痛、強烈得足以灼傷皮膚的電擊。

儘管這位年輕的工程師深信自己一定能設計出更好的心律調整器,但他靈機一動的時刻,來得純屬偶然。一九五六年,現為水牛城大學助理教授的葛瑞巴契正在為附近的醫療研究中心研發一種記錄心跳聲的裝置。一次,他裝錯電路板的電阻器,卻發現它每一秒鐘都會產生穩定的電脈衝——宛如心跳!

葛瑞巴契明白他的電路板可以用來製造小到可以植入病患體內的心律調整器,於是辭去工作,接下來兩年時間,都在工作室裡琢磨他的發明。他的植入式心律調節器在一九六一年問世,改良版(改用鋰電池,使壽命從兩年延長至十年)則在一九七〇年推出。自此之後,葛瑞巴契偶然的發明拯救了世界各地數百萬民眾的性命。

(D) 案答驗測讀閱

Vocabulary Bank

1) **performer** [pə`fɔrmə] (n.) 表演者，演奏者
The audience clapped when the performers walked onto the stage.
表演者走上舞台時，觀眾都拍手喝采。

2) **tempting** [`tɛmptɪŋ] (a.) 誘人的，吸引人的
The cake looks tempting, but I'm on a diet.
這個蛋糕看起來好誘人，可是我正在減肥。

3) **prospect** [`prɑspɛkt] (n.)（成功的）可能性、期望，前景，前途；找礦
Doctors say there is little prospect of saving the patient.
醫生說要救活該名病患的機會渺茫。

4) **boom town** [bum taun] (n.)（經濟、人口快速成長的）新興城市
Many of the boom towns built during the oil rush no longer exist.
許多在石油熱潮期間所建造的新興城市已不復見。

5) **entertainment** [ˌɛntə`tenmənt] (n.) 娛樂，演藝
Hollywood is the center of America's entertainment industry.
好萊塢是美國娛樂產業的中心。

6) **feature** [`fitʃə] (v.) 以⋯為特色，有⋯
The dinner menu features seafood and pasta dishes.
晚餐菜單以海鮮和義式麵食為主。

7) **act** [ækt] (n.) 表演團體、節目
Led Zeppelin was one of the most popular acts in rock history.
齊柏林飛船合唱團是搖滾史上最受歡迎的樂團之一。

8) **relocate** [ri`loket] (v.) 遷居，重新安置
My company relocated me to Tokyo.
我公司要把我派駐到東京工作。

9) **ultimate** [`ʌltəmɪt] (a.) 極致的，終極的
Hawaii is the ultimate vacation destination
夏威夷是絕佳的度假勝地。

10) **cement** [sə`mɛnt] (n.) 水泥
Ross fell and hit his head on the cement floor.
羅斯跌倒後，頭撞到了水泥地。

進階字彙

11) **mecca** [`mɛkə] (n.) 眾人嚮往的地方，聖地。原意（大寫）為「麥加」，即位於沙烏地阿拉伯的伊斯蘭教朝聖地
New York is a mecca for museum lovers.
紐約對於那些博物館迷來說是非常嚮往的地方。

Tongue-tied No More

1 strike it rich 發大財

看到 rich 就知道這個片語應該和錢財有關。該說法原為「挖到大油田」之意，而挖到油田當然就會發大財囉，因此 strike it rich 指的就是「獲得意外的大成功」或「賺大錢」。

A: How are your stocks doing?
你的股票怎麼樣？

B: Well, I haven't struck it rich, but I'm doing OK.
嗯，雖然還不至於靠它發財，不過還可以啦。

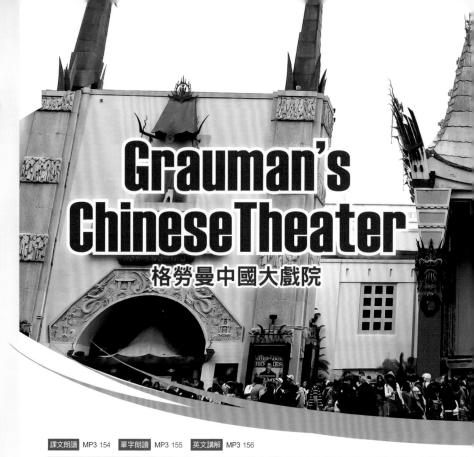

Grauman's Chinese Theater
格勞曼中國大戲院

課文朗讀 MP3 154　單字朗讀 MP3 155　英文講解 MP3 156

Sidney Grauman was born on March 17, 1879 in Indiana. His parents, David and Rosa, were vaudeville [1]**performers**, so the family moved around following touring shows. David never earned much money as a performer, making the Klondike Gold Rush a [2]**tempting** [3]**prospect**. When Sid was nineteen, father and son headed for the Yukon hoping to **1 strike it rich**.

While they didn't find any gold in the Yukon, they did make an important discovery in the [4]**boom town** of Dawson City. Besides prospecting, there was nothing to do in town, so the miners were **2 bored out of their minds**. Seeing an opportunity, David and Sid began promoting boxing matches and other events. By taking advantage of this huge demand for [5]**entertainment**, they were able to leave for San Francisco two years later much wealthier than when they arrived.

In the early 1900s, David and Sid opened two theaters in San Francisco, [6]**featuring** vaudeville [7]**acts** and later motion pictures. When both theaters were destroyed in the 1906 San Francisco Earthquake, Sid [8]**relocated** to the nation's movie capital—Hollywood. After first achieving success with the Million Dollar Theater and the Egyptian, Sid began planning his [9]**ultimate** project—Grauman's Chinese Theater.

In April 1927, Sid invited movie stars Mary Pickford and Norma Talmage to the Chinese Theater's construction site. While

© Palette7/shutterstock.com

exiting the car, Norma stepped in some wet [10]**cement**, leaving a footprint. On seeing this, Sidney had his eureka moment. What better way to advertise his theater than having famous movie stars leave their hand and footprints near the entrance? And it obviously worked. Grauman's Chinese Theater was the most successful movie palace of its day, and is still a [11]**mecca** for movie lovers from all over the world.

Mini Quiz 閱讀測驗

Which of the following is true about Sid Grauman?
(A) He made a fortune as a gold miner.
(B) He moved to Hollywood because of a disaster.
(C) He moved to San Francisco as a child.
(D) He worked as a vaudeville performer.

中 Translation

席德尼格勞曼於一八七九年三月十七日出生在印地安那州。他的爸媽大衛和羅莎都是輕歌舞劇表演者，因此一家人會跟著巡迴演出的地點搬來搬去。大衛靠表演一直賺不到很多錢，因此克朗代克淘金熱對他來說是個誘人的機會。席德十九歲時，父子倆便前往加拿大育空地區，盼能一舉致富。

父子倆儘管未在育空發現任何黃金，卻在新興的道森市有了重要的發現。除了淘金之外，道森市無事可做，因此礦工們無聊至極。見機不可失，大衛和席德開始舉辦拳賽和其他活動。受惠於當地龐大的娛樂需求，他們得以在兩年後帶著遠比來時還多的財富前往舊金山。

二十世紀初，大衛和席德在舊金山開了兩家戲院，先提供輕歌舞表演，後放映電影。當兩家戲院在一九○六年舊金山大地震毀於一旦，席德遷徙至全國電影的首府——好萊塢。在最早設立的百萬美元戲院和埃及戲院獲得成功後，席德便開始進行他的終極計畫——格勞曼中國戲院。

一九二七年四月，席德邀請電影明星瑪麗畢克馥和諾瑪塔瑪芝到中國戲院的工地。下車時，諾瑪踩進還沒乾的水泥，留下腳印。看到這個情況，席德尼靈機一動。要替他的戲院打廣告，有什麼方式比讓知名電影明星在入口處留下手印和腳印更好？這種方式顯然奏效。格勞曼中國戲院是當代最成功的電影皇宮，至今仍是世界各地電影愛好者的朝聖地。

🔑 Tongue-tied No More

❷ bored out of one's mind
（某人）無聊極了

要形容「某人⋯極了」，可以使用 adj. + out of one's mind 的句型來表示。例如 I'm scared out of my mind.（嚇死我了。）或 She's drunk out of her mind.（她醉到一個不行。），諸如此類。

A: Did you have fun during summer vacation?
你暑假玩得還開心嗎？

B: No. I was bored out of my mind.
不開心。我無聊得要死。

🧭 Language Guide

vaudeville 輕歌舞劇

為十九世紀後期至二十世紀三○年代流行於美國和加拿大劇場的一種綜藝娛樂節目，又可稱為通俗喜劇，內容主要是魔術表演、雜技(acrobatics)、喜劇、歌舞等，被譽為「美國演藝界的心臟」。

1906 San Francisco Earthquake
一九○六年舊金山大地震

該起地震發生在一九○六年四月十八日的清晨，震央位在聖安地列斯斷層(San Andreas Fault)上，芮氏規模(Richter scale)為七點九度。地震強烈引發了多起火災，這些伴隨而來的大火重創了舊金山及鄰近地區，整個城市大約百分之八十損毀，為美國大城市遭受最嚴重的天災之一。據估計，約有三十萬左右的居民無家可歸，必須住在臨時搭建的帳篷內，死亡人數大約為三千至六千人，財務損失則高達四億美金。這是首次以相片形式清楚記錄的大規模地震，也使得後來地震學(seismology)研究蓬勃發展。

movie palace 電影皇宮

電影皇宮盛行於一九一○到一九四○年代，為美國一種電影院的建築風格。由於當時電影工業正值蓬勃發展，一些獨立的電影製片公司便大搞噱頭，將旗下的連鎖電影院打造成奢華、精緻的風格來吸引觀眾上門。其特色在於採用復古華麗的外觀、劇院式的天花板等，這種誇張的建築風格直到經濟大蕭條 (Great Depression) 時才逐漸式微。

© Stevietheman/wikipedia

閱讀測驗解答：(B)

Hard Rock Cafe 硬石餐廳

©Sasha Davas / Shutterstock.com

Vocabulary Bank

1) **spiritual** [ˋspɪrɪtʃuəl] (a.) 精神上的，心靈的
The Pope is the spiritual leader of the Catholic Church.
那位教宗是天主教會的精神領導。

2) **quest** [kwɛst] (n.) 探索，追尋
Iran refuses to give up its quest for nuclear energy.
伊恩拒絕放棄發展核能。

3) **longing** [ˋlɔŋɪŋ] (n.) 渴望
The refugees were filled with longing for their country.
那些難民們充滿著對祖國的渴望。

4) **differentiate** [ˌdɪfəˋrɛnʃɪˌet] (v.) 使有差異
The ability to speak differentiates humans from other animals.
人類可以說話的能力使得和其他動物有很大的不同。

5) **motto** [ˋmɑto] (n.) 座右銘，格言
"Service with a smile" is our company's motto.
以微笑服務顧客是本公司的座右銘。

6) **theme** [θim] (n.) 主題
What is the theme of your essay?
你論文的主題是什麼？

7) **packed** [pækt] (a.) 客滿的
The stadium was packed for the big game.
館場因為大球賽而爆滿。

進階字彙

8) **expatriate** [ɛksˋpetrɪət] (n./a.) 移居國外者；移居國外的。常簡稱為 expat [ˋɛksˌpæt]
Most of the foreign reporters hang out at the expatriate bar.
大部分的外國記者都在那家外國酒吧流連。

9) **snooty** [ˋsnuti] (a.) 傲慢的，勢利的
I can't stand the snooty waiters at that restaurant.
我無法忍受那間餐廳裡傲慢的服務生。

10) **establishment** [ɪˋstæblɪʃmənt] (n.) 餐廳，商店，公司
Alcohol isn't served in this establishment.
這間餐廳沒有賣酒。

課文朗讀 MP3 157　　單字朗讀 MP3 158　　英文講解 MP3 159

At the dawn of the 1970s, two young Americans met in London. Isaac Tigrett was born into a wealthy family, and moved as a teenager to England, where his father exported Rolls-Royces to the U.S. After attending private school in Switzerland, he followed the hippie trail to India on a [1]**spiritual** [2]**quest** before returning to London. Peter Morton, son of a successful Chicago restaurant owner, arrived in London after earning a business degree at the University of Denver.

When the two [8]**expatriates** ran into each other, they found themselves wishing they could trade fish and chips for burgers and fries. This [3]**longing** led to their eureka moment. Figuring there were thousands of American expats **1 in the same boat**, they decided to open their own restaurant and serve American staples like burgers, fries, shakes, apple pie and cold beer. To [4]**differentiate** themselves from [9]**snooty** London [10]**establishments**, they chose a rock 'n' roll theme and made "Love All—Serve All" their [5]**motto**. After finding a name they liked on the back of a Doors album, Tigrett and Morton opened the Hard Rock Cafe—the world's first [6]**theme** restaurant—in June 1971.

The restaurant was [7]**packed** from day one, and famous rock [11]**acts** like the Beatles, the Rolling Stones and Led Zeppelin became regular customers. One day, Eric Clapton left his guitar there to reserve his favorite table, and a tradition was born. The restaurant began collecting and displaying rock [12]memorabilia, and would eventually own the largest collection on the planet. This combination of food, music and memorabilia proved to be a successful formula—there are now 134 Hard Rock Cafes in 36 countries around the world!

Mini Quiz 閱讀測驗

Why did Tigrett and Morton establish the Hard Rock Cafe?
(A) Because they didn't like snooty London establishments
(B) Because they didn't enjoy eating fish and chips
(C) Because they wanted to open a rock 'n' roll theme restaurant
(D) Because they figured there was a market for American food

中 Translation

一九七○年代初,兩個美國年輕人在倫敦相遇。艾塞克泰葛特出生於富裕家庭,青少年時期搬到英國,他父親在英國從事勞斯萊斯名車銷美的生意。在瑞士念完私立學校後,他沿著嬉皮之路,前往印度進行心靈探索之旅,然後才回到倫敦。彼得莫頓則是芝加哥一名事業有成的餐廳老闆之子,取得丹佛大學企管學位後來到倫敦。

當這兩名異鄉遊子相遇,發現他們都好希望能夠拿炸魚薯條換漢堡跟薯條。這份渴望讓他們靈光乍現。他們認為有成千上萬美國異鄉客跟他們同病相憐,於是決定自己開一家餐廳,專門販售美國主要食物,好比漢堡、薯條、奶昔、蘋果派跟冰啤酒。為了跟勢利眼的倫敦餐廳有所區隔,他們選擇搖滾為主題,並且以「愛萬物,事萬物」作為服務宗旨。他們在門合唱團的一張專輯背面找到了喜歡的店名之後,泰葛特跟莫頓於一九七一年六月開了世界上第一間主題餐廳:硬石餐廳。

餐廳從開幕第一天就爆滿,許多著名搖滾樂團,好比披頭四、滾石和齊柏林飛船都成為常客。有一天,艾力克萊普頓為了保留他最喜歡的位子,把吉他留在那裡,一項傳統從此誕生。餐廳開始收集並展示搖滾紀念物,最後所擁有的收藏品居全球之冠。食物、音樂和紀念品的組合,結果是一個成功方程式,現在總共有一百三十四間硬石餐廳,遍佈在全球三十六個國家!

©Andrew F. Kazmierski / Shutterstock.com

喬治哈里森的吉他

JOHN LENNON
THE BEATLES

11) **act** [ækt] (n.) 表演者,表演團體
How many acts are going to play at the concert?
有幾個樂團會在這場演唱會中表演?

12) **memorabilia** [ˌmɛmərəˈbɪlɪə] (n.)
(複數名詞)紀念品
Mike likes to collect sports memorabilia.
麥克喜歡蒐集體育紀念品。

Tongue-tied No More

① in the same boat 同病相憐

in the same boat 字面直譯是「在同一條船上」,意指「處境相同,遭遇一樣的困難」。

A: Do you think you could lend me some money? I'm totally broke.
你能借我一點錢嗎?我完全沒錢了。
B: Sorry. I'd love to help, but I'm in the same boat.
抱歉。愛莫能助,我跟你同病相憐啊。

Language Guide

hippie trail 嬉皮之路

「嬉皮之路」是六○到七○年代歐美青年時興的旅遊方式,當時的年輕人崇尚以嬉皮自居,多數從美洲飛往盧森堡,或從倫敦、阿姆斯特丹出發,經過君士坦丁堡、德黑蘭、喀布爾或加德滿都,主要目的地都是南亞的印度或尼泊爾。在經費拮据的情況下,他們絕大多數的旅程都以搭便車 (hitchhiking) 或搭公車的方式完成,以拖延回家的時間。

Hard Rock Cafe 小檔案

Hard Rock Cafe 是全球連鎖的餐廳,台灣也曾經開了兩間,首先於一九九二年在台北成立第一家,接著於一九九四年在台中開了第二家,可惜後來都陸續結束營業。近年來,Hard Rock 集團將事業觸角拓展至會議度假飯店及賭場飯店,主辦熱門音樂會及現場音樂表演,也是重要的經營項目之一。

位於洛杉磯 Universal Citywalk 的 Hard Rock Cafe

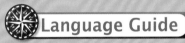

閱讀測驗解答:(C)

©Aija Lehtonen / Shutterstock.com
約翰藍儂的衣服和眼鏡

國家圖書館出版品預行編目 (CIP) 資料

改變人類生活的創意發明Eureka!：EZ TALK總編嚴選特刊 / EZ叢書館編輯部作. --
初版. -- 臺北市：日月文化, 2013.10
144 面；21x28 公分
ISBN 978-986-248-342-8(平裝附光碟片)
1. 英語 2. 讀本
805.18   102016649

EZ 叢書館

改變人類生活的創意發明Eureka!：EZ TALK 總編嚴選特刊

作　　者：EZ TALK 編輯部
總 編 輯：顏秀竹
總 編 審：Judd Piggott
資深編輯：黃鈺琦
執行編輯：韋孟岑
美術設計：管仕豪、徐歷弘、許葳
錄 音 員：Michael Tennant 、Meilee Saccenti 、Jacob Roth

發 行 人：洪祺祥
法律顧問：建大法律事務所
財務顧問：高威會計師事務所

出　　版：日月文化集團—日月文化出版股份有限公司
製　　作：EZ 叢書館 / EZ TALK
地　　址：台北市大安區信義路三段 151 號 8 樓
電　　話：(02) 2708-5509
傳　　真：(02) 2708-6157
網　　址：www.ezbooks.com.tw
客服信箱：service@heliopolis.com.tw

總 經 銷：聯合發行股份有限公司
電　　話：(02) 2917-8022
傳　　真：(02) 2915-7212
印　　刷：科樂印刷事業股份有限公司
初　　版：2013 年 10 月
定　　價：350 元
I S B N：978-986-248-342-8

讀者基本資料

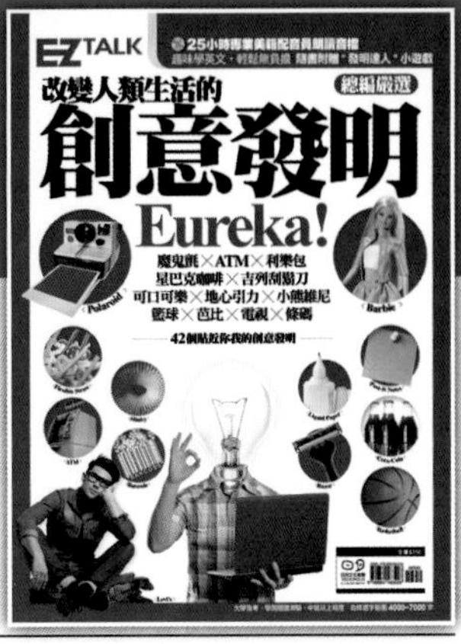

■姓名 ______________________________ 性別 □男 □女

■生日 民國 __________ 年 __________ 月 __________ 日

■地址 □□□-□□（請務必填寫郵遞區號）

____

■聯絡電話（日）______________________________

（夜）______________________________

（手機）______________________________

■ E-mail

____

（請務必填寫 E-mail，讓我們為您提供 VIP 服務）

■職業

□學生 □服務業 □傳媒業 □資訊業 □自由業 □軍公教 □出版業

□商業 □補教業 □其他

■教育程度

□國中及以下 □高中 □高職 □專科 □大學 □研究所以上

■您從何種通路購得本書？

□一般書店 □量販店 □網路書店 □書展 □郵局劃撥

您對本書的建議……

請傳真至 *02-2708-6157* 或投郵筒寄回，感謝你的配合！

廣告回信免貼郵票
台灣北區郵政管理號登記證
第 000370 號

日月文化出版股份有限公司

10658　台北市大安區信義路三段 151 號 8 樓

大好書屋　寶鼎出版　山岳文化　唐莊文化　EZ叢書館　EZ TALK 美語會話誌　EZ Japan 流行日語會話誌　EZ Korea 流行韓語教學誌

請以膠帶封口

發明達人問答樂
怎麼玩

遊戲使用說明

讀完書本內容不確定自己是否都吸收了嗎？別擔心，發明達人問答樂，幫你重拾記憶印象加深。本款遊戲可和朋友一同進行問答，或是自行重溫學習，玩法多樣，既可複習又可收納做為年份圖表，英語學習有趣又好玩！

玩法一：你問我答

「發明達人」小卡拆下後，依據紙板上的問題，進行猜謎遊戲。

玩法二：自製發明年份表

1. 可將所有小卡依照附贈年份表上的問題欄，將正確小卡貼上。
2. 將所有小卡黏畢之後，自製的發明年份圖表完成。

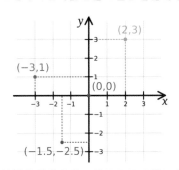

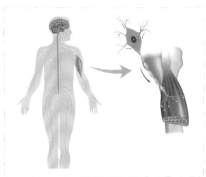

geometry	Isaac Newton	Goodyear
basketball	Coca Cola	Levi's
neuroscience	Nobel Prize	Olymic Games
Winnie the Pooh	television	Grauman's Chinese Theater
flexible straw	Penguin Books	Dr. Seuss

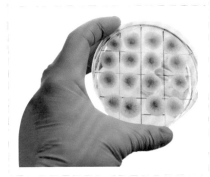

penicillin	Tetra Pak	Sweet'N Low
instant photography	barcode	Liquid Paper
pacemaker	Barbie	Weight Watchers
ATM	Hard Rock Cafe	Post-it Notes
Amazon	Velcro	Netflix